Praise for the bestselling novels of

# IRIS JOHANSEN

## COUNTDOWN

"Johansen delivers a top-notch sequel filled with great chases, original characters, and intricate plot twists, creating a unique supernatural twist on the classic thriller." —*Booklist*

## BLIND ALLEY

"Johansen has become adept at mixing supernatural elements with intriguing suspense, and her new tale will please both fans and new converts with its unpredictable journey from Atlanta to the archaeological digs of Herculaneum in Italy." —*Booklist*

"Johansen's back . . . solid thriller, intriguing suspense." —*Kirkus Reviews*

## FIRESTORM

"[A] rip-roaring thriller . . . just might increase the sale of fire extinguishers." —*Publishers Weekly*

"Terrific . . . [A] thrilling suspense novel."
—*New York Daily News*

# FATAL TIDE

"You'll be swept away by this thriller."
—*Cosmopolitan*

"Part romance novel, part Indiana Jones . . . *Fatal Tide* is a page-turner par excellence." —*BookPage*

"A fun-to-read, fast-paced tale of treasure and intrigue." —*Baton Rouge Advocate*

"Trust crowd-pleaser Johansen . . . what a plot. Fun for fans." —*Kirkus Reviews*

"Johansen is in fine form." —*Booklist*

"Johansen knows exactly what her devoted readers want and gives it to them once again in this impassioned romantic suspense novel. Her lusty characters, both good and evil, preen and snarl as they fight, love and kill with almost superhuman stamina and appetite." —*Publishers Weekly*

# DEAD AIM

"Smoothly written, tightly plotted, turbocharged thriller . . . megaselling Johansen doesn't miss."
—*Kirkus Reviews*

"Readers will stay up all night reading this cat-and-mouse chase." —*Booklist*

"Johansen has once again hit her mark with *Dead Aim*." —*Fort Worth Star-Telegram*

"There's plenty of suspense from beginning to end." —*Oklahoman*

## NO ONE TO TRUST

"With its taut plot and complex characters, [*No One to Trust*] is vintage, fan-pleasing Johansen." —*Booklist*

"Fast-moving plot . . . another zippy read from Johansen." —*Kirkus Reviews*

"Gritty, powerful and fast-paced, *No One to Trust* starts off with a bang and never lets up. . . . This is one thriller that will keep you on the edge of your scat." —*Romantic Times*

## BODY OF LIES

"Filled with explosives, trained killers, intrigues within intrigues . . . it all adds up to one exciting thriller." —*Booklist*

"A romantic thriller whose humanity keeps the readers rooting for its heroine every step of the way." —*Publishers Weekly*

"[Johansen] doesn't let her readers down."
—*Newark Star-Ledger*

# FINAL TARGET

"A winning page-turner that will please old and new fans alike." —*Booklist*

"A compelling tale." —*Atlanta Journal-Constitution*

"Thrilling . . . will have fans of the author ecstatic and bring Ms. Johansen new readers."
—BookBrowser.com

# THE SEARCH

"Thoroughly gripping and with a number of shocking plot twists . . . [Johansen] has packed all the right elements into this latest work: intriguing characters; a creepy, crazy villain; a variety of exotic locations." —*New York Post*

"Johansen's thrillers ooze enough testosterone to suggest she also descends from the house of Robert Ludlum. Johansen pushes the gender boundary in popular fiction, offering up that rarity: a woman's novel for men." —*Publishers Weekly*

"Fans of Iris Johansen will pounce on *The Search*. And they'll be rewarded." —*USA Today*

"A spine-tingler." —*Miami Herald*

"Sabotage, dangerous secrets, and lots of dark action characterize Johansen's enthralling thriller."
—*Abilene Reporter-News*

## THE KILLING GAME

"Johansen is at the top of her game. . . . An enthralling cat-and-mouse game . . . perfect pacing . . . The suspense holds until the very end."
—*Publishers Weekly*

"Most satisfying." —*New York Daily News*

"[A] fast-paced, clever suspense novel that kept me intrigued to the end. In fact, I read it in one sitting." —*Roanoke Times*

"An intense whodunit that will have you gasping for breath." —*Tennessean*

"For a well-plotted thrill-a-minute read, you can't go wrong with this one." —*(NC) Southern Pines Pilot*

## THE FACE OF DECEPTION

"One of her best . . . a fast-paced, nonstop, clever plot in which Johansen mixes political intrigue, murder, and suspense." —*USA Today*

"The book's twists and turns manage to hold the reader hostage until the denouement, a sure crowd-pleaser." —*Publishers Weekly*

"Johansen keeps her story moving at breakneck speed." —*Chicago Daily Sun*

"This is a great mystery with exciting twists and turns." —*Baton Rouge Sunday Advocate Magazine*

## AND THEN YOU DIE

"Iris Johansen keeps the reader intrigued with complex characters and plenty of plot twists. The story moves so fast, you'll be reading the epilogue before you notice." —*People*

"Fans of Mary Higgins Clark will enjoy Iris Johansen's latest, a supercharged thriller. There's peril, romance, and suspense aplenty as the good guys face the clock to stop the villains."
—*Alfred Hitchcock Mystery Magazine*

"A well-crafted romance thriller." —*Kirkus Reviews*

"From the first page, the reader is pulled into a realm of danger, intrigue, and suspense with a touch of romance and enough twists and turns to gladden the hearts of all of her readers."
—*Library Journal*

# LONG AFTER MIDNIGHT

"Iris Johansen is incomparable." —Tami Hoag, *New York Times* bestselling author of *Ashes to Ashes*

"One of the most thrilling books I have curled up with in a long time." —Michael Palmer, *New York Times* bestselling author of *Silent Treatment* and *Critical Judgment*

"You'll be racing through to the last page." —Catherine Coulter, *New York Times* bestselling author of *The Maze*

"Flesh-and-blood characters, crackling dialogue and lean, suspenseful plotting." —*Publishers Weekly*

"A lively, engrossing ride by a strong new voice in the romantic suspense genre." —*Kirkus Reviews*

# THE UGLY DUCKLING

"Outstanding. A real page-turner. Many will add [Iris Johansen's] name to their list of favorite authors." —*Associated Press*

# BOOKS BY IRIS JOHANSEN

# IRIS
# JOHANSEN

___

# COUNTDOWN

___

Bantam Books

COUNTDOWN
A Bantam Book

PUBLISHING HISTORY
Bantam hardcover edition published June 2005
Bantam mass market edition / April 2006

Published by Bantam Dell
A Division of Random House, Inc.
New York, New York

*Book design by Virginia Norey*

Library of Congress Catalog Card Number: 2005046403

ISBN-13: 978-0-553-58651-0
ISBN-10: 0-553-58651-3

Printed in the United States of America
Published simultaneously in Canada

www.bantamdell.com

OPM 10 9 8 7 6 5 4 3 2

# COUNTDOWN

# 1

Find the key.

The hotel room was dark but he didn't dare turn on a light. Leonard had told him that Trevor and Bartlett were usually in the restaurant for an hour, but he couldn't count on it. Grozak had experience with that son of a bitch over the years and he knew Trevor's instincts were still as keen as they had been when he was a mercenary in Colombia.

So he'd give himself ten minutes tops and get out of here.

His penlight flashed around the room. As sterile and impersonal as most hotel rooms. Take the bureau drawers first.

He moved quickly across to the bureau and started going through them.

Nothing.

He went to the closet and dragged out the duffel and searched through it hurriedly.

Nothing.

Five minutes to go.

He went to the bedside table and opened the drawer. A notepad and pen.

Find the key, the Achilles' heel. Everyone had one.

Try the bathroom.

Nothing in the drawers.

The grooming kit.

Pay dirt!

Maybe.

*Yes.* At the bottom of the kit was a small, worn leather folder.

Photos of a woman. Notes. Newspaper clippings with photos of the same woman. Disappointment surged through him. Nothing about MacDuff's Run. Nothing about the gold. Nothing here to really help him. Hell, he'd hoped it was—

Wait. The woman's face was damn familiar. . . .

No time to read them.

He pulled out his digital camera and began to take the pictures. Send the prints to Reilly and show him that he might have the ammunition that he needed to control Trevor.

But this might not be enough for him. One more search of the bedroom and that duffel . . .

The worn, dog-eared sketchbook was under the protective board at the bottom of the duffel.

Probably nothing of value. He quickly flipped through the pages. Faces. Nothing but faces. He shouldn't have taken the extra time. Trevor would be here any minute. Nothing but a bunch of sketches of kids and old people and that bastard—

My God.

Jackpot!

He tucked the sketchbook under his arm and headed for the door, filled with heady exultation. He almost wished that he'd run into Trevor in the hall so that he'd have the chance to kill the son of a bitch. No, that would spoil everything.

I've *got* you, Trevor.

The alarm in Trevor's pocket was vibrating.

Trevor tensed. "Son of a bitch."

"What's wrong?" Bartlett asked.

"Maybe nothing. There's someone in my hotel room." He threw some money down on the table and stood up. "It could be the maid turning down my bed."

"But you don't think so." Bartlett followed him from the room to the elevator. "Grozak?"

"We'll see."

"A trap?"

"Not likely. He wants me dead but he wants the gold more. He's probably trying to find a map or any other info he can get his hands on."

"But you'd never leave anything of value there."

"He can't be sure of that." He stopped outside the door and drew his gun. "Stay here."

"No problem. If you get killed, someone has to

yell for the police, and I'll accept that duty. But if it is the maid, we may be asked to leave this domicile."

"It's not the maid. The room's dark."

"Then perhaps I should—"

Trevor kicked the door open, darted to one side, and hit the floor.

No shot. No movement.

He crawled behind the couch and waited for his eyes to become accustomed to the darkness.

Nothing.

He reached up and turned on the lamp on the end table by the couch.

The room was empty.

"May I join you?" Bartlett called from the hall. "I'm a bit lonely out here."

"Stay there for a minute. I want to make sure . . ." He checked the closet and then the bathroom. "Come in."

"Good. It was interesting watching you tear through that door like Clint Eastwood in a Dirty Harry movie." Bartlett cautiously entered the room. "But I really don't know why I risk my valuable neck with you when I could be safe in London." He looked around. "Everything looks fine to me. Are you becoming paranoid, Trevor? Perhaps that gadget you carry has a short circuit."

"Perhaps." He glanced through the drawers. "No, some of the clothes have been moved."

"How can you tell? It looks neat to me."

"I can tell." He moved toward the bathroom. The grooming kit was in almost the same position as he'd left it.

Almost.

Shit.

He unzipped the kit. The leather case was still there. It was the same black as the bottom of the kit and might not have been noticed.

"Trevor?"

"I'll be with you in a minute." He slowly opened the case and looked down at the articles and then the photo. She was looking up at him from the photo with the challenging stare he knew so well. Perhaps Grozak hadn't seen it. Perhaps he wouldn't think it important even if he had.

But could he afford to risk her life on that chance?

He moved quickly to the closet and jerked out the duffel and tore up the support board.

It was gone.

Shit!

## Harvard University

Hey, I thought you were going to study for that final."

Jane glanced up from her sketchbook to see her roommate, Pat Hershey, bounding into the room. "I had to take a break. I was getting too intense to keep a clear head. Sketching relaxes me."

"So would sleep." Pat smiled. "And you wouldn't have had to study so hard if you hadn't been out half of last night playing nursemaid."

"Mike needed someone to talk to." Jane made a

face. "He's scared to death that he's going to flunk out and disappoint everyone."

"Then he should be studying instead of crying on your shoulder."

Jane knew Pat was right, and she'd had moments of exasperation and impatience last night. "He's used to coming to me with problems. We've known each other since we were kids."

"And you're too soft to send him away now."

"I'm not soft."

"Except about people you care about. Look at me. You've gotten me out of quite a few jams since we started to room together."

"Nothing serious."

"They were serious to me." She strolled over and glanced at the sketch. "Good God, you're drawing him again."

Jane ignored the comment. "Did you have a good run?"

"Upped my distance a mile." Pat flopped down in the chair and began untying her running shoes. "You should have come with me. It's no fun for me running alone. I wanted the satisfaction of leaving you in the dust."

"No time." Jane finished the sketch in three bold strokes. "I told you, I had to study for my chemistry final."

"Yeah, that's what you told me." Pat grinned as she kicked off her shoes. "But here you are drawing Mr. Wonderful again."

"Believe me, he's not wonderful." She snapped the sketchbook shut. "And he's definitely not the type of man you'd take home to meet your mom and dad."

"A black sheep? Exciting."

"Only on soap operas. In real life they're big trouble."

Pat made a face. "You sound like a jaded woman of the world. You're twenty-one, for God's sake."

"I'm not jaded. Jaded is for people who don't have enough imagination to keep life interesting. But I've learned to tell the difference between intriguing and troublesome."

"I could learn to live with that kind of trouble when it's packaged so nicely. He's gorgeous. Sort of a cross between Brad Pitt and Russell Crowe. You must think so too or you wouldn't keep drawing his face."

Jane shrugged. "He's interesting. I find something new in his face every time I draw it. That's why I use him as a distraction."

"You know, I really like those sketches. I don't know why you haven't done a full portrait of him. It would be much better than the one you did of the old lady that won that prize."

Jane smiled. "I don't believe the judges would have agreed with you."

"Oh, I'm not knocking you. The other portrait was brilliant. But then, you're always brilliant. You'll be famous someday."

Jane made a rude sound. "Maybe if I live to be as old as Grandma Moses. I'm far too practical. I have no artistic temperament."

"You always make fun of yourself, but I've seen

you when you're working. You get lost. . . ." She tilted her head. "I've been wondering why you won't admit you have a fantastic future in store for you. It took me a while but I finally figured it out."

"Indeed? I can't wait to hear your take on this."

"Don't be sarcastic. I can be perceptive on occasion. I've decided for some reason you're afraid to reach out and grab the brass ring. Maybe you don't think you deserve it."

"What?"

"I'm not saying you're not confident. I just think you're not as sure of your talent as you should be. Good God, you won one of the most prestigious competitions in the country. That should tell you something."

"It told me the judges liked my style. Art is subjective. If there had been another set of judges, I might not have fared so well." She shrugged. "And that would have been okay. I paint what and who I want. It gives me pleasure. I don't have to be first with anyone else."

"Don't you?"

"No, I don't, Miss Freud. So back off."

"Whatever you say." Pat was still staring at the sketch. "You said he was an old friend?"

Friend? No way. Their relationship had been too volatile to involve friendship. "No, I said I knew him years ago. Hadn't you better take your shower?"

Pat chuckled. "Am I treading on private ground again? Sorry, it's my busybody nature. It comes from living in a small town all my life." She got to her feet and stretched. "You have to admit I restrain myself most of the time."

Jane smiled as she shook her head. "When you're sleeping."

"Well, you must not mind too much. You've roomed with me for two years and you've never put arsenic in my coffee."

"It could still happen."

"Nah, you're used to me now. Actually, we complement each other. You're guarded, hardworking, responsible, and intense. I'm open, lazy, spoiled, and a social butterfly."

"That's why you have a 4.0 average."

"Well, I'm also competitive and you spur me on. That's why I don't find a roommate who's a party girl like me." She pulled her T-shirt over her head. "Besides, I'm hoping Mr. Wonderful is going to show up so that I can seduce him."

"You'll be disappointed. He's not going to show up. He probably doesn't remember I'm alive, and now he's just an interesting face to me."

"I'd make sure he remembered me. What did you say his name was?"

Jane smiled teasingly. "Mr. Wonderful. What else?"

"No, really. I know you told me but I—"

"Trevor. Mark Trevor."

"That's right." Pat headed for the bathroom. "Trevor . . ."

Jane glanced down at the sketch pad. It was curious that Pat had suddenly zeroed in on Trevor again. In spite of what she'd said, she generally

respected Jane's privacy, and she'd backed off before when she'd seen Jane withdraw after she'd
questioned her about him.

"Stop analyzing." Pat stuck her head out of the
bathroom. "I can hear the wheels turning even over
the sound of the shower. I've just decided I need to
take you in hand and find a hunk to screw you and
release all that pent-up tension you're storing.
You've been living like a nun lately. This Trevor
seems a good candidate."

Jane shook her head.

Pat made a face. "Stubborn. Well, then I'll skip
him and go on to the local talent." She disappeared
back into the bathroom.

Skip Trevor? Not likely, Jane thought. She'd been
trying to ignore him for the past four years, and succeeded at times. Yet he was always in the background,
waiting to push into her consciousness. That was the
reason she'd started sketching his face three years
ago. Once the sketch was finished she could forget
him again for a while and get on with her life.

And it was a good life, full and busy and definitely not empty. She didn't need him. She was ac-
complishing her goals, and the only reason his
memory still lingered was that their time together
had taken place under such dramatic circumstances. Black sheep might be intriguing to Pat, but
she'd led a sheltered life and didn't realize how
much—

Her cell phone rang.

*  *  *

She was being followed.

Jane glanced over her shoulder.

No one.

At least, no one suspicious. A couple college guys out for a good time were strolling across the street and eyeing a girl who had just gotten off the bus. No one else. No one interested in her. She must be getting paranoid.

The hell she was. She still had her street kid's instincts and she trusted them. Someone had been following her.

Okay, it could be anyone. This neighborhood had bars on every block catering to college kids who streamed in from the surrounding campuses. Maybe someone had noticed that she was alone, zeroed in on her for a few minutes as a prospective lay, and then lost interest and ducked into a bar.

As she was going to do.

She glanced up at the neon light on the building ahead. The Red Rooster? Oh, for God's sake, Mike. If he was going to get soused, he could have at least picked a bar whose owner had a little originality.

That was too much to expect. Even when Mike wasn't in a panic, he was neither selective nor critical. Tonight he evidently wouldn't care if the place was called Dew Drop Inn if they'd serve him enough beer. Ordinarily, she would have opted to let him make his own mistakes and learn from them, but she'd promised Sandra she'd help him settle in.

And the kid was only eighteen, dammit. So get

him out, get him back to his dorm, and get him sober enough to talk sense into him.

She opened the door and was immediately assaulted by noise, the smell of beer, and a crush of people. Her gaze searched the room and she finally spotted Mike and his roommate, Paul Donnell, at a table across the bar. She moved quickly toward them. From this distance Paul seemed sober, but Mike was obviously royally smashed. He could hardly sit up in his chair.

"Jane." Paul rose to his feet. "This is a surprise. I didn't think you hit the bars."

"I don't." And it wasn't a surprise to Paul. He'd phoned her thirty minutes ago to tell her Mike was depressed and in the process of getting plastered. But if he wanted to protect his relationship with Mike by pretending he hadn't let her know, that was okay with her. She'd never cared much for Paul. He was too slick, too cool for her taste, but he evidently was worried about Mike. "Except when Mike is making an idiot of himself. Come on, Mike, we're getting out of here."

Mike looked blearily up at her. "Can't. I'm still sober enough to think."

"Barely." She glanced at Paul. "You pay the tab and I'll meet you at the door."

"Not going," Mike said. "Happy here. If I get one more beer down, Paul promised to crow like a rooster. A red rooster . . ."

Paul raised his brows and shook his head at Jane. "Sorry to put you through this. Since we've only been rooming together for a few months, he wouldn't listen to me. But he's always talking about you; I didn't think you'd mind if—"

"It's okay. I'm used to it. We grew up together and I've been taking care of him since he was six years old."

"You're not related?"

She shook her head. "He was adopted by the mother of the woman who took me in and raised me. He's a sweet kid when he's not being so damn insecure, but there are times when I want to shake him."

"Go easy on him. He's got a major case of nerves." He headed for the bar. "I'll pay the tab."

Go easy on him? If Ron and Sandra Fitzgerald hadn't been so easy on Mike, he wouldn't have forgotten what he'd learned on Luther Street and would be better able to cope in the real world, she thought in exasperation.

"Are you mad at me?" Mike asked morosely. "Don't be mad at me, Jane."

"Of course I'm mad at—" He was looking up at her like a kicked puppy and she couldn't finish. "Mike, why are you doing this to yourself?"

"Mad at me. Disappointed."

"Listen to me. I'm not disappointed. Because I know you're going to do fine once you work your way through this. Come on, we'll get out of here and go someplace where we can talk."

"Talk here. I'll buy you a drink."

"Mike. I don't want—" It was no use. Persuasion was striking out. Just get him out of here any way she could. "On your feet." Jane took a step closer to the table. "Now. Or I'll carry you in a fireman's lift and tote you out of here on my shoulder. You know I can do it, Mike."

Mike gazed up at her in horror. "You wouldn't do that. Everyone would laugh at me."

"I don't care if these losers laugh at you. They should be studying for their exams instead of pickling their brains. And so should you."

"Doesn't matter." He shook his head mournfully. "I'll flunk it anyway. I should never have come here. Ron and Sandra were wrong. I can never make it in an Ivy League school."

"The school would never have accepted you if they didn't think you could make it. You did fine in high school. This is no different if you work hard enough." She sighed as she realized she wasn't getting to him through that haze of alcohol. "We'll talk later. On your feet."

"No."

"Mike." She bent so that she could stare him directly in the eyes. "I promised Sandra that I'd take care of you. That means not letting you start off your first year like a drunken sot or get thrown in jail for underage drinking. Do I keep my promises?"

He nodded. "But you shouldn't have promised— I'm not a kid anymore."

"Then act like it. You have two more minutes before I make you look like the asshole you're being."

His eyes widened in alarm and he jerked to his feet. "Damn you, Jane. I'm not—"

"Shut up." She took his arm and propelled him toward the door. "I'm not feeling very warm toward you right now. I have a final tomorrow and I'll have to stay up till dawn to make up for this trip to town."

"Why?" he asked gloomily. "You'd ace it anyway. Some people have it. Some people don't."

"That's bull. And a pretty pitiful excuse for being lazy."

He shook his head. "Paul and I talked about it. It's not fair. You've got it all. In a few months you'll graduate with honors and make Eve and Joe proud. I'll be lucky to make it through at the bottom of my class."

"Stop blubbering." She opened the door and pushed him out of the bar. "You won't even make it through the first term if you don't shape up."

"That's what Paul said."

"Then you should have paid more attention." She saw Paul standing on the sidewalk and asked, "Where's his car parked?"

"Around the corner in the alley. All the parking spots were filled when we got here. Do you need help with him?"

"Not if he can walk," she said grimly. "I hope you took his car keys away from him."

"What kind of friend would I be if I didn't?" He reached in his pocket and handed her the keys. "Do you want me to drive your car back to school?"

She nodded, took her keys out of her purse, and gave them to him. "It's two blocks down. A tan Toyota Corolla."

"She worked two jobs and bought it herself." Mike shook his head. "Amazing, brilliant Jane.

She's the star. Did I tell you that, Paul? Everyone's proud of Jane. . . ."

"Come on." She grabbed his arm. "I'll show you amazing. You'll be lucky if I don't deck you before I get you back to the dorm. I'll see you back at your room, Paul."

"Right." He turned on his heel and set off down the street.

"Wonderful Jane . . ."

"Be quiet. I'm not going to let you blame your lack of purpose on me. I'll help you, but you're responsible for your life, just as I am for mine."

"I know that."

"You don't know zilch right now. Listen, Mike, we both grew up on the streets, but we were lucky. We've been given a chance to climb out."

"Not smart enough. Paul's right. . . ."

"You're all muddled." The alley was yawning just ahead. Her hand tightened on the key as she pressed the unlock button and pushed him toward his Saturn. "You can't even remember what—"

*Shadow. Leaping forward. Arm raised.*

She instinctively pushed Mike aside and ducked.

Pain!

In her shoulder, not her head, where the blow was aimed.

She whirled and kicked him in the belly.

He grunted and bent double.

She kicked him in the groin and listened with fierce satisfaction as he howled in agony. "Bastard." She took a step toward him. "Can't you—"

A bullet whistled by her ear.

Mike cried out.

Dear God. She hadn't seen any gun.

No, her attacker was still doubled over, groaning in pain. Someone else was in the alley.

And Mike was falling to his knees.

Get him out of here.

She opened the door of the Saturn and pushed him onto the passenger seat.

Another shadow running toward her from the end of the alley as she ran around to the driver's seat.

Another shot.

"Don't kill her, you fool. She's no good to us dead."

"The kid may already be dead. I'm not leaving a witness."

The voice came from right in front of her.

Blind him.

She turned the lights on high as she started the car.

And ducked as a bullet shattered the windshield.

The tires screeched as she stomped on the accelerator and backed out of the alley.

"Jane . . ."

She looked down at Mike and her heart sank. His chest . . . Blood. So much blood.

"It's okay, Mike. You're going to be fine."

"I . . . don't want to die."

"I'm taking you to the emergency room right now. You're not going to die."

"Scared."

"I'm not." Christ, she was lying. She was terrified,

but she couldn't let him see it. "Because there's no reason to be. You're going to get through this."

"Why?" he whispered. "Why did they— Money? You should have given it to them. I don't want to die."

"They didn't ask me for money." She swallowed. Don't cry now. Pull over and try to stop that bleeding and then get him to the emergency room. "Just hold on, Mike. Trust me. You're going to be all right."

"Promise . . . me." He was slumping forward in the seat. "Don't want to . . ."

Ms. MacGuire?"

A doctor?

Jane looked up quickly at the tall, fortyish man standing in the doorway of the waiting room. "How is he?"

"Sorry. I'm not a doctor. I'm Detective Lee Manning. I need to ask you a few questions."

"Later," she said curtly. She wished she could stop shaking. Dear God, she was scared. "I'm waiting for—"

"The doctors are working on your friend. It's a difficult operation. They won't be out to talk to you for a while."

"That's what they told me, but it's been over four hours, dammit. No one's said a word to me since they took him away."

"Operating rooms are busy places." He came toward her. "And I'm afraid we have to get a statement from you. You showed up here with a victim suffering a gunshot wound and we have to find out what happened. The longer we wait, the greater chance we have of losing the perpetrator."

"I told them what happened when I checked Mike in to the hospital."

"Tell me again. You say robbery didn't appear to be the motive?"

"They didn't ask for money. They wanted—I don't know what they wanted. They said something about the girl not being any good to them dead. That's me, I guess."

"Rape?"

"I don't know."

"It's possible. A kidnapping? Do your parents have a good deal of money?"

"I'm an orphan, but I've lived with Eve Duncan and Joe Quinn since I was a kid. Joe's a cop like you but he has private money. Eve is a forensic sculptor and she does more charity work than professional."

"Eve Duncan . . . I've heard of her." He turned as another man came into the room carrying a Styrofoam cup filled with steaming coffee. "This is Sergeant Ken Fox. He thought you'd need a pick-me-up."

"I'm glad to meet you, ma'am." Fox offered her the cup with a polite smile. "It's black, but I'll be glad to get you another one with cream if you like."

"Are you playing good cop, bad cop with me? It won't work." But she took the cup of coffee. She needed it. "Like I said, I was brought up by a cop."

"That must have come in handy tonight,"

Manning said. "It's hard to believe you were able to fight your way out of that alley."

"Believe what you like." She sipped the coffee. "But find out from the doctors if Mike's going to live. Those nurses gave me all kinds of soothing noncommittal assurances, but I don't know whether to believe them. They'll talk to you."

"They think he has a good chance."

"Just a chance?"

"He was shot in the chest and he lost a good deal of blood."

"I know." She moistened her lips. "I tried to stop it."

"You did a good job. The doctors say you may have saved his life. How did you know what to do?"

"I took EMT training three years ago. It comes in handy. I sometimes go to disaster sites with my friend Sarah Logan, who does canine rescue work."

"You seem to have all kinds of talents."

She stiffened. "Are you being sarcastic? I don't need that kind of hassle right now. I know you have a job to do, but back off."

"I wasn't trying to intimidate you." Manning grimaced. "Lord, you're defensive."

"My friend has just been shot. I think I have a right to be defensive."

"Hey, we're the good guys."

"Sometimes it's hard to tell." She gave him a cool glance. "And you haven't shown me your ID yet. Let's see it."

"Sorry." He reached in his pocket and pulled out his badge. "My error. Show her your ID, Fox."

She examined both IDs closely before handing them back. "Okay. Let's get this over quickly. I'll make a formal statement later but here's what you need to know right now. It was too dark in that alley for me to be able to ID the first man who attacked us. But when I turned on the headlights I got a glimpse of the man who shot Mike."

"You'll be able to recognize him?"

"Oh, yes." Her lips twisted. "No problem. I'm not going to forget him. Not ever. Give me a few hours after I get through this hell and I'll give you a sketch of him."

"You're an artist?"

"It's my major. And I've got a knack for portraiture. I've done sketches for the Atlanta PD before and they haven't complained." She took another sip of coffee. "Check with them if you don't believe me."

"I believe you," Fox said. "That will be a great help. But you only saw him for a moment. It would be hard to remember enough to—"

"I'll remember." She leaned wearily back in the chair. "Look, I'll do everything I can to help. I want to get this bastard. I don't know what the hell this is all about, but Mike didn't deserve this to happen to him. I've met a few people who did deserve to be shot." She shivered. "But not Mike. Will you go check and see if there's any—"

"No news." Joe Quinn's face was grim as he came into the waiting room. "I checked as soon as I got here."

"Joe." She jumped to her feet and ran across the

room toward him. "Thank God you're here. Those nurses were practically patting my head. They won't tell me anything. They're treating me like a kid."

"Heaven forbid. Don't they know you're twenty-one going on a hundred?" He hugged her and then turned to the two detectives. "Detective Joe Quinn. The head nurse tells me you're local police?"

Manning nodded. "Manning, and this is Sergeant Fox. Naturally, we have a few questions to ask the young lady. You understand."

"I understand that you're to leave her alone right now. She's not under suspicion, is she?"

Manning shook his head. "If she shot him, then she did a hell of a lot to keep him alive afterward."

"She's protected him all her life. There's no way she would have shot him. Give her a chance to get herself together and she'll cooperate later."

"So she told us," Manning said. "I was just about to leave when you came. Just doing our job."

Jane was tired of dealing with them. "Where's Eve, Joe? And how did you get here so quickly?"

"I hired a jet as soon as you called, and Eve and I came ahead. Sandra is flying in from New Orleans, where she was vacationing. Eve stayed at the airport to meet her flight and bring her here. Sandra's almost falling apart."

"I promised her I'd take care of him." She could feel the tears sting her eyes. "I didn't do it, Joe. I don't know what happened. Everything went wrong."

"You did your best."

"Don't tell me that. I didn't *do* it."

"Okay, but Sandra had no right to saddle you with that kind of responsibility."

"She's Eve's mother. She loves Mike. Hell, I love Mike. I'd have done it anyway."

"We'll wait in the hall," Sergeant Fox said. "Whenever you're ready to make a statement, Ms. MacGuire."

"Wait a minute. I'll go with you," Joe said. "I want to talk to you about the investigation." He turned to Jane. "I'll be right back. I want an update and then I'll go back to the nurse's desk and see if I can get more info about Mike."

"I'll go with you."

He shook his head. "You're upset and it shows. They'll be walking on eggshells around you. Let me do it. I'll get right back to you."

"I don't want to sit—" She stopped. He was right. She wiped her wet cheeks on the back of her hand. She couldn't stop crying, dammit. "Hurry, Joe."

"I'll hurry." He brushed his lips on her forehead. "You did nothing wrong, Jane."

"That's not true," she said shakily. "I didn't save him. Nothing could be more wrong than that."

# 2

"So what do you know about these sons of bitches?" Joe asked as soon as he was out of the room. "Any witnesses when they took off out of that alley?"

Manning shook his head. "No one's come forward yet. We're not even sure there weren't more than two men."

"Great."

"Look, we're doing the best we can. This is a college town, and every parent of every student is going to be on our ass when they hear about this."

"And they should be."

"Ms. MacGuire offered to sketch the face of one of the perpetrators. Will it be accurate?"

Joe nodded curtly. "If she saw him, you'll be able to use it. She's damn good."

Fox lifted a brow. "You wouldn't be prejudiced?"

"Definitely. All the way. But it's still true. I've watched her do sketches of people she'd seen for only an instant while she was under extreme duress, and they were absolutely correct in every detail."

"The motive seems to be murky. Do you have the kind of money that would tempt someone to make a snatch?"

"I'm not a Rockefeller or a Dupont but I'm comfortable." He shrugged. "Who the hell knows how much money it would take? I've seen drug addicts who'd cut their mother's throat for ten bucks." He glanced at his watch. Eve should be on her way here with her mother. Jesus, he'd hoped to have something to tell them. "What about tire tracks? DNA evidence?"

"We've got forensics going over the alley with a fine-tooth comb." Manning glanced over his shoulder at the waiting-room door. "She's a tough lady."

"You bet she is." Tough and loyal and loving and, dammit, she'd had enough trouble in her life without this happening to her.

"She was your ward?"

Joe nodded. "She's been with us since she was ten. Before that she was in a dozen foster-care facilities and virtually grew up on the streets."

"But she's been on Easy Street since she's been with you."

"If you call working every spare hour to pay her way through college Easy Street. Jane doesn't take anything she can't pay for."

"I wish I could say that about my son." Fox was

frowning. "She looks . . . familiar. She reminds me of someone. There's something about her face."

Oh, Jesus. Here we go again. "You're right. She's damn beautiful." He changed the subject. "Which brings us back to another possible motive. Rape? Or white slavery?"

"We're checking with Vice on any report of—"

"Shit." The elevator doors had opened, and Joe saw Eve and Sandra get out. "Look, there's Mike Fitzgerald's mother. I've got to take her and Eve in to Jane. But I promised Jane a report on Mike. Will you try to pump one of those nurses and see what you come up with?"

"Sure. I'll do it," Manning said as he started down the hall. "You go back and take care of your family."

Tough bastard. For a minute there I felt as if I was getting the third degree. I don't know if I'd be able to keep my mind on the investigation if my family was involved," Manning said as they headed for the nurses' station. "And it's clear he cares about the girl."

"Yeah." Fox was still frowning thoughtfully. "Protective as the devil. Who did you say her—" He suddenly snapped his fingers. "Eve Duncan!"

"What?"

"She said she lived with Eve Duncan."

"So?"

"So I remember who the kid reminds me of."

"Duncan?"

"No, I saw a Discovery Channel show about a year

ago about one of the reconstructions Duncan did of an actress buried in the ruins of Herculaneum two thousand years ago. At least, it was supposed to be her, but there was some kind of big investigation connected with . . ." He shook his head. "I can't remember. I'll have to go back and check on it. All I recall was that there was a big fuss about it at the time."

"You're getting off track. Who does Jane MacGuire remind you of?"

Manning glanced at him in surprise. "I'm not off track. It was the reconstruction. She's a dead ringer for that woman Eve Duncan was supposed to be doing the reconstruction of." He hesitated, searching for a name. "Cira."

Cira.

The name was triggering memory in Manning too. He had a vague recollection of a statue and the reconstruction side by side in a newspaper. "Convenient. Then maybe Duncan isn't as good at her job as she—" He broke off as the door to the operating room opened and two green-garbed doctors strode out. "It looks like we may not have to do any pumping. The operation must be over."

Sandra looked terrible, Jane thought when Joe, Eve, and Sandra walked into the waiting room. Haggard, pale, and twenty years older than when she'd seen her a month ago.

"I don't understand." Sandra stared at Jane accusingly. "What happened?"

"I told you what happened." Eve's hand closed

supportingly on Sandra's arm. "Jane doesn't know any more than we do."

"She has to know more. She was there." Her lips tightened. "And what the hell were you doing in that alley behind a bar with my son, Jane? You should have known that all kinds of drug addicts and criminals could be hanging—"

"Easy, Sandra," Eve said quietly. "I'm sure that she has an explanation. It's not her fault that—"

"I don't care whose fault it is. I want answers." Tears began to roll down her cheeks. "And she promised me that—"

"I tried." Jane's hands clenched into fists at her side. "I didn't know—I thought I was doing the right thing, Sandra."

"He's only a boy," Sandra said. "My boy. He came to me from that dreadful mother and he became *mine*. This shouldn't have happened to him. It shouldn't have happened to us."

"I know." Jane's voice was shaking. "I love him too. He's always been like a little brother to me. I always tried to take care of him."

"You did take care of him," Joe said. "Sandra's upset or she'd remember all the times you pulled him out of scrapes and kept him on the right path."

"You talk as if he was a bad kid," Sandra said. "Sometimes he didn't think, but every boy has moments that—"

"He *is* a great kid." Jane took a step closer. She wanted to reach out and touch her, comfort her, but Sandra stiffened and Jane stopped. "He's smart and sweet and he—"

"Quinn?" Manning stood in the doorway. "The operation is over and Doctor Benjamin is on his way to talk to you all. Fox and I will get in touch with you later."

The detective was carefully looking at no one but Joe, avoiding everyone else's eyes, Jane realized.

Oh, God.

"Mike?" Sandra whispered. "Mike?" She'd interpreted Manning's action the same way Jane had, and her eyes were wide with terror.

"The doctor will talk to you." Manning quickly turned and left the room, passing the surgeon on his way out.

Doctor Benjamin's expression was grave and sympathetic—and sad.

"No," Jane whispered. "No. No. No."

"I'm sorry," the doctor said. "I can't tell you how—"

Sandra screamed.


He's dead, Trevor," Bartlett said. "The kid died on the operating table."

"Shit." It was the worst-case scenario in an already bad situation. "When?"

"Two hours ago. They just left the hospital. Jane looked like hell."

Trevor swore. "Are Quinn and Eve with her?"

"Yes, they showed up at the hospital right before the kid died."

Then at least Jane had family support and

protection. "Do you know when they're having the funeral?"

"Hey, it just happened. And you told me to watch her but not to contact her."

"Find out."

"Are you going to the funeral?"

"I don't know yet."

"Do you want me to come back to the Run?"

"Hell, no. Stay there and keep an eye on her. She's more vulnerable now than ever."

"You think it was Grozak?"

"Good chance. The coincidence is a little too pat for comfort. They wanted Jane and the kid got in the way."

"Sad." Bartlett's voice was heavy. "I can't tell you how sorry I am that I failed her. I had no idea. It happened so fast. She disappeared with the kid into the alley and the next thing I knew the car was roaring out into the street."

"It wasn't your fault. We weren't even sure that Grozak was on the scene. You hadn't seen any suspicious signs."

"Sad," Bartlett repeated. "Life is precious and he was very young."

"So is Jane. And I don't want Grozak to get his hands on her. Watch her."

"You know I will. But I'm not competent enough to handle types like Grozak if the situation becomes dicey. As you know, I have a brilliant mind but no lethal training. You'd better send Brenner or come yourself."

"Brenner is in Denver."

"Then you have no choice, do you?" Bartlett asked. "You'll have to make contact with her and tell her."

"And let Grozak know his guess was on target? No way. He could have been playing a hunch when he sent men to Harvard. I don't want to confirm anything that would indicate Jane may be important to Cira's gold."

"Pretty rough play for a hunch. He killed Mike Fitzgerald."

"Not too rough for Grozak. I've seen him cut a man's throat for accidentally stepping on his toes. He's probably the most vicious son of a bitch I've ever run across. But this was too clumsy. Whoever shot the kid ran off his mouth and tipped his hand. It was probably Leonard, and I'd bet Grozak didn't order the kill. It's more likely Leonard screwed up."

"Then maybe he'll back off now that Jane's on guard and surrounded by family."

"Maybe." He hoped Bartlett was right, but he couldn't count on it. "Maybe not. Stay as close as her shadow." He hung up the phone and leaned back in his chair. Christ, he'd hoped the kid would pull through. Not only because innocent bystanders weren't fair game, but because Jane didn't need another scar. She'd suffered enough wounds growing up in the slums to last her for a lifetime. Not that she'd ever talked about her childhood. Their time together had been too wary for confidences. Too wary for any normal personal interchange. But then nothing about their interaction four years ago had been normal. It had been stimulating, terrifying, disturbing, and . . . sensual. Christ, yes, sensual. Memories he'd carefully suppressed were surfacing and his body was tensing, responding as if she were standing before him instead of being in that college town hundreds of miles away.

Send those memories back where they came from. This was the worst possible time to let sex enter the picture. Not only for him but for Jane MacGuire.

If he could keep her at a distance, it would increase her chances of survival.

She's sleeping now." Eve came out of the hotel bedroom into the sitting room and carefully closed the door. "The doctor gave her a sedative strong enough to knock an elephant out."

"The only problem with that is she'll have it all to face again when she wakes up," Jane said. "I knew it would be bad for her, but I had no idea she'd completely fall apart. Ever since I was a kid, she seemed almost as strong as you are, Eve."

"She is strong. She kicked the drug habit, she helped me through that nightmare when my Bonnie was killed. She built a new life and a new marriage for herself and then survived a divorce from Ron." Eve rubbed her temple. "But the loss of a child can destroy everything. It almost destroyed me."

"Where's Joe?"

"He's making arrangements for the funeral. Sandra wants to take Mike home to Atlanta. We're leaving tomorrow afternoon."

"I'll go with you. You're staying with her tonight?"

Eve nodded. "I want to be here when she wakes up. She may not sleep as well as we hope."

"Or she might have nightmares." Jane added wearily, "But it seems being awake is the nightmare. I can't believe it happened. I can't believe Mike is—" She had to stop as her voice broke. She started again a moment later. "Sometimes life doesn't make sense. He had everything to live for. Why did it—" She stopped again. "Dammit, I lied to him. He was so scared. I told him to trust me, that I'd make sure he was okay. He believed me."

"And it gave him comfort. You didn't know it was a lie. In a way it was more of a prayer." Eve leaned back in the chair. "I'm glad you were there for him. When some of the pain fades for Sandra, she'll be glad too. She knows how much Mike cared about you, how much you helped him."

"Maybe he didn't really feel like— He said a few things last night when I came to get him that— Mike wasn't the most secure kid in the world, and I was tough on him sometimes."

"And you were wonderful to him ninety percent of the time. So stop playing what-might-have-been. You can't ever win that game. Think of the good times."

"It's hard to do right now. All I can remember is that bastard shooting Mike. Perhaps it was my fault. I acted instinctively when he attacked. Maybe if I hadn't resisted, he would have just robbed us. Mike asked me why I didn't give him the money. He didn't ask for money, but perhaps if I'd given him a chance to—"

"You said that the other man said something about getting the girl. That doesn't sound like robbery."

"No. You're right. I'm not thinking clearly." She wearily pushed back her chair and stood up. "Maybe it was going to be a rape or a kidnapping, like Manning said. Who the hell knows?" She headed for the door. "I'm going back to my dorm and pack. I'll see you in the morning. Call me if you need me."

"What I need is for you to remember the good things about your years with Mike."

"I'll try." She paused and then looked back over her shoulder. "Do you know what I remember most? It was when we were kids together and Mike had left home and was hiding out in an alley a few blocks from his house. His mother was a prostitute, and you know how bad it was for Mike whenever his father came home. I'd bring him food and at night I'd slip out of the house and go to keep him company. He was only six and he was scared at night. He got scared a lot. But it was better when I was there. I'd tell him stories and he'd—" Jesus, she was choking up again. "He'd go to sleep." She opened the door. "And now he's never going to wake up again."


You can't go, Trevor," Venable said sharply. "You don't even know that it was Grozak."

"It was Grozak."

"You can't be sure of that."

"I'm not asking your permission, Venable. I told

you what you had to do and gave you the courtesy of informing you that there's a problem. If I decide it's best, I'm gone."

"What you're doing there is more essential. Why go off on the chance that Grozak was involved? Sometimes I think Sabot is right and Grozak isn't going to be able to pull this off anyway. He's vicious but definitely small potatoes."

"I told you that I believe Thomas Reilly may be involved. That changes the whole complexion of the situation."

"And you're relying on pure deduction. There's no proof. And she's *not* important. You can't risk endangering the—"

"You do your job. I'll decide what's important." He hung up.

Christ, Venable could be difficult. Trevor would have preferred to just leave him in the dark about Jane. He couldn't do that. In an operation this delicate, to have any player stumbling around in ignorance would be foolhardy, if not actually suicidal. Even if he hadn't made a decision about whether to leave the work here at MacDuff's Run, he had to have Venable cover his bases.

He rose to his feet and moved down the hall to the studio Mario was using. Mario had already gone to the adjoining bedroom, and Trevor crossed the study to stand before the statue of Cira. The moonlight was pouring into the room and illuminating the features of the bust. He never got tired of looking at it. The high cheekbones, the winged brows that looked a little like Audrey Hepburn's, the lovely curve and sensitivity of that mouth. A beautiful woman whose attraction lay more in the strength and personality of her spirit than in her features.

Jane.

He smiled as he thought how angry she would be to have him compare her to Cira. She'd been fighting it for too long. And it wasn't really true. The resemblance was there, but since he'd met Jane he no longer saw Cira when he looked at the statue. It was Jane, alive, vibrant, intelligent, and very, very direct.

His smile faded. And that directness could be her worst enemy right now. She only knew one way to go, and that was straight ahead, jumping over all obstacles. She wouldn't be content to sit and wait for the police to find clues to Fitzgerald's death.

He touched the statue's cheek and it felt smooth and cold beneath his finger. Right now he wished he still did think of the statue as Cira.

Smooth and cold.

Without life . . .

His phone rang. Venable again?

"Trevor, Thomas Reilly."

Trevor stiffened.

"We haven't met, but I believe you've probably heard of me. We have a common interest. We almost ran into each other several times in Herculaneum over the years when we were pursuing that common interest."

"What do you want, Reilly?"

"What we both want. But I'll be the one to get it, because I want it more than you or anyone else. I've been studying your background and you appear to have a streak of softness, a certain idealism I wouldn't have attributed to you. You may even be willing to hand the gold over to me."

"Dream on."

"Of course, I'd be willing to let you have a percentage."

"How kind. And what about Grozak?"

"Unfortunately, my friend Grozak is fumbling, and I feel the need for a backup."

"So you're double-crossing him."

"That's up to you. I'll deal with whoever can supply what I want. I'll probably even tell Grozak I've contacted you to stir up a little competition."

"You want the gold."

"Yes."

"I don't have it yet. I wouldn't give it to you if I did."

"I'd judge you have an excellent chance of finding it. But the gold isn't everything I want."

"The Cira statue. You can't have it."

"Oh, I'll have it. It belongs to me. You stole it away from me when I was trying to buy it from that dealer. I'll have it all."

"All?"

"I want something else. I'll make you a proposition. . . ."

That was Joe Quinn calling from the airport," Manning said as he hung up the phone. "He wants protection for Jane MacGuire when she comes back to school after the funeral."

"Are you going to request it?" Fox asked as he leaned back in his office chair.

"Of course I'm going to request it." Manning shook his head. "But after that budget cut, the captain is going to go ballistic unless I can show definite cause. Can we tie anything into that case you said you read about on the Internet?"

"Maybe. Let's see. . . ." Fox leaned forward and typed an access code into his computer. "I pulled up this old newspaper article when we came back to the precinct from the hospital. It's interesting, but I don't believe we're going to see a connection to anyone with homicidal tendencies. Unless we're talking about ghosts." He pressed a button to bring up the article and then swung the laptop around on his desk so that Manning could read it. "Evidently this serial killer, Aldo Manza, had a father who had an obsession with an actress who lived two thousand years ago, at the time of the eruption of Vesuvius that destroyed Herculaneum and Pompeii. The father was an archaeologist who wasn't above peddling illegal artifacts, and he'd found a statue of the actress, Cira, in the ruins of Herculaneum."

"So?"

"Aldo developed an obsession too. He couldn't stand to let any woman live who bore a resemblance to the statue of Cira his father possessed. He'd go after them and slice off their face before he killed them."

"Gory bastard. And you said Jane MacGuire looks like this Cira?"

Fox nodded. "The spitting image. That's why she became a target."

"Stalked?"

"Yes. But Eve Duncan and Quinn managed to turn the tables on him. They set a trap in the tunnels below Herculaneum. Duncan reconstructed the face of one of the skulls the scientists found in the marina at Herculaneum, and they publicized it as being the skull of Cira. It wasn't, of course. It was a deliberate phony done by Duncan. The real skull looked nothing like Cira. But the combination of the skull and the presence of Jane MacGuire drew Aldo close enough so that they could take him out."

"He's dead?"

"As a doornail. Like his father."

"Any relatives who might want revenge?"

"Wouldn't they have tried before this? It's been four years."

Manning frowned. "Maybe." He was reading the article. Everything checked out as Fox had described, but there was one line that puzzled him. "It mentions that Duncan, Quinn, the girl, and a Mark Trevor were at the scene. Who's Mark Trevor?"

Fox shook his head. "I accessed a couple of other articles, and some of them have a mention of him. None of the other people present in that tunnel would make a comment about him. He was clearly at the scene but he left before either the police or media could interview him. One article indicated there were hints he had a criminal background."

"And yet Quinn's protecting him for some reason?"

"I didn't say that. He's just not talking about him."

"But if Trevor was involved with Fitzgerald's killing, I can't see Quinn not serving him up to us. He's too protective of the girl. Does Trevor have a record?"

"Maybe."

"What do you mean? Either he does or he doesn't."

"I can't seem to get through to the right database. It bounces me out."

"That's crazy. Keep trying."

Fox nodded as he turned the laptop back around to face him. "But you said you didn't think Quinn would protect Trevor if he suspected him. Why waste the time?"

"Because there's always the possibility that Quinn might want to leave us out of it and cut Trevor's throat himself."

"He's a cop, for God's sake. He wouldn't do that."

"No? How would you feel if it was your kid, Fox?"

Lake Cottage
Atlanta, Georgia

What are you doing out here on the porch?" Eve asked as she came up the steps. "It's the middle of the night."

"I couldn't sleep." Jane pushed her dog, Toby, to one side to make room for Eve on the top step. "I thought you'd be staying with Sandra at her condo."

"I was planning on it, but Ron showed up and I felt a little de trop. They may be divorced, but they both loved Mike. I'm glad he's there for her."

Jane nodded. "I remember all the fishing trips he took Mike on when he was a kid. Is he going to the funeral tomorrow?"

"Today," Eve corrected. "Probably. Did Joe go to bed?"

"Yes. He wasn't expecting you either. You'd better get some sleep. It's going to be a difficult day." She looked out at the lake. "A nightmare of a day."

"For you, too. It's been a nightmare since the moment you met Mike in that bar." She paused. "Do you ever have those dreams of Cira anymore?"

Jane looked back at her, startled. "What? Where did that come from?"

Eve shrugged. "Nightmares. It just popped into my mind."

"Now? It's been four years and you've never mentioned anything about them."

"That doesn't mean I haven't thought about them. I just figured it would be better if we forgot about everything connected with that time."

"That's not easy to do."

"Obviously," Eve said dryly. "You've been on three archaeological field trips back to Herculaneum since you entered Harvard."

Jane gently stroked Toby's head. "You never argued with me about it."

"That would have been placing too much importance on something I wanted to fade from your memory. That didn't stop me from hating it. I didn't want you to spend your youth chasing an obsession."

"It's not an obses— Well, maybe it is. I only know I have to find out about Cira. I have to know if she lived or died when that volcano erupted."

"Why? It was two thousand years ago, dammit."

"You know why. She had my face. Or I have her face. Whatever."

"And you dreamed about her for weeks before you actually knew she existed."

"I probably read about her someplace."

"But you haven't been able to verify that."

"That doesn't mean it didn't happen." She made a face. "I like that explanation better than some wacky psychic bullshit."

"You didn't answer me. Have you dreamed about her?"

"No. Satisfied?"

"Partially." She was silent a moment. "Have you been in contact with Mark Trevor?"

"What is this? Twenty questions?"

"It's me, loving you, and making sure that you're okay."

"I'm okay. And I haven't talked to Trevor since that night he left Naples four years ago."

"I thought you might have run into him on one of those excavations."

"He wouldn't be on his knees spooning dirt with college kids. He knows where those scrolls are buried, blast him." Trevor had been involved in the smuggling of ancient Roman artifacts when he was contacted by a less than legitimate professor of antiquities and his son, Aldo. They'd discovered a library in a tunnel leading from the villa of Julius Precebio, one of the ancient town's leading citizens. The library had proved to contain a number of bronze tubes holding priceless scrolls, which had escaped the lava flow that destroyed the villa. Many of the scrolls had been devoted to describing Julius's mistress, Cira, who had been a bright star in the theater at Herculaneum. Aldo and his father had blown the tunnel to kill everyone who had knowledge of its location, including Trevor. But he'd managed to escape. "Trevor's the one who camouflaged the site after the cave-in. He doesn't want anyone to find that tunnel before he can go back and get that chest of gold Julius mentioned in the scrolls."

"Maybe he's already found it."

"Maybe." Jane had often wondered that same thing, but she had still kept searching. "But I have a feeling . . . I don't know. I have to keep looking. Dammit, I should be the one to find those scrolls. I deserve it. I'm the one who had that crazy after me trying to slice off my face because I looked like Cira."

"Then why didn't you tackle Trevor and get him to tell you where they were?"

"Persuading Trevor to do anything is never an option. He wants the gold, and he believes he deserves it after he lost his friend Pietro in that tunnel. Besides, how was I supposed to find him when Interpol couldn't keep track of him?"

"I rather thought he might have contacted you when you were over there."

"No." On Jane's first expedition she had fought that irrational thought for the entire time she was in Herculaneum. She had found herself looking over her shoulder, remembering Trevor's voice, fighting the feeling that he was around the corner, in the next room, somewhere—near. "It's not likely that he'd stay in touch. I was only seventeen and he thought I was too young to be interesting."

"Seventeen going on thirty," Eve said. "And Trevor was no fool."

"You'd be surprised."

"Nothing Trevor would do would surprise me. He was one of a kind."

Eve's tone was almost affectionate, Jane realized. "You liked him."

"He saved my life. He saved Joe. He saved you. It's hard to dislike a man who's stacked up that kind of credit. That doesn't mean I approve of him. His intelligence may be off the charts, and he definitely has a way about him. But he's a smuggler, a con man, and God knows what else."

"What else indeed? He's had four years to get into all kinds of nefarious pursuits."

"At least you're not defending him."

"No way. He's probably the most brilliant man I've ever met and could coax the birds from the trees. Other than that, he's an enigma, he's proficient in all manner of violence, and he has an addiction to walking a tightrope. None of those qualities tend to endear themselves to a hardheaded, practical woman like me."

"Woman . . ." Eve sadly shook her head. "I still think of you as a girl."

"Then that's what I'll stay." Jane leaned her head against Eve's shoulder. "Whatever you want me to be. You name it."

"I just want you to be happy." She brushed her lips against Jane's forehead. "And not waste your life chasing after a woman who's been dead two thousand years."

"I won't waste my life. I just have to have my questions answered before I can walk away."

Eve was silent a moment. "Maybe you're right. Maybe I was wrong to want to bury the past. Maybe it would have been healthier to just let you go for it."

"Stop blaming yourself. You never said a word to me when I went back to Herculaneum."

Eve stared out at the lake. "No, I never said a word to you."

"And it's not as if I'm devoting all my time to Cira. I've won a couple art competitions, I've gone on several search-and-rescue missions with Sarah, and I've kept my grades up." She looked up with a smile. "And I haven't been toying with gorgeous ne'er-do-wells like Mark Trevor. I'm golden."

"Yes, you are." Eve straightened and rose to her feet. "And I want to keep you that way. We'll talk more after this funeral is over." She headed for the door. "We'd both better get some sleep. I told Sandra we'd pick her up at eleven."

"I'll come in soon. I want to stay out here with Toby for a while." She gave the dog a hug. "Lord, I miss him when I'm at school." She paused. "Why did all this come tumbling out now, Eve?"

"I don't know." She opened the screen door. "Mike. That horrible, senseless murder. I guess it reminded me of Aldo and his fixation on Cira, all those killings . . . and the way he stalked you. And now Mike's murder may have something to do with you too."

"Maybe not. We don't know anything for sure."

"No, we don't." The door closed behind her.

It was odd that Eve had connected Mike's murder with that nightmare time in Herculaneum. Or maybe not so strange. She, Joe, Eve, and Trevor had been bound together in a common purpose to put an end to that monster, Aldo, and then had put it behind them. Only how could you truly abandon the memory of an experience like that and walk away? She and Trevor had been knit so closely that she felt as if she had known him forever. It hadn't mattered that his past was murky or that he was totally ruthless and self-serving. She had been motivated by self-preservation and he had been driven by greed and revenge. Yet they had come together and gotten the job done.

Stop thinking about him. Talking to Eve about Trevor had caused the flood of memory to rush back to her. She had put him firmly in the back of her consciousness and only brought him out at her convenience. That way she remained in control as she had never succeeded in doing when she was with him.

What could you expect? She had only been seventeen and he had been almost thirty and experienced as hell. She had handled him very well considering the emotional storm she'd been going through at the time.

She stood up and moved toward the door. Forget Trevor and Cira. They didn't belong in her life right now. She had to concentrate on her family and the effort it was going to take to get through today.

# 3

She hated funerals, Jane thought numbly as she stared down at the coffin. Whoever thought they were some kind of catharsis must be nuts. Every moment hurt, and she could see no healing coming from this ritual. She'd said her own good-byes to Mike during these last three days since that senseless murder. She was only here for Sandra.

And Sandra looked like she was going to collapse any moment and was paying attention to no one. Eve was standing beside her, but Sandra probably didn't even know she was there. Several of Mike's friends were gathered at the grave site. Jane knew a few of them: Jimmy Carver, Denise Roberts, and Paul Donnell. Her roommate, Pat, had also flown down for the funeral and was looking uncharacteristically solemn. Nice of her to come. Nice of all of them.

Only a few more minutes and they could leave the cemetery. Those minutes seemed to take a lifetime.

It was over.

She stepped forward to throw her rose on the coffin.

"Is there anything I can do?" Pat asked as Jane turned away from the grave. "I'm supposed to get back to school, but I'll bail if you need me."

Jane shook her head. "Go on. I don't need you. I'll see you tomorrow or maybe the next day."

Pat made a face. "I should have known. You don't need anyone. You're always willing to step up to the plate if I'm in a jam but heaven forbid if I try to return the favor. Did it ever occur to you that I'd feel good to be on the giving end?"

"You don't know how much you've already given me." She swallowed to ease the tightness of her throat. "I should have told you. Sometimes it's difficult for me to . . . When I first met you, I was so serious and responsible I couldn't even think about just relaxing and having a good time. You taught me that having a good time isn't a crime and that joy can come from some pretty bizarre situations."

Pat smiled. "You mean like the time we got stuck in the car in that snowstorm because you had to come and get me when I drank too much? Not much joy there. You gave me hell."

"You deserved it. But even from that fiasco there will be good memories. We sang stupid songs and talked for hours while we waited to be rescued. It . . . enriched me. You enriched me."

Pat didn't speak for a moment. "I do believe I'm choking up. I'd better get out of here." She gave Jane a quick hug. "I'll see you tomorrow."

Jane watched her walk away. Pat was almost as awkward at personal interchanges as Jane was. Strange they shared that reticence when they were so different in other ways. Pat had been caught off guard by Jane's words at this sensitive moment. It was because of the very sadness of this time that the words had tumbled from Jane's lips. She had lost one friend, and she wished with all her heart that she'd been able to tell him how much he meant to her. She wasn't going to make that mistake again.

"Jane." Paul Donnell was standing beside her, his face pale. "I'm sorry. I didn't get a chance to talk to you before, but I want you to know how— I can't tell you how I regret not walking you back to the car that night. I didn't think— I hope you don't blame me for—"

"I don't blame anyone but the bastard who killed Mike. And how could you know it would happen?"

He nodded quickly, jerkily. "That's right. I couldn't know, but I still regret— I liked Mike. I never wanted anything to happen to him. I just had to tell you that I—" He turned away. "I just wanted to say I'm sorry."

She watched him walk away. He was truly upset. Upset enough to disturb that slick facade he usually maintained. Perhaps he and Mike had been closer friends than she'd thought. Or perhaps he did feel guilty for not being there when Mike had needed him. A thought occurred to her. Or perhaps it was—

"Come on, Jane." Joe was beside her, taking her arm. "I'll drive you back to the cottage."

"Okay." Then she suddenly shook her head. "No, I have to go to the airport. I'm going to say good-bye to Sandra and then go back to school. There's something I have to do there."

"Jane, take a few days off. You need—"

"There's something I have to do." She turned away. "I'll be okay, Joe."

"The hell you will. You're not okay right now. Look, Sandra's upset. She doesn't really blame you. It wouldn't make sense."

"She blames me," she added sadly. "She blames everyone and everything right now. She can't even stand to look at me. I know she doesn't want to hurt me. She can't help it. Her world's upside down. You and Eve need to comfort her and it's better if I'm not around."

"She's not the only one who needs comforting," Joe muttered. "You need us, dammit."

"I have you. You're always with me." She tried to smile. "I don't have to have you in the same room or holding my hand. I believe Sandra does right now. I'll call you after I get back to my dorm. Okay?"

"No. But I guess it will have to be. You're not going to give in." His lips tightened. "But I'm not going to let you go back there unprotected. I've hired a security guard to tail you until Manning's investigation turns up a reason for that attack. He'll be waiting at your dorm when you get there."

"I don't care. If it makes you feel better."

"You're damn right it makes me feel better." He opened the door of the car for her. "No one is going to hurt you."

It was too late. She was already hurting. She couldn't erase the image of Mike lying in that car with the blood pouring from his chest, begging her to help him.

She could feel her eyes stinging. Not now. Don't start crying again now.

The time for tears was over.

$P_{aul}$."

Paul Donnell stiffened and turned around as he was climbing the steps to his dorm. "Jane?" He smiled. "What are you doing here? I thought you'd be staying behind in Atlanta. May I help you?"

"I believe you can." She reached over and opened the passenger door of her car. "Get in."

His smile faded. "I'm afraid you've caught me at a bad time. I'm behind in my homework since I took time out to go to the funeral. Suppose I call you tomorrow."

"Suppose you get in the car," she said curtly. "Don't play games with me, Paul. Do you want to talk to me or do you want to talk to the police?"

"That sounds like a threat. I've been upset enough because I lost my friend, and I don't need—"

"Was he your friend? Do you betray your friends, Paul?"

He moistened his lips. "I don't know what you mean."

"Do you want me to explain? Do you want me to get out of this car and shout it so that everyone on the campus can hear me? I'll do it. Mike must have told you that I'm not in the least shy."

He was silent for a moment. "Yes, he told me."

"He confided a lot of things to you. Because he trusted you. Mike was vulnerable to anyone he thought was his friend."

"I was his friend. I resent you—"

She opened the driver's door and started to get out.

"No!" He strode around the car. "If you won't be reasonable, I'll have to—"

"I'm not reasonable." She locked the doors as soon as he got in the car, and took off. "I'm angry and I want answers."

"You have no reason to be angry with me." He paused. "Just what do you think I did?"

"I think you set Mike up." Her hands tightened on the steering wheel. "I think you worked on him until he was so depressed and scared that he was like putty in your hands. I think you got him drunk and then called me. I think you knew someone was waiting in that alley."

"Crap. Look, I know Mike said some weird stuff that night, but he was drunk."

"That's what I believed until it all came together after the funeral and I was wondering why you were so nervous. There were plenty of parking meters available on that street. Why risk being towed off by parking in the alley?"

"There weren't any spaces when we got there."

"When I got to the airport today, I went straight to the Red Rooster and questioned the bartender. He said that it was a slow night and there were plenty of available spaces on the street when he came on duty at seven. You got there at seven-fifteen, right?"

"I'm not sure."

"That's what the bartender said."

"Pull over. I don't have to take this."

"Yes, you do." But she pulled over to the side of the road and turned off the car. "Talk to me. Who paid you to set Mike up?"

"No one."

"Then you did it because you had a grudge against him?"

"Of course not."

"Then we're back to square one."

"I didn't have anything to do with it."

"Bullshit." She stared him straight in the eye. "You're scared stiff. I could almost taste it at the cemetery. You weren't grieving. You were putting on a front because you were afraid someone would suspect the truth."

His gaze slid away. "The police didn't think so."

"They will when I have a talk with them. I'm a cop's kid. That's almost family. They'll pay attention when I ask them to look closer at you."

"They won't find anything. It's not as if I'm some juvenile delinquent. I come from a good family."

"And I come from one of the lousiest neighborhoods in Atlanta, where whores and pimps and every kind of scum walk the street. That's how I can recognize scum when I see it."

"Let me out of the car."

"When you tell me who paid you and why."

His lips tightened. "You're only a woman. I could force you to open this door anytime I choose. I'm just placating you."

"I'm a woman brought up by a cop who was a SEAL and wanted me to be able to keep myself safe. Joe's first rule was don't waste your time if you're attacked. Assume you're going to be killed and react accordingly. Kill them."

"You're bluffing."

"I'm telling you the way it is. You're the one who threatened me. All I want right now is information."

"You're not going to get it. Don't you think I know you'll go running to the police?" He burst out, "And it wasn't my fault. None of it was my fault."

A crack in the armor. "No one's going to believe that if you don't go to the police and confess."

"Confess? Criminals confess. I didn't do anything criminal. I didn't know." He gave her a panicky glance. "And I'll tell them you lied if you say I—"

"What didn't you know?"

He was silent. Yet she could feel his sick fear. He was almost there. Push him a little bit more. "You were an accessory to murder. They'll put you away and throw away the key. Or does this state have a death penalty?"

"Bitch."

Breaking. Push a little harder. "I'll go straight from here to the police. They'll probably pick you up in a few hours. If you tell me what I want to know, I'll let you turn yourself in and try to schmooze your way out of this."

"It's not my *fault*. Nothing was supposed to happen. They said that they just wanted to talk to you and you weren't cooperating."

"Who wanted to talk to me?"

He didn't answer.

"Who?"

"I don't know. Leonard . . . I don't remember."

"Was Leonard his first name or his last name?"

"I told you—I don't— His last. If it was his real name."

"Why should you doubt it?"

"I didn't, until— I didn't want Mike to die—I didn't want to hurt anyone."

"Do you know Leonard's first name?"

He was silent a moment. "Ryan."

"What was the other man's name?"

"I have no idea. He never introduced himself. Leonard did all the talking."

"Where did you meet them?"

"I didn't meet them exactly. I was sitting in a bar a few weeks ago and they sat down and started talking. I needed the money and they promised it would be okay. All I had to do was make sure you came to the alley so they could talk to you."

"And it wasn't difficult, was it? Because Mike was

so easy to manipulate. Just jerk a few strings and he'd dance."

"I liked Mike. I didn't want to hurt him."

"You did hurt him. You made him feel inadequate and then you set him up."

"I need the money. Harvard's expensive, and my parents can barely afford the tuition. I was living like a pauper."

"Did you think of getting a job?"

"Like you did?" he asked sourly. "So perfect. Mike hated that about you."

Don't show him how that jab hurt. "How do we find this Ryan Leonard?"

He shrugged. "I have no idea. They gave me half the money when I agreed to do it, and they put an envelope with the rest of the cash in my post office box when I called and told them I'd bring you to the Red Rooster that night. I haven't heard from them since."

"Do you still have the envelope?"

He nodded. "I didn't spend the money. It's still in the envelope. After Mike was— I was afraid to even put it in the bank. I thought it might look incriminating if I had to go to the police. But there's no address. It's just a blank envelope."

"Where is it?"

"In my room at the dorm."

"Where?"

"In my English lit book."

"And you saw the other man that night?"

"I told you I did. Why?"

"Because I only saw one. I need a description."

"Now?"

"No, not now." She couldn't take any more. She unlocked the door. "Get out. I'll give you two hours to get to a police station and try to convince them how innocent you are. If you take off, I'll send them after you." Her lips tightened. "And I'll come after you too."

"I'm not a fool. I'll turn myself in. Not that I'm afraid of you. It's just the smart thing to do." He got out of the car. His fear was fading, and he smiled with a touch of bravado. "I'll get off. Maybe I'll only have to plea-bargain. I've got everything going for me. I'm young and smart and they'll just believe I'm a clean-cut kid who made a mistake in judgment."

She felt sick. God, he might be right. "Tell me. How many pieces of eight, Paul?"

"What?"

"How much did they pay you?"

"Ten thousand when I agreed. Another ten when I set it up."

"And you didn't question why they'd spend that kind of money just to talk to me?"

"It wasn't my business. If they wanted to fork out that kind of—" He broke off as he met her gaze. "Screw it." He turned on his heel and strode down the street.

Jesus, he was cocky. She wanted to gun the car and drive over the bastard. He'd betrayed his friend and he was only worried about his own neck. She leaned her head against the steering wheel for a moment, gathering her composure.

Then she started the car and reached for the phone. Joe answered on the second ring.

"I want you to do something for me." She stared after Paul as he reached the corner. "Paul Donnell is going to turn himself in to the police in the next couple hours."

"What?"

"He set Mike up. He took twenty thousand dollars to get Mike to bring me to that alley." She interrupted him as he started to curse. "He says they told him they only wanted to talk to me. He accepted it and didn't ask questions. He didn't give a damn."

"Son of a bitch."

"Yes. He said the name of the man who gave him the money was Ryan Leonard and that he knew nothing else about him. He didn't get the name of the second man but he saw him close enough to give me a description. I want you to call Manning and tell him to get that description before Donnell tries to use it as a bargaining point. He's capable of it."

"Done. Anything else?"

"Tell him not to make it easy on him." Her voice was shaking. "He may not have pulled that trigger, but he was guilty as sin. I don't want to see him walk."

"I'm surprised you got him to talk."

"So am I. But he was already scared and I used it. I'm on my way to his dorm to get the envelope with the last payment Leonard gave him. It just occurred to me that he might decide to double back and pick it up to use the money for his defense."

"Let the police do it. There might be prints."

"I'll be careful. But there are too many restrictions on the police. It might take too long to get a writ to search his room, and there's no way I'll let him get his hands on that money. I've got to go. I'll call you later, Joe." She hung up before he could argue with her.

She pulled away from the curb, made a U-turn, and started back toward the dorm.

Bitch. Whore.

Paul Donnell was seething with fury as he hurried down the street.

He'd always had a distaste for bossy women, and Jane MacGuire was a prime example of everything he hated. It was too bad Leonard hadn't taken care of her in that alley.

Get rid of the anger. When he talked to the police, he had to appear heartbroken but straightforward and blame only himself. He could handle this. He could be very persuasive and he had to marshal all his talents. He'd call his father to get a lawyer to meet him at the police station. He'd read too many times of convictions that were caused by those first interviews with the police. He'd be respectful but tell those flatfeet that he'd been advised to get an attorney.

Yes, that was the strategy. But lawyers cost money and he wasn't about to rely on a public defender. He'd have the best, and that would take—

*Headlights.*

He glanced behind him. No, it wasn't the bitch coming after him. This was a bigger car, the beams of the headlights spearing the darkness of the quiet residential street. He glanced away and quickened his pace. He'd better move fast and get to that police station in case the bitch decided to break her word and pay them a visit before he could get in his innings. He wouldn't put it past her to—

Light. All around him. A motor gunned, roaring.

What the hell was—

Jane parked in front of the dorm and jumped out of the car.

It shouldn't be too difficult to get into Paul's room, she thought as she moved quickly toward the steps. She'd visited Mike numerous times, and if security questioned her, she could tell them that she'd left something in the room and wanted to retrieve it. If that didn't work, she'd play it by—

"Jane."

She stiffened. No. She was imagining— It couldn't be him.

She slowly turned around.

Trevor.

He was dressed in jeans and a dark green sweater and he looked the same as the day she'd left him at the airport four years ago.

He smiled. "It's been a long time. Have you missed me?"

She was jarred out of her shock. Arrogant ass. "Not at all. What are you doing here?"

His smile faded. "Believe me, I'd have preferred to stay away from you. It wasn't possible."

"You've done a good job of it for the last four years." She shouldn't have said that. It sounded reproachful, and the last thing she wanted was for him to think she cared whether or not he'd forgotten her. "So have I. Water under the bridge."

"I wish I could say the same." His lips tightened. "We need to talk. My car is parked down the block. Come with me."

She didn't move. "I have something I have to do. Call me later."

He shook his head. "Now."

She started up the steps. "Go to hell."

"You'll find out more by coming with me than you will from that envelope in Donnell's room."

She stiffened and slowly turned to face him. "How did you know I was going after—"

"Come with me." He started down the street. "I'll have Bartlett keep an eye on the dorm to make sure Donnell doesn't come back for the money."

"Bartlett's here?"

"He's waiting in the car." He looked back over his shoulder. "You trust Bartlett even if you don't trust me."

She was trying to clear her mind. "You know my friend Mike was killed?"

"Yes, I'm sorry. I understand you were very close."

"And how did you know about what happened tonight with Donnell?"

"I had Bartlett bug your car."

"What?"

"And your dorm room." He smiled. "Does that make you angry enough to follow me and give me hell?"

"Yes." She came down the steps. "You're damn right it does."

"Good." He moved down the street. "Then come along and I'll give you the first five minutes to scold me."

Scold? She wanted to murder him. He was just the same. Totally confident, totally contained, and totally without concern for anyone's plans but his own.

"You're thinking bad thoughts about me," he murmured. "I can feel the vibes. You should really give me time to explain before you get angry."

"You just told me you bugged my car."

"It was done with the best of intentions." He stopped before a blue Lexus. "Bartlett, I need to talk to her. Watch the dorm for Donnell and call me if he shows up."

Bartlett nodded as he got out of the car. "My pleasure." He smiled at Jane. "I'm glad to see you again. I'm sorry it's under such unhappy circumstances."

"I agree. Since you were evidently busy bugging my car and dorm room."

Bartlett gazed reproachfully at Trevor. "Was it really necessary to tell her that?"

"Yes. Give him the keys to your car, Jane. He might as well be on stakeout in comfort."

She started to refuse and then she met Bartlett's

gentle, dark eyes, which had always reminded her of Winnie the Pooh. It was no use being angry with Bartlett. He'd only been following Trevor's orders. She tossed him the car keys. "You shouldn't have done it, Bartlett."

"I thought it best. Maybe I was wrong."

"You were wrong." She got into the passenger seat. "And don't you let Donnell into that dorm if he comes back."

"You know I'm not good at violence, Jane." He added earnestly, "But I'll be sure to let you know right away."

She watched him walk away as Trevor got into the driver's seat. "You shouldn't have involved him. He's no criminal."

"How do you know? It's been four years and he's been associating with me. Maybe I corrupted him with my wicked ways."

"Not everyone is corruptible." Although the chances of anyone being able to withstand Trevor if he chose to exert that magnetism and intelligence that had drawn her to him were very slight. He was a Pied Piper who could persuade anyone that black was white. She had watched him twist situations to suit himself during those weeks they had been together, and knew the dazzling power of that silver tongue. "And you like Bartlett. You wouldn't respect him if you were able to make a yes man of him."

He chuckled. "You're right. But there's no danger of Bartlett becoming a yes man. He has too much character."

"How did you persuade him to bug my car?"

"I told him it would help keep you safe." His smile disappeared. "Though I didn't expect you to waylay Donnell. That could have been dangerous. A desperate man is always a wild card."

"He was scared. I could see it."

"Frightened men have been known to strike out."

"He didn't and it's over. It's none of your business." She turned to face him. "Or is it? You said you could tell me more than that envelope. Do it."

"The other man's name is probably Dennis Wharton. He generally works with Leonard."

"How do you know?"

"I've run into him in the past."

"Then why didn't you tell the police you knew who killed Mike?"

"I didn't want them to go on the run."

"Why not?"

"I want them for myself," he said simply. "The police aren't always efficient. I didn't want to risk Leonard and Wharton getting another chance at you."

"And you thought they'd try?"

"As long as the situation isn't too dicey. The police aren't making much headway. I'd bet those two will make at least one more try before someone else is sent to complete the job."

"Sent by whom?"

He shook his head. "Really, Jane, I can't tell you everything. Then I'd have nothing to use as a bargaining chip."

"Why did they come after me?"

"They considered you a valuable asset in the game."

"Game?" Her hands clenched. "It was no game. Mike died in that alley."

"I'm sorry," Trevor said gently. "I don't believe he was meant to die. It was an accident."

"That's no comfort. And how do you know what was meant to happen? What did you have to do with this?"

"Everything. It was probably my fault."

"What?"

"I should have come sooner. I was hoping that I was wrong and there wouldn't be a fallout, so I sent Bartlett instead. I should have bundled you up and taken you back with me."

"You're not making sense. What's this all about?"

"Cira."

Jane froze. "What?"

"Or to be more precise, Cira's gold."

She stared at him, stunned.

"A chest filled with gold over two thousand years old. The antiquity alone would make it exceptionally valuable. The fact that Julius Precebio gave it to his mistress, Cira, would even add to the mystique."

"You found it?"

"No, but I'm on the trail. Unfortunately, there are others who know I'm on the trail and are looking for an edge." He inclined his head at her. "And they found it."

"Me?"

"Who else?"

"Why would they think—"

He glanced away from her. "I'd bet they're guessing you may be my Achilles' heel."

"Why?"

"Perhaps our past? That time we were together in Herculaneum was pretty highly publicized."

"Ridiculous. You have no Achilles' heel."

He shrugged. "Like I said, they're looking for an edge. I never said they found it. But I didn't want to come here in case it seemed to confirm that they were right, so I sent Bartlett."

"And they used Mike to get to me," she said dully. "And that damn gold."

"Yes."

"Damn them." She was silent a moment. "And damn you."

"I thought you'd feel like that. But there's nothing I can do now but damage control."

"The damage is done."

"It may have just started. They used Mike Fitzgerald to get to you. Who's to say they won't use someone else you care about?"

Her gaze flew to his face. "Eve? Joe?"

"Bingo. You'd go anywhere, do anything for them."

"No one's going to hurt them," she said fiercely.

"Then your best bet is to avoid their involvement entirely. Get the hell away from them and go someplace where you'll be safe."

"And where is that?" she asked sarcastically.

"With me. I'll keep you safe and I won't have to worry about you being a thousand miles away."

"I don't give a damn about your blasted worries.

And I'll keep myself safe. You should never have—" She stopped as her phone rang. She glanced at the caller ID. "It's Joe."

"Donnell's dead," Joe said when she picked up the call. "And the police want to talk to you."

"Dead?" She went rigid. "What are you talking about? He can't be dead." She saw Trevor stiffen next to her. "I just saw him a little over an hour ago."

"Where?"

"I let him out of my car on one of the side streets about four miles from here." She tried to think of the street name. "I don't remember which one. I wasn't paying any attention."

"Donnell was killed by a hit-and-run driver on Justine Street. There was a witness in one of the houses who saw a light-colored car drive up on the sidewalk and hit him."

"No accident."

"Not likely. After the driver hit him, he backed over him."

"Did the witness get a license number?"

"No. The kid had had a couple drinks and was feeling no pain. He was lucky to be able to dial the police and report what he'd seen. Where are you? I'll send Manning to pick you up and get a statement."

She still couldn't believe it. "They killed him. . . ."

"That's what you've got to convince Manning."

"What do you mean?"

"He was killed by a light-colored sedan. You drive a tan Toyota Corolla. Donnell had admitted to you that he was an accessory to Mike's death. You'd just come back from your friend's funeral and were understandably upset."

"But you called Manning and told him that Donnell was going to turn himself in."

"And that you were concerned he'd get off. Do the math, Jane. Isn't it reasonable that you might have changed your mind and gone back to take justice into your own hands?"

"No." She had a sudden memory of that moment when she'd actually thought how much she'd enjoy running the cocky bastard down. "I might have been tempted, but I'm not an idiot."

"And we'll convince them you didn't do it. It will take a little time, but we'll do it. I'll have a lawyer meet you at the station and I'll be there myself in the next couple hours."

"Good God, you actually think they're going to charge me?"

"I don't want to take the chance without being prepared. Where are you now?"

"I'm still at Donnell's dorm."

"Stay there." Joe hung up.

She slowly pressed the disconnect.

"Donnell's dead?" Trevor asked.

"Hit-and-run. Light-colored sedan." She shook her head. "It's crazy. Joe thinks they may charge me."

"No." He started the car and pulled away from the curb. "That's not going to happen."

"Where are you going? Joe told me to stay here until Manning—"

"And I'm sure he had the best of intentions, but

there's no way I'm going to risk them putting you in a cage even temporarily. There are too many ways to get to prisoners." He pulled even with Bartlett sitting in Jane's car. "Get out. We're heading for the airport."

"The hell we are," Jane said. "I'm not going anywhere with you."

"You're going to the airport," Trevor said as Bartlett jumped into the backseat. "After that, it's up to you. But you might consider that Donnell was murdered to eliminate a possible witness. It will give you some indication of how high the stakes are. Mike Fitzgerald and Paul Donnell are both down and they were only minor players. You, on the other hand, are a prime target. And Eve and Joe may be put on the agenda if you go near them. How are you going to take care of them if you're locked up?"

"There's no certainty that I'll be locked up. If they examine my car, they won't find any damage."

"But they might impound it for an in-depth test. They may hold you temporarily until you can be cleared. Are you willing to take that chance? Think about it." His foot pressed the accelerator. "And let me know when we get to the airport."

# 4

"This is the airport?" Jane raised her brows as Trevor pulled off the secondary road outside Boston and stopped beside a large hangar.

"I didn't say it was a major airport." Trevor got out of the car. "But I guarantee it's a very private airport."

"In other words, you're here illegally."

"It was necessary. When I knew I had to come here, it had to be fast and unobserved."

"You didn't have to come. You chose to."

"Yes, it's all about choices." He stood there looking at her. "Have you made yours?"

"No." But she slowly got out of the car. "I don't think that I'm in any danger of being arrested. I believe you were giving me bull to persuade me to do what you wanted. Manning would probably just take my statement and send me home."

"Possibly."

"I'll tell Brenner we're ready to take off," Bartlett said as he hopped out of the backseat and smiled at her. "Good-bye, Jane. I hope you won't decide to abandon us. I've missed you."

She didn't answer as she watched him hurry across the tarmac toward the Learjet sitting on the runway. She hadn't realized until this moment that she had missed Bartlett too. Small, plump, with that beaming smile radiating warmth and a kind of innocent joy in life, he was totally unique. "Did he ever marry again?"

"No, maybe he decided three was enough." Trevor smiled. "Or maybe he was waiting for you. He always liked you."

"I'd have to stand in line. Every woman has a soft spot for Bartlett. Even Eve."

"How is Eve?"

"Not so good. Dealing with her mother's grief and her own is pretty tough. Otherwise, she's just the same." Jane couldn't take her gaze from the plane sitting on the runway. Bartlett had disappeared inside and she could dimly make out two figures in the cockpit. "Who's Brenner? The pilot?"

"Yes, among other things. He's an Aussie I brought on board to facilitate a few matters."

"He works for you?"

"God, no. The arrogant bastard works for himself. But in his infinite wisdom he's decided to let me run the show."

"What show?"

He didn't answer. "Are you coming with me?"

"Where?"

"Aberdeen."

"What?" Her eyes widened. "Scotland?"

He smiled faintly. "You expected Naples?"

"You said you were on the trail of Cira's gold. That chest was in a tunnel outside Herculaneum."

"We might pay a visit there later. Right now we go to Aberdeen."

"Why?"

"Are you going?"

"Answer me."

He was silent.

"Damn you. Mike died because you wanted that gold. I deserve to know what's happening."

"But then I might not get what I want from you. And you know what a selfish bastard I am."

"In spades. But why should I give you anything you want?"

"Because you know I want you to stay alive?"

"I don't know anything about you anymore. It's been too long."

"True." He tilted his head, considering. "Then because I can give you something you've been searching for?"

"I don't want that gold."

"No." He smiled. "But you'd give your eyeteeth for a glance at Precebio's scrolls in that library we discovered in the tunnel outside his villa. And so you should. They'd really fascinate you."

She stiffened. "The scrolls?"

"Isn't that why you went back to Herculaneum?

You chose not to volunteer for the digs in the city it-self. You worked on the outskirts of Herculaneum, in the countryside. Were you disappointed that you never found the tunnel?"

"Disappointed, not surprised. You told me that after the cave-in you'd camouflaged it so well no-body could find it." Her tone was abstracted as her gaze narrowed on his face. "You went back and dug your way into that library?"

He nodded. "And came out with Precebio's scrolls written about Cira."

Excitement seared through her. "All of them?"

"All of them. I'd read about half before the ex-plosion that caused the cave-in. The rest had to be carefully handled to preserve them from damage before I could have them translated."

"But you had it done?"

He smiled. "I had it done."

"What did they say?"

"Read them yourself." He turned and headed for the plane. "There are a few surprises. . . ."

"Are you lying to me?"

He glanced over his shoulder. "I suppose I de-serve your suspicion. As you know, I'm not above ly-ing. It's all part of the game."

"Are you lying?"

He met her gaze and the mocking smile van-ished. "Not to you, Jane. Never to you." He disap-peared into the plane.

* * *

She's a hard sell." Bartlett came out of the cockpit as Trevor entered the plane. "Is she coming with us?"

"Yes, have Brenner start the engines."

Bartlett gazed skeptically at Jane still standing beside the car. "She hasn't moved."

"She's coming."

"How can you be sure?"

He wasn't sure. There was no way to be certain of anyone as strong-willed as Jane. He'd done his best to persuade her, but his success depended on how well he'd read her. "I made her an offer she couldn't refuse. She wants Mike Fitzgerald's killer and she knows I know something about him she doesn't. And she wants to find out what's in those scrolls so bad she can taste it. I dangled both in front of her like juicy carrots."

"What if you're wrong? What if she turns and walks away?"

Trevor's lips tightened. "Then I go after her, knock her out, and carry her on the plane. Either way she comes."

Bartlett gave a low whistle. "I wouldn't like to be in your shoes when she wakes up."

"Me either. But there's no way I'll leave her where I can't protect her. There are too many variables to deal with here now."

"Joe Quinn can protect her."

"And he'll try, but Eve always comes first with him. I need Jane to get top priority."

Bartlett's eyes left Jane to gaze curiously at

Trevor. "You have a few other items on your plate that are pretty high in priority. I'm surprised you believe that—"

"Here she comes." Trevor turned away from the window and headed for the cockpit. "It's better that she doesn't see me until we're airborne. She regards me as something of an irritant, and the balance could swing either way once she steps on the plane. Close the door, make her comfortable, and soothe the hell out of her."

"Irritant?" Bartlett murmured. "And I thought I was the only one who could see past that charm to the beast you really are."

"Just soothe her." Trevor closed the door of the cockpit behind him.

You decided to come. Capital. I'm so glad I don't have to be alone on such a long trip." Bartlett beamed as he closed and latched the door behind Jane. "Just sit down and fasten your seat belt. Brenner will be taking off any—"

"Where's Trevor?"

"Up front with Brenner. He said for me to make you comfortable." His eyes were suddenly twinkling. "And to soothe you. He very much thought you'd need soothing."

She did need soothing. She was uneasy and uncertain and not at all sure she was doing the right thing. That damn Trevor had played her to the hilt, using every weapon he knew to get her to do what he wanted. And here she was on a plane bound for

Scotland and she hadn't even told Joe or Eve she was going or why.

Because she didn't know why, dammit.

But she knew that she had to take any opportunity to find out more about Mike's death.

And she knew she wanted to see those scrolls. She'd devoted years to trying to find them, and Trevor had them in his hands.

Perhaps Trevor was even right about the death of Donnell tonight putting her in greater danger.

And perhaps he wasn't and was using the circumstances to bend her in the direction he wanted her to go.

What the hell? She'd find out. But first she had to act like a responsible human being instead of flitting away like a damn butterfly. She took out her phone. "I'm not going anywhere without letting Eve and Joe know."

"By all means. That wouldn't be considerate. I'm sure you still have time before we take off."

"We'll make time." She dialed Eve. "Did I wake you?"

"No, Joe called me ten minutes ago. What the devil is happening, Jane?"

"I'm not sure, but I'm not going to risk getting jailed right now. Tell Joe that I'll send Manning a statement later."

"That's hardly correct procedure, Jane."

"It's the best I can do." She paused. "I may be on a trail that could lead me to answers. I have a better chance if I go my own way."

"You're scaring the hell out of me. What are you up to?"

"Something popped up and I need to look into it."

"Not alone, dammit."

"I'm not alone."

"That's even worse. I want names, your location, and the reason you're being so damn cagey."

How much to tell her? Eve would be obligated to tell Joe, and Joe was a cop who had a duty to his badge. Okay, tell her enough to cut down her worrying, but no details.

"I may be able to find out who hired Leonard and where he is."

"How?"

"I believe I know someone who's familiar with the entire picture."

"Jane."

"I know. I know. I'm sorry. It must be frustrating to listen to me yammer and pick and choose my words when—"

"Who are you with?"

Jane was silent a moment. Oh, what the hell. "Trevor."

"Shit."

"You should feel better. You know Trevor knows what he's doing."

"He walks a mean tightrope, but that doesn't mean you'll survive if you follow him."

"I'm not following him. I'm only going to find out—" Cut it short. "I'll call you again as soon as we get where we're going. Don't worry, Eve. I'm not doing anything dumb. I'm being careful."

"That word isn't in Trevor's vocabulary. I want to talk to him."

"He's busy. I'll phone you in six or seven hours. I have to go now." She hung up the phone.

"I take it she didn't consider Trevor a suitable escort," Bartlett said. "I can't say I really blame her."

"Neither can I." Jane sat down and buckled the seat belt. "Okay, start soothing, Bartlett. First, tell me why you're still with Trevor."

He smiled. "He promised me that he'd get me enough money to retire on a South Seas island."

"You'd hate living on an island. You're much too urban-oriented."

He nodded. "It was only an excuse. I like the life I live with Trevor. Being an accountant in London wasn't very thrilling."

"Being a criminal is thrilling?"

"I'm not a criminal." He thought about it. "Or perhaps I am, but it doesn't seem like it. I just trail around with Trevor and do a few things he asks me to do. Of course, that probably makes me an accessory, but I don't really do anything bad, as I see it. I don't hurt anyone."

The plane had started down the runway and she had an instant of panic. Calm down. She'd made her decision. "What about this Brenner? I suppose he doesn't do anything bad either."

He smiled. "You'll have to ask Brenner. He's an Australian. On the surface he's not at all lethal. But he doesn't discuss what he does for Trevor, and I suspect he's been a very bad boy in his time."

"So has Trevor. Like to like."

"Perhaps. I understand years ago they were mercenaries together in Colombia."

"They were?" Her gaze flew to the door of the cockpit. "Interesting."

"I found it revealing. Trevor has difficulties becoming close to people these days, but evidently he was more open when he was younger."

"Open?" Jane shook her head. "Not Trevor."

"Wrong word?" He thought about it. "No, I believe I'm—"

"How do you do?" A tall, thirtyish, sandy-haired man stood in the door of the cockpit. "I'm Sam Brenner, and I couldn't resist the temptation to come back and get a good look at you. Introduce us, Bartlett."

"Jane MacGuire," Bartlett said. "And I'm surprised Trevor decided to let her be exposed to you, Brenner."

"I persuaded him that it would be better for her to know the best as well as the worst of the situation. Go up front and keep Trevor company, will you, mate?"

Bartlett glanced at Jane. "It's up to you."

Jane's gaze was narrowed on Brenner's face. He was very tanned and had the bluest eyes she'd ever seen. His face was too long, his nose and mouth too big to be handsome, but his brows had an arched curve that was almost Pan-like.

He smiled, and his Australian accent was even

more evident as he asked, "And do I pass inspection?"

"Not until you tell me who the hell's flying the plane."

He chuckled. "Trevor. He's not as good a pilot as I am, but he's adequate, and he wanted to have something to do that would let him avoid you. But I wasn't about to sit up there and twiddle my thumbs when I could be back here satisfying my curiosity about you."

"Curiosity?"

"I guess I'm not needed." Bartlett rose to his feet and headed for the cockpit. "I'll come back and get you something to eat a little later."

"Do that." Brenner dropped down in the chair Bartlett had vacated. "Call me if Trevor gets bored."

"I'm sure he'll let you know," Bartlett said dryly. "And he'll be back here even quicker if he thinks you're upsetting Jane."

"I disagree." He stretched his long legs in front of him. "I think he decided that it was time to go into phase two. You were to soothe and comfort and I'm here to allow myself to be probed and generally intimidated by the lady. He knows I have no discretion."

"Curiosity?" she repeated as the door closed behind Bartlett.

"You must get a good deal of that after all the publicity you were subjected to four years ago."

"You know about that?"

"Not firsthand. I was in a jail in Bangkok when all the furor was going on, and by the time I liberated myself you were yesterday's news. It wasn't until Trevor brought me on board a year ago that I even knew you existed."

"Trevor mentioned me?"

He shook his head. "Nary a word. But when he started sending me to Naples to retrieve the scrolls, Bartlett dropped a word here and there about you and I did a little research."

She went still. "The scrolls. You have the scrolls?"

"No, Trevor has them. I was only the courier."

"Where are they?"

He smiled. "I'm not that indiscreet." He studied her. "You really do look like the statue of Cira. Much more beautiful, of course."

"Bull. Does Trevor have all the scrolls now?"

"You'll have to ask him. I brought him everything he sent me for and he's usually pretty thorough. I know he was very determined I get them out of Italy without the government confiscating them."

"Because he thought there might be a mention of the location of the gold in them?"

"Possibly."

"Was there?"

He smiled.

"Don't try to play games with me," she said coldly. "I have enough of that with Trevor. Why don't you just go back and fly the damn plane?"

"Ouch." His smile disappeared. "Sorry. I admit I was doing a little exploratory assessing to see how far I could push you. It's my inquisitive nature."

"Screw your inquisitive nature."

"I've heard that before, and not from such exceptionally attractive lips." He paused. "And you've had a rough time, according to Trevor. You deserve not to have to put up with bastards like me."

"I agree."

He chuckled. "Okay, then why not call a truce?"

"I'm not at war with you. You don't mean anything to me."

"You mean something to me. I've lived with you at MacDuff's Run since Trevor leased it."

"What?"

"Well, not you. Cira's statue. But the resemblance is remarkable."

"It's only a resemblance. That's *not* me."

"Okay. Okay. I didn't mean to upset you. You're a bit sensitive on that score, aren't you?"

"You're damn right I am. I have a right to be. Or maybe your 'research' didn't delve that deep. What did you find out about me and Cira?"

"From the newspaper stories on the Internet? That a serial killer was murdering and mutilating every woman he could find who resembled the statue of an actress who was the toast of Herculaneum at the time of the Vesuvius eruption. That he thought you were the reincarnation of Cira and targeted you. The rest was pretty much about how he was trapped and killed." He paused. "And I was amazed how few photos there were of you in the stories. I was wondering how your family managed to keep the spotlight on Cira and made you fade into the background."

"They did their best. Eve and Joe are very smart, but the first year was pretty rough for me." She smiled sardonically. "But, as you put it, after that I was yesterday's news. Thank God." She returned to something he'd said earlier. "Trevor keeps his statue of Cira at this MacDuff's Run? Is that in Scotland?"

Brenner nodded. "Oh, yes. The statue's a truly splendid work of art. Even a rough-and-ready bloke like me can appreciate it. I can see why Trevor had to have it."

"Enough to negotiate with a collector who'd bought it illegally to get it," she said dryly. "And I'm not sure that he wanted it for its artistic value. He's like the rest of you. He has an obsession with Cira."

"The woman with your face." He smiled faintly. "An interesting connection."

"No connection. She's been dead two thousand years and I'm very much alive. Why did he send you to Naples instead of going himself?"

"It was a little too hot for him."

"The Italian police? They found the tunnel where Trevor discovered those scrolls?"

Brenner shook his head. "No, evidently he'd camouflaged the entrance too well, but there was a leak by a scholar Trevor was using to translate the scrolls. He was trying to sell them to the highest bidder, and before Trevor found out and yanked the scrolls away from him he'd talked a little too much to the wrong people. Evidently the gold was mentioned prominently in the scrolls."

"Yes, that's what Trevor told me. Who were these 'wrong' people?"

"Trevor's made a lot of enemies over the years,"
he said evasively. "I'm sure he'll discuss it with you."

"But you're not going to do it."

"Not at the moment. I've got to leave something
for Trevor. After all these years you're probably going to have ghastly conversation gaps." He got to his
feet. "And perhaps I'd better go and relieve him before you convince me to bare all."

"I didn't convince you of anything. You told me
exactly what you wanted to tell me. What you
wanted me to know. What Trevor wanted me to
know. Isn't that right?"

He grinned. "Well, Trevor didn't want me to tell
you that I had a crush on Cira. He thought you'd
not be pleased."

"Why should you be different?" she said wearily.
"Evidently she was the femme fatale of the ancient
world. I suppose you read some of the translations
describing her?"

"Racy. Very racy. It seems she was as talented in
bed as she was on the stage."

"That doesn't mean she was a prostitute. She was
born a slave and she did what she had to do to survive."

"A moment ago you were very adamant that
you're nothing like her. Now you're defending her."

"Of course I'm defending her. She couldn't help
the fact that she was born in a world where sex was
one of the only weapons a low-born woman possessed. She was strong and smart and she deserved
more than to have all you chauvinists lusting after
her."

"Caught." He smiled over his shoulder as he started up the aisle. "But that's what she gets for making herself a legend. Make sure you profit by her example."

"No danger. As I said, we're nothing alike."

"Oh, I've noticed a few similarities besides that face. You're intelligent; you're definitely not weak. And you like to shape circumstances to suit yourself." He opened the cockpit door. "And if you consider the Internet and media publicity you've already acquired, you're well on the way to becoming a legend yourself."

"That's bull. I don't have any desire to—"

He'd already closed the door behind him, and she wearily leaned back in her seat. Brenner was wrong. She liked everything clear-cut and aboveboard and she hated being in the limelight. Not like Cira, who had effortlessly manipulated the hearts and minds of both her audiences and the people around her. Yes, she felt as if she understood Cira, but that didn't mean she would ever react in the same way. It seemed as if she'd been making that argument with everyone since the day that nutty killer had decided she was some sort of modern-day reincarnation of the woman his father had worshipped and he had hated. She had thought she was on the way to putting it behind her, but here it was again. Lord, she was tired of it.

Trevor," Joe echoed. "Where the hell is he taking her?"

"I told you everything Jane told me," Eve said. "That's the big question. And the second one is how Trevor became involved in this."

"I don't give a damn. The only thing that matters is that he stay away from Jane. Dammit, I thought he was out of her life for good."

"I didn't. There were too many loose ends when she left Herculaneum. But I hoped for a few more years."

"What loose ends? It was finished. We caught that killer and Jane got on with her life."

"So it would seem."

"You're being enigmatic as hell. Talk to me."

"I don't mean to be. I'm just trying to say that we were so desperate to get Jane away from that nightmare and back to normalcy that we may have rushed things. We may have made a mistake."

"Bull," Joe said flatly. "There's no way I'd have let her hang out in Italy searching for those scrolls while Trevor was on the same continent. She's got a good head on her shoulders, but it was clear he was something new in her experience and he fascinated her. He's like a hypnotist, and I didn't want her deciding she wanted to follow him."

She had said something of that nature to Jane, Eve remembered. Trevor and Jane had been thrown together too closely, and toward the end Eve thought she'd seen signs that Jane was not unaware. "Well, she's following him now. She said she'd call us in six or seven hours." She paused. "It's Cira again, Joe. Cira and that damn gold. And now it's killed Mike and that Donnell boy."

"We don't have any proof of a connection yet."

"Why else would Trevor appear out of nowhere after all these years? The hunt for that gold has always been a passion with him. And he held up Leonard as bait to get Jane to go with him. There *is* a connection."

"Then we'll find it. Let me get off the phone and I'll call Interpol and see if we have any word on what Trevor's been up to lately." He paused. "She's calling you in six or seven hours? What destination would take that long from Boston? Naples?"

"God, I hope not."

Bartlett tells me that you called Eve before we took off." Trevor was coming down the aisle toward Jane. "And that you mentioned me. That must have pleased her."

"No, but I couldn't leave her completely in the dark, and I thought the devil she knew . . ." She shrugged. "Maybe I was wrong. She's quite aware of how reckless you are, and in spite of herself, she still has moments of thinking of me as a child stumbling around in the dark."

"No, she doesn't. But she's protective of the people she loves and she's never really trusted me. That's why I'm surprised you mentioned me."

"She trusts you—within limits."

"Because she's a wise woman." He sat down beside her. "She's been through too much to let outsiders get close enough to hurt her."

"You're wrong. Eve opens herself to hurt every time she starts a reconstruction."

"That's different. That's her job, her vocation. You and Joe are her life, and she'd do anything to protect you and keep you happy and safe."

"That's not unusual."

"I'm not saying it is. I admire her and we have a lot in common."

"She'd argue that statement," Jane said dryly. "And so would I."

"Oh, I don't know." Trevor met her gaze. "I protected you once."

She felt a sudden breathlessness, a heat . . . Oh, Christ, she'd thought it was gone, and here it was rushing back. No, she wouldn't *have* it. "My God, how arrogant can you get? Am I supposed to thank you for saving the poor underage Lolita from her lustful cravings?" she asked through clenched teeth. "You didn't want me? Fine. I wouldn't have wanted you if I'd had more experience. I suppose you've been patting yourself on the back all these years because you saved me from myself. Well, I may have been only seventeen, but I wasn't stupid and I had a right to free choice. You treated me as if I was a child with no—"

"Hold it." He held up his hand to stop the flow. "How do you know that's what I meant when I said I protected you? After all, I did my best to keep Aldo from killing you."

She blinked. "Oh." Then she studied his bland expression and said through gritted teeth, "Damn you. That isn't what you meant."

"But it could have been." He smiled slyly. "And it was the only way I could defuse all that abuse you were heaping on me."

"You didn't defuse anything, and I—" But the clever bastard had done just that. The anger and hurt ignited by those memories had been lessened. "I meant every word I said, and it's just as well it's out in the open."

"Right. And did it occur to you that might be why I did it? There was no use having a festering sore that might erupt any minute when we had other problems to address."

"What a disgusting metaphor. And you flatter yourself. I wasn't festering."

"Maybe I wasn't talking about you."

Heat, again. Jesus, what was wrong with her?

She jerked her gaze away. "Don't try to con me. I know how much you like to control situations. You're not going to control this one, Trevor. Stop trying to manipulate me and tell me why you wanted me to come with you."

"I told you, to eliminate one more weapon to be used against me."

"By whom?"

He didn't answer.

"I came with you because I couldn't see an immediate alternative that would give me what I needed. But I'm not going to stay around if you keep me in the dark."

He nodded. "I hoped for a little more time, but I knew it would come down to this."

"You're darned right. Who?"

"An extremely nasty fellow by the name of Rand Grozak."

"Nasty? How?"

"Murder, smuggling, drugs, prostitution. He dabbles in a good many areas to get what he wants."

"And what did he have to do with Mike's death?"

"Leonard works for him. I don't believe Grozak told him to kill Fitzgerald. It was a blunder. It was a kidnapping attempt and you were the target."

"Why? And don't tell me about your Achilles' heel. If he knows you as well as you say he does, he must know that you're too tough to be influenced."

"It's heartwarming to realize how well you read me," he murmured. "But perhaps Grozak senses another, more sensitive side to my character."

"Why did he want to target me?" she repeated.

"He wants Cira's gold and he's looking for an edge. He probably believes you may know where it is."

"That's crazy. Why? You're the one who's been searching for it for years. You're the one who found the scrolls."

"Perhaps he believes I may have shared information with you. We were together in Herculaneum four years ago. You've gone on three archaeological digs to Herculaneum since then. Add it together and he'd assume you were on the hunt for the gold too."

"Not everyone prefers money to knowledge."

"You won't convince Grozak of that. Money makes his world go around."

"And yours too."

"I won't deny I like it. It doesn't make my world go around, but it intrigues me. It's the prize in the big game." His lips tightened. "And I keep to the rules. Grozak doesn't."

"Screw you. Life isn't a board game. And you're just as bad as Grozak if you think it is."

"No, I'm not. I assure you, once you become acquainted with him you'll agree with me."

"I don't want to become acquainted with him. I want him behind bars." She met his gaze. "And I'm going to call Joe and give him Grozak's name as soon as we reach Scotland."

"I thought you would. That's why I wanted a little time for you to get over your first emotional response and be able to reason again."

"It's reasonable to call in the law."

"Reasonable, but not effective if you want Grozak. He's been dodging the law for years and he's good at it. You don't want him to suspend operations and disappear if he scents trouble."

"I don't want that smirking bastard who killed Mike walking around free either."

"You're a cop's kid. You know the large percentage of murderers who are never caught. And most of them don't have as many contacts and people protecting them as Grozak."

"He's not going to get away."

"I never said he would. I can't afford to let him. He's a danger and he has to be eliminated." The words were spoken simply but with absolute coldness, sending a ripple of shock through her. Trevor was usually so understated that she sometimes forgot how lethal he could be.

"And how do you intend to do it?"

"He wants me dead, he wants the gold. Since he can't have either one, I let him come near enough for me to pounce." He smiled. "I pounce very well, Jane."

"I imagine you do." She looked away from him. "But I'm still not convinced I should trust you instead of the police."

"Shall I tell you? Because I'll make it worth your while."

"I don't want the gold."

"We've already covered that ground. I know what you want." He leaned toward her and his voice lowered to velvet softness. "And I'll give it to you. Everything, anything you want."

Her gaze flew back to his face and she was caught, held captive by the intensity, the charisma that electrified his expression. She had drawn that face a hundred times and knew every line and indentation of his lips, the blue of eyes that could often be cold and yet sometimes were warm as a tropic sea. Those eyes were very warm now. He couldn't mean— No, of course not. With an effort she pulled her glance away. "The scrolls. You're talking about the scrolls."

"Am I?" He smiled faintly. "Of course I am. What else?" He reached into his jacket pocket. "I brought you a present."

A cabochon-cut blue stone lay in his palm.

"It's one of the lapis stones on the bronze

containers for the scrolls. Not very pretty, but I thought you'd like it."

Two thousand years old.

She reached out and tentatively touched the lapis. "So old . . . You shouldn't have taken it out of its setting."

"I didn't. It fell out when we were opening the tube." His hand brushed hers as he placed the lapis in her palm.

She flinched and then forced herself to steady her hand. Jesus, he'd barely touched her and she felt as if an electric charge had rippled between them. She looked up to see him studying her expression. "And I was right, it's better off with you."

"Is this some kind of bribe?"

"More like a promise. I promise to let you read the scroll that was in that tube if you'll give me a little time to find that chest and remove Grozak from this earthly sphere."

"Only this scroll?"

He chuckled. "Greedy. No, I'll let you read all of them. But this one was particularly interesting, and I think you'll be as excited as I was."

She could feel the excitement as she looked down at the lapis. "Why? How was it different?"

"Cira wrote it."

She glanced up, startled. "What?"

"Cira. The rest were written by Julius Precebio and his scribes, but this one was definitely Cira."

"My God," she whispered.

"Just a little time," he said persuasively. "Stay with me. Let me keep you safe. You want Grozak? It will happen. You want to read the scrolls? You'll get them. It's a win-win situation for you."

Her resolution was bending, swaying with every word. She had to block him out, think. She could feel herself falling under Trevor's spell.

*Just a little time.*

He hadn't asked for an irrevocable commitment.

*A win-win situation.*

Lord, she didn't know whether he was right, but she suddenly knew she was going to find out.

She leaned back in her seat. "Two days. I'll give you two days, Trevor."

# 5

*R*ocks flying everywhere.
*Pain.*

*Blood!*

*She would not die in this hellish tunnel, Cira thought through the haze of pain. They had to be somewhere near the end of the passage. She wouldn't be stopped now. She'd give herself just a second and then she'd—*

*"Run." Cira could hear Antonio cursing as he grabbed her arm and pulled her down the tunnel. "Pamper yourself later."*

*Pamper? she thought indignantly. It was pampering to pause because she was dazed and bleeding? The anger sent the blood rushing through her veins and into the sluggish coldness of her legs.*

*She ran.*

*Rocks were falling all around them.*

*Heat.*

*No air.*

*Night with no air.*

*Antonio's hand holding hers in the darkness.*

*Darkness?*

*No, the darkness was less now.*

*And up ahead . . . light?*

*Her heart leaped and she put on speed.*

Antonio chuckled as he kept pace with her. "I told you I'd lead you out of here."

*Don't look at him.* "If I stopped pampering myself," she said tartly. "And I would have got myself out eventually."

"May I point out that there's little time for trial and error?" Antonio asked. "Admit you were right to trust me."

They were closer to the light now. Almost safe. *If anyone could be safe while the world ended around them,* she thought grimly. "I don't trust you. I just know you want out as much as I do. You could still betray me. You've done it before."

"I made a mistake. I was hungry and poor and—"

"Ambitious."

"Yes, ambitious. And you're not? Tell me that you didn't claw and fight to get out of the gutter and win a place for yourself."

"I didn't take money to abandon you. We were going to go away and start a life together," she said bitterly. "You left me."

"All right. I left you. Julius offered me either money if I left Herculaneum or a knife in the back if I stayed with you. I took the money." His hand tightened around hers. "But I came back."

"Because you wanted more gold. You wanted the chest

*of gold Julius gave me. Or maybe the portion Julius was willing to dole out to you for bringing him my head."*

*"I wanted you," he said. "And I was willing to connive and lie and risk my neck to get you."*

*"And the gold."*

*"Yes, but I'd take you without it." He grimaced. "By the gods, what a confession from me. I never thought I'd say those words."*

*She glanced at him, and even in the dimness she could see how beautiful he was, perfect of form and face. He had been the most popular actor to walk the stage at Herculaneum, and every woman in the audience had desired him. But it was his intelligence and volatile recklessness that had drawn Cira from the beginning. She had always been able to control her lovers but she had never been able to control Antonio. Perhaps that danger had been part of the excitement. Yet at this moment his expression was grave and his words had the ring of truth.*

*Don't listen to him. He had betrayed her. He would betray her again.*

*"I'm taking you away from here," he said. "If Julius tries to stop me, I'll kill him. If you want to leave the gold, I'll walk away from it." He scowled. "Though you'd be a fool to do it. And I'd be a bigger fool to try to prove that it meant nothing to me. It does mean something to both of us. It means freedom and the chance to—"*

*Someone was standing at the end of the tunnel, framed against the light!*

*"What?" He frowned and followed her glance. He stiffened and stopped in his tracks. "Julius?"*

*"You know it is, damn you. You led me right to him."*

*Fury. Disappointment. Sadness.*

*Accept the fury but not the sadness. What a fool she was. She'd almost believed him again. Would she never learn?*

*"Damn you."* She lunged forward and grasped the hilt of *Antonio's sword. "I'm not going to let you bastards do this to—"*

"Jane. Wake up."

*She had to get away from Antonio. Had to get past Julius at the end of the tunnel.*

"Jane, dammit." She was being shaken. "Open your eyes."

"Julius . . ."

Her lids lifted sluggishly.

Trevor.

"I thought you didn't dream about Cira anymore," he said grimly. "That was one hell of a nightmare."

Her gaze wandered around the jet as she tried to get her bearings. That's right. Trevor. Mike was dead and they were on their way to Scotland. She shook her head to clear it. What had Trevor said? Something about Cira . . . She sat up straighter in the chair. "I haven't dreamed about Cira for more than four years."

"Well, this one must have been a doozy. You were scared to death."

"I wasn't scared." It was Cira who had been frightened and angry. Cira who thought she had been betrayed. Cripes, stop thinking like that. It had been Jane's dream, and any emotion generated was her own, not some long-dead actress's. "How do you know I was dreaming of Cira? Did I call her name?"

"No, Julius's. And since Julius Precebio was the villain of the piece, it had to be a Cira dream."

"Very logical." She took a deep breath. "I suppose it was perfectly natural for me to dream of Cira. You brought it all back with your talk of the scrolls and her gold she'd hidden away."

"I didn't have to bring it back from very far," he said dryly. "She must have always been with you if you went to the trouble of going on those archaeological excavations." He got to his feet. "I'll get you a cup of coffee. You look like you need it."

She did need it, she thought as she watched him head toward the galley at the back of the plane. As usual, the dream of Cira had been vividly lifelike and it was difficult to bring herself back to reality. She felt a desperate need to dive back, finish what Cira had started.

Crazy. Get a grip. It was a dream.

"Black, right?" Trevor was beside her, handing her a Styrofoam cup. "It's been a long time since I made you a cup of coffee."

But he'd remembered the way she took it. There wasn't much that Trevor didn't remember. As Eve had said, he was totally brilliant, with an IQ off the charts, and that amazing memory went with the territory. "Yes, black." She sipped the coffee. "How much longer before we land?"

"Another hour or so."

"I slept longer than I thought."

"You needed it. It's been a hell of a day for you." He sat down beside her again. "Too bad you couldn't have pleasant dreams. But the Cira dreams are never pleasant, are they?"

"I wouldn't say that. You told me once that you dreamed of Cira after you first read the scrolls, and your dreams were disgustingly pleasant."

He chuckled. "What the hell? I'm a man. What do you expect?"

"A little respect for a woman who did the best she could in a time when she should have been ground into the dirt by the system."

"I respect her. But those scrolls written about her by Julius were as erotic as the Kama Sutra. You'll see when you read them." He lifted his cup to his lips. "You never did tell me about your dreams."

"Yes, I did."

"Not much. She's in a cave or a tunnel running, it's hot and she can't breathe. The night Vesuvius erupted?"

"Probably. It seemed as if the conditions would have been the same." She looked down at her coffee. "And if the dreams were triggered by something I read somewhere, then the eruption might have figured in them. It was the most famous event that happened in that era."

"But you've never been able to track down any reference to Cira in any history book or other source?"

"That doesn't mean it doesn't exist. I was a bookworm from the time I was a toddler. It could have been just a line or two that stuck in my mind and later—"

"Whoa. I'm not arguing with you. There are too

many bizarre happenings in this world for me to question anything. Your explanation sounds as good as any to me."

She had sounded defensive, she realized, and she didn't have to defend herself to Trevor. "If you can think of a better one, I'm open. I've been searching for a logical answer for four years and I haven't found one. That's one of the reasons I want to read those scrolls. Maybe there's something in them that will trigger a memory."

"Maybe." He smiled. "Or maybe you're just plain curious about Cira. You told me before you left Herculaneum that you had to find out if she survived the eruption."

"The scrolls wouldn't tell me that."

"But they might point you on the right path."

Her gaze flew to his face. "Do they?"

"You'll find out for yourself in a few days."

"I may strangle you. And if you're conning me I'll find a way to make you wish you'd never been born."

"I wouldn't dare. You'd see right through me." He stood up. "I believe I'll go and relieve Brenner for a while. It will give you a break from my company."

"And keep me from asking questions?"

"Just delay them." He paused, looking down at her. "I'm not trying to keep you in the dark, Jane. I have a lot to do, and having to worry about you halfway across the world will get in my way."

"So you're dribbling information to keep me intrigued and heading in the direction you want me to go."

"Whatever works."

"Well, then dribble this information. Why are we going to Scotland instead of back to Herculaneum?"

"I'm sure Brenner told you it's a trifle uncomfortable for me in Italy at the moment."

"Because that's what you told him to tell me. I don't believe it would make any difference to you if Grozak was on your tail. You'd enjoy the adrenaline rush. It's why you do what you do instead of becoming a solid citizen."

"True, but unfortunately most of the people around me aren't similarly inclined. I have to take their feelings into consideration and act responsibly."

"Responsibly?"

"I can be responsible when it's important to me." He met her gaze. "That's the reason I came to get you. You're important to me."

Every word, every nuance, every expression breathed sensuality. And her body was responding to that sensuality; the palms of her hands were tingling, her breasts felt suddenly sensitive. Even her pulse was beginning to race, she realized with frustration.

Son of a bitch. She wouldn't look away from him, dammit. He knew what he was doing to her. He was expecting it. Ignore it and face him down. "I wasn't even on the scene when you set up shop in

Scotland. Who were you being responsible for then? Bartlett?"

He stared at her defiant face for a long moment before he smiled. "Do you know there's no one in the world like you? God, I've missed you."

Stop this melting warmth that flowed through her. Crazy. They were over a foot apart, but she felt as if they were touching. "Bartlett?" she repeated.

"Bartlett and Mario."

"Who's Mario?"

"Mario Donato, another innocent bystander who's doing some work for me at MacDuff's Run."

"If he's doing work for you, then he's not innocent."

"Relatively speaking. He's the translator finishing up the scrolls. I had to get someone else to do the work after Dupoi sold me down the river to Grozak."

"I'm surprised you were able to get the scrolls back from him."

"I was keeping an eye on Dupoi. I'm not the most trusting man around. At the first sign that he was negotiating I moved in and took the scrolls away."

Her gaze narrowed on his face. "He double-crossed you. What did you do to him?"

"Nothing. I didn't touch a hair on his head." He tilted his head. "You don't believe me?"

"Why should I? I know you spent years and traveled thousands of miles to get revenge on that murderer who was after me four years ago. You wouldn't walk away from someone who betrayed you."

"But that's exactly what I did." He paused. "After

I planted evidence that the bastard was really in the process of double-crossing Grozak. I thought the punishment should fit the crime. I understand Grozak was very upset and took a very long time to dismember that son of a bitch."

She shivered as she saw his expression. Cool, casual, yet there was an underlying savagery in that very carelessness.

"You shouldn't ask questions if you don't want answers," he said as he read her expression. "Because I'm going to tell you the truth. Well, as much as I can. If it doesn't violate a confidence. But I'll never lie to you if I can help it. That's quite a gift from a con man like me, but you may find it uncomfortable as hell." He turned and headed for the cockpit. "Too bad. Live with it."

It's like something from *Macbeth*," Jane murmured as the car glided toward the huge stone castle on the cliff overlooking the sea. "Very dark and moody."

"But it's got modern plumbing," Bartlett said. "One can put up with dark and moody if you can have a hot shower every day."

"You have a point," Trevor said. "There's a lot to say about the delights of an efficient hot-water heater. But that isn't why I leased MacDuff's Run."

"Why did you?" Jane asked.

"A number of reasons. It's an interesting property. It was built by Angus MacDuff back in 1350, and the family has a fascinating history. Unfortunately, they recently fell on hard times and have had to rent out the place. It's private, easily protected, and we were able to move in and out of the area without nosy neighbors asking questions. The people in the village believe in keeping to themselves." He glanced at Brenner, who was driving the car. "Though Brenner's been doing more moving than I have lately. I stashed the scrolls in several different areas after I took them away from Dupoi, and he had to be very careful retrieving them."

"You mean smuggling them."

"She does believe in calling a spade a spade," Brenner murmured. "I prefer to refer to it as Trevor's salvaging operation."

"I don't believe the Italian government regards these artifacts as salvage." She turned to Trevor. "What have you been doing here if Brenner has been doing all the fetching and carrying for you?"

"Oh, I've been hanging around the place doing research and keeping an eye on Mario."

"The translator? You don't trust him either?"

"I didn't say that. He just requires watching." He reached for his phone and dialed a number. "We're nearing the Run, James. Is everything okay? . . . Good. I'll talk to you later." He hung up and said to Brenner, "We're still under surveillance but there's not been any move from Grozak since I left. That could change anytime once he knows Jane's here. Make sure security is doing its job."

Brenner nodded. "I'll do a round after I drop you off."

"Security?" Jane glanced around the barren terrain. "I don't see any security."

"If you did, I'd fire them." Trevor smiled as they passed through the gate and pulled up before the massive front door of the castle. "You'll meet several locals who guard the castle proper, but the outlying sentries are ex-marines who specialize in not being seen until it's too late."

"And all this is to keep Grozak away from you," she said slowly. "It seems a little . . . overkill. You believe he wants the scrolls that bad?"

"I believe he wants what the scrolls may lead him to." He met her gaze. "And, no, it's not overkill." He got out of the car and held out his hand to help her. "Come in and—" He stopped, his gaze going beyond her. "Well, well, I believe you're going to meet MacDuff," he murmured. "I hope you appreciate the honor."

She turned her head to follow his gaze. A tall, muscular man was crossing the courtyard toward them. As he drew closer, she realized that he was in his mid-thirties, with an olive complexion and pale eyes, but she couldn't tell whether they were gray or blue in this dim light. His dark hair was pulled back from his face and he reminded her of someone. . . . No, she couldn't think of who it was. He was dressed in casual slacks and a crewneck sweater, but there was nothing casual about his demeanor. Guarded. Yes, every muscle of his body breathed wariness. "Who is he?"

"The laird. The earl of Cranought, lord of Mac-Duff's Run. John Angus Brodie Niall . . . I forget the other names." Trevor smiled at the man as he reached them. "Would you care to elaborate, MacDuff?"

"Not particularly. A name is just a label." He was staring at Jane. "Who is she? I told you I had to approve anyone you brought to—" His lips tightened as he drew closer. "Dammit, she's Jane MacGuire. I don't want her here. It will give Grozak all the more reason to target—"

"I don't care if you want her," Trevor said coldly. "She's here and she's going to stay. That's the end of it. I'm not going to have her in danger just to protect this blasted stack of rock you call home."

"Indeed?" MacDuff's expression didn't change, but Jane could almost feel the chill he was emitting. "That wasn't our agreement, Trevor."

"Then I'm putting in an addendum."

"Which I may choose to ignore. You do what you wish outside these gates, but don't expect me to—"

"This argument is stupid," Jane interrupted. "I won't be here more than a day or two. And I'm the one who'll decide whether I'm staying or going." She stared MacDuff in the eye. "You're very rude and I'm tired of you both treating me as if I weren't here."

He met her gaze for a moment and then smiled slightly. "Aye, you're right, I'm an ass and a bore. My apologies. You are most definitely here, and that's the bone of contention." His glance shifted to Trevor and his smile disappeared. "I can tolerate two days. After that we renegotiate." He turned on his heel and strode back across the courtyard.

"Not exactly welcoming," she said dryly. "And I'll be damned if I'll be a bone of contention for anyone."

"I was hoping he'd ignore you like he does the rest of us. I should have known he'd be on the alert. He probably knew I'd brought someone with me the minute we got off the plane."

"How?"

"MacDuff knows everyone in Scotland, and he's considered something of a folk hero."

She grimaced. "He's no Rob Roy."

"No, but he won a gold medal in archery in the Olympics fifteen years ago and then joined the 45 Commando of the Royal Marines and later won a chestful of medals for bravery. It's a country that still has a healthy respect for a man who handles himself well in battle. Primitive, but true."

She raised her brows. "And you don't?"

He smiled. "When it doesn't get in my way. MacDuff can be arrogant as hell on occasion. It's natural, I guess. He's the laird, and everyone around here kowtows to him."

"That's true." Bartlett made a face. "The laird and god. And I'm not sure which one has more sway. His people here won't do anything I ask of them without his permission."

"His people?" Jane asked.

"MacDuff insisted on providing the guards inside the gates of the castle itself. He may be short on cash, but he still commands the loyalty of his old buddies from his marine days. They'd work for him for zilch if he asked them," Trevor said. "I let him have his way as long as I had the right to check them out. They're okay. Tough as hell."

"Let him have his way? That doesn't sound like you. He mentioned Grozak. How much does he know about what's going on?"

"As much as he has to know. He has a certain vested interest."

"What kind of interest?"

"You'll have to ask him. He came to me with an offer and I took it. One of the conditions was that I wouldn't discuss it with anyone."

"And one of the perks was the use of his castle?"

"For a hefty sum. MacDuff charged me a small fortune but I'd have paid more. I told you, this is an ideal place for my purposes. It was worth a little negotiating." He took her arm. "Come on, I'll introduce you to Mario."

"I'll go on and make sure her room is ready." Bartlett was already climbing the steps. "We may have hot water but Trevor is paranoid about letting strangers into the house, so there's no maid service. I chose a room and straightened it before I left, but it's probably dusty now and—"

"Wait a minute," Jane interrupted. "You expected me to come here?"

"Expected?" Bartlett shook his head. "We'd never take you for granted. But Trevor said that it was an option, and I didn't want you to be uncomfortable." He opened the door. "You have nothing to wear, but I'll go to Aberdeen and take care of that first thing tomorrow. In the meantime, I'll rifle through all of our wardrobes and see what I can find for you."

"I'll go to Aberdeen myself."

"No," Trevor said. "Let Bartlett. It will please him, and he knows a lot about women's clothes. Three wives gave him a wide education."

"Yes, they did," Bartlett said. "Nice women, all of them. And they were stylish dressers. I won't disappoint you, Jane." He disappeared into the castle.

She turned to Trevor and asked coldly, "You told him it was an option that you'd bring me here?"

"Do you expect me to deny it? It was always an option. But I honestly hoped I wouldn't have to do it."

"And I most definitely didn't want to be here."

"But here we are." He opened the door. "So let's make the best of it." He added softly, "And it can be a very good best, Jane. We just have to work at it."

"The only thing I'm going to work at is making sure this Grozak is the man who killed Mike and finding a way to put a noose around his neck." She looked around the huge hall. It wasn't as barren as the exterior of the castle hinted. Carpets warmed the stone floors and a muted, threadbare tapestry hung by the curving staircase. There was another tapestry on the opposite wall. In fact, practically all the walls appeared to be covered with tapestries. "And where is this Mario?"

"Here I am. Mario Donato, at your service." A young, dark-haired man was hurrying down the stairs. He was good-looking, rosy-cheeked, and looked as if he was in his early twenties. He was smiling eagerly. "Bartlett told me you were here." He stopped on the second step, staring at her. "Sweet Jesus, it's true. You're Cira."

"I'm no such thing. I'm Jane MacGuire."

"And I'm a fool," he said apologetically as he came down to stand before her. "Forgive me. I didn't mean to offend you. I was just so excited to see you. I've been reading the scrolls and looking at Trevor's statue, and then I came down and saw you standing there and it was as if—" He made a face. "I'm an idiot. You must be sick and tired of people telling you how much you look like that statue."

"Yes, I am." But Mario was young and appealing and he was clearly sorry for that blunder. "But I'm probably more sensitive than I should be about it." She smiled. "And if you've been that immersed in Cira, it's understandable."

"Thank you." He turned to Trevor. "I'm down to the last four scrolls. I should have the translations for you within a few days." His dark eyes glittered with excitement. "One of them is another Cira."

"Another Cira?" Jane asked. "How many Cira scrolls have you found?"

"Just one until now." He smiled. "And her scroll is much more interesting than Julius Precebio's. She was totally amazing, wasn't she? She was only seventeen when this was written, born a slave, and still managed to learn to write. That's more than most high-born women accomplished. Smart, very smart." He turned back to Trevor. "I kept an eye out for the reference you asked about but there's nothing yet. Maybe in these other scrolls."

"And maybe not," Trevor said. "Just let me know if something pops up." He said to Jane, "Why don't you go along with Mario and let him show you your room? I have to make a few phone calls. Dinner is at six. We take turns with the cooking and cleanup."

"Even MacDuff?"

"No, he doesn't occupy a room here in the castle. I invited him to stay, but he moved into an apartment over the stable when we took over here. Mario or Bartlett will show you to the dining room. When we moved in, it resembled something from King Arthur's court, but Bartlett's managed to make it look almost cozy." He was heading down the hall. "We'll let you off kitchen duty for the next couple days. After that, you're on the roster."

"I may not be here more than a couple days," she called after him. "I didn't promise you anything, Trevor."

He smiled over his shoulder. "But you lit up like a fireworks display when Mario was talking about Cira's scrolls. I believe I'm safe until you've finished your reading." He opened a paneled door. "And Mario's not finished with his work yet. He's very slow and meticulous. I'll see you at dinner."

"He's right, you know," Mario said gravely as the door closed behind Trevor. "I'm sometimes over-careful, but it's a great responsibility. I'm working with photocopies of the actual scrolls, but the translation is very important. They're part of living history."

"And you have to give Trevor what he paid for."

His expression clouded. "You're right to be cynical. I'm taking money for my work but that's not why I'm here. Do you know how little chance I'd have to do work like this for anyone else? I'm fresh out of graduate school and I don't have any experience to speak of. I wanted this job. I fought to get it. I wasn't the only one he was interviewing. I had to do everything from assuring him I had no immediate family to doing a test translation on one of the scrolls. A project like this comes once in a lifetime."

"And it may land you in prison."

"Trevor promised to protect me and see that that doesn't happen. It's worth the risk." He smiled with an effort. "And having you here makes it that much more exciting. I hope I can convince you that I'm telling the truth when I say that I wouldn't do it for just the money."

"Why does it matter to you?"

"You're close to my age. Trevor and the others are . . . different. I get lonely here sometimes. I thought maybe—"

He was appealing, insecure, and for an instant he reminded her of Mike. What the hell? She was feeling a little insecure herself at the moment, and he was the only one who seemed in the least vulnerable. She smiled. "Trevor is definitely different. And I can see why you're not best buddies. I'd like to see where you work after dinner. Will you show me?"

"My privilege." A luminous smile lit his face. "Trevor told me to take any room I wanted when I came here. I chose the bedroom and study suite where Trevor kept his statue of Cira. It will be wonderful to have you in that same room with her." He added hurriedly, "Though I'm sure I'll notice many differences once I see you together."

"I hope you will." She started up the stairs. "Now will you show me my room so that I can get cleaned up?"

You're not pleased." Jock was frowning anxiously, his gaze on MacDuff as he entered the stable. "Is she going to be a problem for you?"

"Hell, I don't know." MacDuff scowled. "And, no, I'm damn well not pleased. She shouldn't be here."

"She's making you unhappy." Jock's gaze went beyond him to the castle. "Do you want her gone?"

"I told you that I—" He stopped as he realized what Jock meant. If he wasn't careful, Jock would be figuring a way to get to Jane MacGuire to permanently rid MacDuff of his "problem." He was usually more careful with his words around Jock, and it was the measure of his annoyance that he'd almost made the mistake of setting the boy off. "I'll take care of it, Jock. It's not a serious problem."

"She's making you unhappy."

"Not really." Christ, he didn't feel like reassuring the boy right now. He was angry and annoyed and wanted to lash out at someone. Suck it up. He'd accepted the responsibility of Jock and this went with the territory. He clapped the boy on the shoulder and spoke slowly and clearly. "She may even be able to help us. It's Jane MacGuire. You remember I showed you the picture of her on the Internet?"

Jock thought about it, trying to recall. Then he smiled. "Cira. She looks like Cira. The same as that statue that Trevor brought here."

"That's right." Distract him. It didn't take much if Jock wasn't already focused. "I'm hungry. Is supper ready?"

Jock frowned uncertainly. "No, did you tell me to fix it?" He headed for the stairs that led to the apartment. "I'm sorry. I'll get to it right away."

"No hurry."

"But you're hungry," Jock said. "You told me that you were—"

"I can wait." He moved after him. "We'll make it together."

"We will?" A brilliant smile lit Jock's face. "Together? That would be nice." His smile faded. "But you don't have to help. Don't you want to go back to Angus's place? I don't want to bother you."

"You're not bothering me. I need a break. What's quick?"

"Fresh salmon." Jock frowned. "Or perhaps a steak. I'll have to check to make sure what we have."

"You do that."

Distraction in place. And if MacDuff was lucky, Jane MacGuire would live through the night without any other intervention from him.

# 6

Bartlett was standing at the casement window across the large bedroom when Mario opened the door for Jane a few minutes later. "I was just getting some air in here." He threw back the thick red velvet drapes and opened the window. "Close them when you come back from dinner. It can get a bit drafty. I hope you don't find it damp and cold."

"Not too bad." She glanced around the room. It was generally pleasant, with Persian carpets and a secretary and cushioned chair against one wall. Another one of the seemingly never-ending number of faded, threadbare tapestries occupied the wall opposite the bed. But a huge four-poster with drapes that matched those at the window loomed with intimidating majesty across the room. "I'm supposed to sleep in that?"

"It will be fine." Mario chuckled. "I have one in my room too, and I had the same reaction. But the mattress is very comfortable and definitely not from the fourteenth century."

She grimaced. "If you say so. I'm a slum kid, and I'm not used to beds that are almost as big as one of the foster homes where I grew up."

"But you have your own bathroom," Bartlett announced proudly, nodding toward a door across the room. "MacDuff's father converted a few bedrooms to very practical uses."

She smiled. "You're obsessed with the glory of modern plumbing. Not that I'm knocking it. I'm aching to wash up and get rid of some of this travel grime."

"Then we'll leave you." Mario turned toward the door. "Shall I come to get you and take you down to dinner?"

"I'm sure I can find—" His expression was so disappointed that she said instead, "That would be very kind of you."

"Good." He gave her another brilliant smile. "But the kindness is yours." He hurried from the room.

"I believe he's smitten," Bartlett said. "Not that I'm surprised."

"He's not the type of man I'd expect to be working for Trevor. Where did he find him?"

"Through the university in Naples. Trevor was trying to avoid the scholastic contingent, but after Dupoi double-crossed him, he decided that he'd risk it. Since Grozak was on the radar he couldn't afford to take a chance on a freelance translator. So he interviewed several brilliant antiquity students before he hired Mario and brought him here under his eye."

"He said he had to watch him." She shook her head. "But I can't imagine him being a threat."

"No, the threat is to Mario. He'd be vulnerable out on his own. Trevor didn't want to risk him getting his throat cut."

"But not enough not to use him."

"Mario knew there was a risk. Trevor was honest with him." He headed for the door. "There are a few items of clothing in the cupboard in the bathroom. If there's anything else I can do, call me. I left my phone number on the card on the secretary. I hope you'll be comfortable. I did my best."

"Thank you. I'm sure I'll be very comfortable."

He smiled as he opened the door. "I try. Perhaps I'm a little smitten too." He chuckled as he saw her eyes widen. "Strictly on a platonic basis. You aroused my brotherly protective instincts when I met you when you were only seventeen. I'm afraid they're still in place. Good thing. My life is much too interesting these days to complicate it. I'll see you at dinner."

After the door closed behind him, she moved over to the window and looked out at the courtyard below. She could see lights across the way. The stable apartment where MacDuff stayed? He was as strange as everything else connected to this place, and she didn't like Trevor's silence regarding him. She felt tired and disoriented and everything seemed surreal. What the devil was she doing in this place?

What was wrong with her? She knew why she was here and what she was doing. Things had just been moving too fast for her to absorb. Donnell's death, Trevor's appearance, and being whisked here to this castle far away from everything familiar had unsettled her.

But she could bring the familiar to her and she would. She crossed to the phone on the bedside table. A few minutes later Eve picked up the phone. Lord, it was good to hear her voice.

"It's Jane. I'm sorry I didn't call you right away. We had to travel a good distance from the airport before we arrived here."

"Are you all right?"

"I'm fine."

"Then what airport? And where the hell are you?"

How much to tell her? She'd hedged the last time she'd asked herself that question and she wouldn't do it again. Eve and Joe meant too much to her to be dishonest with them. "Aberdeen, Scotland, and I'm at a place called MacDuff's Run."

"Scotland," Eve repeated. "Joe was guessing Italy."

"So was I. At the moment Trevor prefers to handle his affairs at a distance. It seems Italy is too hot to be comfortable for him."

"I can believe that." Eve paused. "Trevor may be hot in other countries besides Italy. Joe sent out in-

quiries to Scotland Yard and Interpol to check and
see what Trevor's been up to lately."

"And?"

"Nothing. It came back classified information."

She frowned. "What the devil does that mean?"

"Joe doesn't know. Scotland Yard, maybe. But Interpol has a muzzle too. It may mean he's messing
around in something extremely ugly, or stepping on
someone's toes who has the power to black out the
official information networks. Either way it makes
me uneasy."

It made Jane uneasy too. "It doesn't make sense."

"It makes enough sense to send Joe digging like a
ferret to get around that block. And it makes
enough sense for you to get out of there and come
home."

"Not yet."

"Jane—"

"I don't feel threatened. Trevor has this place
surrounded by security guards."

"And who's going to protect you from Trevor?"

"I can protect myself." She drew a deep breath.
"And I need to stay here. I'm finding out what I
need to know. Tell Joe to check on a Rand Grozak.
Trevor says he's the man who ordered Leonard to
grab me in that alley."

"Why?"

"I'm not sure yet. Maybe Cira's gold. Oh, I don't
know. That's why I have to stay for a few days."

"I don't like it."

"It's going to be okay. I'll call you every day."

"You'd better." She paused. "MacDuff's Run?"

"It's a castle on the coast. But don't you dare launch an attack. As I said, I'm perfectly safe."

"Bullshit. But we won't make a move unless you skip checking in with us one day."

"It won't happen. Bye, Eve."

"Keep safe." Eve hung up.

Keep safe. Jane didn't feel safe. She felt alone and disconnected from the two people she loved most in the world. Hearing Eve's voice had warmed her, but it had also emphasized her remoteness from them.

Stop whining. She had a job to do. It wasn't as if she was surrounded by vampires. Bartlett was here, Brenner didn't seem intimidating, and Mario was very sweet. MacDuff was fairly forbidding, but he obviously intended to ignore her unless he decided she was going to cause trouble. If there was a vampire, it was Trevor. Yes, she could see that comparison. He'd managed to hold her imagination captive and mesmerize her for four years.

And that was too damn long.

"Trevor's back at MacDuff's Run," Panger said when Grozak answered the phone. "He arrived late today with Bartlett, Brenner, and a woman."

Shit. "A young woman?"

"Early twenties. Good-looking. Reddish-brown hair. You know her?"

He cursed. "Jane MacGuire. I told that idiot Leonard that he was going to push too hard. He's been scurrying around trying to protect his ass since he killed Fitzgerald. Damn fool panicked last night and killed Donnell too. It triggered Trevor to make a move."

"So what do I do?"

He thought about it. "I can't have Leonard picked up by the police, and he's made one mistake too many. Get rid of him."

"You want me to stop watching the castle?"

"If you're not as much of a fool as Leonard, it won't take you long."

"What about Wharton?"

"It's up to you. He's Leonard's partner but I doubt if he's going to object to finding a new one. If he gets in your way, I won't give you an argument if you dispose of him. Then you can come back and watch and wait. That's all the hell you're doing anyway." He hung up the phone and leaned back in his chair. It might not be too bad. Jane MacGuire was tucked under Trevor's wing, but at least she didn't have Joe Quinn to protect her. Grozak had his own men stationed around MacDuff's Run and an opportunity might present itself to get the girl.

No, what was he thinking? Fools and weaklings relied on chance. He'd think and plan and make his own opportunity. If he couldn't make a direct assault on the woman, then he'd circle around and try to come at Trevor from another angle.

But Reilly wasn't going to see it that way. He was only interested in getting the gold and Jane MacGuire. Crazy bastard. He sat there in his compound fat and arrogant as a Siamese cat giving orders and telling Grozak what to do.

And he had to do it, dammit.

He glanced at the calendar on his desk. December 8. Fourteen days left until the deadline Reilly had given him of December 22. Could he delay the operation if Reilly didn't come through on time?

No, everything was in motion. Bribes in place. The explosives on their way from the Middle East. It was his big chance and he'd be damned if he'd let it slip through his fingers. Reilly had told Grozak outright that if he couldn't produce he'd deal with Trevor and leave Grozak with nothing.

It wasn't going to happen. Everyone had a weak spot, and Reilly's was his love of power and his obsession with Cira's gold. If Grozak could tap those weaknesses, then he'd be the one with power over Reilly.

But to do it he had to have Jane MacGuire.

Thank God, he had an alternate plan in mind to pull the rug out from under Trevor. But he was done with using incompetents like Leonard. He needed someone who had nerve, someone with brains enough to follow orders.

Wickman. He'd never met a colder human being, and Wickman would do anything if the price was right. Grozak would make sure it was. He had no choice with Reilly breathing down his neck.

Time was running out.

D id you enjoy the casserole?"

Jane turned away from laughing at something Mario had said to see Trevor's gaze on her. He had been watching her all through the meal, she thought in exasperation. Every time she'd looked up she'd encountered that critical stare. It was like being under a microscope.

"What's not to like? It was very tasty," she said as she leaned back in her chair. "Who cooked it?"

"I did." Brenner grinned. "My talents as a cook have grown by leaps and bounds since I took this job. Trevor never mentioned that as part of the job description." He glanced slyly at Trevor. "Maybe I've gotten too good. I've been tempted to serve up a little snake stew on my next cook day."

"You'll get no quarrel from me," Trevor said. "As long as you eat it too. I don't think you will. As I recall, when there were times we had nothing to eat in Colombia but what we could hunt and gather, I was able to stomach the more exotic fare better than you." He smiled. "Do you remember when García brought in that python?"

Brenner made a face. "I could have eaten it, but when I saw what was in its stomach I decided I wasn't that hungry."

There was a bond of companionship between the two men that was almost visible, Jane thought. She had never seen this side of Trevor. He seemed less guarded. Younger . . .

"I don't think that's a discussion for the dinner table," Mario said with a frown. "Jane will think we're barbarians."

"And we aren't?" Trevor asked with lifted brows. "You and Bartlett are civilized, but Brenner and I have a tendency to slip back into the jungle occasionally." But he nodded and said to Jane, "He's absolutely right. My apologies if our crudeness offended you."

"You didn't offend me."

Trevor turned to Mario with a smile. "You see? You didn't need to be defensive. She's no delicate flower."

"But she's a lady." Mario was still frowning. "And she should be treated with respect."

Trevor's smile faded. "Are you telling me how to treat our guest, Mario?"

"I'll get the coffee," Brenner said as he quickly got to his feet. "No dessert, but there's a cheese tray. Come help me bring it in, Bartlett."

Bartlett's glance went from Trevor to Mario. "Maybe I should stay and—" Then he shrugged, rose to his feet, and followed Brenner from the room.

"You didn't answer me, Mario," Trevor said.

Mario stiffened as he caught the underlying menace beneath the softness in Trevor's voice. The color mantled his cheeks and he lifted his chin. "It wasn't right."

He was afraid of Trevor, Jane realized. And why not? In that moment Trevor was intimidating as hell. But, scared or not, Mario was still sticking to his guns, and Trevor was obviously in no mood to be tolerant. "I don't want coffee." She pushed back her chair. "You promised to show me where you work, Mario."

Mario eagerly grasped at the rope she'd thrown

him. "Of course. At once." He jumped to his feet. "It's time I got back to work anyway."

"Yes, it is," Trevor said. "So you can show Jane your workroom later. Perhaps she'll change her mind and stay with us and have her coffee. We don't want you distracted." He glanced at Jane. "And she's definitely a distraction."

Mario gazed at her uncertainly. "But she wanted to—"

"She wouldn't want to interfere with your work." Trevor looked at her. "Would you, Jane?"

It was clear he didn't want her to go with Mario and was using Mario's nervousness as leverage to ensure she didn't. And it was going to work, dammit. She wasn't going to cause Mario trouble just because she was irritated with Trevor and wanted to make a gesture. She slowly sat back down. "No, maybe I will have that coffee." She smiled warmly at Mario. "You go ahead. I'll see you later."

"If that's what you want." Regret and relief fought for dominance on Mario's face. "It will be my pleasure to show you my work at any time. Perhaps tomorrow?"

She nodded. "Tomorrow. No perhaps about it."

He smiled brilliantly before turning and leaving the room.

She stood up the moment he was out of sight. "I'm out of here."

"No coffee?"

"I wouldn't give you the satisfaction." She glared at him. "Are you proud of yourself?"

"Not particularly. It was too easy."

"Because you're a bully."

"Not usually. I was annoyed. I watched you murmuring and giggling with him all through dinner and it had its effect. I had it pretty well under control until he decided to lecture me."

"Mario's only a kid. He's no match for you."

"He's older than you."

"You know what I mean."

"That he's soft and full of dreams." He met her gaze. "And some of those dreams are of Cira. If you're looking for someone at MacDuff's Run who won't compare you to Cira, come to me."

"Bull. You can't separate the two of us in your mind."

He shook his head. "I never said that. You're the one who jumped to conclusions. From the moment I saw you I knew exactly who and what you were to me." He paused. "And it wasn't Cira."

Heat tingled through her, catching her unaware. Christ, she didn't want this response. It made her feel confused and weak. She'd been angry only a moment ago and now she was— She was still angry, dammit. "You weren't fair. Mario's like a friendly puppy."

"I know, and you like puppies." His lips twisted. "Maybe that's my problem. I've never resembled a puppy in my life." He got up. "Don't worry, I'll make it right with Mario. It was only a temporary blowup. I like the kid."

"You didn't behave like it."

"Actually, I did. I was very restrained for the way I was feeling. But if I upset you, I should probably make amends. If you want to go running after Mario and soothe his feelings, I won't stop you."

"What a sacrifice."

"You have no idea." He stood looking at her. "I suppose this isn't the moment to ask you to go to bed with me?"

She stiffened in shock. "What?"

"I didn't think so." He turned and headed for the door. "It's too soon and you're mad as hell at me. But I thought I'd throw it out there and let you become accustomed to the idea that it was coming. I've got some work to do, so I'll leave and get to it." He smiled at her over his shoulder. "Since I'm ridding you of my presence, there's no reason that you can't stay and have your coffee. I'll see you in the morning."

She couldn't find the words to speak. She could only stare after him with her mind and emotions in chaos.

"Well, evidently we took long enough to resolve the situation," Bartlett said as he came in carrying a platter of cheese. "I trust there was no violence?"

"No," she said absently. "Mario went up to work."

"Very wise. Young men tend to want to challenge all comers, but I thought Mario was smarter than to do it with Trevor."

"Mario's a sweet boy."

"If he was a boy, Trevor would have less trouble with him." He put the platter down on the table. "I'll go see what's keeping Brenner with the coffee. I thought he was right behind me."

"Not for me. I don't want anything." She turned

toward the door. "I think I'll go to my room. It's been a long day."

"Yes, it has. Perhaps that would be best. Sleep brings a clear head."

"My head is clear, Bartlett." She was lying. Her thoughts were in a turmoil and she couldn't get the memory of Trevor's words out of her mind. Admit it, she couldn't get *him* out of her mind. Since the moment she had seen him outside the dorm, the sexual tension had been growing, developing, but she'd tried to ignore it. There was no ignoring it now that he had spoken that one sentence. It was there before her and she had to confront it and come to terms with it.

"I'm glad," Bartlett said gently. "You look a bit disturbed. Is there anything I can do to help?"

"No, I'm fine." She forced a smile as she started for the door. "Thank you. Good night, Bartlett."

"Pleasant dreams."

The pleasantest prospect she could have would be no dreams at all. Not of Cira and her damned run through that tunnel. And not of Trevor, who had dominated too much of her thoughts since he had entered her life four years ago.

Jesus, she had worked so hard to block him out of her memory. When that failed, she had used the memory, lived with it, in an attempt to render it powerless. She had thought she'd succeeded.

The hell she had. He hadn't even touched her and her body was tingling, alive, needing. . . .

No, she didn't need him. She *wouldn't* need him.

The word indicated weakness, and she wasn't weak. She didn't need anyone.

She started to climb the stairs. She'd go to her room and take advantage of that hot shower Bartlett had waxed eloquent about. Then she'd call Eve and talk to her and gradually this turmoil would lessen or vanish entirely.

She was lying to herself. It would take more than a chat with the person she loved the most to quiet this disturbance. She'd have to do what she always did with a problem. She'd have to face it, make it her own, and then find a way to rid herself of it.


I've brought your coffee, Trevor," Bartlett said as he opened the library door. "Someone has to drink it after Brenner went to the trouble of making it. He gets a bit touchy."

"We wouldn't want that." Trevor watched Bartlett put a tray on the desk. "Two cups?"

"I didn't get mine either. We were all too busy tip-toeing around trying to avoid your bad manners." He poured coffee into the cups. "That display wasn't worthy of you."

"I've had my fill of lectures tonight, Bartlett."

"He only wanted to impress her. Any other time you'd have ignored it. He's not in your league."

"I know that." He sipped his coffee. "Or I would have been a hell of a lot harder on him. I was in a lousy mood."

Bartlett nodded. "The green-eyed monster. It was

refreshing to see you raked over the coals. I was very amused."

"I'm sure you were. Why don't you get out of here? Venable called while I was at dinner and I have to return his call."

"After I finish my coffee." Bartlett leaned back in his chair. "You handled the situation very clumsily. Jane was bound to be defensive of him. It's her nature."

"Now I have to take advice from a man who's been divorced three times? Your qualifications suck, Bartlett."

"I may not have been able to keep a woman but I was always able to acquire them."

"I don't want to 'acquire' Jane. When have you ever known me to want that kind of baggage?"

"Well, I'm sure lust figures significantly in your attitude. After four years of anticipation, it's quite reasonable."

"You're off the track, Bartlett."

He shook his head. "Oh, I know you've had other women since you left Herculaneum. I really liked that Laura person. She reminded me of my—"

"Out."

He smiled and finished his coffee. "I'm going. I just wished to give you the benefit of my vast experience. You proved you needed it tonight. Considering what a smooth operator you are, it surprised me. I was feeling wonderfully superior until I began to feel sorry for Jane."

"She can take care of herself." Trevor's lips twisted. "Or are you saying she's still too young to know what she wants? That she'd be better off with some idealistic kid like Mario?"

"I didn't say that." He stood up. "But I've seen you when you're on the attack. Once you make up your mind you don't stop. You have years and years of experience over Jane, and that could—"

"I'm thirty-four," he said through his teeth. "I'm *not* Methuselah."

Bartlett chuckled. "I thought that would prick you. I'll leave now."

"Bastard."

"You deserved it for making an ass of yourself at dinner. I enjoy my meals, and anything that interferes with my digestion is in danger of annihilation." He headed for the door. "Remember that when you're tempted to roast any other *younger* men with your bad temper."

He closed the door behind him before Trevor could answer.

Puckish son of a bitch. If he didn't like him so much, he'd throw him off the parapets of this damn castle. He might anyway if Bartlett kept on jabbing at him. His temperament was obviously not at all stable at present or he wouldn't have handled Mario that stupidly. Bartlett was right, it was clumsy, and he prided himself on his deftness.

And he'd been equally clumsy with Jane in the conversation afterward. He should have kept his distance, let her become accustomed to him again.

Hell, no. She didn't need to become accustomed to him. It was as if they'd never been apart. And he couldn't act any other way when he was with her. He was no Bartlett, and he wouldn't—

His phone rang. Venable.

"I haven't got it yet," he said before Venable could speak. "Maybe in the next few days. Mario's working on another Cira scroll."

"And what if that one doesn't pan out either?" Venable's voice was charged with tension. "We have to move."

"We will. But if we can find out anything else, then we'll go that route. We have time."

"Not much. I'm tempted to come in there and take over those scrolls and—"

"You do that and you'll get ashes."

"You wouldn't do that. Those scrolls are priceless."

"To you. Once I've read them they're nothing to me. I'm such a philistine."

Venable started to curse.

"I believe I'm going to hang up. I've taken enough abuse for one evening. I'll call you when I have something concrete."

"No, wait. We intercepted a call tonight from the MacGuire woman. She phoned Eve Duncan."

"So?"

"She told her about Grozak, about MacDuff's Run, everything."

"That's not unexpected. They're very close."

"You shouldn't have brought her there."

"Don't tell me what to do, Venable."

He pressed the disconnect. In two minutes Venable would call back apologizing and telling him it was desperation that had sent him over the edge.

Screw him. Venable wasn't a bad guy but he was beginning to get on Trevor's nerves. He was a frightened man and he was scared Trevor was going to blunder.

Blundering seemed to be the name of the game tonight, Trevor thought ruefully. Well, he was tired of analyzing everything he did or said. He'd lived by instinct most of his life and that's the way he'd handle this situation.

He went to the window. The moon was bright tonight and he could see the stark cliffs and the sea beyond. How many times had Angus MacDuff stood here, looking out, and thought about the next voyage, the next raid, the next game?

The game.

He turned and moved toward the door. He needed to get his head straight and his priorities in order, and he knew where to go to do that.

The Run.

Jane took a long shower before slipping on one of Bartlett's oversize flannel shirts and heading for that huge bed.

Go to sleep. Forget about Trevor and that scene downstairs. He was the grand manipulator, and who knew what he'd intended by telling her he wanted to sleep with her. Maybe he really was anxious to have her, or maybe he was just using his knowledge of her own desires to push her in the way he wanted her to go. The smart thing would be to pretend it had never happened and go on and do what she had to do here.

But that wasn't her nature. She couldn't stand pussyfooting around and ignoring the stick of dynamite Trevor had hurled at her. She'd have to confront him, and she wasn't looking forward to it.

Lord, she was hot. The heavy velvet draperies of the room were smothering. Or maybe she was so charged it only seemed warm. It didn't matter. She needed air. . . .

*Night with no air.*

No, that was the dream, Cira's dream.

She threw back the curtains and opened the heavy casement window.

Bright moonlight shone on the ancient courtyard below.

Ancient? Compared with the ruins of Herculaneum this castle wasn't old at all. Yet it seemed old when she thought of the comparative youth of the United States and the city of Atlanta where she'd been born. MacDuff's Run had a haunting quality that was different from Herculaneum. There you were forced by the weight of thousands of years to accept the death of the city and its inhabitants. Here you could still imagine that the Scots who'd lived here would come marching down that road that led to the castle or out that gate to do—

Someone was standing by the stable door across the courtyard, looking up at the castle.

MacDuff?

No, this man was slender, almost gangly, and his

hair appeared to be light, not dark. Definitely not MacDuff. Yet there could be no doubt of the intensity of his body language.

The man stiffened, his gaze on someone or something on the front steps. Then he faded back into the stable. Who had he seen?

Trevor.

She saw him walk toward the gate. Even after all these years she had no problem recognizing that springy gait. The cars were parked in the courtyard, but he was making no attempt to use any of the vehicles.

Where the hell was he going?

Evidently she wasn't the only one asking that question. A man in a windbreaker stepped out of the shadows as Trevor approached. One of the guards Trevor had told her about? They spoke for a moment and then Trevor passed him and went through the gate. The guard faded back into the shadows.

The terrain was rough and stark outside the castle and not inviting for a casual stroll. Was he going to meet someone? If he was, they must already have arrived, for there were no car lights piercing the darkness.

And what was he doing going out without protection when he'd told her it was dangerous for her to do it? If Grozak hated him as much as he'd said, then Trevor would be a prime target.

Fear iced through her. She instantly rejected it. Jesus, Trevor wasn't her concern. If he was idiot enough to go strolling out there in no-man's-land, then he deserved what he got. He could take care of himself.

And she wouldn't stand here and watch to see if he came safely back through that gate. She shut the window and drew the drapes. A moment later she was crawling beneath the sheets and closing her eyes.

Go to sleep. It's not going to do any good to worry about the arrogant bastard. Don't think about him.

But where the hell had he gone?

# 7

I went to the village and bought you a perfectly splendid wardrobe," Bartlett said as he met her at the bottom of the steps the next morning. "Well, perhaps not splendid. The village only has a few shops. Splendid indicates ball gowns and velvet wraps, and I went for slacks and cashmeres. But very fine quality. Though you look much better in our clothes than we ever did."

"Sure I do." She wrinkled her nose as she looked down at the loose jeans and navy crewneck sweater she was wearing. "I appreciate the sacrifice but I'll be glad to get into something that I don't trip over. Were you able to get my sketchbook?"

Bartlett nodded. "That was a little more difficult. But I found a drugstore and they had a meager supply."

"I'm surprised you were able to get anything this early. It's only a little after nine."

"The lady who owned the clothes shop was kind enough to take pity on me and open early. I guess I must have looked a bit forlorn standing out in front of her window. Nice lady."

And Jane could see how that nice lady's heart would have melted enough to open her doors to Bartlett. "Thank you for going to the trouble. You could have waited."

"A woman always feels better when she's not at a disadvantage, and most women connect fashion with self-esteem. Of course, you're not most women, but I decided it wouldn't hurt." He turned toward the door. "I'll go get the packages out of the car."

"Wait."

He looked back at her. "You need something?"

She shook her head. "I saw someone standing outside the stable last night. Blond, thin, boyish. Do you know who it was?"

"Jock Gavin. One of MacDuff's employees. He has a room in the stable and trails around behind MacDuff like a puppy dog. Nice lad. Very quiet. Appears to be a little slow. He didn't bother you?"

"No, I only saw him from the window. He seemed to be very interested in something in the castle."

"As I said, Jock isn't quite there. No telling what he was doing. If he troubles you, just let me know and I'll have a talk with him."

She smiled as she watched him hurry out into the courtyard. What a dear man he was, she thought af-

fectionately. There weren't many people who were
as caring as Bartlett.

"Good God, Bartlett strikes again."

Her smile vanished as she turned to face Trevor.
"I beg your pardon?"

He gave a mock shiver. "Just a comment. I wasn't
insulting Bartlett. I stand in awe of his power over
your sex."

"He's a gentle, caring man."

"And I suffer by comparison. I accept my lot after
being with Bartlett all these years." He gazed after
Bartlett. "Why was he being so protective about Jock
Gavin? Did he approach you?"

"No, I just noticed him staring at the castle last
night and wondered who he was."

"I'll tell MacDuff to keep him away from you."

"I'm not worried about the poor kid talking to
me. I only wondered who he was."

"And now you know. Breakfast?"

"I'm not hungry."

He took her elbow. "Then juice and coffee." He
felt the muscles of her arm stiffen beneath his
touch and said roughly, "For God's sake, I'm not going to jump you. You don't have to be afraid of me."

"I'm not afraid." It was the truth. It wasn't fear
that had caused her to tense. Shit, she didn't want
this. She pulled her arm away from him. "Just don't
touch me."

He took a step back and held up his hands. "Is
this good enough?"

No, because she wanted those hands on her

again, dammit. "Fine." She turned and strode toward the kitchen.

He caught up with her as she opened the refrigerator door. "It's not fine," he said quietly. "You're as prickly as a porcupine and I'm—well, we won't discuss my state at present. But we'd both be more comfortable if we could reach a compatible relationship."

"I've never been comfortable with you." She took out the carton of orange juice. "You never wanted me to be. You have to know someone to be comfortable with them, and you don't want anyone to know you. You just want to glide along on the surface and occasionally dip your tail feathers."

"Dip my tail feathers?" His lips twitched. "Is that a euphemism for what I think it is?"

"Take it for whatever you like." She poured orange juice into a glass. "It means the same. You want it down and dirty? I can give it to you. Street kids learn every filthy term in the book. As you told Mario, I'm no delicate flower."

"No, you're not. Actually you rather resemble that vine that grows down in Georgia. Gorgeous, strong, resilient, and give it a chance and it takes over the world."

She took a sip of her orange juice. "Kudzu? It's a nuisance weed."

"That too. Very troublesome." He smiled. "Because you're unpredictable. I fully expected you to go on the attack this morning. You can't stand anything not being out in the open. But you're not doing it. You're drawing back. I had to go after you."

He studied her. "I must have really upset you. You're not ready. You're biding your time."

Christ, he knew her well. "You didn't upset—" She stared him in the eye. "Yes, you upset me. You wanted to upset me. You can't stand not being in control and you thought you'd throw me a curve. You were trying to manipulate me."

"Why would I do that?"

"You didn't want me to ask questions and it was easier to distract me with—"

"Sex?" He shook his head. "Nothing easy about it. You want to ask questions? Do it."

She drew a deep breath. "Joe says you're into something very ugly. Are you?"

"Yes."

"And you're not going to tell me what?"

"I will eventually. Any other questions?"

She didn't speak for a moment. "Where did you go last night when you left the castle?"

His brows lifted. "You saw me?"

"I saw you. Where did you go?"

"The Run."

"What?"

"It's better seen than described. I'll take you there if you like."

"When?"

"Tonight after dinner. I have work to do today."

"What kind of work?"

"Research."

"You said that before. Studying the scrolls, no doubt."

He nodded. "Among other things. I'm trying to put the pieces together."

"What pieces?"

"I'll go over it with you after I have the whole picture."

Her hands clenched in frustration. "And what am I supposed to be doing until then?"

"Explore the castle, take a walk in the courtyard, sketch, call Eve again and have her tell you what a scoundrel I am."

"Again? You know I called Eve?"

"You told me that Joe had found out I was dabbling in sin and brimstone."

That's right, she had. "But I didn't tell you Eve called you a scoundrel."

"She probably didn't. She likes me. Grudgingly, but the feeling's there. But I'm sure she felt it her duty to express her distrust." He tilted his head, studying her expression. "And I assure you that I wasn't listening in on your call. I don't care what you tell Joe and Eve."

She believed him. "I came here because I want answers. I'm not going to stay if I don't get them. Two days, Trevor."

"Ultimatum?"

"You bet your life." Her lips twisted. "Does that phrase stimulate you? You like to gamble. You love the tightrope. For years you made a living counting cards in the casinos, didn't you?"

"You always stimulate me. Are you coming to the Run with me tonight?"

"Yes. I want answers and I'll get them any way I

can." She put down her glass in the sink. "Which is why I'm not going to go for a walk in the courtyard or explore the castle." She turned toward the door. "I'm going to see Mario and see if he's willing to be any more communicative." She looked over her shoulder in sly satisfaction at his reaction. "Want to bet on that, Trevor?"

"No bet." He met her gaze. "But you might remember that I'll hold him responsible for any fall from grace and act accordingly."

Her smile faded. Bastard. He couldn't have said anything that would have been more likely to deter her. "What if I said I didn't care?"

"You'd be lying." He added curtly, "Run along. You've gotten the rise you wanted out of me. I'm sure Mario will be ecstatic to see you."

Yes, she'd gotten the response for which she'd aimed, but she felt no triumph. She'd wanted to get her own back, anger him, pierce that cool, smooth facade. She'd done it, but he'd managed to turn victory into a stalemate.

"What did you expect?" Trevor's gaze was on her face. "I'm not one of the boys you fool around with at Harvard. You play for high stakes, you should be ready to have your bluff called."

She looked away from him and headed for the hall. "It wasn't a bluff."

"It better be."

His soft words trailed after her as she started up the staircase. She wouldn't look back. She wouldn't let him see that his velvet threat disturbed her. Not frightened. Disturbed. There was an excitement, a tingling awareness of uncertainty and danger that she'd never experienced before. Was this Trevor's tightrope? Is this what he felt when—

Forget it. Shrug it off. She'd find out what she could from Mario without making trouble for the boy, and tonight she'd find out more from Trevor.

The Run . . .

No, put Trevor aside, don't think of him, smother this eagerness. Concentrate on Mario and Cira.

Keep Jock Gavin away from Jane," Trevor said as soon as MacDuff picked up the phone. "I don't want him near her."

"He won't hurt her."

"Not if you don't let him within a hundred yards of her. She saw him last night and asked about him."

"I'm not going to pen him up like an animal. He's a twenty-year-old boy."

"Who nearly killed one of my security guards because he thought he was a threat to you."

"He startled Jock. He shouldn't have been in the stable. I told you that was the only place in the castle that was off-limits to you."

"You didn't tell me you were keeping a pet tiger there. He had a garrote around James's neck in two seconds, and if you hadn't interfered, he'd have been dead in another three."

"It didn't happen."

"And it's not going to happen to Jane MacGuire.

She has damn good instincts. If she asked about him, she must have sensed something wrong."

"I'll take care of it."

"See that you do. Or I will." He hung up.

Dammit to hell.

MacDuff stuffed his phone into his pocket and turned and strode through the stable to the potting shed Jock had created in one of the back stalls. "I told you to stay away from her, Jock."

Jock looked up, startled, from the gardenia he was transplanting into a terra-cotta pot. "Cira?"

"She's not Cira. Jane MacGuire. I told you that I wasn't upset with her. Did you try to go to see her last night?"

He shook his head.

"Then how did she see you?"

"They gave her the room you usually use. I could see her standing at the window." He frowned. "They shouldn't have done that. It's your room."

"It's fine with me. I don't care where I sleep."

"But you're the laird."

"Listen to me, Jock. I don't care."

"I care." He looked down at his gardenia. "This is a special gardenia from Australia. In the catalog it said it's supposed to be able to stand very harsh winds and still live. Do you think that's true?"

He felt his throat tighten as he looked at the boy. "It could be true. I've seen creatures go through unbelievable hardship and cruelty and still survive."

Jock gently touched the creamy white petal. "But this is a flower."

"Then we'll have to see, won't we?" He paused.

"Your mother called me again. She wants to see you."

"No."

"You're hurting her, Jock."

He shook his head. "I'm not her son anymore. I don't want to see her cry." His gaze shifted to MacDuff's face. "Unless you tell me I have to do it."

MacDuff wearily shook his head. "No, I'm not going to tell you that." He added, "But I'm going to tell you not to go near Jane MacGuire. Promise me, Jock."

He didn't answer for a moment. "When she was standing at the window, I could only see a kind of . . . silhouette. She stood very straight, with her head high. It reminded me of an iris or a daffodil. . . . It made me sad to think of breaking—"

"You don't have to break anything or anyone, Jock. Don't go near her. Promise me."

"Not if you don't want me to." He nodded. "I won't go near her." He looked back at his gardenia. "I hope it lives. If it does, maybe next spring you could give it to my mother?"

Christ, sometimes life could be pure shit. "Maybe I could." He turned away. "I think she'd like that."

She saw the statue the moment she entered Mario's study after she'd knocked.

The bust was on a pedestal by the window, and the brilliant sunlight touched it, surrounding it with radiance.

"Magnificent, isn't she?" Mario got up from his

desk and came toward her. "Come closer. She's quite perfect." He took her hand and led her toward the statue. "But perhaps you know that. Have you seen the statue before?"

"No, I've seen pictures of it but I've never seen the real thing."

"I'm surprised Trevor didn't show you. You've known him for a long time, haven't you?"

"Sort of. But the time was never right," she said absently, her gaze on Cira's face. Even she could see the resemblance, but she was too caught up in the idea that this artist had actually seen Cira. Perhaps she'd even posed for him two thousand years ago. Yet the statue didn't look old, and Cira's expression was as modern as a photo in *People* magazine. She looked boldly out at the world, alert, intelligent, with a hint of humor in the curve of her lips that made her come vividly alive. "You're right, it's magnificent. I've been told there were many statues created of Cira, but this one has to be the finest."

"Trevor thinks it is. He's very possessive of her. He didn't want to let me work in here but I told him that I needed inspiration." Mario smiled mischievously. "It was a real victory for me. I don't get many with Trevor."

It was strange standing here staring at this face that had already twisted her life in a multitude of different ways. The dreams, the episode four years ago that had nearly taken her life, and now the circle was returning, closing, with Cira in the center. Strange and mesmerizing. She forced herself to look away. "And is it inspiring?"

"No, but I enjoyed looking up at her after working on her scroll. It was almost as if she were in the room talking to me." He frowned. "But didn't I read on the Internet that Ms. Duncan did a forensic sculpture of a skull that resembled the statue of Cira?"

"No, that was pure hype. She did do a reconstruction of a skull from that period, which Trevor borrowed from a museum in Naples. But it looked nothing like Cira."

"My mistake. I suppose I was so absorbed in her scroll that I was working on that I didn't pay enough attention."

"Her scroll," Jane repeated. "I didn't know anything about those before Trevor told me when I was coming here. All he said was that there were scrolls about Cira."

"These were in a separate chest enclosed in the wall at the back of the library. Trevor said he hadn't seen them before and the cave-in might have toppled the wall. He believes she tried to hide them."

"She probably did. I'm sure when she was Julius's mistress she wasn't encouraged to do anything with her mind. He was only interested in her body."

He smiled. "That's evident from the scrolls he had written about her. Would you like to read a few of them?"

"How many are there?"

"Twelve. But they're pretty repetitive. He was besotted with Cira and he evidently had a fondness for porn."

"And what about Cira's?"

"They're more interesting but much less titillating."

"What a disappointment. Could I read the Cira scrolls?"

He nodded. "Trevor called me last night and gave me permission. He said those would be the ones that you'd be most interested in." He nodded toward an easy chair in the corner of the room. "I'll bring the translation of the first one to you. That corner has plenty of light."

"I could take it to my room."

He shook his head. "When I first started to work for Trevor, I promised him I wouldn't let the scrolls or the translations out of my sight."

"Did he tell you why?"

"He told me that they were very important and what I was doing was dangerous because a man named Grozak was after them."

"That's all?"

"That's all I wanted to know. Why should I be curious? I don't care what Trevor and Grozak are fighting about. It's only the scrolls that are important to me."

She could see that. His dark eyes were glowing and his hand gently touching the scroll was almost caressing. "I suppose Trevor has a right to set up rules about the scrolls, but I believe I'd be a little more inquisitive than you seem to be."

"But then, you're not me. Our lives were probably very different. I grew up in a village at the foot of a monastery in Northern Italy. I worked in the garden when I was a little boy and later they let me

work in the library. I'd scrub the tiles on my hands
and knees until they bled. And at the end of the
week the fathers would give me an hour to touch
the books." His lips curved reminiscently. "So old.
The leather of the binding was smooth and rich. I'll
remember the smell of those pages all my life. And
the script . . ." He shook his head. "It was fine, a
thing of beauty and grace. It seemed magical to me
that those priests who'd written them could have
been so learned and wise. It just shows that time
doesn't really matter, doesn't it? Yesterday or thousands of years ago, we go through life and some
things change, some things stay the same."

"How many years did you work for the monastery?"

"Until I was fifteen. At one time I wanted to become a priest. Then I discovered girls." He shook
his head ruefully. "I fell from grace and committed
sin. The priests were very disappointed in me."

"I'm sure your sin wasn't too extreme." She remembered the tough streets where she'd grown up,
where sin was a daily fact of life. "But you're right,
our upbringing was completely different."

"That doesn't mean we can't enjoy each other's
company. Please stay." He smiled. "It will be very exciting for me to see you sitting there and reading
what was written in Cira's scrolls. And bizarre. It will
be like having her—" He broke off guiltily. "But of
course now that I see you next to the statue, I can see
there are many differences. You actually don't—"

"Liar." She couldn't help smiling. "It's okay,
Mario."

"Good." He let out a deep breath of relief. "Come sit down." He carefully leafed through the pile of papers on his desk. "I translated the scrolls first from Latin to modern Italian, then to English. Then I went through them again and did it all over just to make sure I was accurate."

"Good heavens."

"It's what Trevor wanted, and I would have done it anyway given the choice." He drew out a thin folder containing several sheets of paper stapled together and took them to her. "I wanted to hear her speak to me."

She slowly took the papers. "And did she?"

"Oh, yes," he said softly as he turned and went back to his desk. "All I had to do was listen."

*Cira I* was printed on the title page.

Cira.

Dammit, she was actually nervous to start reading Cira's words. She'd lived with her image and the story of her life for years, but that was different from reading her actual thoughts. It made her . . . real.

"Is something wrong?" Mario asked.

"No, nothing." She sat up straight in the chair and turned the page.

Okay, speak to me, Cira. I'm listening.

## Lucerne, Switzerland

May I sit down? All the tables seem to be filled."

Eduardo looked up from his newspaper at the

man holding a cup of espresso. He nodded. "You must get here early to get a table. The lake is particularly beautiful from this vantage point." He gazed out at the sunlight glinting on Lake Lucerne. "Although it's lovely from wherever you view it." He shifted his newspaper to make room. "It moves the heart."

"It's my first time here but I must agree."

"You're a tourist?"

"Yes." He smiled. "But you look very much the native. You live here in Lucerne?"

"Since I retired. I share an apartment with my sister in the city."

"And you get to come here every morning and enjoy this bounty. What a lucky man."

Eduardo made a face. "One can't eat scenery. My pension doesn't allow me more than a cup of coffee and a croissant to start my day." He gazed out at the lake. "But perhaps I am lucky. You're right, beauty feeds the soul."

"You know Lucerne well?"

"It's a small town. There's not that much to know."

He leaned forward. "Then perhaps I could persuade you to show me other sights like this wonderful lake? I'm not a rich man, but I'd be glad to pay you for your trouble." He hesitated. "If it wouldn't insult you to accept my money."

Eduardo sipped his coffee and thought about it. The man was courteous, well-spoken, and he didn't throw his weight around like many of the tourists who flocked to Lucerne in droves. Perhaps he was a teacher or civil servant, because his clothes were casual and not expensive. And he obviously knew that pride was important to the poor. He was respectful, and the tentative eagerness with which he was gazing at Eduardo was very flattering.

Why not? He could always use a little extra money, and he would enjoy having a purpose again. The days were long and boring, and retirement was not what he'd believed it was going to be. He could understand why seniors gave up and faded away when they had no reason to get up in the morning. He slowly nodded. "Perhaps we could come to an arrangement. What do you wish particularly to see, Mr. . . ."

"Forgive me. How rude I am. Let me introduce myself." He smiled. "My name is Ralph Wickman."

*The scribe, Actos, who gave me this scroll says I should not write anything that I would not want Julius to read, that I must be careful.*

*I'm weary of being careful. And perhaps I no longer care whether he reads this and is angry. Right now life seems very dreary and I cannot bear to have him suffocate my mind as he does my body. I must not be seen talking to anyone for fear Julius will find a way to hurt them, but I may be able to send this scroll to you, Pia. He does not know about you, so it may be safe. Julius is watching me all the time now since he found out that I took Antonio for a lover. Sometimes I wonder if he's mad. He tells me he's crazed by love, but he loves no one but himself. When he* bribed Antonio to leave me, he thought that I'd come meekly back and live beneath his yoke.

I will not be a slave to any man. The only thing they understand is what lies between my thighs and the gold that crosses their palms. So I told Julius he could have my body again if the price was high enough. Why not? I tried love and Antonio betrayed me. But a chest of gold would keep us safe and free for the rest of our lives.

He fell into a rage but in the end he gave it to me. He said I had to keep it in a room in the tunnel under guard so that he would know that I wouldn't break our bargain, take it, and leave him. I know he hoped that he would tire of me and take back his gold. He will not tire. I will see that he doesn't. If there's one thing I've learned, it's how to please a man.

And he will not keep that gold hostage. It's mine and will stay mine. I've already started to talk to the guards who are assigned to watch over it. It won't be long before I get them into my camp.

Then it's you who must help me, Pia. My servant, Dominic, will bring the gold to you with instructions on what to do with it. Then he must leave Herculaneum and hide in the countryside before Julius finds out that he's helped me. I've told him he must take Leo with him because Julius will kill anyone who's close to me once I leave him. He will not care that Leo is only a child. As I said, he's mad.

You must also hide. I'll ask Dominic to have you tell him where you'll be and he will get word to me.

I hope I have a chance to send this to you. I don't know whether it's better to risk sending this missive to prepare you or just to rely on Dominic to show up at your door with the gold. I'll have to decide soon.

*I want to reach out and touch you with my words in case I won't be able to see you again. I fear it's a very real possibility.*

*Nonsense. All will go well. I won't have Julius defeat me. Just do what I've said.*

> *With all love I remain,*
> *Cira*

Good God, her hands holding the paper were shaking, Jane realized. She drew a deep breath and tried to compose herself.

"Powerful, yes?" Mario was gazing at her across the room. "She was quite a woman."

"Yes, she was." She looked down at the pages. "Evidently she decided it wasn't safe to send this. You're translating another scroll by her?"

He nodded. "I've just started."

"Then we don't know whether she was able to send the gold out of the tunnel before the eruption?"

"Not yet."

"Do we know who Pia was?"

He shook his head. "Evidently someone she loved. Perhaps an actress friend from the theater?"

"Trevor told me that according to Julius's scrolls she had no family or close friends. There was only a servant, Dominic, an ex-gladiator, and she took a street child into her home."

Mario nodded. "Leo."

"Trevor didn't mention any name. I suppose it might be. But who the devil is Pia?"

"It's possible Julius didn't know as much as he thought he did about Cira."

That was true. Cira didn't want Julius to be intimate with her in any way but the physical.

As Mario saw her frustrated expression, he lifted his brows and shrugged. "I'm sorry. I told you, I've just started."

But she wanted to *know*.

"I understand," Mario said gently. "I'm just as eager as you are. But it all takes time to translate, not only the words but the nuances. I have to be very careful not to make mistakes. Trevor made me promise that there would be no possibility of misinterpretation."

"And we wouldn't want to disappoint Trevor." She nodded resignedly. "Okay, I can wait." She wrinkled her nose. "Impatiently."

He laughed, picked up another folder from his desk, and got to his feet. "Would you like to read a few of Julius's scrolls?"

"Sure. It might be interesting to get his view on Cira. But from what you've said I don't believe I'm going to get any surprises." She took the folder and curled up in the chair. "And maybe you'll have something for me from Cira's scroll later in the afternoon?"

He shook his head. "I'm having difficulty with this one. It's not as well preserved as the first scroll. The tube containing it was partially damaged."

She mustn't feel frustrated. Cira's letter to Pia had confirmed not only Cira's character but had opened a new avenue of information. Julius's scrolls might also prove interesting, and she had nothing else to do until after dinner, when Trevor had promised to show her this Run. She sighed. "Well, then I'll just have to stay here and be an inspiration to goad you to work a little faster."

# 8

_____

She'd made her way through four of Julius's scrolls before she got up from her chair and carried the rest back to Mario's desk. "Good God, he was a horny bastard."

Mario chuckled. "Had enough?"

"For now. He's not telling me anything about Cira but what remarkable private parts she possessed. I'll try again later. I need a break. I'm going down to the courtyard and do a little sketching." She smiled. "Then I'll come back and nag you again."

"I look forward to it." His tone was abstracted. He was obviously already back in his translation.

She wished she could be so involved, she thought as she left the room. After all these years of antici-pating reading Julius's scrolls, they were definitely a disappointment. She'd already been told the details

of Cira's life by Trevor, and Julius's sexual fanta-
sies about her were degrading and annoying. She
couldn't wait to read the other Cira scroll.

Well, she'd have to wait. So forget about Cira and
get involved in her own work. That would make the
time pass until she could brace herself for another
onslaught of Julius's porn.

An hour later she was sitting on the edge of the
fountain and finishing a sketch of the battlements.
Boring. The castle was interesting and she was sure
there was a colorful history connected to the place,
but there wasn't anything she could get her teeth
into. It was rock and mortar and—

The stable door opened. "You're angry again,
aren't you?"

Her gaze flew to the man who was standing in the
doorway. No, not a man. He was a boy in his late
teens or early twenties.

And, my God, that face.

Beautiful. He couldn't be called good-looking
any more than the statues she'd seen of Greek he-
roes could be described by that term. His tousled
blond hair framed perfect features and gray eyes
that were staring at her with a kind of troubled in-
nocence. That's right, Bartlett had said Jock Gavin
was slow, childlike.

"Are you still angry with the laird?" he asked, his
frown deepening.

"No." Even that scowl couldn't spoil the fascina-
tion of that face. It only gave it more character,
more layers. "I'm not angry at anyone. I don't really
know MacDuff."

"You were angry when you came. I saw it. You made him unhappy."

"He didn't make me overjoyed." He still had that troubled frown and she could see she wasn't getting through to him. "It was a misunderstanding. Do you know what I mean?"

"Of course. But sometimes people don't tell the truth." His gaze shifted to the sketchbook. "You're drawing something. I saw you. What?"

"The battlements." She made a face as she turned the sketch around so that he could see it. "But I'm not doing it very well. I don't really like drawing structures. I'd rather sketch people."

"Why?"

She shrugged. "Because it's life. Faces change and age and become something different from minute to minute, year to year."

He nodded. "Like flowers."

She smiled. "Some of the faces I've drawn haven't been in the least flowerlike. But, yes, it's the same idea. Do you like flowers?"

"Yes." He paused. "I have a new plant, a gardenia. I was going to give it to my mother in the spring, but I could give her a picture of it now, couldn't I?"

"She'd probably rather have the flower."

"But it might die." His expression became shadowed. "I might die. Sometimes things die."

"You're young," she said gently. "Usually, the young don't die, Jock." But Mike had died, and he had been as young as this beautiful boy. She said impulsively, "But I could draw your flower now and you could still give the real plant to your mother later."

His expression lit with eagerness. "Would you? When could you do it?"

She glanced at her watch. "Now. I have time. It won't take long. Where is it?"

"In my garden." He stepped aside and gestured inside the stable. "Come on. I'll show you where—" His smile disappeared. "But I can't do that."

"Why not?"

"I promised the laird I wouldn't go near you."

"Oh, for God's sake." She remembered Bartlett's and Trevor's words about not letting the boy bother her. They'd evidently gone ahead and talked to MacDuff in spite of her protest that the idea of the kid accosting her didn't worry her. Now that she'd met him she was definitely feeling defensive. "It's all right, Jock."

He shook his head. "I promised him." He thought about it. "But if I go ahead and you follow me I won't really be near you, will I?"

She smiled. He might be childlike, but he wasn't as slow as Bartlett thought. "By all means, keep your distance, Jock." She crossed the courtyard to the stable. "I'll be right behind you."


"Why are all the stalls empty?" Jane called ahead as she followed Jock through the stable. "MacDuff has no horses?"

He shook his head. "He sold them. He doesn't come here very often anymore." He had reached the door at the back of the stable. "This is my garden." He threw open the door. "It's only potted plants, but the laird says I can plant them outside in the earth later."

She followed him out into the sunlight. Flowers. The tiny cobblestone area resembled a patio, but there was barely room to walk for the vases and pots overflowing with blossoms of every description. A glass roof overhead made it into a perfect greenhouse. "Why not now?"

"He's not sure where we'll be. He said it's important to take care of flowers." He pointed to a terracotta pot. "This is my gardenia."

"It's beautiful."

He nodded. "And it will live when the winter winds blow."

"That's beautiful too." She opened her sketchbook. "Is the gardenia your favorite flower?"

"No, I like all of them." He frowned. "Except lilacs. I don't like lilacs."

"Why not? They're very lovely and I'd think they'd grow well here."

He shook his head. "I don't like them."

"I do. We have lots of them at home." She began to sketch. "The blossoms of your gardenia are drooping a little. Could you tie up the branches until I finish?"

He nodded, reached in his pocket, and drew out a leather cord. A moment later the gardenia was upright in the pot. "Is that what you want?"

She nodded absently as her pencil raced over the pad. "That's fine. . . . You can sit down on that stool at the potting table, if you like. It will be a little while before I finish."

He shook his head as he moved to the far edge of the patio. "Too near. I promised the laird." His gaze went to the cord around the gardenia. "But he knows I really don't have to be near. There are so many ways . . ."

W̲hat the hell are you doing here?"

Jane glanced over her shoulder to see MacDuff standing in the doorway. "What does it look like?" She turned back and made the last few strokes on the sketch. She tore it off her pad and held it out to Jock. "Here it is. It's the best I can do. I told you I did faces better."

Jock stood still, not moving, his gaze on MacDuff. "I'm not near her. I didn't break my promise."

"Yes, you did. You knew what I meant." He took the sketch from Jane and thrust it at the boy. "I'm not pleased, Jock."

The boy appeared totally crushed and Jane felt a surge of anger. "Oh, for Pete's sake. I could *hit* you. Stop it. I offered to make the sketch. He didn't do anything."

"Oh, shit." MacDuff's gaze was on Jock's face. "Shut up and get the hell out of here."

"I will not." She went to the gardenia and carefully untied it. "Not until you tell him you're sorry for being a complete ass." She crossed to Jock and handed him the cord. "I don't need this anymore. I hope your mother likes the sketch."

He was silent, looking down at the cord in his hand. "You're going to hurt him?"

"MacDuff? I feel like throttling him." She heard MacDuff mutter something beside her. "He shouldn't treat you like that, and if you had sense you'd take a punch at him."

"I couldn't do that." He stared down at the sketch for a long moment and then slowly put the cord in his pocket. "And you mustn't do it either. I have to keep anyone from hurting him." He glanced at the sketch again and a slow smile lit his face. "Thank you."

"You're welcome." She smiled back at him. "If you really want to thank me, you could do me a favor. I'd like to sketch you. I promise it will turn out much better than your gardenia."

Jock looked uncertainly at MacDuff.

He hesitated and then slowly nodded. "Go ahead. As long as I'm present, Jock."

"I don't want you, MacDuff." She saw Jock begin to frown again and sighed with resignation. There wasn't any use in making the boy fret. The laird seemed to have him firmly under his thumb. "Okay. Okay." She turned and headed for the door. It was time she got back to Cira and Julius and away from this beautiful boy and the man who seemed to control his every move. "I'll see you tomorrow, Jock."

"Wait." MacDuff was following her down the row of stalls toward the courtyard entrance. "I want to talk to you."

"I don't want to talk to you. I don't like the way

you treat that boy. If he has problems, he should have help, not coercion."

"I am helping him." He paused. "But you might be able to help him too. He didn't react the way I thought he would back there. It could be ... healthy."

"To be treated like a human being and not a robot? I'd say that's healthy."

He ignored her sarcasm. "The rules are the same for you as for him. I'm with you when you're sketching Jock. No exceptions."

"Anything else?"

"If you tell Trevor, he won't let you do it. He'll think Jock will hurt you. He knows he isn't stable." He met her gaze. "It's true. He could hurt you."

"He couldn't have been more gentle to me."

"Believe me, all it would take is a trigger."

She gazed at him, going over the scene that had just taken place. "And you're the trigger. He's very protective of you. You should try to talk him out of—"

"Do you think I haven't?" he said roughly. "He won't listen."

"Why not? You don't appear to be in need of protection."

"I did him a favor and he feels obligated. I'm hoping it will gradually fade away."

She shook her head as she remembered Jock's expression when MacDuff had told him he was displeased with him. Total devotion. Total dependence. "If you wait for that to happen, it may take a long time."

"Then it will take a long time," he said harshly. "I'm not stuffing him behind bars and having him prodded and poked by a bunch of doctors who care not a whit about him. I take care of my own."

"Bartlett said he was from the village, and Jock mentioned his mother. Does he have any other family?"

"Two younger brothers."

"And his family won't help him?"

"He won't let them." He added impatiently, "I'm not asking that much. I'll keep you safe. Just be with him, talk to him. You said yourself you wanted to draw him. Have you changed your mind because there may be a risk? Yes or no?"

She had enough on her plate right now without helping that beautiful boy. Yes, she wanted to draw him, but she didn't need another complication. She found it hard to believe that he was as unstable and dangerous as MacDuff claimed, but there was no doubt that it must have some substance if MacDuff felt it necessary to warn her. "Why me?"

He shrugged. "I don't know. He saw Trevor's statue of Cira and asked me questions about what Trevor was doing here. He's very visual, so I dug up the story on the Internet about Cira and you figured prominently in it."

Cira again. "And he believes I'm Cira?"

"No, he's not stupid. He just has problems." He amended, "Well, maybe sometimes he gets confused."

And MacDuff was obviously as protective and defensive about Jock as the boy was about him. For the first time she felt a surge of sympathy and under-standing for MacDuff. It wasn't only duty that was driving the laird to take care of the boy. "You like him."

"I watched him grow up. His mother was head housekeeper and he was in and out of the castle from the time he was a lad. He wasn't always like this. He was bright and happy and—" He broke off. "Yes, I like Jock. Will you do it or not?"

She slowly nodded. "I'll do it. But I don't know how long I'll be here." She grimaced. "You obvi-ously don't appreciate me being here."

"The situation is already too complicated." He added gravely, "But it's good that you're going to be of use to me."

She looked at him in amazement. "I'm not one of your damn 'people' and I won't be used by—" He was smiling and she realized that he was joking. "Good Lord, do I detect a sense of humor?"

"Don't tell Trevor. One mustn't lower one's guard. Are you going to tell him you're going to draw Jock?"

"If I feel like it." But she knew what he meant. She'd been on guard with Trevor since he'd come back into her life. "But it doesn't concern him."

"He won't agree. He wouldn't have brought you here if you didn't concern him." He opened the sta-ble door for her. "If you're not here tomorrow, I'll understand."

The bastard was saying the one thing that would firm her determination to come. He was almost as much a manipulator as Trevor, she thought in amusement. Why wasn't she irritated, as she would have been with Trevor? "I'll be here at nine A.M."

"I'm . . . grateful." He met her gaze. "And I repay my debts."

"Fine." She started across the courtyard. "It's good that I can make use of *you*, MacDuff."

She heard a surprised chuckle behind her but she didn't look back. She was probably making a mistake becoming involved with Jock Gavin. He wasn't her concern. No sketch was worth the risk MacDuff had warned her about.

To hell with it. Orphans and lame ducks seemed to be her downfall. She'd never been able to walk away just because the going got tough. It wasn't her nature. If it was a mistake, then it was *her* mistake and she'd live with it.

Had that been Cira's attitude when she'd taken the boy, Leo, into her home?

Jock Gavin wasn't Leo and she wasn't Cira. So stop making comparisons and get back to Mario and see if she could nudge him into speeding up the work on Cira's scrolls.

Bartlett was standing in the hall when she came in the front door, his expression concerned. "I saw you go into the stable with the boy. You were there a long time. Is everything all right?"

"No problem. He's very sweet." She gestured to the sketchbook she carried. "I was just doing a little work."

He shook his head reproachfully. "You shouldn't have gone into the stable. Trevor's put it off-limits to all of us. That's MacDuff's territory."

"MacDuff didn't kick me out, so I guess it was okay with him." She started up the stairs. "I've got to get back to Mario. I'll see you later." As she reached the landing, she glanced back and saw him still staring after her with a troubled expression. She said gently, "It's okay, Bartlett. Stop worrying."

He forced a smile and nodded. "I'll work on it." He turned away. "It used to be easier. The older I get, the more aware I become of how many things there are to worry about in this world. You wouldn't know about that. The young always think they're immortal."

"You're wrong. I never thought I was immortal even when I was a kid. I knew you had to fight to stay alive." She continued up the stairs. "But I'm not about to spoil even one minute of it fretting unless I decide there's cause."

May I come in, Trevor?" MacDuff asked after he opened the library door. He nodded at Bartlett, who was standing beside the desk. "I thought you'd come running here after I saw you outside in the courtyard looking at the stable as if it were a windmill and you were Don Quixote." He dropped down in the visitor's chair and smiled at Trevor. "I decided to save you the trouble of seeking me out. You're such a busy man."

"You said you'd keep him away from her," Trevor said coldly. "Get him the hell out of here."

His smile faded. "Jock's home is with me. Such as it is."

"I believe I'll leave you to your discussion." Bartlett moved toward the door. "But I never tilt at windmills, MacDuff. Though I do believe Don Quixote's nobility overshadowed his foolishness."

As the door closed behind Bartlett, Trevor repeated, "Get Jock the hell away from here. Or I'll do it myself."

MacDuff shook his head. "No, you won't. You need me. If he goes, I go."

"Don't try to bluff me." His gaze was narrowed on MacDuff's face. "You may not even be able to help me. If Mario comes through, I may be able to find the gold myself. How the hell do I know you have any valid lead at all? Maybe it's a con."

"Give me what I want and see."

"Bloodthirsty bastard."

"Ah, yes. That I am. But you should have realized that when you saw everything I was willing to give up to get my chance." He leaned back in the chair and his gaze wandered around the library. "It's strange sitting in this visitor's chair when I always sat where you are. Life takes odd turns, doesn't it?"

"You're changing the subject."

"Just a wee detour." His gaze shifted back to Trevor. "I did tell him not to go near her, but it didn't work out. It won't happen again."

"He'll stay away from her?"

"No, but I'll always be with them." He held up his hand as Trevor started to curse. "She wants to sketch him. I warned her about him. I'm not sure she believed me, but that won't matter as long as I'm there to intercede."

"It's not going to happen."

"Then talk to her, tell her not to do it." He tilted his head. "If you think it will do any good."

"You son of a bitch."

"Actually, my mother was a quintessential bitch, so I'll not take offense at that remark." He got to his feet. "I'll make sure Jane sketches him in the court-yard so that you can have someone you trust keep watch on them. I'm quite aware that wouldn't be me." He shook his head as he gazed around the library again. "Strange . . ."

"I hope it sticks in your throat to see me here," Trevor said through his teeth.

MacDuff shook his head. "No, this place doesn't define who I am. Do I love it? With every breath. But I don't have to be here. I carry it with me." He smiled. "You look very good in that chair, Trevor. Quite the laird. Enjoy." His smile faded as he turned and headed for the door. "If you choose not to in-terfere, I'll be grateful. It's the first time since I found him that he's responded positively to anyone but me. I believe she's good for him. That's the bot-tom line for me."

"I won't trade—"

But MacDuff had already left the library.

Trevor drew a deep breath and tried to smother the frustration that was tearing through him. He did need MacDuff, dammit. He'd begun thinking of the laird as a long shot, but the more he found out about MacDuff's visits to Herculaneum, the more Trevor was beginning to believe he might be the answer.

Was MacDuff bluffing? Maybe, but Trevor couldn't risk it. Okay, so consider the situation calmly. MacDuff wouldn't want anything to happen to Jane. It wasn't in his best interests. He'd promised to be on-site during any encounter, and Trevor trusted him to keep his word. Not that he wouldn't have Brenner on hand to keep an eye on Jock.

Hell, the entire situation could be resolved if he could go to Jane and tell her that those damn sketching sessions were unacceptable. But that wasn't an option.

If MacDuff had warned her about Jock and she was still planning on seeing the boy, then Trevor's interference would do no good. She'd do as she pleased, and any protest from him would be useless.

But she never let stubbornness get in the way of good sense. So try to get ammunition to convince her that it was reasonable for her to turn her back on the boy. Until then he'd take measures to protect her and try to keep himself from obviously stepping between them.

Ammunition. He reached for the telephone and dialed Venable. "I have a favor to ask. I need information."

Jane was still with Mario when Trevor knocked on the door at eight-fifteen that evening. He opened the door without waiting for an answer. "I do hate to interrupt, Jane." His tone was sarcastic. "But I can't have you distracting Mario from his work any longer."

"She wasn't distracting me," Mario said quickly. "Her presence is very quiet and soothing."

"Soothing? Amazing. And Bartlett tells me she went down to the kitchen late this afternoon and fixed you both a tray. You must have discovered a side of her that she's never shown me."

"People respond differently to different people," Jane said. "I didn't want to disturb Mario."

Mario grinned. "Because she wanted me to finish the scroll I'm working on."

Jane nodded with a rueful smile. "I was hoping you'd speed through it and give me something to read tomorrow."

"I told you I was having trouble with it. There are entire words missing and I have to guess. Or perhaps I'm stretching out the translating so that I can look up and see you sitting there."

"You'd better not be," Trevor said.

"Just a joke," Mario said quickly. "It's going well, Trevor."

"Any reference?"

"Not yet."

"Reference to what?" Jane asked.

"The gold. What else?" Trevor said. "If you read Cira's first letter, you must know there's a doubt that the gold was in the tunnel, that she might have hidden it somewhere else."

"And if she did, you're out of luck."

"Unless I find a clue to where she stashed it."

"You mean where Pia stashed it. Who is Pia?"

He shrugged. "If you read the scroll, you know as much as I do." He met her eyes. "You said you wanted to go to the Run. Have you changed your mind?"

"No. Why should I?"

"You seem to be fascinated by Mario and his scholastic bag of tricks." He turned on his heel. "Come on."

"Wait a moment." He wasn't waiting. He was already halfway down the hall. "Bye, Mario, I'll see you tomorrow."

Trevor had reached the staircase by the time she caught up with him. "You're being exceptionally rude."

"I know. I feel like being rude. It's a privilege I allow myself occasionally."

"I'm surprised anyone puts up with you."

"They don't have to. It's their privilege to tell me to go to hell."

"You're right." She stopped on the stairs. "Go to hell."

He glanced back over his shoulder. "Now, that's what I expected. You mustn't treat me too—" He broke off. Then a smile lit his face. "I'm being an uncivilized bastard, aren't I?"

"Yes."

"And you did your best to provoke me today." He made a face. "I made it easy for you. You knew just where to strike. I've always prided myself on my self-confidence, but you managed to undermine it. I was actually jealous of Mario." He lifted his hand to stop her as she started to speak. "And don't tell me that you didn't want to rake me over the coals. You were frustrated about your situation here and you wanted me to be frustrated too. Well, you succeeded. We're even. *Pax?*"

They weren't even, but she welcomed the possibility of ignoring the tension between them. The past twenty-four hours had been unbearable. "I'd never encourage Mario to get my own back against you. I don't play with people's feelings. I like him too much."

"Oh, I believe you. But you wouldn't mind letting me wonder. I showed you a weakness and you jumped on it. Maybe in the back of your mind you were punishing me for being fool enough to push you away four years ago."

She moistened her lips. "I don't want to talk about this now. Are you going to take me to the Run or not?"

He nodded and turned to the door. "Let's go."

They were stopped by a guard at the gate, as Trevor had been last night. "Jane, Patrick Campbell. We're just going to the Run, Pat. All clear tonight?"

Campbell nodded. "Douglas had a sighting three hours ago, but nowhere close to the castle." He took out his phone. "I'll just give your security boys on the perimeter a warning to keep sharp."

"Do that." Trevor took Jane's elbow and nudged her through the gates. "We take the path around the castle to the cliffs. It's about ten minutes' walk." He looked up at the sky. "It's a full moon. You should be able to see well enough. . . ."

\* \* \*

When they turned the corner and began walking toward the edge of the cliff, Jane first noticed only the sea stretching before her. "What is this? What am I supposed to—"

They had reached the top of a knoll, and below them, stretching toward the steep cliff, was a level grassy plain that bordered the entire rear of the castle. The grass was perfectly manicured and on either end of the long expanse were several rows of boulders.

"MacDuff's Run," Trevor said.

"What the devil is it? It looks like some Druid meeting place."

"It was a meeting place, all right. Angus MacDuff had a passion for athletic games. He was something of a robber baron and admired might in any form. He finished building his castle in 1350 and the next spring he held the first Scottish Games in this area."

"That long ago?"

Trevor shook his head. "In 844 Kenneth MacAlpine, King of Scots, organized a three-day game to keep his army occupied while waiting for good-luck omens before his battle with the Picts. Malcolm Canmore, who took the throne in 1058, held regular games to select the strongest and fastest Scots to join his elite guard."

"And I thought they were called the Highland Games."

"The MacDuffs originated in the Highlands, and I guess they brought their games with them. According to their journals the games were the highlight of their year. Curling, wrestling, racing, and some local sports that were a bit weird. All the young men in MacDuff's service participated in them." He smiled at Jane. "And an occasional woman. Fiona MacDuff was mentioned as being permitted to run in the races. She won two years in a row."

"And then I suppose they decided to outlaw women?"

He shook his head. "She got pregnant and stopped of her own accord." He stopped beside one of the boulders at the end of the Run. "Sit down. I imagine that the later generations brought out chairs to view the games, but these were the first seats."

She slowly sat down on the boulder beside him. "Why do you come here?"

"I like it." His gaze traveled down the stretch of grass to the rocks at the end of the Run. "It's a good place to get your head straight. I feel at home here. I believe I would have enjoyed knowing Angus MacDuff."

As she stared at his profile, she believed he would too. The wind from the sea was lifting his hair from his forehead and there was that hint of recklessness about his mouth. His eyes were narrowed as if gauging the difficulty of the next competition. She could imagine him sitting here, laughing with the laird and preparing for his turn at the Run. Jesus, she wished she had her sketchbook. "Which event would you have entered?"

"I don't know. The run, maybe curling . . ." He turned to her and his eyes were glittering with mischief. "Or maybe I'd have been better suited taking book on all the events. I'm sure there was plenty of gambling going on during the games."

She smiled back at him. "I can see you carving out a niche in that area."

"Perhaps I could have done both. I'd have gotten bored with only betting on one game a year."

"Heaven forbid." She looked away from him. "I didn't expect this when you brought me here."

"I know you didn't. You probably thought the Run was one of my more wicked criminal enterprises."

"Or had some connection with Grozak. Why didn't you tell me?"

"Because I wanted you here," he said simply. "I like it here and I wanted you to like it too."

He was telling the truth, and she did like it here, dammit. It was as if this place reduced everything to the basic and primitive. She could almost hear the pipes and feel the earth vibrate beneath the feet of those long-ago runners. "Would it have been so difficult to just say that?"

"Hell, yes. You're having trouble even looking at me these days without throwing up a cast-iron barrier. And then I made it worse by letting sex— See, you're tensing again. Look at me, dammit. This isn't like you, Jane."

"How do you know? You haven't seen me in four years." But she forced herself to turn her head and look at him. Oh, God, she wished she hadn't. Now how was she going to look away?

"Tough, isn't it? Me too." He stared down at her

hand resting on the boulder. "Christ, I want to touch you."

He wasn't touching her but he might as well have been. Her palm pressing against the rock was tingling and she felt again that queer breathlessness.

His gaze stayed on her hand. "You touched me once. You put your hand on my chest and I had to stand there and keep myself from reaching out for you. It nearly killed me."

"It should have. You were being stupid."

"You were seventeen."

"I was old enough to know what I wanted." She added quickly, "Not that you were so special. You were just the first man that I'd felt that way about. I was a little backward where sex was concerned."

"You didn't act backward. I thought you were going to slug me."

"You called me a schoolgirl."

"I was trying to make you angry enough to protect myself."

She was still angry, hurt—and filled with bitter regret. "Poor Trevor."

"I hurt you."

"Nonsense. I don't let people hurt me. Did you think you'd scarred me for other relationships? No way."

He shook his head. "You warned me you'd search until you found someone better than me. You kept your word." He looked out at the sea. "Clark Peters, nice boy, but he got possessive after two months. Tad Kipp, very smart and ambitious but he didn't like your dog, Toby, when you brought him home to

Eve and Joe. Jack Ledborne, archaeology professor who supervised the second dig you went on. He didn't tell you he was married and you cut him dead when you found out. Peter Brack, a K-9 cop in Quinn's precinct. A match made in heaven. A dog lover and a cop. But he must have done something wrong, because you—"

"What the devil?" She couldn't believe it. "Have you been having me watched?"

"Only when I couldn't do it myself." His gaze shifted back to her. "And most of the time I could. Do you want me to go on with your little black book? Or do you want me to tell you how proud I was when you won the Mondale International Art Award? I tried to get them to sell that painting to me, but they keep them for five years to put on tour to display around the country." He smiled. "Of course, I considered stealing it, but I didn't think you'd approve. But I did steal something else that belonged to you."

"What?"

"A sketchbook. Two years ago you left it on a bench at the Metropolitan Museum when you went off with your friends to the cafeteria. I flipped through it and I couldn't resist. I was always going to return it to you but I never did."

"I remember that happening. I was mad as hell."

"It didn't seem to be anything that you'd develop into a painting. It seemed more . . . personal."

Personal. She tried to remember if she'd had any sketches of Trevor in that sketchbook. Probably. "Why?" she whispered. "Why did you do all this?"

"You told me when you left Naples that it wasn't finished. I found it wasn't finished for me either." His lips twisted. "Jesus, sometimes I prayed for it to be finished. You're tough, Jane."

"Then why didn't you—"

"You told me I had no place in your life for the next four years. I was giving you your chance to find out if that was true."

"And if I had?"

"The truth? I'm no martyr. I'd have stepped in and ruined the tidy little life you'd structured for yourself."

"What are you saying? What's the bottom line?"

"The bottom line?" His hand moved to within an inch of hers on the boulder. She could feel its warmth. "I want to go to bed with you so bad it's a constant ache. I respect you. I admire you. You accused me once of being obsessed with Cira, but it's nothing to what I feel for you. I don't like it. I don't know if it will go on. Sometimes I hope it doesn't. Is that bottom line enough for you?"

"Yes." Her throat was tight and she had to clear it. "If it's true."

"There's a way to test at least the most obvious portion of it."

He moved his hand that last inch. He touched her.

She shuddered, but not with cold. Heat.

Too much. Too intense.

She jerked her hand away. "No."

"You want it."

She couldn't lie about that. She felt as if she were

sending out signals like an animal in heat. "It's too fast."

"The hell it is."

"And sex is—it's not everything. I don't even know if I trust you."

"And you're still wary as hell."

"I have reason."

"Do you? Your friend died. Do you think I'm to blame?"

"I don't know."

"You know. I want everything clear between us. That's why I brought you here. Think. Make a decision."

"Mike might have lived if you hadn't gone after the gold and become involved with this Grozak."

"So are you blaming me for the domino effect?"

"No, I guess not," she said wearily. "Or maybe I am. I'm not sure anymore. I don't know what the hell is happening."

"I'd have saved him if I could. I wish I could turn back the clock."

"But you'd still go after the gold, wouldn't you?"

He was silent a moment. "Yes. I won't lie to you. I have to get the gold."

"Why? You're a brilliant man. You don't have to do this. I don't believe it even means anything to you but the game itself."

"You're wrong. This time it does mean something. If I get it, then Grozak won't."

"Revenge?"

"Partly. You're not above taking revenge yourself, Jane."

"No, I'm not." She got to her feet. "But I wouldn't do it by depriving a killer of a pocketful of gold. We don't think alike."

"Sometimes it's not necessary to think."

That wave of heat again. "It is for me."

"We'll see." He stood up. "But I should warn you, if you decide you want to put your hand on me again, you're not going to get the same answer." He started toward the path. "And Angus MacDuff would understand perfectly."

# 9

---

"I've got the old man," Wickman said as soon as Grozak answered. "What do you want me to do with him?"

Satisfaction surged through Grozak. Now, this was efficiency. He'd been right to call in Wickman. He'd only been on the job a matter of a few days and he'd done what he'd been paid to do.

Well, not entirely what he'd been paid to do.

"Has he written the note?"

"I have it."

"Then it's time to finish the job."

"How?"

Grozak thought about it. In order to have maximum effect the method had to arouse shock, fear, and horror.

"How?" Wickman repeated.

"I'm thinking."

And then it came to him.

I've got a line on Grozak," Joe said when he called Eve that evening. "He's bad news."

"We knew that from what Trevor told Jane. Details?"

"I don't have details. The FBI has put a lock on his computer records."

"Why would they do that?"

"Maybe the same reason Interpol wouldn't let me access Trevor's records." He paused. "And the CIA bounced me off the Internet so fast it made my head swim. Five minutes later I got a call from my captain asking me what the hell I was up to dealing with classified material. Those sites are being monitored damn closely."

Eve felt a ripple of fear. "Did you find out anything at all?"

"I was able to access Grozak's local police records. He was born in Miami, Florida, and had a record by the time he was thirteen. He belonged to a particularly vicious teenage gang. They were involved in a number of hate crimes ranging from the rape and torture of a black girl to joining with a Nazi group to beat up a Jewish shopkeeper. He was sent to a juvenile facility for killing a Hispanic cop when he was fourteen. He was paroled at eighteen and disappeared from the radar screen after he got out of prison. That was over twenty years ago."

"He evidently expanded his horizons and moved

on to the international scene if the CIA is involved."
She shivered. "Hate crimes. You're right. He's bad
news."

"He appeared to have a grudge against the
world. And his psychological profile indicated he'd
only get worse."

"Then why the hell did they let him out of
prison?"

"The system. Got to give every murdering kid a
fighting chance to kill again. It's the American way."

"And according to Trevor, he killed Mike. Christ,
it's not fair." She drew in a shaky breath. "Are we going to phone Jane right away?"

"Not until we know more. It's not going to help
her to know what he did as a kid. We need an update. And maybe she'll be the one to get us one. I'm
sure she's not sitting around that MacDuff's Run
and wringing her hands."

Venable called on the land line." Bartlett
was coming out of the library when Jane and Trevor
came in the front door. "He said he couldn't reach
you on your cell. Neither could I."

"I turned it off. I figured I could give myself an
hour of peace," Trevor said. "Important?"

"He wouldn't confide in me. But I'd say we can
assume he considers everything he does important." He turned to Jane. "You didn't eat any supper.
Would you like me to fix you a sandwich?"

"No, I'm not hungry." She started up the stairs.

"I'm going to bed. Unless one of you would like to tell me who Venable is?"

"A man who shares our fears about Grozak," Trevor said. "Unfortunately, he's uncertain what to do about it."

"And you're not uncertain?"

"Not in the least." He headed down the hall. "But it's a problem when the Venables of the world get in the way."

"Yet you're evidently allowing him access to you." She stopped on the third step. "I'm not going to be shut out any longer, Trevor. I'm tired of it. You've used Cira as a red herring to keep me from focusing on Grozak, and I let you do it because she meant so much to me. I said a few days. It's over."

"Cira wasn't exactly a red herring." He studied her expression. "But you're right, it's gone on too long. You've got to start to trust me. I'll work on it." He smiled. "Tomorrow." He disappeared into the library.

It was just as well he hadn't picked up the challenge she'd issued, she thought wearily. Her emotions were raw and she was confused and, yes, frustrated. The night had been too intense and had sent her spiraling through a tornado of sexual tension. She'd barely been able to keep her composure on the way back from the Run. She'd been aware of every movement of his body as he walked beside her. It was idiotic to respond like this. Jesus, it wasn't as if she was the inexperienced kid she'd been when she first met him.

"You can trust him, you know," Bartlett said

gravely. "He's a bit erratic, but Trevor's never let me down when it counted."

"Really? But then, your relationship is a good deal different, isn't it? Good night, Bartlett."

"Good night." He started down the hall toward the library. "I'll see you in the morning."

Yes, tomorrow. She'd go to Mario's study first thing and stay there a few hours to get ready to confront Trevor. Those hours with Mario had been tranquil, and she needed that peace. Tonight she'd sleep and block out Trevor, try not to think how much she'd wanted to touch him. Hell, touch him? She'd wanted to pull him into bed and rut like a damn nymphomaniac. She couldn't think of a bigger mistake. She had to keep a clear head and she didn't know if she could if she became sexually involved with Trevor. She'd never had this kind of intense response to any man, and the bond between them was as strong now as it had been four years ago. She couldn't afford for it to gain any more power.

Then don't remember how it felt sitting beside him on that boulder at the Run. Concentrate on this Venable.

Trevor had just hung up when Bartlett came into the library.

Bartlett raised his brows. "That was quick. I take it Venable was overreacting?"

"Maybe." Trevor was frowning thoughtfully. "But

I'd rather he overreact than sit on his ass and live in la-la land like Sabot."

"What was the problem?"

"Quinn's been trying to access the CIA records on Grozak. It made Venable nervous." He shrugged. "It was bound to happen. Quinn's an ex-FBI man and he has contacts. He'll find a way to get the info he wants. I'll deal with it when it happens."

"And that's all Venable wanted?"

Trevor shook his head. "He said that he had an informant in Switzerland who said something important was going down in Lucerne."

"What? Grozak?"

"Vague. But a possibility."

Bartlett tilted his head. "It's bothering you."

"Grozak always bothers me if I'm not sure where he's going to jump next."

"Maybe Venable's informant got it wrong."

"And maybe he got it right." He leaned back in the chair, his mind trying to process those possibilities. "Lucerne . . ."


Jock is going to meet us at the fountain," MacDuff said as he crossed the courtyard toward Jane. "If that's all right with you?"

"I don't care." She sat down on the rim of the fountain and opened her sketchbook. "When is he coming?"

"In a few minutes. He's watering his plants." He frowned. "What are you doing?"

"Sketching you. I hate wasting time." Her pencil

was moving rapidly over the page. "You've got a very interesting face. All hard lines, except for the mouth. . . ." She added a few lines to the cheekbones. "I knew you reminded me of someone. Did you ever see that TV program *Highlander*?"

"No, I was spared that."

"You look like the actor who plays the lead."

"Oh, God."

"He was very good." She smiled slyly, wondering how far she could take this. "And pretty, very pretty."

He didn't rise to the bait. "Jock is the one who you're supposed to be sketching."

"I'm loosening up. It's like stretching before you run." She paused. "By the way, Trevor took me to the Run last night."

"I know."

"How do you know?"

He didn't answer.

"Oh, of course, Trevor said you had your people all over the castle." Her gaze fastened on the sketch. "It must be difficult having to lease out this place. I grew up in the streets, and there's never been a place I could really call mine. But for a few minutes last night I could imagine what it must be like." She raised her eyes from the pad. "I believe Trevor could too. That's why he likes the Run so much."

He shrugged. "Then he'd better enjoy it while he can. I'm taking it back."

"How?"

"Any way I can."

"But Trevor said your family couldn't afford not to rent out the place."

"Then that's the way to get it back, isn't it?"

"With Cira's gold?"

"The gold seems to be the goal for all of us. Why should I be any different?"

"Then that's why you're concerned about Grozak?"

"What did Trevor say?"

"He said to ask you."

He smiled faintly. "I'm glad he kept his word."

"I'm not. I want to know how you're involved. Is it just the gold?"

He didn't answer directly. "The gold should be enough to motivate any man, especially a man who needs money as desperately as I do." His gaze went beyond her shoulder. "Here comes Jock." He made a face. "Try to refrain from calling me names while he's around. It will be healthier for all of us."

She turned to see the boy coming toward them. He was smiling and there was a hint of eagerness in his expression. Lord, that face . . . She automatically turned the page of her sketchbook. "Good morning, Jock. Did you sleep well?"

"No. I have dreams. Do you have dreams, Jane?"

"Sometimes." She began to sketch. Could she catch the haunted expression that lingered behind that smile? And did she want to? The vulnerability of the boy was almost tangible, and capturing it seemed an intrusion. "Bad dreams?"

"Not as bad as they were." He was looking at MacDuff, and the devotion in his expression made her shake her head in amazement. "They're getting better, sir. Honestly."

"They'd better be," MacDuff said gruffly. "I told you it's only a question of will. Use it." He sat down on the rim of the fountain. "Now stop yammering at me and let the woman sketch you."

"Yes, sir." Jock looked at Jane. "What do I do?"

"Nothing." She looked down at the pad. "Be natural. Talk to me. Tell me about your flowers. . . ."

"Good morning," Jane said as she carried a tray into Mario's study. "How are you today?" She shook her head as she saw the pile of papers on his desk. "I'd say you either worked late or started early. Whichever it is, you can use a break for a cup of coffee and some toast."

He nodded. "Thank you. Actually, I didn't get much sleep last night and I've probably had too much coffee already." He reached for the carafe. "But that doesn't mean I'm not going to have some more."

She studied him. "You're wired."

"It's getting interesting again." He took a drink of his coffee. "There are hours and hours of just painstaking deciphering and then it starts to open up for me." He smiled eagerly. "Like the curtain swinging open in a theater when the play begins. Exciting . . ."

"I can see it is." She went to her chair in the corner and sat down. "But you've been translating too much Cira if you're starting to do comparisons with theaters and plays."

He glanced at the statue by the window. "There's never too much Cira." He looked down at the photocopy on the desk in front of him. "I have to call Trevor. I believe I may have found a reference he's looking for."

"Ah, the gold?"

"Yes, anything to do with the gold." He frowned. "No, I'll wait until the final translation. I have to check over the inserts I had to make. I have to make sure that—"

"Mail call." Trevor stood in the doorway with a small package and two letters in his hands. "For you, Mario. Just arrived by special messenger." He came toward the desk. "Who do you know in Lucerne?"

Trevor's tone was without expression, but Jane was suddenly aware of an underlying tenseness in his demeanor.

"Lucerne?" Mario's gaze focused on the mail Trevor had placed before him. "For me?"

"That's what I said." Trevor's lips tightened. "Open it."

A chill went through Jane. She knew how careful Trevor was with all aspects of security. She didn't like this. There was something wrong. "Have you checked it?"

"Of course I've checked it." He never took his gaze off Mario. "No bombs. No powder."

"Then why are you—" She broke off as she watched Mario open the letter and start to read it.

"Or maybe there was a bomb," Trevor murmured.

She knew what he meant. Bewilderment and then horror froze Mario's expression as his gaze flew across the page. "What's wrong, Mario?"

"Everything." He lifted his eyes. "Everything. How could you do this? Why didn't you give me the other letters, Trevor?"

"What letters?" Trevor asked.

"I have to see the tape." He frantically tore the wrappings off the package and took out a black VHS case. "Where's a VCR?"

"The library," Trevor said. "I'll go with you and set it up."

"No, I'll go by myself," he said jerkily. "I don't want your help." He ran from the room.

"What happened?" Jane asked as she got to her feet.

"I don't know, but I intend to find out." He crossed to the desk and picked up the letter.

Jane frowned. "That's a breach of privacy."

"Sue me." Trevor was already reading the letter. "I've an idea the content's aimed at me anyway. Mario was— Shit!" He thrust the letter at Jane and headed for the door. "Read it. Son of a bitch . . ."

Jane looked down at the letter.

*Mario,*

    *Why do you not answer them? They've sent you letter after letter and told you what they'll do to me if you don't stop what you're doing. Surely blood is more important than your work. What evil have you become mixed up in that would cause these men to do this to me?*

*I don't want to die. Answer them. Tell them you will stop.*

*Your father,*
*Eduardo Donato*

Then below the handwritten letter was one type-written line.

*Since we're not sure that you're receiving these letters, our patience is at an end, and we must show both you and Trevor we mean what we say.*

The tape!

"Christ." She threw the letter on the desk and flew from the room.

The door of the library was open and she heard the sound of sobbing as she ran down the hall.

"Oh, God."

The TV screen was blank but Mario was bent double, his shoulders heaving. "*Santa Maria.* Dear God in heaven."

Trevor's hand gripped his shoulder in comfort. "I'm sorry, Mario."

"Don't touch me." Mario wrenched away from him. "They butchered him. You let them kill him." Tears were running down his cheeks. "He was an old man. He worked hard all his life and he deserved to live in peace. He didn't deserve—" He swallowed. "Dear God, what they did to—" He brushed past

Jane as he ran out of the room. She didn't believe he even saw her.

Jane stared at the flickering screen. She didn't want to know the answer but she had to ask. "What happened to him?"

"He was beheaded."

"What?" Her gaze flew to his face. "Beheaded?"

"Barbaric, isn't it?" His lips twisted. "And they threw in all the trimmings, including holding up the old man's head after the act."

She felt sick. It was more than barbaric, it was the act of a monster. Poor Mario. "Grozak?"

"Not personally. The executioner wore a hood, but he was taller, thinner."

She rubbed her temple. It was hard to comprehend when all she could see was the image that Trevor had described. "He said . . . letters?"

"There were no letters. This was the only letter Mario received since he came to MacDuff's Run."

"Then why would Grozak say—"

"He wanted to put a spoke in the wheel," Trevor said harshly. "I needed Mario to translate, and Grozak wanted to stop me or slow me down until he could make a move. If Mario thought I was keeping his father's ransom letters from him for my own purposes, that would do the trick."

"He beheaded that old man without giving anyone a chance to ransom him?"

"Ransom wasn't the aim. That would have dragged it out too long, and Grozak doesn't have that much time. He needed the translating stopped now. This was the quickest and most likely way to do it."

"His father . . ." She remembered something Mario had said on the first day she'd arrived at the castle. "But he said he'd told you he had no close relatives. That you'd made it one of the requirements for the job."

"It seems he lied. Stupid . . ." For an instant his expression was more agonized than Mario's had been. "He didn't give me a chance. I could have—" He flipped open his telephone and pressed a number. "Brenner, I'm in the library. I need you now." He hung up. "Get out of here, Jane."

"Why?"

"Because as soon as Brenner walks through that door I'm going to start rerunning the tape. I don't think you want to see it."

She stared at him in horror. "Why would you do that?"

"Between us, Brenner and I have run across most of the hit men who Grozak would deal with. If we look at the tape enough, we may come up with an identity."

"How can you sit and watch—" She knew the answer. You could do anything you had to do. But watching and rewatching that tape would be hard even for the most callous person. "It's necessary?"

"I'm not letting Grozak get what he wants without paying the price." He repeated wearily as Brenner came into the room, "Get out of here. I'll let you know if we come up with anything."

She hesitated.

"You can't do anything," Trevor said. "You'll only get in the way."

And he didn't want her to see that tape. Dear God, she didn't want to see it either. And he was right, it would serve no purpose. She turned and headed for the door. "I'll go and see if I can help Mario."

She felt numb with horror as she went down the hall and started up the stairs. She had known that Grozak was evil, but this took malevolence to a new level. The sheer calculated coldness of the act was stunning. What kind of creature was he?

Mario wasn't in the study as she'd expected. No, of course not. He wouldn't be able to face the work that had been the cause of his father's death. She knocked on the door of the adjoining bedroom. "Mario?"

"Go away."

She was tempted to do as he said. He probably needed time alone to get over the shock.

No, she couldn't leave him to cope with that shock and horror alone. She opened the door. He was sitting in a chair across the room, and the tears were gone but his expression was ravaged. She came into the room. "I won't stay long. I just want you to know I'm here if you need to talk to someone."

"I don't need you. I don't need any of you." He stared at her accusingly. "Did you know about the letters?"

"There were no other letters," she said gently. "Grozak wanted you to think there were so that you'd stop work and blame Trevor."

He shook his head.

"It's true. Grozak's a terrible man. That's why Trevor wanted to make sure that he didn't have a target."

"He let them kill my father."

"You told me yourself that you told Trevor you had no close living relatives."

He looked away from her. "He wouldn't have given me the job. It was clear what he wanted from the man he hired. And it wasn't exactly a lie. My mother divorced my father years before she died. He moved to Lucerne and I didn't see him often." His voice broke. "But I loved him. I should have taken the trouble to see him more. I was too busy." He covered his eyes with a shaking hand. "And I let Trevor kill him."

"Grozak killed him. Trevor didn't even know he existed."

"The letters."

She shouldn't argue with him. He was upset and grieving. Then she remembered Trevor's expression in the library. Silence was assent, and she found she couldn't do that to Trevor. "Listen to me." She knelt before him and took his hand from his eyes. "Look at me. You're not being fair, and I won't let you get away with it. I think Grozak counted on you blaming Trevor. He set you up and you're falling for it."

Mario shook his head.

"You're looking for someone to blame and Trevor's the closest target. But it's not true. It's a terrible, terrible tragedy, but the only one to blame for it is Grozak."

Mario was gazing at her in scornful disbelief. "You believe Trevor? You actually trust him?"

She was silent. If he had asked her that last night, she wasn't sure what she would have told him. What had changed?

The answer came with unerring certainty. The terror and shock of this monstrous killing had burned away all the confusion and hesitancy, and, for the first time since she'd seen Trevor outside that dorm at Harvard, she was responding with instinct and not emotion.

"Yes," she said slowly. "I do trust him."

Wickman?" Trevor asked as he put the video on pause. "Same height."

Brenner frowned. "I was thinking maybe Rendle. I'm not sure Wickman is that thin. Of course, you've run across him more than I have, haven't you?"

"Twice. Once in Rome, another time in Copenhagen. He's smooth. Everything about him is smooth. The way he talks, the way he moves . . ."

"I remember. But Rendle is thinner."

"Weight can vary. It's difficult to change your body language." He punched the rewind button. "But you may be right. We'll watch it again."

Brenner grimaced. "Great."

Trevor knew how he felt. He'd seen many atrocities in his life, but the sight of that old man's bewilderment and terror was enough to make him want to throw up. "We have to get a handle on who we're dealing with."

"And take him out?"

Trevor nodded curtly. "Particularly if it's Wickman. He's good, and I don't want him turned loose on Jane or anyone else here." He pressed the button and Eduardo's face appeared on the screen. "So we'll watch this damn video until we go blind if we have to. Wickman or Rendle?"

# 10

They're still in the library," Bartlett told Jane when he met her coming down the stairs an hour later. "Trevor told me to keep you out. I didn't ask him how I was to do that since you're probably more martially adept than I'll ever be." He frowned. "But *please* has always worked for me. Will you please not cause me undue distress by barging in there?"

"Yes, I don't need to see that video to know what we're dealing with. My friend was killed by them." She shuddered. "But I admit the sheer callousness of what they did to Mario's father is almost beyond belief. It's . . . barbaric."

Bartlett nodded. "Attila the Hun comes to mind. Trevor told me Grozak was vicious, but one can't take it in until—"

"I need to charter a plane, Bartlett." Brenner had

left the library and was coming down the hall toward them. "Get a helicopter to take me to Aberdeen and have a jet ready to take off when we land there."

"Right away." Bartlett turned toward the phone on the hall table. "Where are you going?"

"Lucerne. Trevor and I aren't agreeing on the possible executioner. I'm going to see if I can nose around and narrow it down and try to get confirmation." He looked at Jane. "How's Mario doing?"

"Not good. Devastated. What would you expect?"

"I'd expect him to be mad as hell and not cave. I'd expect him to be on his feet and fighting me for a seat on that plane that's going to Lucerne."

"He's not you, Brenner." She started down the hall toward the library. "Give him a chance."

"I'll give him a chance if he doesn't open his mouth to me about Trevor being to blame." His tone was cold. "If he does, his luck is going to run out." He headed for the front door. "Trevor told me to make sure security is at high alert before I leave. Call me when you have an ETA on that helicopter, Bartlett."

Bartlett was talking on the phone and merely nodded.

Things were moving, stirring. Bartlett was operating with meticulous efficiency, and Brenner was no longer the easygoing Aussie she'd met on the plane. He was impatient, machete-sharp, and very defensive of his friend. She could understand his reaction. She was feeling that impatience and stirring to action herself.

The door of the library was open and she saw Trevor sitting at the desk, putting the videotape in an envelope. He looked drained. She'd never seen him with that expression of extreme weariness and disappointment. She hesitated. "Are you okay?"

"No." He tossed the envelope aside. "I'm sick to death. And I'm wondering why the human race hasn't evolved to a higher state that could prevent us from producing the Grozaks of the world." He looked at her. "So has Mario convinced you what a callous bastard I am?"

"Don't be stupid. Sometimes I have a soft heart, never a soft head. How could you be to blame? Grozak lied to Mario." She paused. "And there's no way you'd be capable of the kind of coldness it would take to deliberately ignore a ransom letter to keep Mario working."

"I wouldn't?" His brows lifted. "Are you sure?"

"Yes, I'm sure." She frowned. "And I didn't come down here to defend you to yourself. I just got through trying to talk sense into Mario."

"And did you succeed?"

"No, he's too busy trying to blame everyone but himself for his father's death, which I guess is understandable." Her lips tightened. "So I stopped being diplomatic and patient and told him he needed to face up to the truth."

One corner of his lips lifted in a faint smile. "Well, that's certainly not diplomatic."

"He didn't have any right to blame you, even if he has just had the most incredible shock. If you need him to continue with the translating, you'll have to try to soothe him."

"Good God, I believe you're defending me."

"I just don't believe in unfairness. Don't let it go to your head."

"I wouldn't think of it."

"And I may not have completely alienated Mario. He's a nice guy and he may be able to face his guilt and stop blaming you if we give him enough time."

"I don't know how much time we have."

"What's the hurry?" She sat down in the chair in front of his desk. "Why would Grozak kill that poor man just to stall for time?"

"Grozak and I are in a bit of a competition. First one who crosses the finish line gets the prize."

She shook her head. "Another one of your games? And what's the damn prize?"

"Initially? A chest full of gold."

"Initially? What's that supposed to mean?"

"It means the prize may be a hell of a lot bigger down the road."

"Stop being cryptic. Give me a straight answer."

"I'm not trying to be cryptic." He leaned wearily back in his chair. "I told you last night that I'm not hiding anything anymore. I guess I'm just tired." He reached in the drawer, drew out a rolled document, and spread it out on the desk to reveal a map of the United States. "You want to know what the prize is?" He pointed to Los Angeles. "That's a prize." He pointed to Chicago. "That's a prize." He tapped his index finger on Washington, D.C. "And that may be the biggest prize of all."

"What are you talking about?"

"On December twenty-third there will be nuclear explosions set off in two cities. I haven't been able to find out which ones. But it will be a sizable blast, and enough radioactive material will be released to kill thousands."

She was staring at him in horror. "9/11," she whispered.

"Maybe worse. It depends on how many kamikaze are put into play."

"Kamikaze?"

"The modern-day terrorist version of kamikaze: the suicide bomber. It doesn't work nearly so well unless the man who's setting off the bomb is willing to put his neck into the noose."

"Wait a minute. You're talking about terrorists? Grozak is a terrorist?"

He nodded. "Since 1994. After his stint as a mercenary he finally found his niche. Over the years he's hired himself out to several terrorist groups for fun and profit. He hated practically every minority anyway and it allowed him to expend that hatred in violence and get paid for it. He operated in Sudan, Lebanon, Indonesia, and Russia that I know about. He's clever. He has contacts. And he has no problem taking that final step."

"Final step?"

"Many terrorists go so far and if the risk proves too great they back down. Grozak builds a bolt-hole and goes for it anyway."

"If he's that dangerous, why hasn't the CIA picked him up?"

"They've made several attempts, but they're stretched pretty thin and he's not at the top of their priority list. They get hundreds of tips every week about potential terrorist threats. I told you he was clever. He's aimed his attacks at other countries in Europe and South America. He's not gone for U.S. targets either at home or abroad—so far."

So far. That qualification sent a shiver through her. "So why now?"

"I think he's been biding his time, building his contacts. He's always had a grudge against the U.S. and there was no question he'd be targeting them eventually. It was only a question of when."

"Why now?" she asked again.

"It's all come together for him. He's got the weapons, the money for the operation, all he needs is the manpower." His lips twisted. "Or should I say cannon fodder? It's more apt. The most valuable tools a terrorist has are accessories who are willing to sacrifice their lives for the cause. That was proved on 9/11. They'll take any risk, and after they execute their mission there's no chance of them talking and leading trails back to home base. But it's become increasingly difficult to recruit fanatics who won't back down at the last minute. Of course, there's the Middle East religious contingent, but the CIA is watching them like a hawk."

"And so is Homeland Security."

He nodded. "I'm sure Grozak's prepared to have half the world on his tail for the pleasure of bringing the U.S. to its knees, but he doesn't want to take any additional chances."

"It's crazy. He'd have to crawl into a hole like Saddam Hussein."

"His hole would be gold-lined, and he has the arrogance to believe he'd be able to wait out the search. He'd be a hero to the terrorist world and have plenty of support."

She shook her head. "You said he was clever. This is mad."

"He is clever. He's also full of venom and bitterness and ego. He's going to go for it. He's been nurturing this goal for years."

"How do you know?"

"We were in Colombia together. I knew he was a son of a bitch then and had no love for the U.S. He was always ranting about the pigs who put him in prison. It's rather ironic that by putting him in jail for hate crimes the U.S. turned all that hatred against the government instead. But I was more interested in keeping the bastard from trying to run over me than listening to his political views. I ended up breaking his arm before I left Colombia." He grimaced. "That could be why he hates my guts. What do you think?"

"I'd say that would do it," she said absently. "How did you know Grozak was planning this?"

"I didn't know the exact details. I've kept an eye on him through the years because he's a vengeful bastard and I knew he'd eventually come after me. Eight months ago I began to get some weird reports on Grozak's movements. Six months ago I got hold of an informant in Grozak's circle, who I persuaded to talk."

"Persuaded?"

"Well, forcefully persuaded, but afterward I gave him enough money to make him disappear."

Her mind was whirling, overflowing with what he'd told her. Unbelievable. Yet she was terribly afraid it was true. "What can we do to stop it from happening?"

"Find Cira's gold."

"What?"

"Grozak needs his suicide bombers. He's negotiating to get them from Thomas Reilly. Hell, it may be Reilly who first approached Grozak. Reilly needed muscle to get what he wanted, and he might have decided to manipulate Grozak to go after the gold."

"Manipulate?"

"Possible, even probable. Reilly likes to stay in the background and pull the strings. He has a tremendous ego and loves to show how clever he is. He was actively involved with the IRA for years and later branched out to other terrorist organizations and moved to Greece. Then five years ago he pulled up stakes and disappeared from view. He was rumored to have gone underground in the U.S."

"And how could Reilly help Grozak?"

"Reilly had a special interest that made him invaluable. He was a brilliant psychologist and would pick up dissidents and kids who could be easily influenced and brainwash them into doing almost anything he wanted. They'd take crazy chances and several times they were killed planting bombs at his orders. Later he was rumored to be training suicide bombers at a terrorist camp in Germany. I know he approached al Qaeda at one point and tried to make a deal."

She stiffened. "Al Qaeda?"

He shook his head. "No, they're not involved in this. Al Qaeda doesn't like to deal with non-Muslims. They didn't greet Reilly with open arms years ago when he offered his services. And Grozak doesn't want to deal with al Qaeda right now. That would send up a red flag and tip his hand. He's more interested in another sideline Reilly's been exploring. Reilly's rumored to have recruited a team of American ex-GIs who have a grudge against the U.S. and to have been training them."

"You mean brainwashing."

"That's right. The potential is very attractive for Grozak. Americans with American papers and backgrounds who are willing to kill themselves to get back at the U.S. government."

"I can't believe they'd do it."

"I had my doubts. Reilly sent me a film clip of one of the GIs blowing himself up in front of the U.S. embassy in Nairobi." His lips tightened. "He made sure the kid wasn't too near the embassy and didn't have enough firepower to do any damage and get Reilly in trouble. After all, it was only a sales presentation."

"Sent *you* the clip?"

"He wanted me to know how much power he had. He doesn't trust Grozak to be able to deliver. He said that if I can come up with Cira's gold, he'll call off the deal with Grozak. He'll even help me trap him."

She stared at him in bewilderment. "You don't have Cira's gold. And what difference would it make to a slimeball like that anyway?"

"Even slimeballs have their weaknesses. He's an antiquity collector and has a passion for anything connected with Herculaneum. I've run into him several times over the years while he was trying to acquire stolen artifacts. I bought Cira's statue before he could get his hands on it, and he was mad as hell. He probably knows more about Herculaneum than most university professors. He's acquired ancient letters, ships' journals, documents, supply lists. Anything that would give him the Herculaneum experience. His collection has to be mind-boggling. He has a particular passion for antique coins. He'd give his eyeteeth for the gold from Precebio's tunnel."

"How did you know that?"

"I got a list from Dupoi of the people he'd approached to sell the scrolls. He told me that Reilly was near the top of the list of people he knew would be interested. He didn't notify Grozak; he was on the second rung to be contacted." He paused. "To Dupoi's surprise, Reilly didn't make an offer. But Grozak approached Dupoi almost at once after he'd contacted Reilly and started negotiations."

"Reilly sent Grozak?"

"That was my guess. And I hadn't expected it. It made me damn nervous that Reilly was in Grozak's camp. Grozak was small-time as long as he couldn't put a total package together. Reilly could supply the missing links."

"Christ."

"According to what Reilly told me later, he was going to supply suicide drivers for Grozak's trucks in exchange for Cira's gold. I told Reilly that Grozak didn't have a chance in hell of coming up with it and agreed that I'd give the gold to him if he'd cancel the deal with Grozak."

She shook her head in disbelief. "You're both nuts. Neither of you has it."

"But I told him I knew where it was, that the location was in the scrolls Grozak didn't get his hands on."

"He believed you?"

"I'm a pretty good poker player. He gave me until December twenty-second to deliver if I could come up with everything he wanted. After that he goes through with the deal with Grozak. And who knows? Maybe it wasn't a bluff. That's why I wanted Mario to finish that Cira scroll."

"And what if he won't finish it now?"

"Then I'll get someone else."

"And it might not have any clue about where the gold is."

"That's true. But at least it gives me time to work out something else to do."

"You can't take chances with a potential disaster like this. We have to notify the authorities."

He picked up the phone and handed it to her. "The number is in my memory list. Carl Venable. Special agent. CIA. If you're going to call him, you might tell him about Eduardo Donato. I haven't gotten around to it yet."

She stared down at the phone. "Venable. You're working with the CIA?"

"As much as I can. There seems to be a break in the ranks. Sabot is Venable's superior, and he disagrees that Grozak is a threat. He believes Grozak is a minor player, uninterested in targeting the U.S., and not capable of an operation of this scope." He grimaced. "And either Grozak or Reilly has set up a cry-wolf scenario that's keeping Sabot from believing an attack is coming."

"Cry wolf?"

"Over the last year there have been leaks to the CIA, FBI, and Homeland Security several times warning of attacks at specific sites by Grozak. They raised the alert, sent out teams, and nothing happened. Except they came back mad as hell and with egg on their face. Sabot's not willing to be made a fool of again. He thinks this is just another threat."

"He cried wolf on himself. . . ."

"Right. And Reilly has been off their radar for years—there's no proof he's even alive." He made a face. "Except my word about our conversation, and I'm not exactly a reputable character."

"And Venable?"

"He's a nervous man and doesn't want to be called before a congressional committee to answer questions after an attack. He'd rather cover his bases. Sabot's giving him limited authority to save his own ass if anything goes wrong. God, I hate bureaucracy."

"And Reilly can't be found?"

"Not yet. I've been sending Brenner back to the U.S. to try to pick up word about him. That word is that he may be in the Northwest. Brenner followed two false leads but he thinks he may be on to something now."

"He has to be found."

"I'm doing everything I can, Jane. We'll find him. Third time lucky."

"Luck?"

"Sorry. But I am what I am. I assure you that I'm not relying on chance this time." He grimaced. "And, even though it goes against the grain to give up that gold, I'll do it if I can locate that chest."

"It's a long shot." She frowned. "And I can't believe that Grozak would delay his move on the chance of getting Reilly's support."

"It's either Reilly or an indefinite delay, and Grozak is chomping at the bit after all these years. He wants to be perceived as this mastermind who has the power to shake the world."

"But the chance is so slim of that gold showing up."

"Grozak doesn't know that." He reached in the desk drawer and drew out a velvet pouch. "He's sure that he's on the right track." He tossed the pouch to her. "I sent this to Dupoi with the scrolls and asked him to get an estimate on the age and value."

She slowly opened the pouch and poured the contents into her palm. Four gold coins. Her gaze flew to his face. "You found the chest?"

He shook his head. "No, but I was able to locate

these ancient coins and buy them. I figured they'd be a good lure."

She stared down in wonder at the face imprinted on the coins. "You're sure these are from Cira's time?"

"The face on the coins is Vespasianus Augustus, the emperor at the time of the eruption. Dupoi had them examined and the estimate was A.D. 78. The volcano blew in A.D. 79." He added, "Dupoi authenticated them as coming from Herculaneum. He asked where I'd found them and if there were any more. I told him about the chest."

"What?" Then it hit home. "A trap. You deliberately fed him the information. You knew Dupoi would betray you to Grozak."

He shrugged. "There was a good chance. The word was out that Grozak was trying to find any and all artifacts connected with Herculaneum. He was asking particularly about artifacts connected with Cira. There had been a lot of buzz about Cira after the story came out four years ago, but I couldn't figure out why Grozak was interested when he was no collector himself. I didn't have any idea that he'd taken on a partner."

"Reilly."

He nodded. "Just a guess, but enough to make me think."

"And when you took the scrolls and coins back from Dupoi, Grozak had to go after you to get what he wanted. You had Dupoi set up as a lure and to authenticate the find. And that's what you planned."

She shook her head. "My God, you're a devious son of a bitch."

"But this time I'm on the side of the angels. That should make you happy."

"I'm too scared to be happy about any of this." She shivered. "And then you went to the CIA?"

"Not right away." He grimaced. "I have a problem with all this self-sacrificing bullshit. I decided to verify and do a little soul-searching. There was the possibility that Grozak wouldn't get his act together this time either. But then Reilly appeared, hovering in the background, and I knew it could happen." He shrugged. "The opportunity seemed too good not to take advantage of it. I could rid myself of Grozak before he found a way to take me out. I could save the world." He smiled. "And if I played the game right, I could still end up with the gold. How could I resist?"

"How indeed?" she murmured. She stared at the envelope containing the videotape. "The ultimate tightrope."

His smile faded. "But I didn't want you to be involved. Believe me, if I could have found a way to lock you up in a nunnery until this was over, I would have done it."

"A nunnery?"

"A bit extreme. In case you haven't noticed, I'm a jealous son of a bitch where you're concerned."

"I'm not going to be locked up anywhere." She raised her gaze from the envelope. "And I'm not going to have what happened to Mario's father happen to Eve or Joe."

"The first thing I did when I thought there was a possibility of a danger to you was to tell Venable that he had to have twenty-four-hour coverage for both of them."

"But you're not impressed by the CIA's efficiency."

"I told him if anything happened to them that I'd take the CIA out of the loop. As I told you, Grozak is a nervous man."

"I'm going to warn them anyway."

"As you like."

She had another thought. "How are they going to do it? What are the specific targets?"

"I don't know. I was lucky to get as much information as I did. I doubt if anyone but Grozak knows all the details." He took the telephone back from her. "If you're not going to call Venable, then I'd better do it. I don't want his men getting in Brenner's way when he reaches Lucerne."

"Brenner said you think you know who the murderer is."

"Ralph Wickman. Brenner thinks it's Tom Rendle. I could be wrong but I don't believe so. Brenner is going to scout around and see if he can determine if anyone has an idea of his next move."

"Any hope?"

"Very little. But it doesn't hurt to explore the possibilities. If Wickman is working for Grozak, we have to keep tabs on him."

She shuddered. "He must be a horrible man."

"Yes. But no more horrible than the man who hired him." He reached into his desk drawer and drew out two photos. He threw one in front of her. "Grozak." The face in the photo was that of a man in his forties, not bad looking but nothing extraordinary about him. "If Grozak had to do the job himself, he'd have wielded that sword without a qualm. And enjoyed it." He tossed the other photo down. "Thomas Reilly." Reilly was older, somewhere in his fifties, and his features were almost aristocratic, with fine bones, a long nose, and thin, well-shaped lips. "And, in his way, Reilly makes Grozak look angelic in comparison." He took out his phone. "Do you want to talk to Venable?"

She got to her feet. "Why should I?"

"To see if I've told you the truth."

"You've told me the truth."

"How do you know?"

She smiled slightly. "Because you promised you'd never lie to me."

"Good God, I believe we have a breakthrough."

"And if you wanted to fool Venable, you're capable of doing it with no problem. I've seen you in action."

"Now you've spoiled it."

"Live with it." She paused. "Who knows about Venable?"

"No one but Bartlett, Brenner, and MacDuff. Do you think I'd let the whole world know that I was dealing with the CIA? The more people who know, the greater the chance of a leak."

"Well, Eve and Joe are going to know it."

"Then they'd better be damn discreet about it."

"You know they will." She headed for the door. "Make your call. I have to get back to Mario."

"Why?"

"Because he's not going to be allowed to blame you and curl up in a ball and shut out the rest of the world. It's too important that he finish those scrolls. I'm going to make sure he does it."

His brows lifted. "What determination."

"You're damn right." She looked him in the eye as she opened the door. "I'm an American, Trevor. No bastard is going to blow up any city, town, or podunk junction in my country. Not if I can help it. You play all the games you like as long as it doesn't interfere with that. But it's no game to me. Grozak's going down."

I told you I didn't want you here," Mario said as she came into his room. "You have no heart."

"But I have a brain and I'm using it. Which is a hell of a lot better than you're doing." She sat down in the chair across from him. "I'd like to be gentle and patient with you but there's no time. I can't let you go on feeling sorry for yourself. There's too much work to do."

"I don't work for Trevor anymore."

"Okay, then work for yourself. Don't let that bastard get away with what he did to your father."

"It was Trevor's fault."

She studied his expression. "You don't believe that." She added deliberately, "And you don't believe it was the man who beheaded your father that's responsible."

"Of course I do."

"No." Say it. Cruel or not. It had to be said or Mario would continue to hide from the truth. "You think it was your fault. You think you should never have taken the job. Or if you did, you should have told Trevor about your father."

"No!"

"Maybe it's true, but you'll have to decide that for yourself. You thought your father wouldn't be in danger, but were you fooling yourself? I don't know. All I know is that the man's dead and you should be ready to avenge him instead of blaming everyone in sight, including yourself."

"Get out of here." His voice broke. "It's lies."

"It's truth." She stood up. "And I believe you're man enough to face it. I'm going into the next room to sit in my corner and look at the statue of Cira and wait for you to come in and start working again."

"I won't come."

"You'll come. Because it's the right thing to do. There aren't many things that are right in this mess, but you have the chance to do one of them." She started for the door. "If you find what Trevor is looking for, those murderers who killed that help-less old man won't win."

"Lies . . ."

She opened the door. "I'll be waiting."

* * *

She was still sitting in the chair in the corner when Mario's door opened four hours later.

He stood in the doorway. "You don't give up, do you?"

"Not when it's important. And this couldn't be more important."

"Why? To get Trevor what he wants?"

"In this case what Trevor wants is what we all should want." She paused. "And it's important that you see things clearly for your own sake. Even if it hurts."

"Oh, it does." He came toward her. "Damn you, Jane." As he drew close to her, she could see his dark eyes glistening with tears. "Damn you." He fell to his knees in front of her chair and buried his face in her lap. "I'm not ever going to forgive you."

"That's okay." She gently stroked his hair. She felt an aching maternal tenderness. "Everything will be okay, Mario."

"No, it won't." He lifted his head, and the desolation in his expression made her ache with sympathy. "Because I'm lying. It's not you I'm not going to forgive. I . . . killed him, Jane."

"No, you didn't. Grozak killed him."

"I should have— Trevor told me there was a threat but I didn't believe it would affect anyone but me. I was selfish. I didn't want to believe. I couldn't imagine anyone doing anything like this." Tears were running down his cheeks. "And I'm not the one who paid the price. I was an idiot and I should have—"

"Shh." Her fingers touched his lips. "You made a mistake and you have to live with it. But the guilt is Grozak's and you have to accept that too."

"It's hard." He sat back on his heels and closed his eyes tightly. "I feel like I should be crucified."

He was being crucified, she thought. He was blaming himself with the same passion with which he'd earlier blamed Trevor. "Then get busy. Block it out. I felt guilty when my friend Mike was killed. I went through all the scenarios of what I could have done differently that might have saved him. But in the end you have to put it on the back burner and get on with life. It will creep back in the middle of the night sometimes, but the only thing you can do is endure and learn from it."

His eyes opened. "I'm being a child. You don't deserve this." He forced a smile. "But I'm glad you're here."

"So am I."

He shook his head as if to clear it and got to his feet. "Now get out of here. I need to go back to my room and take a shower." His lips twisted. "Isn't it strange how instinct tells us that if we get our bodies clean it will somehow cleanse our soul?"

"Shall I come back?"

"Not right away. I'll be down later to talk to Trevor." His gaze went to the desk. "But I have to get back to work. It's not going to be easy. I'll keep remembering why— I may only be able to do a few lines, but it will be a start. What is your phrase? Getting back on the horse that threw you?"

She nodded.

"It's a good phrase." He turned away. "I feel as if that horse broke all my bones. But he didn't, and he won't. Maybe my heart . . . But hearts heal, don't they?"

"So I understand."

He glanced back at her. "All that wisdom you've been spouting and you don't know the most important thing? I can tell you're not Italian."

It was almost a joke, thank God. The pain was still there, but he was not quite as devastated as he had been. She smiled. "I realize that's a great handicap."

"Yes, it is, but you're exceptional enough to overcome it." He paused before he added, "Thank you, Jane."

He didn't wait for a reply before he left the room.

She slowly rose to her feet. She had gotten what she needed from Mario, but it had been an experience that was painful for both of them. And she had seen something in Mario that last few minutes that had surprised her. It was as if she had witnessed a rebirth or a coming of age or . . .

She didn't know. It could be imagination born from the emotional state they'd both gone through today. Personality changes seldom came with such rapidity.

But changes were rarely initiated by such shock and horror.

And hadn't her attitude toward Trevor been clarified by that horror too? Life around her was shifting, moving as Grozak and Reilly pulled the strings.

It had to stop.

# 11

"How is he?" Trevor asked as she came into the library ten minutes later. "Still hating my guts?"

"No." She grimaced. "Hating himself. But he's going to give you what you want. He's going to go back to translating this evening."

"You must have cast a spell."

She shook her head. "I told him the truth, but I think he would have come to it anyway if we'd given him a little more time. I believe you're going to find he's . . . different."

"How?"

She shrugged. "I'm not sure. But I don't think I'll be tempted to call him a 'nice boy' anymore. Judge for yourself. He'll come down to talk to you later." She changed the subject. "Did you find out anything from Venable about Wickman?"

"He's going to get back to me. He sent a man to talk to Eduardo Donato's sister, and she said she hadn't seen him since yesterday morning. Eduardo called and told her he was going to take a job acting as a guide for a tourist he met in a coffeehouse."

"Did he tell her his name?"

He shook his head. "He was interrupted in the middle of the conversation and hung up quickly."

"Can we get a photo of Wickman from Venable?"

"In time. So far he hasn't been able to pull up a record. Wickman seems to be the invisible man. But I'll have Brenner zero in on the coffeehouse and see if he can get us a description from one of the waiters."

She went still. "I can do better than that."

He understood at once. "No. Not only no, but hell no."

"If I can get a good description, I can do a sketch. Since I've never seen Wickman, that sketch would tell you what you want to know without question."

"Then I'll have Brenner ask the questions and relate the answers over the phone to you."

"It doesn't work that way. I have to show the sketch to the witness as I'm doing it to get a confirmation on the features." Her lips tightened. "And I'm not sitting here and waiting for Brenner to waste time trying to pin down the ID when I can do it faster."

"It's not safe for you to go traipsing all over Lucerne. I can keep you secure here."

"I'm not going all over Lucerne. I'm going to one café, and presumably you'll have Brenner there to meet me at the airport. Can you arrange for a helicopter and a private plane in Aberdeen piloted by someone you trust?"

"I could. I won't."

"Yes, you will. Because you know I'm going anyway." She turned on her heel. "I'll go up and pack an overnight case and my sketchbook."

"What part of no didn't you understand?"

"The part where you gave me orders that go against good sense. Call Brenner and tell him I'm coming, or I'll find my own way to that café."

Mario met Jane as she left her bedroom and was heading for the stairs. He frowned as he glanced at the overnight case she was carrying. "Where are you going?"

"I have to do a job. I'll be back tonight or tomorrow."

"What kind of job?"

She was silent a moment, unsure how he would accept the truth. "I'm going to Lucerne to try to do a sketch of your father's killer, if I can get a good description."

"Is that possible?"

She nodded. "I'm pretty good. I have a knack for it."

"Someone saw him?"

"We think there's a good chance. Your father was well known at the café and—"

He turned back to his room. "I'm going with you."

"No."

"It's got to be dangerous. What if he's still around? I'm not going to let you run a risk. My father was killed and he didn't do—"

"No, you're more valuable here." He started to protest and she said quickly, "I don't need you. I'm going to have Brenner to help me."

He was silent a moment before his lips twisted in a mirthless smile. "Then I guess you don't need me. I wouldn't be much good to you, would I? I'm better at dealing with books than the real world. I never realized that I'd ever have to know how to fight people like Grozak." He paused. "You're sure that you'll be safe with Brenner?"

"I'm sure. Good-bye, Mario." She hurried down the stairs before he could protest again. Trevor was standing at the front door. "You've phoned Brenner?"

"Yes, and I'm going with you myself." He opened the door for her. "Bartlett's arranged for a helicopter. It will be landing in five minutes."

"No."

"I beg your pardon?"

"No." She repeated his words to her. "What part of that word don't you understand? You're not going with me. You have no purpose except to protect me, and Brenner is doing that. You told me that one of your jobs here at the Run was to keep an eye on Mario. Well, that's more important than ever now."

"And what about keeping an eye on you?"

"Grozak appears to have changed targets and is

aiming at Mario. All the more reason for keeping him safe." She saw his lips tighten and added fiercely, "I talked Mario into going back to work, and I'm not letting that go to waste. It's important that he get that scroll done as soon as possible. Someone's got to be here to encourage and reinforce him. That's either me or you. And I'm going to Lucerne." She opened the door. "Don't try to stop me, Trevor."

"I wouldn't think of it," he said sarcastically. "You'd probably push me out of the helicopter."

"Right."

"And I wouldn't dream of trying to quench that fire I seem to have lit."

"You couldn't." She looked him in the eye. "You were born in Johannesburg and you've been roaming most of your life. I don't know whether you consider yourself a citizen of the world or a man without a country. Well, I do have a country, and I protect what's mine. So you're damn right I'm on fire. We'll do what's best to keep Grozak away from my people no matter who's at risk."

"My God, a patriot."

"I'm not ashamed of it. Mock all you please."

"I'm not mocking. I'm envious." He turned away. "Go on. Get on that helicopter before I start remembering that video of Eduardo Donato. I'll take care of Mario."

A few minutes later Trevor watched the helicopter take off and circle east over the sea. His hands clenched into fists. Dammit, he wanted to call the pilot, Cookson, and tell him to bring her back. Instead, he called Brenner. "She's on her way. Cookson just took off. I want her back here in twenty-four hours. If anything happens to her, I'll have your ass."

"You can try." Brenner paused. "I'll keep her safe, Trevor."

"If she lets you. She's full of piss and vinegar and the star-spangled banner."

"What a combination," Brenner said. "It may prove an interesting twenty-four hours." He hung up.

Interesting? Trevor watched the helicopter as it flew toward the horizon. That wasn't the word he would have used. It was going to be one hell of a—

"She's gone?"

Trevor turned to see Mario standing behind him, his gaze on the helicopter. He nodded curtly. "She'll be back as soon as she does the sketch."

"I wanted to go with her."

"So did I. She wasn't having it."

Mario smiled slightly. "She's a very strong woman." His smile disappeared. "Have they found my father yet?"

"No."

He shuddered. "I hate the idea of his body being tossed aside with no respect by that—" He drew a deep breath. "Have you shown the police the video?"

"No, but I'm sending it to the authorities right

away." He looked the boy in the eye. "If you still don't trust me, I'll let you talk to them if you like."

Mario shook his head. "I don't have to talk to them." He added awkwardly, "I'm sorry that— I shouldn't have believed that swine when he wrote that you—No, I didn't believe him. Not really. I just couldn't accept that I—"

"Forget it. It's understandable."

"I can't forget it. I blinded myself to the truth because it wasn't what I wished it to be. I closed myself up in my cocoon just as I've always done." His lips tightened. "I can't do that any longer."

Trevor's gaze narrowed on Mario's face. "Is this leading somewhere?"

"Yes. Jane wouldn't let me go with her because she knew she'd be safer with Brenner." He frowned. "I'm not equipped for life outside my ivory tower. That has to change. I won't be a helpless pawn with my head in the sand."

"You're not a pawn."

"Grozak thinks I am. He killed my father to make me do what he wanted. He'll kill Jane if he can, won't he?"

"He'd rather take her alive. But, hell yes, he won't hesitate to kill her if it suits him."

"You see, I have to ask these questions that I should have asked when I first came here. I didn't want to know anything that might make me feel uncomfortable and keep me from my work." He shook his head. "What a fool I was. . . ."

"You didn't need to know. It was your job to translate those scrolls. It was my job to protect you."

"And now I have another job. I didn't protect my father, but I can avenge him."

"No, we'll handle it."

He smiled sadly. "Because you believe I'm not man enough to do it myself. I will show you. I may seem useless, but I'm not afraid."

"You should be, dammit." Trevor frowned. "If you want to get revenge, get that scroll translated."

"I will. That goes without saying. But how fast I do it depends on you."

"Do I smell a touch of blackmail?"

"Only a bargain. There are things I must learn."

"Such as?"

"I know nothing about weapons. I'm sure you could teach me."

"Mario—"

"Guns. That shouldn't take too long."

Trevor studied him. Jane was right. Mario was changing, maturing, hardening by the minute. "You're serious about this."

"And I should know some self-defense."

"I don't have time to conduct a course in—" He stopped as he saw Mario's jaw square with determination. Oh, what the hell. He couldn't argue with the boy's motives. He would have done the same under similar circumstances. But those circumstances had never existed for him. He couldn't remember a time when he hadn't been fighting for survival in one way or another. Ivory towers were the stuff of myths. "Okay, two hours a day. I'll set up a target range on the Run. The rest of the time you're working on the scrolls." He held up his hand as Mario opened his lips. "And MacDuff owes me a favor. I'll ask him to teach you some karate moves. That's it, Mario."

"Starting today?"

"Okay, today."

"It's enough—for now." Mario added, "Just one more thing."

"You're pushing."

"It's something I have the right to know. It's what I should have asked in the beginning. Why is Grozak after the scrolls? Why did he kill my father?"

Trevor nodded. He was too volatile to tell everything, but he deserved to know the basics. "You're right. It's not fair to keep you in the dark." He turned toward the front door. "Come on in and we'll go to the library and have a drink. You may need it—it's a nasty story."

You've upset Trevor," Brenner said as he met Jane at the plane. "He's threatening me with mayhem if I don't take proper care of you."

"Then do it. I understand you're pretty good at mayhem yourself." She changed the subject. "Have you talked to the waiters at the café yet?"

He nodded. "It's pretty busy early in the morning. Evidently there are a lot of regulars like Donato who show up every day. Albert Dengler, the man behind the counter, says he got a close look at the man Donato was sitting with. The café is sort of like your Starbucks, and he served him when he came to the counter. I thought it best to only tell him that Donato is missing and no details."

"Will he be working today or do we have to go to his home?"

Brenner checked his watch. "He should be starting his shift in about an hour and forty minutes."

"Then let's go."

"Yes, ma'am." He opened the passenger door of the car for her. "Anything else?"

"You can make sure I have sufficient time with him to get a good enough description to do the sketch."

"I'll do my best." He smiled. "It shouldn't be a problem. If I have to do it, I'll take over his shift. Of course, I can't promise that the caffe mocha won't turn out to be caffe latte. But I'll be such a charming lad that no one will care."

"Just so you don't make Dengler too nervous to concentrate."

"I wouldn't judge him to be the nervous type. Or if he is, it's not when he's on his favorite pot."

"Oh, great. He's on drugs?"

"Marijuana. There's no mistaking the odor that clings to him, and he appeared very mellow."

"Maybe too mellow to be detail oriented."

"Well, if he's on the stuff regularly, he's not going to have a great memory. You'll have to see, won't you?" He started the car. "But if he's on the happy weed, he'll be laid-back enough to give you all the time you need."

* * *

He usually sat over there." Dengler nodded at a table by the wrought-iron railing overlooking the lake. "A nice old gentleman. Always dressed neat and tidy. Not like some of the kids who come in here. I have to tell them to wear shoes. You'd think they'd realize this is—"

"Had you ever seen him with the other man?"

He shook his head. "He was always alone. No, once he came in with a woman." He wrinkled his brow. "Late fifties, gray hair, a little plump."

Donato's sister, Jane guessed. "How long ago was that?"

He shrugged. "I don't know. Six months, maybe."

The description was good—excellent, for the length of time from the sighting. Brenner was right about the smell of pot that clung to Dengler, but it must not be habitual if he had this decent a memory.

"Was there anything unusual about the man who sat down at Donato's table?"

He thought about it. "He was tall, thin. Long legs. He seemed to be all legs."

"No, his face."

Dengler thought about it. "Nothing really unusual. Large eyes. Hazel, I think."

"No scars?"

He shook his head. "His complexion was a little pasty, as if he worked inside a lot." He paused, looking at her sketchbook open in front of her. "Can you really do this?"

"If you'll help me."

"Oh, I'll help you. It gets boring here. This is the first interesting thing that's happened to me in months." He made a face. "That sounded very callous. It's not that I'm not concerned about finding the old man. As I said, he was pleasant, never a cross word to anyone. You say he's disappeared? Foul play?"

Nothing fouler on this earth, she thought as she remembered Donato's death. "We'll have to see when we find him."

"Are you with the police?"

"No, I'm a friend of the family." That was the truth. "They're very concerned. Naturally, I'll turn the sketch over to the authorities after we get a good likeness."

"You're very sure."

She smiled at him. "Of course I am. You're obviously an intelligent man with a fine memory. If we work together long enough, we'll do it."

"You're flattering me." He suddenly smiled. "But I like it. How do we start?"

She picked up her pencil. "The shape of the face. We have to have a canvas to work on. Square? Round? Angular?"

Almost done?" Brenner came to stand beside her. "It's been over four hours."

She didn't take her gaze from the sketchbook. "I want to be as sure as I can be." She shaded a few more lines to the left cheek. "It's not easy, is it, Albert? So many choices . . ."

"Leave her alone," Dengler said. "We're doing the best we can."

*We.*

Brenner smothered a smile. She had obviously charmed Dengler into considering the two of them a team. It surprised him, since he had only seen the tough, wary side of Jane MacGuire. It had been interesting watching her skillful handling of Dengler. She was clearly a multifaceted woman. "Sorry." He turned away. "Just thought I'd check. I'll go back to my counter and clean the coffee machine or something."

"Wait." Jane added feathering to the hair of the man in the sketch. "Like this, Albert?" She turned the sketch to face him. "Is this the man?"

Dengler stared at the sketch. "My God."

"Is it him?"

Dengler nodded and then smiled proudly. "Close as a photograph. We did it."

"No changes?"

"You did the thinner hair. The rest was perfect before."

"Does this mean that I don't have to make any more caffe latte?" Brenner asked.

"He's certain." She handed Brenner the sketch. "Who is it?"

S he nailed him," Brenner told Trevor when he answered the phone. "You were right. It's not Rendle, it's Wickman."

"Good. Is she on her way back?"

"We're just leaving the café. She's still talking to Dengler. She spent forty minutes or so after the sketch was finished complimenting Dengler and making him feel like a big man. She said that if you have to use someone you should at least leave them with a good feeling about it." He paused. "She's . . . interesting."

"Put her on the plane and get her back here. You weren't followed?"

"I'm not an amateur. I'll get her safely on that plane. Then I'll scout around and talk to a few contacts and see what I can find out about Wickman. He'll be long gone from here, though."

"Try Rome. That's one of the places I ran into him."

"He may be with Grozak now."

"We still need to know everything we can about him. If he's going to be the one doing Grozak's dirty work, we have to take him down." He paused. "But before you leave Lucerne, see what kind of rumors you can gather about the location of Donato's body."

"Hey, is that important? There's no doubt he's dead."

"It's important. Mario is hurting and he's going to need closure."

"Okay. I'll get on it. If Venable was able to tell you there was something going down here before Donato's death, then there must be sources I can tap. But I thought you wanted me to get back to Colorado. Though, heaven knows I haven't found out anything yet about Reilly."

"Give Donato twelve hours. Then hop on a plane to Colorado."

"Right." He paused. "You're still going to be able to control Mario?"

"Control? Hell, I don't know. He went back to work. I'll take one day at a time. Just find the old man's body."

Jane arrived back at MacDuff's Run after nine that night.

The minute she got off the helicopter, she handed Trevor the sketch. "Brenner says it's Wickman."

He nodded after he glanced at it. "I called Venable as soon as Brenner told me you'd ID'd him, but I'll fax this to him right away. You did a good job."

She shivered. "He looks ordinary. Like a school-teacher or a clerk in a bank. It seems impossible that he could do that horrible killing."

"That's what makes him so valuable to his clients. He's everyman, and who'd suspect him of being Jack the Ripper?" He took her elbow and nudged her toward the front door. "Go on. You need something to eat before you go to bed. You look beat."

"I ate on the plane. Brenner packed me a pastry and a ham sandwich he took from the café. He said it was the least they could do after all the hard work he did behind the counter. How's Mario?"

"Turning into the Terminator."

"What?"

"I spent two hours this afternoon giving him the

basics of firing a pistol. I told him unless he wants to become a sniper he can forget about rifles for a while." He made a face. "He accepted my advice, but I don't know how long I can hold him off."

"Why does he—" She broke off as she understood. "No, you can't let him do it. It would be like putting a gun into the hands of a child."

"I'm not sure. He has an aptitude." He glanced at her as he opened the door. "We made a bargain. He continues working on the scrolls and I make him the Terminator."

"It's not funny."

"I don't think it is either. But it's going to happen. You told me to make sure Mario kept working, and I'm doing it. Tomorrow morning he starts working out with MacDuff on hand-to-hand martial arts."

"MacDuff agreed?"

"Reluctantly. I called in a debt." He followed her into the hall. "Think about it. If you were in Mario's shoes, wouldn't you do the same?"

"Go after a man who beheads—" She drew a deep breath. Yes, there was no question she would want revenge and would go after it any way she could. It was just that Mario was a gentle soul and it seemed impossible to equate him with violence. "Where is he?"

"Working on the scrolls. Don't bother him, Jane." His lips twisted. "And I'm not saying that because I'm jealous of that soft spot you have for him. We made a deal and he's got to keep his part of it. You know that as well as I do. Time's getting too short to play around."

"I'm not playing. Nothing could be further from my mind." She started up the stairs. God, she was tired. "But I won't bother Mario tonight. Tomorrow will be soon enough."

She could feel his gaze on her as she climbed the steps. "You don't have to watch me. I told you I'm not going to see Mario tonight. I'm going straight to my room and to bed."

"I like to watch you. I don't have to have an excuse."

She stiffened and then continued up the stairs. No, she wouldn't let him do this to her. Not now. There was too much at stake to let herself be sidetracked. "Good night, Trevor."

"It will be a good night now that you're back here and not skittering all over Switzerland."

"Skittering? I wasn't—" When she looked back over her shoulder he was walking down the hall toward the library. That's right, he was going to fax the sketch to Venable. She had done her job and now he was going to follow up. That's what they should be concentrating on. Stopping Grozak was far more important than the emotions that were drawing them to each other. They had worked well together four years ago and they could do it again.

They *had* to do it again.

She knows who I am," Wickman said as he came in to the hotel room. "She sketched a goddamm picture of me at the café."

"A mistake?" Grozak raised his brows. "I told you that I couldn't tolerate inefficiency, Wickman. How do you know that she did it?"

"I'm not inefficient. I went back to remove the witnesses. She was there before me. Sam Brenner was with her or I'd have been able to take care of it."

"But you didn't take care of it." He smiled. "And now Trevor knows who you are. What a pity. You'll have to remove him for sheer self-preservation. I shouldn't even have to pay you."

"I wouldn't try to cheat me, Grozak." Wickman's face was without expression. "I carried out your job and did it well. I'll do the wrap-up well too."

"It's not cheating you to point out that we now have a common goal." He added persuasively, "You can't have any love for those smug sons of bitches in the U.S. Help me bring them down."

Cheap bastard, Wickman thought with contempt. He'd run across men like Grozak before, who were so caught up in their own hatred that they couldn't see beyond it. "I've no goal other than to collect as much money as I can before I walk away from the business."

"I'll be very well funded by our Muslim extremist friends for any future projects if I can pull this off. You can share."

"I don't want to share. I want my money up front."

Grozak was clearly not pleased. "You haven't finished."

"Do you want me to hand you Donato's head? Sorry. It's at the bottom of a bog near Milan."

"I don't care about Donato. What about Trevor?"

"Not until you pay me."

Grozak scowled and then reached in the top desk drawer and tossed him an envelope. "Half."

Wickman counted the cash. "You want his head too?"

"Maybe later. I want you to get the woman first. Alive. I need her."

"Why?"

"That's none of your concern. All you need to know is that I want the woman alive and Trevor has to be able to talk to me before he dies."

"About what?"

"He may be able to lead me to something I need."

Money? Wickman thought. Perhaps. But with fanatics like Grozak it could just as well be a hydrogen bomb. Still, it was something to keep in mind. "It's more risk for me. Quick and clean is better. I'll want more money."

Grozak muttered a curse before nodding. "You'll get it. Not now. It's not easy to gather your kind of money together. I've thrown everything I have into this project."

"Get it from Reilly."

"Reilly's being very stingy with everything but the manpower."

Wickman thought about pushing and then decided against it. He had never had a problem squeezing money from his patrons after a job. It always surprised him how quickly they caved when he focused his full attention on them. "I'll give you a few days." He dropped down in a chair. "But if you want the woman, you have to give me something to work with. Tell me everything you know about her."

# 12

I t's good to have you back," Bartlett said as he met Jane in the hall the next morning. "I was worried."

"Brenner was with me. I had to go."

He nodded solemnly. "So Trevor told me."

"Have you seen Mario? He isn't in his room."

"I understand he's at the Run with MacDuff. Would you like breakfast?"

"Later," she said absently as she headed for the door. "I want to talk to Mario."

It took her ten minutes to go through the gates and around the castle to the Run.

She stopped several yards from the rocks when she saw Mario and MacDuff. They were both stripped to the waist and despite the chill they were gleaming with sweat. As she watched, MacDuff dropped Mario to the ground by sweeping his leg in a round kick.

Mario muttered a curse and struggled to his feet. "Again."

"You're not going to have time to learn anything," MacDuff said grimly. "Except how to fall without hurting yourself. That's not going to save your life."

"Again," Mario said, and lunged toward him.

MacDuff flipped him over his hip and then straddled him. "Give it up. It will take weeks. Use a damn gun."

"I'm learning." Mario glared up at him. "I'm learning something with every fall. Again."

MacDuff muttered another obscenity.

"He's angry." Jane turned to see Jock standing behind her. He was frowning as he came toward her, his gaze on the two men. "He could hurt the laird."

"Mario? It's not likely." She watched as MacDuff got off Mario and the boy jumped to his feet. "It's not MacDuff I'm worried about. Mario's the one who's the most vulnerable. He could be—"

She broke off as Mario lowered his head and butted MacDuff in the stomach. MacDuff grunted and fell to his knees, struggling for breath. "Dammit, that's not anything I showed you. You're not supposed to— No!"

Jock was behind Mario, his arm around his neck. He had moved with such dazzling speed that Jane was stunned.

But MacDuff was there, giving Jock a numbing

blow to the arm tightening around Mario. "Stop it, Jock. Let him go."

Jock didn't move.

"Jock."

Jock slowly released Mario. "You should have let me do it. He could hurt you."

"He doesn't want to hurt me. We were just working out. Playing."

"It's not playing. He hit you in the stomach. There are ways to break a rib and send it into the heart."

"He doesn't know those ways." MacDuff spoke slowly, patiently. "He knows nothing. That's why I'm trying to teach him."

"Why?"

"What is this?" Mario was staring at Jock in bewilderment.

MacDuff ignored him, his gaze on Jock. "Someone hurt his father. He needs to be able to protect himself."

Jock's gaze shifted to Mario. "You mean he wants to kill someone."

"For God's sake, not with his bare hands. I told you, he only wants to protect himself."

Jock frowned. "He might hurt you. I'll teach him what he needs to know."

"Not bloody likely. You might forget. And as I keep telling you, I'm not as good as you, but I'm fully capable of taking care of myself."

"I know that."

"Then go on back to the stable."

Jock shook his head and moved over to the large

rocks at the end of the Run. "I'll just sit here and watch."

MacDuff stared at him in exasperation before turning to Mario. "Meet me here at two this afternoon. This isn't a good time."

Mario hesitated and then grabbed his shirt from the ground. "Two." He grimaced at Jane as he passed her. "Weird. Very weird."

She agreed completely, and was so absorbed in the interplay between Jock and MacDuff that Mario had disappeared around the side of the castle before she remembered she had come here to talk to him.

"I don't remember sending out invitations." MacDuff was looking at her as he wiped the sweat from his chest and arms. "Why are you here?"

"I wanted to try to persuade Mario to drop this craziness."

"It wouldn't be crazy if there wasn't a time restraint. It would be entirely reasonable. Revenge is completely understandable." His gaze went to the path where Mario had disappeared. "And he's not going to be bad if he lives long enough. That last move took me by surprise."

"Jock's the one who took me by surprise." She looked at the boy, who was sitting absolutely still on the rocks some distance away. He smiled at her as he saw her staring at him, a sweet smile that lit his face with radiance. She couldn't believe that it was the same face that had tightened to cold ferocity as his arm snaked around Mario's throat. She returned his smile with an effort and turned back to MacDuff. "He was going to kill him, wasn't he?"

"Yes." He pulled a sweatshirt over his head. "In a matter of seconds. Jock is very quick."

She shook her head in wonder. "I wouldn't have believed it if I hadn't seen— He seems so sweet natured."

"Oh, he is. When he's not committing murder."

Her eyes widened at the bitterness in his voice. "Murder? But he was just angry because he thought Mario was going to hurt you."

He didn't answer.

"That was it, wasn't it?"

He was silent a moment and then shrugged. "He wasn't angry. He was on a mission, and this time I was the mission."

"What?"

"He feels duty-bound to keep me safe. I started out letting him do it because I didn't know if I could keep him alive unless I gave him a motivation. Now he's stronger and I'm trying to wean him away from it. But it's not easy."

"Keep him alive," she repeated.

"He tried to commit suicide three times after I got him away from that son of a bitch Reilly."

Reilly. The man Trevor had said he and Grozak were battling over.

"You've heard of Reilly." MacDuff's eyes were narrowed on her expression. "Trevor told you about him?"

She nodded. "But he didn't tell me anything

about a connection between Reilly and you or Jock."

"He doesn't know about the connection with Jock. He only knows I want Reilly." He glanced at Jock. "Dead."

"Then why are you telling me?"

"Because Jock likes you and you've chosen to help him. I thought I could control him, but some time I may not be around and you may need information to guide him. I'm not letting you go in blind."

"Is he . . . insane?"

"No more than any one of us would be if we'd gone through what he has. He blocks things out; at moments he goes back to the simplicity of childhood. But he's getting better every day."

"What things does he try to block out?"

MacDuff didn't answer for a moment. "I know he's killed at least twenty-two people. Probably a good many more. That's all he'll allow himself to remember."

"My God."

"It wasn't his fault," MacDuff said harshly. "If you could have known him as a boy, you'd realize that. He was wild as a hare but there was no one with a kinder heart or a sweeter nature. It was that son of a bitch Reilly."

"He can't be more than nineteen," she whispered.

"Twenty."

"How . . . ?"

"I told you, he was wild. He ran away from home

when he was fifteen to knock about the world. I don't know when or where he ran across Reilly. All I know is that not long ago his mother came to me and asked me to go get her son. He was in an asylum in Denver, Colorado. The police had picked him up wandering on a highway near Boulder. No papers. And they couldn't get him to tell them anything. He was in the asylum for two weeks before he spoke one word. Then it was to ask for pen and paper to write to his mother." He paused. "It was a good-bye letter. She was hysterical when she came to me and asked me to go get him. She thought he was going to commit suicide."

"Why didn't she go to him herself?"

"I'm the laird. They're used to coming to me in emergencies."

"Then why didn't she come to you when he ran away?"

"I wasn't in the country. I was in Naples trying to find enough money to bail out the Run." His lips thinned. "I should have been here. I was almost too late. When I got to the hospital, he'd already gotten hold of a razor and cut his wrists. They barely managed to save him."

"What did you do?"

"What do you think I did? He was one of mine. I rented a chalet in the mountains and took him out of that hospital and stayed with him for the next month. I held him while he raved and ranted and wept. I talked to him and made him talk to me."

"Did he tell you what happened to him?"

He shook his head. "Only bits and pieces. Reilly was very clear in Jock's mind, but he couldn't decide whether Reilly was Satan or God. Whatever entity he was to Jock, he dominated and punished. And controlled. Oh, yes, he definitely controlled."

"Brainwashing? Like Trevor told me he did with those GIs?"

"Evidently he was doing in-depth experimentation this time. How do you make an assassin of a good-hearted lad like Jock? Drugs? Sleep deprivation? Torture? Give him hallucinations? Prey on his mind and emotions? Or combine them all into one package? He was trained in all forms of murder and then sent out to do Reilly's bidding. It must have been difficult to keep control of Jock over an extended killing spree like that. Reilly was very clever."

"And a monster."

"Without doubt. And monsters don't deserve to walk this earth. And he won't for much longer. I made a deal with Trevor. I get Reilly. I don't care about anything else."

Jane thought of something. "Why Jock? It's too great a coincidence that he'd just pick him out of the blue."

"No coincidence. I've made it no secret that I've been looking for Cira's gold. That story on the Internet drew me the way it drew everyone else. The pot of gold at the end of the rainbow. The answer to my prayers. I've made five trips to Herculaneum in the past three years and it must have gotten back to Reilly. Trevor says he's been keeping an eagle eye on everything and everyone who looked like he might have a chance at finding the gold before he does. He's obsessed with those gold coins, and he probably wanted to find out if I'd learned anything important. Jock was in and out of the castle all the time before he decided to go off and see the world. Who better to ask?" His lips tightened bitterly. "He probably tracked him down to ask him a few crucial questions and then decided to make use of him in other ways when Jock couldn't tell him anything."

"So you went after Reilly. Could Jock tell you anything about him?"

"Not much. Every time he'd start to remember he'd go into convulsions and start screaming with pain. A little posthypnotic gift from Reilly. He's getting better, but I haven't tried since that first month. I'm waiting for him to heal. If he ever does."

"And you're teaming up with Trevor instead. Why?"

"I'm one of the people who Dupoi notified when he was trying to double-cross Trevor. Everyone in Herculaneum knew I was interested, and he thought I might have enough money to make the bidding interesting." He grimaced. "Wrong. But I learned enough about Trevor and his background from Dupoi to know that he could have the same goals I did—and the contacts to find Reilly." He stared her directly in the eye. "Are you afraid to be around Jock now?"

She looked back at Jock. "A little."

"Then I've blown it. I thought you might understand."

"It's hard to understand twenty-two murders."

"If he'd been an assassin for your government, you'd accept it. In some circles he'd be a hero."

"You know that argument doesn't wash. I feel sorry for him, but there's no way I can understand how Reilly could twist him like that." She squared her shoulders. "So I won't try. I'll accept that it happened and go on from there."

"But in what direction? Are you going to abandon him?"

"Damn you. He's not my problem." What was she going to do? Jock had touched and haunted her from the moment she had seen him. The story of horror had shocked her but had also made her heart ache for the boy. "I don't know what I'm going to do." But whatever she decided to do, she had to confront it. She strode across the Run toward Jock.

His gaze was on her face as she went toward him. "He told you about me, didn't he? You're going to tell me you don't want to draw me anymore."

"Why would you think that?"

"Because I'm ugly," he said simply. "You see it now, don't you?"

Oh, hell. She could feel that aching pity begin again. "You're not ugly. You just did ugly things. But you won't do them again."

"Maybe I will. He said it's what I am. That I can't do anything else."

"Reilly?"

"Sometimes I'm sure he's right. It's so easy. I don't have to think."

"He's not right. MacDuff will tell you that."

He nodded. "He always does."

"And I'm telling you too." She looked him in the eye. "So stop talking foolish and get on to forgetting that bastard." She turned away. "And meet me in the courtyard in an hour. I have to finish that sketch."

It was only a small commitment and she could still back away. She glanced over her shoulder as she reached the path. MacDuff had come to sit beside Jock on the rock and he was frowning, talking fast and low to the boy. Jock was nodding, but his gaze was still fixed on Jane.

And then he smiled. A smile full of sadness and acceptance and, dammit, hope.

She sighed. Caught.

Were you followed?" Reilly asked Chad Norton when he delivered the package to him.

"No. I was careful, but there wasn't anyone following and I checked the box out for tracking devices. It's safe." Norton was looking at him hopefully, waiting for praise.

Should he give it to him? Praise or condemnation. It was always a delicate balance with the subjects he kept close to him for daily labor. You would have thought it would be easier, but propinquity had a habit of dulling the command effect. Perhaps a mix in this case. "You took too long. You kept me waiting."

Norton stiffened and Reilly could see the panic begin. "I tried to be quick. I was afraid to speed. You told me to be sure and not attract attention."

"I didn't tell you to take half the day." It was enough, the sting of the whip; now rub in a soothing unguent. He smiled at Norton. "But I'm sure you were only being careful because you wanted to keep me secure. On the whole you did well."

He could see the relief in Norton's expression. "I tried. I always try." He paused. "Better than Gavin?"

Reilly's brows lifted. "Kim's been talking."

Norton shook his head. "She only said that I'd never be as good as— She said Jock Gavin was special to you."

"Indeed he was. But you're special also. So I'll let you pick up the mail next week." Reilly waved his hand to dismiss Norton as he turned to the box. "And tell Kim I said to increase your ration tonight."

"Thank you."

Reilly smiled at the eagerness in the young man's voice as he heard the door close behind Norton. The extra cocaine ration always brought the pleasure and excitement intended, and he'd never found a suitable substitute. He'd tried several times to use posthypnotic suggestion in combination with various forms of deprivation to make the subjects believe they were being given hard drugs. In some cases the ploy had worked, but the effects were too short-lived to be satisfactory. Pity. It would have been the ultimate power trip to be able to give intense pleasure as well as pain. Like being God.

But he mustn't be too disappointed. It was an exhilarating experience to control other human beings as if they were slaves and he the master. It was clear Grozak had no concept of the complicated and difficult methods he used to bring about the desired results. He thought the subjects were weak of mind and will, and in the beginning Reilly had experimented with just that type of personality. But he'd grown bored and exasperated very soon and moved on to test himself with more difficult subjects. That was the reason he'd taken Norton when Jock Gavin had slipped away from him. He'd wanted to prove that he could overcome all resistance, even if Gavin had been a failure.

Not really a failure, he reminded himself. The boy might have broken down, but his basic conditioning had stayed in place. If it hadn't, he'd have had Homeland Security and CIA crawling all over Montana and Idaho looking for him. He'd had Grozak monitoring Jock after MacDuff had taken him to Scotland, but he'd gradually begun to feel more comfortable. It was almost worth Jock's defection to prove how impregnable that basic conditioning was. Jock would die before betraying him. He almost hoped he'd try. It would be a heady victory.

"Norton said you'd okayed an extra cocaine ration." Kim Chan stood in the doorway. "You shouldn't have done it. You were never that soft with Jock."

"Jock was different. I had to keep the reins tight.

Norton is no problem." He leaned back in his chair. "And you've evidently been undermining his training by comparing him to Jock. It's okay to voice your displeasure to me, but don't do it to anyone else."

Kim's cheeks flushed. "It's true. A little pain and Norton caves. He disgusts me."

"But not enough to stop inflicting that pain." He smiled. "And until you reach that point, don't come and tell me how to do my job." His voice lowered to steely softness. "You've forgotten. You're not my partner. You work for me. And if you annoy me too much, I'll toss you back into that whorehouse in Singapore where I found you."

"You won't do that. You need me."

"I need someone like you. You're not unique. Perhaps if you'd done your job more efficiently, I wouldn't have lost Jock."

"You can't blame it on me. You're the one who—" She stopped as she met his gaze. He could see her struggling with her anger and outrage, but she finally backed down as he knew she would. She muttered, "It wasn't my fault. I had complete control when he was with me." She turned away. "I'll give Norton his extra ration, but it's a mistake."

And she realized that she'd made a mistake too, Reilly thought. She'd been arrogant when he'd chosen her, and he'd had to keep that arrogance in check over the years. He'd been tempted to try training her, but that might have destroyed the domination factor in her that was her most valuable asset.

But she was right: Norton was no Jock Gavin. Though he'd been a brilliant student at the University of Colorado, president of the student council, a star on the basketball team, all of which had given him that touch of youthful arrogance that had made him interesting for a while.

No longer. Reilly would have to dispose of him soon and get someone else to pique his interest. It was getting increasingly difficult to avoid that boredom. Norton would be no use to him as a suicide bomber, because those subjects had to have a certain initial bitterness and concentrated special training that took months. He'd have to write off the training he'd put into Norton and have Kim give him an overdose when he had a replacement on hand.

He opened the box and carefully took away the protective plastic wrappings.

He sighed with pleasure. Beautiful . . .

Trevor met Jane as she reached the courtyard. "Bartlett said you were going after Mario. Did you talk to him?"

She shook her head. "But I talked to MacDuff. He told me that you'd made a deal to turn over Reilly to him."

"Did he?" He paused. "And what do you think about that?"

"I don't care who gets rid of Reilly as long as it's done. And MacDuff seems to have a good reason for wanting him dead. Reilly has to be a complete slimeball."

"I told you that before."

"I understood it. I didn't have an example thrown at me until MacDuff told me about Jock. Reilly is evidently a fit partner for Grozak." She searched his expression. "MacDuff said you didn't know about Jock's connection with Reilly, but I find that hard to believe."

"I suspected and I put out feelers to Venable to see if I could confirm it one way or the other. He hasn't gotten back to me." He smiled slightly. "And now he doesn't have to. Jock was brainwashed and trained by Reilly?"

"And he almost sent him around the bend. He tried to commit suicide."

"And that of course made you want to mother the poor lad." His smile disappeared. "He's a victim, but a victim who's a trained killer and unbalanced to boot. Stay away from him, Jane."

She shook her head. "Don't you think I told myself that? It didn't work. I can't walk away from him. He was brutalized by that son of a bitch. He deserves help."

"Then let MacDuff help him."

"He's doing his best." She paused. "MacDuff said Jock refuses to remember anything much about Reilly, but he must know a lot. If we could tap that knowledge . . ."

"MacDuff must have tried like hell to do that."

"He did. But maybe it was too soon. Maybe a different person, a fresh approach would do the trick."

Trevor swore an oath beneath his breath. "You try to stir up memories and you're likely to get your neck broken. He's volatile as hell."

"I wouldn't deliberately hurt Jock." She thought about it. "But having those memories buried can't be doing him good either. If I could find a way to make him face reality that wouldn't make him take a step back——"

"Dammit, no!"

"Don't tell me no." She glared at him. "You can't find the gold and Brenner can't find Reilly. I'm not going to let Grozak have time enough to get what he wants from Reilly." She started across the courtyard. "If Jock can help, then I'm going to do my damnedest to get him to talk to me. I don't want to do it. I'm afraid I'll damage the progress MacDuff has made with Jock. So you get on the ball and give me a reason to back off from that poor boy."

She could feel Trevor's gaze on her as she entered the castle. She grimaced as she remembered the term she'd used to describe Jock. That "poor boy" had killed a number of people and had almost broken Mario's neck. Yet she couldn't think of him with anything but pity.

Well, she'd better get over it. It was going to take toughness as well as a certain ruthlessness to make Jock remember that horror he'd been through. It was going to hurt her but not nearly as much as it was going to hurt Jock.

But it had to be done. The stakes were too high for her not to make the attempt.

\* \* \*

Reilly waited two hours after opening the box Norton had brought him to call Grozak. "How are you doing, Grozak? Progress?"

"Yes," Grozak said warily. "Why do you ask?"

"Because I'm sitting here staring at an old book on ancient coins that I bought from a dealer in Hong Kong. I've been hearing stories about a certain coin and sent to get this book to find out more about it. Did you know that one of the coins Judas took for betraying Christ is rumored to still be in existence? Can you imagine how much that coin would be worth today?"

"No. I'm not interested."

"You should be interested. The coin is said to have been taken to Herculaneum by a captured slave destined to be a gladiator. Did you know Cira had a servant who was once a gladiator? Wouldn't it have been reasonable for him to put it in her hands for safekeeping? That it might be in that gold chest?"

"What are you getting at? It's all a bunch of fables."

"Perhaps. But I thought you should know how unhappy I'd be if I had even the slightest chance of obtaining that coin and was cheated out of it. What news of Cira's chest?"

"I'm working on it."

"And you haven't been able to rid me of Jock Gavin. That was part of our deal too. He knows too much."

"You told me yourself that Gavin might not be a threat, that he wouldn't be able to remember you."

"There's the slightest chance. I don't take chances. Find a way to kill him."

"Then evidently you're not all that sure your training is effective."

"You don't know what you're talking about. You have no concept of what I can do." He paused. "You promised me Jane MacGuire. I've been looking at her photograph, and the resemblance to Cira is remarkable. She couldn't look more like her. To have Jane MacGuire would be like having Cira come to life."

"So?"

"From what you tell me MacGuire is young, smart, and strong-willed. Like Cira. What a challenge for a man of my talent."

"You're going to train her?"

"It may come down to that, but I hope not. All I want is information. Women are difficult to train. Most of them break before they bend. But this one might be different."

"What kind of information?"

"The gold. It's all about the gold, isn't it?"

"If she knew anything she'd have gone after the gold herself."

"She probably knows more than she thinks she does. She's visited Herculaneum three times in the last four years. She's been an intimate of Trevor's. And she's clearly been completely absorbed by Cira for years. Why not? They're practically twins."

"That doesn't mean she knows where Cira's gold is hidden."

"It's worth a shot. Maybe she's picked up some information she's not aware of knowing. I can't tell you how many times I've run across facts a subject didn't remember about himself without my help."

"And you can dig it out of her?"

"I can dredge up everything she ever knew. A clean sweep is dangerous and can end with the subject never being able to function again. But even if she can give me only a hint, a fragment, it's worth doing." He paused. "Unless you can save me the trouble by giving me that chest. But I'm sensing a bit too much eagerness in those questions you're putting to me."

"Things aren't working out as I hoped." Grozak paused. "What if I get the woman and have to wait awhile to deliver the gold?"

Reilly's hand tightened on the phone. "I don't like the sound of that."

"Oh, I'm on the trail," Grozak said quickly. "I have a few aces up my sleeve. But I might not be able to deliver before the twenty-second. Suppose I give you a cash down payment and deliver the gold after the attack?"

Good God, did the man think he was a fool? "I don't care about your cash. I have all the money I could ever need, and if I want more, I only have to send one of my men out to get it. I want Cira's gold. I want to be able to see it, touch it."

"And you will. Later."

"You may not be around later. What's to stop you from reneging after I deliver?"

"Naturally, I'll have to go underground for a while after the attack. But I'm not fool enough to try to cheat you. You only have to turn loose one of your zomb—people to hunt me down."

Reilly thought about it. It wasn't as if he hadn't considered this possibility. When you dealt with men like Grozak, you had to be prepared. "That's true. I might be willing to accept a delay on the gold if you get me the woman. Only a delay, Grozak."

"And you'd still furnish me with the men on the target date?"

"I'll work with you. You'll have your men a few days ahead of the target date. That will give you time to brief them on exactly what to do. But they'll need a phone call from me to initiate the action. I'll do that right before the attack if I get the woman." Time to insert the goad. "If I don't get the woman, I'll give Trevor a call and offer him your head on a platter and start negotiations again."

"Bluff. He'll never give you the woman."

"He might. Some people would think any woman was expendable when weighed against a Judas coin. Wouldn't you?"

"I'm not Trevor."

And Reilly was grateful he wasn't. Trevor was much tougher to deal with and wouldn't be manipulated like Grozak. "We'll see. It's a moot point if you deliver. Let me know when I can expect her and we'll set up a meeting place." He hung up the phone.

Enough pressure?

Perhaps. If not, he'd apply more.

He rose to his feet and moved over to the shelves. There were several priceless coins on display from all the ancient worlds. For years he'd gathered all the artifacts he'd been able to get his hands on from Egypt, Herculaneum, and Pompeii, but coins were his passion. Even in those times they'd signified power.

What an age, he thought. He should have lived then, during that golden period in history. A man could shape his life and the lives of others with ruthless efficiency. It was what he had been born to do. Not that he hadn't been able to do that in the present day. But then slaves were not only accepted, their owners were admired and respected. Slaves lived and died at their owners' whims.

Cira had been born a slave and yet had never been conquered.

He would have conquered her. He would have found a way to break her, even without the tools he used now. What a subject she would have been, he thought wistfully. To control a woman of that strength would have been totally exhilarating.

But Jane MacGuire was also strong. He'd read how she trapped that killer who'd been stalking her. Not many women would have risked what she had and managed to pull it off.

He'd been intrigued and his imagination had been sparked by the resemblance to Cira. Lately he'd been fantasizing about how he was going to interrogate her. Only, Jane MacGuire kept blending together with Cira in his mind.

He smiled in sudden amusement as a thought struck him. What better way to dredge her mind and memory than to make her think she was Cira? He must consider that possibility more carefully. . . .

# 13

"What are you thinking about, Jock?" Jane's pencil flew over the sketch pad. "You're a million miles away."

"I was wondering if you were angry with me," Jock said soberly. "The laird is angry. He said I shouldn't have tried to protect him from that Mario this morning."

"He's right. Mario was doing nothing wrong and you can't just go around killing people." Good God, how simplistic that sounded. "If MacDuff hadn't stopped you, you'd have done something terrible."

"I know that—sometimes." Jock frowned. "When I think about it. But when I get worried, I can't think, I just do it."

"And you worry about MacDuff." She looked down at the sketch. "What else do you worry about?"

He shook his head and didn't answer.

Don't push him. She sketched in silence for a few minutes. "Mario is very sad. It wasn't MacDuff he wanted to hurt."

"That's what the laird told me. He wants to punish the man who works with—" The last name came out with difficulty. "Reilly."

"Yes. And Reilly too. That should please you. Don't you want Reilly punished?"

"I don't want to talk about him."

"Why not?"

"I'm not supposed to talk about him. Not to anyone."

A fragment of that damn brainwashing was obviously still in place. "You're supposed to do anything you want to do."

A sudden smile indented his lips. "Except kill Mario."

Good God, a flash of bitter humor. For an instant as she met his eyes there was nothing childlike about him. "Except kill anyone innocent of wrongdoing. But no one should be able to control your mind or free speech."

"Reilly." Again he struggled to get the name out. "Reilly does."

"Then you have to stop him."

He shook his head.

"Why not? You have to hate him."

He looked at her.

"Don't you?"

"Not allowed."

"Don't you?"

"Yes." He closed his eyes. "Sometimes. Hard.

Hurts. Like a fire that won't go out. When the laird came for me, I didn't hate Reilly. But lately—it's there, burning me."

"Because you remember what he did to you."

His eyes opened and he shook his head. "I don't want to remember. Hurts."

"If you don't let yourself remember, if you don't tell us where we can find Reilly, then there will be other people who are hurt and killed. It will be your fault."

"Hurts." He stood up. "I have to get back to my garden. Good-bye."

With a feeling of helplessness, she watched him walk away. Had she even made a dent? She called after him. "I'm not finished with the sketch. Meet me here at five."

He didn't answer as he disappeared into the stable.

Would he come?

"You upset him." MacDuff was walking toward her from the stable. "You were supposed to help him, not stir him up."

"It will help him to remember that bastard Reilly. You must think so too. You told me yourself that you tried to get information out of him about Reilly."

"And failed."

"Maybe it was too soon."

"And maybe the wounds are so deep that he'd bleed to death if he started probing them."

"People are going to die, dammit."

"I'm trusting Trevor to find Reilly before that."

"But maybe it would only take a few words from Jock."

"He may not even know where Reilly's located. I tried everything when I first found him, including hypnosis. But it sent him into a tailspin. I'd think that would be one of the first mental blocks Reilly would instill."

"What if he does know?" She snapped the sketchbook shut. "What if he can point the way and we don't try to prod him to do it?" She met his gaze. "For a moment I saw something in Jock's expression— I think he could be changing, maybe . . . coming back." She made a frustrated gesture. "Hell, I'm not going to hurt him. Why are you so against me trying?"

"Because he may not be ready to come back." His gaze shifted to the stable. "I've been aware of those moments too. It's like the sun coming out on a cloudy day. But what if he does come back before he's ready? For God's sake, he's a killer who makes Rambo look like a kindergarten kid. He's a time bomb ready to go off."

"He loves you. You could control him."

"Could I? I'm glad you're so confident." He studied her expression. "And ruthless. I should have known. Women are always the deadlier of the species."

"Trite. Very trite. I'm not ruthless. Or maybe I am. All I know is that I won't let those bastards hurt my people." She turned away. "You and Trevor aren't playing on the same field I am. Are you going to stop me from talking to Jock?"

He didn't answer for a moment and then said slowly, "No, I'll let you have your try. Be careful. If you set him off, it won't be pretty."

She'd be careful, she thought as she went back toward the castle. Not only for her own safety, but for the sanity of that poor tormented boy. Everything she heard about Reilly made her angry and sick. She had thought Grozak was horrible, but he was matched by that thug who twisted minds and wills and traded in mass destruction.

Damn you, Reilly.

You don't approve of what I'm doing," Mario said when she walked in to his studio five minutes later. "It's necessary, Jane. I'm helpless with these people. It has to change."

"I'm not going to argue with you." She sat down in her corner chair. "I can understand how you feel. I just don't want you to go out thinking you're capable when you're not. It takes a long time to become proficient at weapons and martial arts. You're not going to have that time. Things are moving too fast."

"I can start. It may help. You're not going to convince me. Sometimes I have a very hard head." He suddenly grinned. "As MacDuff found out. I believe I caught him off guard."

She smiled back at him. "I believe you did too." She'd had her say and it obviously was falling on deaf ears. Drop it and maybe come back to it later.

Not that she had any confidence it would do any good. "How's the translation going?"

"Slowly." He looked down at the sheet of paper in front of him. "I've been abstracted."

"I can understand that. And yet it may be our best chance to stop this horror from happening."

"It seems a long shot." He looked up at her. "Two thousand years is a long time. Finding a lost treasure would be like a fairy tale. Do you believe it could happen?"

"I believe anything can happen."

"That's a generalization."

She thought about it. She was generally a pragmatic, cynical person, but somehow she had never doubted that the gold still existed somewhere. Perhaps it was because of the dreams that had plagued her all these years. Perhaps it was because Cira seemed alive to her and so the gold was also very real. "Do you believe those scrolls were written by Cira?"

"Yes."

"And what were the odds of them ever being found in that tunnel? That's a fairy tale in itself."

He smiled. "I guess you're right."

"Damn right I am."

"Back to work." He looked down at the scroll. "Get out of here and let me get to it."

Her brows rose. "I didn't bother you before."

"You did, but I was willing to be distracted. I'm not now." His smile faded. "To me all this has been more of a horror story than a fairy tale, but I want some part of this to have a happy ending. I'll tell you if I find something."

He was businesslike, even curt, and seemed years older than the man she had first met. She felt a ripple of sadness for the loss of that boyish eagerness. "Okay." She got to her feet. "It's time I called Eve and Joe and filled them in anyway. I meant to do it last night, but I was exhausted when I came back from Lucerne."

"You're telling them everything?"

"Of course. We need all the help we can get. Joe has contacts all over the country. Maybe he can shake the authorities up enough to put a full-scale effort into finding Grozak and Reilly."

Mario shook his head. "Judging by what Trevor told me, it's not likely. No proof. Who will they get to listen?"

"Joe will listen." She headed for the door. "Eve will listen. And I'd rather have them on my team than any authority in existence."

Christ," Joe murmured when Jane finished. "What a god-awful mess."

"We need to find either Grozak or Reilly to stop it. You know people. There should be some way to find and get rid of them before this happens. It *can't* happen."

"No, it can't," Eve said from the other extension. "And it won't. We'll work on it from this end. Joe still has lots of contacts with the FBI. And I'll call

John Logan and see if he can push some buttons."
She paused. "Come home, Jane."

"I can't do that. At least I'm doing something here. I may be able to get information from Jock."

"Or you may not."

"I have to try. This is where the action is, Eve. If I don't get a breakthrough with Jock, we may still find out about the gold from the scrolls. That could be almost as important if Trevor can negotiate a deal with Reilly."

"Bastard. I hate the idea of negotiating with that slime."

"So do I, but I'll take any way out right now."

"But you said that according to that scroll Cira was going to try to move the gold from the tunnel. If she succeeded, it will be much harder to find."

"Unless Cira tells us in the scroll Mario is working on where this Pia hid it."

"And if it isn't still buried beneath all that hardened lava that flowed over the city," Joe said.

"Yes, we need a break." Jane was silent a moment. "But, you know, I've been thinking. This whole thing with Cira and the dreams and the gold has been bizarre. It seems to be reaching out and touching all of us. Maybe Cira is trying to stop—" She broke off and then said in disgust, "Jesus, I can't believe I said that. All this tension must be affecting my mind. Just call me and let me know what you're able to do."

"Don't sound so discouraged," Joe said. "The bad guys don't always win. They won't this time. We just have to work until we find a way to blow their sorry asses out of the water. I'll phone you later."

* * *

I never thought it would be this bad," Eve whispered as she hung up the extension. "And I don't like it that Jane's 'where the action is,' dammit. I don't care if she feels sorry for that boy. If she starts pushing him too quickly, he's likely to explode. We both know how quickly a trained murderer can kill."

"It may not come down to that. Jane's right, there are actually two options. Maybe they'll find Cira's gold and manage to negotiate with Reilly to refuse Grozak." He grimaced. "Though I wouldn't like to bank on a long shot like that."

Eve was silent, thinking. "Maybe it's not such a long shot."

Joe gazed at her inquiringly. "Why not?"

She glanced away from him. "Anything can happen. Mario could translate that scroll and it might tell them exactly where the gold is."

"That's not what you meant." Joe's eyes were narrowed on her face. "And I don't believe it's just wishful thinking."

"You're wrong. I'm wishing with all my heart they find that gold. And soon." She picked up her phone and dialed John Logan. She got his message service and left a call-back. "I'll phone John again when I get back." She moved toward the front door. "I'm taking Toby for a walk by the lake. I need to blow off some steam." She whistled for the dog. "He's been moping around since Jane left again. Are you getting on the phone with Washington right away?"

"You bet I am." He flipped open his phone. "Like you said, there's not much time."

"And you'd rather they close in on Reilly and kill the bastard than negotiate with him."

"Hell, yes. Give him the gold and he'll take it and bury himself somewhere only to surface again. You know that's true."

"Yes." But it might also give Jane time to come out of this nightmare safely. "I'll be back soon."

The screen door slammed behind her and she hurried down the porch steps. Toby ran ahead of her down the path. She let him go. He needed the exercise and she needed a little time to think.

Jesus, she was scared. What the devil should she do? She could do nothing. Joe was right about the odds of finding the gold.

And wrong. It might be—

Barking.

Toby was standing in the middle of the path, barking at something in the trees. He was tense, back on his haunches, and the tone of his barking became shrill.

"Toby. Come."

He didn't pay any attention to her, dammit. It wasn't unheard of for a bear or mountain lion to stray from the hills down here. She didn't want Toby tearing in there and getting himself hurt.

"Toby!"

He was starting toward the trees.

She ran after him and grabbed his collar. "No, there's nothing there."

But there *was* something there.

The hair was rising at the back of her neck.

She jerked Toby back as he lunged forward. "Home! Go home, boy." He turned and ran back toward the cottage, she saw with relief.

And she was right after him. Silly that her heart was beating this hard. It might not have been a dangerous wild animal at all. Toby wasn't the brightest dog in the world. It could have been an owl or a possum.

Yet she breathed easier when she reached the porch. She sank down on the step and Toby sat down beside her. "I'm going to have to tell Jane you need a refresher course in obedience," she whispered as she threw her arm around his back. "*Come* doesn't mean *attack*. You could have gotten yourself torn up, boy."

He wasn't looking at her. His stare was intent on the path.

She felt a chill run through her. Imagination.

The path was empty. Nothing was coming toward them.

Nothing and no one.

But that knowledge didn't chase the chill away. She stood up and headed for the front door. She hadn't had the chance to do that thinking she was going to do, and she couldn't put it off. "Come on. I'm going in and getting a cup of hot chocolate, Toby. I'll let you have a treat even though you don't deserve it."


Jane was smiling as she hung up the phone. She always felt better after she talked to Joe and Eve.

She hadn't realized how desperate and discouraged she'd been feeling until this moment. In only these few minutes of conversation, they'd managed to share their strength with her.

A knock at the door. Trevor opened it before she could answer. "You're about to receive a visitor," he said grimly. "Venable just called and he's frothing at the mouth."

"Why?"

"He didn't like your recent discussion with Eve and Joe. He's talking breach of security, interference with CIA business, and posing a threat to the national interest."

"What?" Then his words hit home. "He bugged my phone?"

"Yes. Hell, he bugs *my* phone. I let him do it. It made him feel more secure, and there are always ways around it." He made a face. "I told him I didn't give a damn what you told Eve and Joe, but evidently you crossed his line of comfort. What did you ask Joe to do?"

"Stir everyone up so that we could get some help finding Reilly and Grozak."

"That would do it. Government agencies are extremely touchy about interference in their jurisdictions."

"Tough."

"I agree." He gestured toward the door. "So shall we go down and tell him so? He should be arriving any time now."

"Cripes, he must be upset." She frowned as she

passed him. "And I do care if my phone is bugged, dammit."

"Talk to him, not to me."

"You didn't tell me he'd done it."

"You were feeling insecure enough." He preceded her down the stairs. "And I wanted you to stay. It was important to me."

"But you're letting me know now."

"I don't think a hydrogen bomb blast would budge you from here at the moment. You're involved." He looked at her over his shoulder. "Right?"

He was right, dammit. As she'd told Eve and Joe, this was the one place where she could be of use. "I'm involved," she repeated. "But that doesn't mean I'm willing to put up with this kind of bullshit to stay here."

"I know. That's why I'm letting Venable clear the decks and put everything out in the open." He turned as he reached the bottom of the stairs. "And to convince you that Venable does exist and that I'm telling you the truth about working with him."

"I didn't think you were lying."

"Perhaps not consciously. But maybe on a subliminal level? You know I'm capable of fairly complicated chicancry. I wanted to make sure that you knew I was being entirely aboveboard." He turned and opened the front door. "Ask Venable any question you like." He smiled. "Of course, now that you're considered a security risk, he may not answer you."

\* \* \*

Carl Venable didn't look like the nervous individual Trevor had described, Jane thought as he got off the helicopter. He was big and burly with a shock of graying red hair and held himself with confidence and authority.

But the frown on his face and the jerkiness of his movement belied that confidence as he came toward them. "I told you that you shouldn't have gone to get her," he said curtly to Trevor. "Sabot's furious. He threatened to pull me off the case."

"He won't do it. Quinn will undoubtedly stir up the waters, but he's going to paint you as the good guy. Sabot will be too busy answering questions and trying to make his position seem credible to undermine you."

"So you say." He turned to Jane. "You don't know what a mess you've made of this. It's going to be twice as hard for us to get anything done efficiently. Quinn is bound to involve Homeland Security, and that means that we'll have to answer to them. You might have blown any chance we have of capturing Grozak."

"You don't seem to have done such a great job to date," Jane said. "And if it will keep another 9/11 from happening, I don't care how difficult I've made your job. Screw it. I'll do what I please."

His cheeks flushed. "Not if I arrest you and put you under our protection as a material witness."

"Stop right there, Venable," Trevor said. "I know you're upset, but we both know that's not going to happen."

"I should do it. It would be safer for all of us. Hell, it would be safer for her. It would keep Reilly's hands off her. You told me yourself that he said he wanted to make a trade for her. And now she's becoming a thorn—"

"I also told you to keep your mouth shut about what Reilly said, you son of a bitch," Trevor interrupted in disgust. "Now you've blown it."

"Wait a minute," Jane said. "What are you talking about?" She whirled on Trevor. "Trade?"

He was silent a moment and then shrugged. "When he called me, he had a list of demands to stop him from going along with Grozak."

"And what was on this list?"

"The gold, my statue of Cira." He paused. "And you. You figured very prominently on his list."

"Why?"

"Why do you think? I told you he was a fanatic about everything to do with Herculaneum, and Cira's gold in particular. What's more to do with Cira than you? The spitting image. He believes you may know more than you think you do. Or that you may know and are lying low and waiting for the opportune moment to reach out and grab."

"That's absurd." She tried to think. "And I can't see how he could make me tell him any—" And then it came to her. "Jock . . ."

"Bingo. Mind control. Making you open your mind and letting him explore every inch of it," Trevor said. "No doubt with some of his dirty little tampering along the way."

A chill went through her at the thought. "That bastard."

"I told him no sale. I offered him the gold if I found it, and my statue, but I told him he'd have to do without you."

"Why didn't you tell me?"

"He should have told you," Venable said. "I told him that we might be able to use that—"

"And I told you it wasn't going to happen."

Jane tried to work her way through the first horror of that threat. "Venable's right. We should explore every—"

"Screw it," Trevor said. "I knew you'd react like this. That's why I didn't tell you. I risked you once four years ago; it's not happening again."

"You didn't make the decision. I made the choice then. I'll make it now."

"Reilly tentatively accepted the offer of the statue and the gold. It's really the gold that he wants. There's no reason to make any decision."

"We haven't found the gold yet."

"We've still got time." He glanced at Venable. "Damn you."

"It slipped," Venable said. "But maybe it's a good thing. She has to realize that every action she takes can affect us all. I'm still tempted to take her away and put her—" He broke off and then sighed wearily. "No, I won't do it. But we all might be a hell of a lot safer if I did." His lips twisted. "Including your Joe Quinn and Eve Duncan."

She stiffened. "What do you mean?" She swung on Trevor. "You told me they were guarded, safe."

"They are," Trevor said. "Stop trying to scare her, Venable."

"Is that what you're doing?" she demanded.

"They're guarded. We won't let anything happen to them." Venable shrugged. "There have just been reports from the agents on duty of a few signs of disturbance in the woods near the cottage."

"What kind of disturbance?"

He shrugged. "Nothing concrete." He turned back to the helicopter. "I've got to get back to Aberdeen. I shouldn't have come. I was going to be all diplomatic and try to convince her that we were doing the best job we could and ask her to call off Quinn and Duncan." He grimaced. "It didn't work out that way. I lost it. Sabot would never tolerate or understand a slip like that. Hell, maybe I should turn in my resignation. I haven't been a company man since this started. I've been too scared."

"Scared?" Jane echoed.

"Why not? I have a wife and four kids. I have three brothers, a father in a nursing home, and a mother who takes care of all of us. We don't know where those explosives are supposed to go off." He looked at Jane. "They might be targeted at your Atlanta. It's a big city and a major airline hub. Aren't you tempted to run home and whisk the people you love to a cave in the nearest mountain? I am."

Yes, she was tempted. She'd been trying to smother that fear since Trevor told her about Grozak's plans. "Eve and Joe wouldn't go." She stared him in the eye. "And you didn't run home. You stayed here and tried to make a difference."

"Not a very good attempt, according to Trevor." He shrugged and turned away. "But I'll keep on trying until Sabot gets sick of me and gives me a pink slip. Don't worry, Ms. MacGuire, nothing is going to happen to your people. I made Trevor a promise." He got back on the helicopter. "I'll call you, Trevor."

"Do that. Don't come in person just because you're angry. I'm doing my damnedest to keep Grozak from knowing that the CIA has any involvement. Did you cover your ass?"

"I'm no amateur. The helicopter is rented in the name of Herculaneum Historical Society. We might even make Grozak a little worried that you located the gold and sent for someone to have it authenticated. From Aberdeen I board a flight direct to Naples. Satisfied?"

"No, I'd have been satisfied if you'd just kept your mouth shut."

"I couldn't do that." Venable's gaze shifted to Jane. "You opened a whole can of worms. You've no idea how fast and hard Homeland Security can act if they decide to do it. It may only be a token foray, since they don't believe Grozak is a threat any more than Sabot does. But it will be enough to blow any cover you have. I'm probably too late, but I thought I'd try." The door of the helicopter closed behind him.

Trevor glanced at Jane. "You didn't ask him any questions about me."

"I didn't get a chance." She turned toward the front door. "And I never said I wanted to ask him questions. That was your idea."

"What did you think of him?"

"Sad." She shook her head. "And very human. I believe he'll do the best he can."

"We're all doing the best we can." Trevor opened the door for her and let her precede him into the hall. "And I could use a little of that tolerance you're showing Venable."

"You should have told me what Reilly said."

"No, I shouldn't. I never make it hard on myself if I can help it. I could help it this time."

"But I'm the one at risk. Every time I think we're working together, I find out you haven't told me something. Dammit, I don't even understand how you think."

He smiled. "Then skim the surface. I'll guarantee to make it worth your while."

She felt the familiar heat flow through her as she looked at him. He was standing there, his stance casual, but there was nothing casual about that smile. It was intimate, sensual, and devilishly seductive. Why did she let him do this to her? Christ, that tingling response had erupted out of nowhere. One moment she'd been upset, almost indignant with him, and then that physical response had come. "I'm not a skimmer. I don't know how."

"I'll teach you. I'm an expert." He was watching her expression. "Not now?"

"It's not . . . my nature." She hurried toward the staircase. "I've got to check on Mario and then I'm meeting Jock in the courtyard at five."

"He seemed upset when he left you this morning. He might not show."

"You were watching?"

"Brenner wasn't here, and I trust MacDuff but he has his own agenda. Of course I was watching. And I'll be watching this afternoon."

"I don't believe he'll hurt me."

"I want to be sure." He paused. "I'm going to the Run tonight after dinner. I want you there. Will you come?"

"I don't . . . know. I'm still angry with you."

"But there's something else going on too, isn't there?" His gaze was fixed intently on her face and his voice was suddenly rough with feeling. "I want it very much. So much that I've got to get away from you or I'll show you right here, right now. I'll be waiting." He headed toward the library. "And I'm damn human too, Jane. Come and see for yourself."

It was five-fifteen when Jane saw Jock coming across the courtyard toward her.

"You came back." She tried to hide her relief as she opened her sketchbook. "I'm glad."

"The laird told me I should." He frowned. "I didn't want to do it."

"Because I made you uneasy?" She started to sketch. "I didn't mean to—" She stopped and then said, "I'm not telling you the truth. I wanted you to be worried, Jock. We're all worried, and why should you be different? We have to stop that man who hurt you. It's your job to help us."

He shook his head.

"Do you believe it's over? It's not over, Jock. Reilly

is going to hurt a lot of people because you're burying your head in the sand. If he does, it will be your
fault."

"Not my fault."

"Yes, it is." She searched wildly for a way to get
through to him. "And it's not only strangers he's going to hurt. He'd be angry that MacDuff is trying to
stop him. Are you going to let Reilly hurt him?"

He looked away from her. "I'll take care of the
laird. No one will hurt him."

"MacDuff won't let you. He wants to find and kill
Reilly because of what he did to you. MacDuff is a
strong, determined man. You won't be able stop
him. In your heart you know that. The only way to
keep him safe is for us to strike at Reilly before he
can strike. But we have to know where he is."

"I don't know where he is."

"I think you do."

"I don't. I don't." His voice sharpened. "Stop talking about it."

"When you tell me about Reilly."

"I can make you stop." He took a half step toward
her and his hand reached into his pocket. "It's easy.
I know how to do that."

She went rigid. The garrote. He was reaching for
the garrote. She forced herself not to take a step
back. "I'm sure you know all kinds of ways to quiet
your enemies, but I'm not your enemy, Jock."

"You won't shut up. You *bother* me."

"And is that reason to kill? Is that what Reilly
taught you? Are you still doing what he orders you
to do?"

"No! I ran away. I knew it was bad, but I couldn't stop."

"You still haven't stopped. You're letting it go on and on. And soon it will kill MacDuff."

"It won't." His face was pale and he was no more than a step away from her. "It won't happen."

"It will. Unless you help him."

Pain twisted his face. "I can't," he whispered. "He's . . . always there, talking to me. I can't shut him out."

"Try." She took a step toward him and put her hand gently on his arm. "Just try, Jock."

He shook her off, his expression panicked. "Shut up. I can't listen to you."

"Because Reilly told you not to do it? Because he told you to kill anyone who asked you about him?" she called after him as he almost ran away from her toward the stable. "Don't you see how wrong it is to let him get away with that?"

He didn't answer as he disappeared into the stable.

She drew a long shaky breath as she gazed after him. Close. She didn't know how near she'd come to having that garrote around her neck, but she didn't want to think about it. Had it been worth it? Had she made him think or would he just block her words out? Only time would tell.

Maybe she shouldn't have rushed him. It hadn't been her intention, but the words had tumbled out. She was getting increasingly panicky about finding a way to stop this horror. And Jock was the only game in town right now.

"My God, what were you trying to do, get yourself killed?"

She turned to see Trevor coming toward her across the courtyard. "Not much chance. You were keeping guard, and I'm sure MacDuff would have sprung out of that stable like Superman if Jock had touched me."

"We might not have been in time," he said grimly. "I saw him in action with one of my men when we first came here, and he was fast, very fast."

"Well, nothing happened." She passed him and hurried toward the steps. "With the emphasis on *nothing*. I'm not sure he'll even remember talking to me. Reilly still has him under his thumb."

"Then you won't mind not talking to him again."

"I would mind. I have to keep chipping away at him."

His hands clenched into fists. "The hell you do. I want to shake some sense into you."

"Then you'd better work on that control. You lay a hand on me and I'll deck you. I'll do what I think is right." She slammed the front door behind her. She was in no mood to argue with him. She was still a little shaken from her encounter with Jock. It had taken all her stamina to stand there and confront him. It had been hard for her to believe the stories about his deadliness when MacDuff told her about the boy. But the lethal vibes Jock had been sending out in those last few minutes had been unmistakable. He might be as beautiful as Lucifer before the fall, but he was every bit as tormented and dangerous.

But there was no question she'd try again. Jock was unstable, but he was vulnerable. And he hadn't hurt her. He'd been close but he hadn't taken that final step. Who knows how hard that restraint might have been for him? Reilly had done terrible things to his mind that were still lingering.

The fear was fading and she felt a sudden surge of heady optimism as she started up the staircase. She'd been dragging around, almost as afraid of Grozak and Reilly as Jock. It wasn't as if the situation couldn't be turned around. Eve and Joe were going to help. She'd made a little progress with Jock. They weren't standing still and waiting for the worst to happen.

She'd take a shower and then work on the background of the sketch of Jock. Then maybe she'd go and check on Mario.

*I'm going to the Run. I want you there.*

She'd backed away from Trevor when he asked her to come. Why? She prided herself on her confidence and boldness. Yet ever since she'd come to this place she'd been a complete wimp. It was time she took herself in hand and started behaving normally. The decision sent a tingle of excitement through her. The memory of Trevor standing there in the moonlight, the breeze lifting his hair, and the slight smile that had made her compare him to those wild, ancient Scots was filling her with a mixture of tension and anticipation.

*I want you there. . . .*

# 14

"I was wondering if you'd come." Trevor stood up from the rock on which he'd been sitting. "I was betting you wouldn't."

"It was fifty-fifty." Jane came toward him. He was dressed in jeans and a dark sweatshirt that appeared black in the moonlight. He looked younger, less hard, more vulnerable. Yet when was Trevor ever vulnerable? "I didn't like the fact that you didn't tell me about Reilly's offer. And I've been pretty mixed up."

"And you're not now?"

"It's getting more clear." She looked around the craggy rocks that bordered the Run. "Why did you want to come here this evening?"

He smiled. "Not because I wanted to be soothed. You want to know the truth? This place is atmospheric as hell. You can almost see Angus and Fiona and their Scottish cronies. I'm a manipulative bastard, and I could see that you responded to the vibes here. I need all the help I can get where you're concerned."

She felt the heat tingle through her. "Do you?"

His smile faded as his gaze searched her face. "Don't I?"

"It's not like you to be uncertain about anything." She took a step closer to him. "And when you come right down to the basics, atmosphere doesn't mean a damn."

He tensed. "And what are the basics?"

"That life can be very short. That there's death all around and you never know when—" She looked him straight in the eye. "I'm not going to let any pleasure go by because I don't believe it's the right time. There's no right time except now."

"Right time for what?"

"Do you want me to say it?" She took another step forward, until she was only a scant foot from him. She could feel the heat emanating from his body and it sent a ripple of heat through her. "I wanted to go to bed with you when I was seventeen. You were stupid and noble and you left me frustrated and empty for those four years. Heaven help me, I still want to go to bed with you, and it's going to happen, dammit." She laid her hand on his chest. A shudder went through him and she felt a heady sense of power. "Isn't it?"

"Hell, yes." His hand covered hers and he rubbed it slowly over his chest. "I told you I wouldn't send you away if you touched me."

She could feel his heartbeat beneath her palm and it was quickening, pounding. Jesus, she could feel that pounding in her own body. It seemed as if they were joined already. She leaned against him until their joined hands pressed against her breast. Dear God, she was melting. "Where?"

"Here," he muttered as his lips buried themselves in her neck. "Behind the rocks. I don't care." His tongue was warm on the pulse in the hollow of her throat. "Anywhere."

She was burning up. She wanted to jerk him down on the hard earth, pull him in and move against him, take all of him. Her arms slid around his shoulders. "Here," she murmured "You're right, it doesn't matter."

He went rigid and he pushed her back. "Yes, it does." He was breathing heavily, his eyes glittering wildly in his taut face. "I don't want MacDuff or one of the guards stumbling over us. I've waited this long. I can wait another ten minutes. Get the hell back to your room. I'll be right behind you."

She stood there, staring dazedly at him. "What?"

"Don't just stand there. I promise this is my last act of nobility. After this, all bets are off." His lips tightened. "And if you change your mind and lock your door on me, I'm going to break it down."

She didn't move. She didn't know if she could wait ten minutes, and she knew it would only take one touch to send him over the edge.

"I want to do it right," he said harshly. "Move!"

What the devil. Just give in and give him what he wanted. Anything he wanted. Maybe he was right.

At the moment her body wasn't letting her mind reason any too well. She turned and streaked toward the path around the castle.

Jock watched the light go on in Jane's room. He had seen her run through the gates and in the front door only a few moments ago and had been wondering if he should go after her.

Then he had seen Trevor stride across the courtyard, and his every sense had gone on alert. Trevor's expression was intent, hard. Was he going to hurt her? Jock took out his garrote and started across the courtyard.

"Come back, Jock."

He turned to see the laird standing in the stable doorway. "He's going to hurt her."

"No. Or if he does, it's because she wants it." He smiled. "And I don't think she will."

"His face . . ."

"I saw his face. It's not what you thought. Life isn't always about death and hurting. Don't you remember that?"

Jock thought about it and then nodded. "Sex?"

"By all means, sex."

Yes, Jock remembered that wild, joyous coupling. Megan in the village and then later other girls as he'd traveled from place to place around the world.

And then Kim Chan at Reilly's place.

He shied quickly away from the thought of her. "And Jane wants it?"

"He won't force her, Jock." MacDuff paused. "Do you mind?"

"Not if he doesn't hurt her." He tilted his head. "Did you think I would?"

"You're attached to her. I just wondered."

"I . . . like her." He frowned. "But sometimes she makes me feel . . . It hurts. She keeps talking and prodding and I want to put a gag on her mouth."

"But not a garrote around her throat."

He shook his head. "I wouldn't do that. But even after I left her, I kept hearing what she said. I'm still hearing it."

"Then maybe your mind is telling you it's time to listen."

"You want me to remember too."

"Deep down, isn't that what you want?"

*Four eight two. Four eight two.*

Not now. Block it out. Block it out. The laird would see his suffering and be upset.

But the laird didn't understand, Jock thought in agony. He didn't understand the chains or the pain that he fought every night. He didn't want him to know. "She said . . . you wouldn't wait. That you'd go after Reilly without my help."

"If I have to do it."

"Don't," he whispered. "Please."

MacDuff turned away. "Come and help me clean up the supper dishes. I have work to do."

"Reilly will—"

"Unless you can tell me what I want, I don't want to hear any arguments about Reilly, Jock."

Despair tore through Jock as he watched MacDuff

go into the stable. Memories of death and guilt and pain swirled around him, tearing through the web of scar tissue that had formed since MacDuff brought him back from Colorado.

*Four eight two. Four eight two.*

Hurt. Hurt. Hurt.

Trevor stood framed in the doorway of Jane's bedroom. "You left the door open."

"I didn't want there to be any mistake about my intentions." Jane could hear the trembling in her voice and tried to steady it. "No locks. No closed doors. Now take your clothes off and get over here. I don't want to be the only one naked. It makes me feel vulnerable." She suddenly tossed the cover aside. "Hell, I am vulnerable. I'm not going to lie about it."

"Give me one minute." He closed the door and pulled the sweatshirt over his head. "Less."

His body was as beautiful as she'd known it would be. Narrow waist, powerful legs, and wide shoulders that made her want to dig her nails into them. She wanted to sketch him. No, the hell she did. She wanted only one thing from him at this moment. "You're too slow."

"Tell me that after I get in that bed." He was coming toward her. "I'll try to be slow then, but I don't promise."

She held out her hand and pulled him down. "I don't want promises." She wrapped her legs around him. She arched upward as she felt him. "I want you to—"

His mouth covered hers to smother her cry as he started to move. "This? And this?" His breath was coming harshly. "Tell me. I want it to be good for you. God, do I want it to be good. . . ."

Jane's lips brushed Trevor's shoulder before she nestled closer. "Are you tired? I'm going to want to do it again."

"Tired?" He chuckled. "Are you impugning my stamina? I believe I can keep up with you." He licked delicately at the tip of her breast. "Now?"

"Pretty soon. When I catch my breath." She stared into the darkness. "It was good, wasn't it?"

"Superb. Wild. Mind-blowing."

"I was afraid I'd be disappointed. Sometimes anticipation spoils the real thing."

"And did you anticipate?"

"Sure." She lifted herself on one elbow to look down at him. "I tried not to, but when you're denied a candy bar, that's the only thing you want to eat. Now I'm getting my fill of you."

"You'd better not. I'll make damn sure I'm much more appetizing than a candy bar." He smiled up at her. "And what did you anticipate?"

"*The Joy of Sex*, the Kama Sutra."

"Good God, what a challenge."

"Can you meet it?"

"Oh, yes." He moved over her, his eyes gleaming down at her. "Can you?"

* * *

It wasn't Julius barring the way, Cira saw as she neared the end of the tunnel. Thank the gods, it was her servant, Dominic.

"Dominic, what are you doing here? I told you to leave the city."

"The Lady Pia sent me." He looked beyond her at Antonio and stiffened. "Do you wish him dead?"

"I told you I didn't betray you, Cira." Antonio was beside her, taking his sword from her hand. "Now let's get out of here."

Dominic took a step toward Antonio. "He made you unhappy. Shall I kill him?"

A low rumble shook the floor of the tunnel.

"Out," Antonio said. "I'm not going to let us all die to satisfy Dominic's bloodlust." He grabbed Cira's arm and pulled her toward the tunnel opening. "Or yours."

Dominic took a step toward him.

"No, it's all right," Cira said as they burst out into daylight that was like night. Smoke. She could scarcely breathe. She stopped in horror, staring at the mountain burning like a flaming sword, fingers of lava streaming down its side. "Later, Dominic. We have to get to the city. Pia—"

"That's why she sent me," Dominic said as he ran after them down the hill. "The Lady Pia was afraid Julius had found out about her. She thought someone had been following her since yesterday. She told me to tell you she'd meet you at the ship."

"What ship?" Antonio asked.

"It's moored down the coast," Cira said. "I paid Demonidas for passage away from here."

"You did?"

"Why are you surprised? I'm no fool. Julius will never rest when he finds me gone. I have to get far away from Herculaneum."

"I'm only surprised that you were able to get anyone to help you. Julius is very powerful."

"I managed. Pia helped. Demonidas is waiting for me."

"Perhaps," Antonio said, gazing at lava running down the volcano. "Or maybe he sailed when the mountain exploded."

That had been one of Cira's fears as she ran through the tunnel. "He's a greedy man and I paid him only half. He'll take his chances. The lava flow doesn't seem to be going in that direction. It's heading straight toward—" She stopped in horror. "Toward the city." She gazed at Dominic over her shoulder. "How long ago did the Lady Pia send you?"

"An hour."

"And she was leaving right away for the ship?"

Dominic nodded, his gaze on the lava. "She said to tell you that she'd be waiting for you."

And it seemed as if the mountain had erupted a century ago, but it couldn't have been very long. Surely Pia was out of the city.

"Do you wish me to go and make sure?" Dominic asked.

Send him into that fiery trap? That deadly lava was flowing faster every second. But what if Pia . . .

She forced herself to look away. "If someone is going to go, it will be me."

"No!" Antonio said. "It would be insane. You wouldn't even be able to reach the outskirts before—"

"This isn't your concern."

"By the gods, it couldn't be more my concern." His expression was grim. "What have I been trying to tell you? Do you want me to go after this Pia? I'm mad enough to do even that for you." He stared directly into her eyes. "Tell me and I'll go."

She believed him. He would go rather than let her risk her life.

Another rumble shook the earth.

She tore her eyes away from Antonio's and asked Dominic, "Is Leo with her?"

"No, she told me to take him to the ship last night. He's with Demonidas."

And Demonidas would be only as compassionate with the boy as his payment dictated. She couldn't risk leaving him alone and unprotected. She had to assume and pray that Pia left the city as she'd told Dominic she'd do. "Then we go to the ship." She turned away from the city and started to run. "Hurry."

"I left two horses at the bottom of the hill." Antonio passed her. "Dominic?"

"I also brought a horse for her," Dominic said. "I did not expect you to return. You betray—" He stopped, his gaze on the mountain, and muttered an oath. "It's coming this way."

He was right, Cira realized.

Though the main flow was heading for the city, a rivulet of molten lava was making a path toward Julius's villa, coming directly toward them.

"We still have time to reach the horses." Antonio's hand

tightened around Cira's. "We'll go north and skirt the flow."

If they could. Smoke and lava seemed to be attacking, smothering, surrounding them on all sides.

Of course they could, Cira thought impatiently. She hadn't gotten this far to be brought down now. "Then stop talking and get me to those horses."

"I'm trying, you demanding woman." Antonio was pulling her toward a stand of trees. "Go get your horse, Dominic. Let the other animal free. Slap his rump and send him north."

Dominic disappeared into the smoke.

She could hear the horses ahead neighing in fear and fighting their ropes.

Then Antonio was tossing her onto the back of one of the horses and handing her the reins. "You lead. I'll be right behind you."

"How unusual for you."

"No choice. I'll keep close. I wouldn't doubt you'll try to lose me." He looked into her eyes. "It won't work. I left you once and I found that out. It's forever, Cira."

Forever. Hope and joy mixed with the fear soaring through her. She kicked the horse into a gallop. "Words have little value. Prove it."

Incredibly, she heard him chuckle behind her. "Only you would make a condition like that. We'll discuss it later. Right now we have to get out of this inferno."

And an inferno it was. The tops of the tall trees along the road were aflame from the sparks. She glanced at the stream of lava coming down the mountain. Was it closer? They had to go at least a mile before they were out of the path. Pray they weren't cut off before they reached it. . . .

*A burning tree crashed across the road in front of her! Her horse screamed and reared. She felt herself slipping from the saddle. . . .*

*"Antonio!"*

Jane jerked upright in bed, gasping. "No!"

"Easy." Antonio's soothing hand was on her shoulder. "Easy."

Not Antonio. Trevor. Not two thousand years ago. Here. Now.

"Okay?" Trevor was pulling her down, cuddling her against his naked body. "You're shaking."

"I'm all right." She moistened her lips. "I guess I should have expected bad dreams after you told me what Reilly wanted to do to me. I can't imagine anything worse than having someone able to control your mind and will. It makes me go berserk to think about it. Cira was born a slave. I probably associated—"

"Easy. Take a deep breath. You're not Cira, and Reilly's not going to get his hands on you."

"I know that." She was silent a moment. "Sorry."

"Nothing to be sorry about. What kind of nightmare?"

"I thought everything was going to be fine for her, and then the tree—"

"Cira?"

"Who else? I seem to be under siege by her." She made a face. "Cripes, that sounds weird. I'm still half convinced that I must have read something about her somewhere that's causing these dreams."

"But only half convinced."

"I don't know." She nestled closer. "They seem so

real, and it's like a story unfolding. As if she were trying to tell me something." She got up on her elbow. "You're not laughing at me."

"I wouldn't dare." He smiled. "Cira's spirit might strike me down with a bolt of lightning." His smile faded. "Or you might decide to leave me. Either way I face disaster."

"Now you are joking," she said uncertainly. Trevor's expression was odd, taut, and without humor.

"Am I? Perhaps I am." He pulled her down again and his lips were pressed in the hair at her temple. "You'd say it was too soon. You're probably right. But I know damn well I want the chance to find out." His arms tightened around her as he felt her stiffen against him. "Okay, I'll stop making you uneasy. God knows, I'm unsettled enough myself. I was expecting a hell of a good roll in the hay with a woman I've wanted for years. I didn't expect—" He broke off. "I believe a change of subject is in order. Would you care to tell me about your latest Cira dream?"

She hesitated. She'd avoided telling anyone details of those dreams, with the exception of Eve. Eve was not only like her other self, but she had her own secrets that she had not divulged even to Joe. Jane could understand that instinctive avoidance. She was as private a person as Eve, and it was difficult to trust anyone with these dreams that seemed not like dreams at all.

"I'll understand if you don't want to talk about it," Trevor said quietly. "But I want you to know that whatever you believe, I'll believe. I trust your instincts and your judgment. Screw everything else."

She was silent a moment. "I don't know what to believe," she said haltingly. "Cira's out of the tunnel. Antonio's with her. So is Dominic. They're heading toward a ship moored down the coast. Cira paid Demonidas to take her away from Herculaneum."

"Demonidas?"

"He's greedy. She believes he'll wait for her, even though—" She shook her head. "Even though their world's ending. Antonio's not so sure." She stared into the darkness. "There's fire all around them. The cypress trees bordering the road are all burning. One fell across the road in front of Cira. She slipped from the horse. She called out for Antonio. . . ." She closed her eyes. "It sounds like something from *The Perils of Pauline,* doesn't it? Thank heaven there were no railroad tracks back then. I'd probably have Cira tied to them with an engine roaring toward her."

"Cira seems to be doing fine in that department herself." Trevor said. "Demonidas . . ."

She opened her eyes to look at him. "What are you thinking?"

"Well, you haven't been able to find any reference to Cira that you could have come across before you started dreaming about her. Demonidas is a new player in the mix. Maybe he's a well-known merchant and trader. Perhaps we can track Cira through him."

*We.* She felt a surge of warmth at the word. "If he existed."

"Don't be a pessimist. He exists until proven otherwise. I'll see what I can do about finding a reference to him tomorrow."

"That's my job."

"Then we'll both do it. Lord knows, there are enough alleys to explore for the two of us."

"Too many. And we don't have time to do this now. Not with Reilly and Grozak—"

"We have a little time now. And it might prove important. If Cira was running away from Julius, is it likely she'd go without the gold?"

She stiffened. "No."

"Then wouldn't it be logical that the gold was on that ship?"

"Yes." She added, "You're talking as if there really was a Demonidas."

"You said you half believed. I'll work on that assumption. Could you have run across the name Demonidas sometime in the past and woven it into fantasy? Possibly. But why not check it out? It can't hurt."

"It might be a waste of time we don't have."

"I told you I'd believe what you believe. I have a hunch you believe in Cira and Antonio and Demonidas more than you'll admit. You don't trust me enough yet."

"I . . . trust you."

He laughed. "That was a pretty lame response." He moved over her. "But that's okay. You respond very enthusiastically in other areas. I'll just have to work on making a major breakthrough." He parted her thighs and whispered, "But there are all kinds of breakthroughs. I think we can make a very interesting one right now."

The heat was moving through her again as she looked up at him. He didn't realize that he had already made a breakthrough tonight. Not the sexual one that had shaken her to her core. She had let him beyond the barriers into her mind and this private part of her that she trusted to no one. She felt joined, part of him. That they were so fantastic sexually together almost paled in comparison.

Almost. What was she thinking? There was nothing pale about sex with Trevor. It was completely mind-shattering. She pulled him closer. "I'm all for breakthroughs." She tried to steady her voice. "Show me. . . ."

W hat are you doing out here?" Joe came out on the porch and sat down beside Eve on the top step. "It's almost three in the morning. Worried?"

"Of course I'm worried." She leaned against him as he put his arm around her. "And scared to death. Why not? All the politicians are still arguing about responsibility for 9/11. I'm afraid that we won't do enough to stop that crazy Grozak."

"We're doing all we can. Did John Logan call you back?"

She nodded. "He's flying to Washington to talk to the bigwigs in Homeland Security. He has enough clout with Congress because of his campaign contributions to have them at least listen. He

says he can promise that if nothing else they'll ele-
vate the warning. He'll call me back tomorrow."

"And I contacted the director of the Bureau. He
was cagey, but I told him if he didn't step in with the
CIA that I'd call in the media. So stop fretting, Eve."

"I'm not fretting." She made a face. "I'm trying to
avoid making a painful decision. No luck. I don't
think there's any way I can get around it."

"What the hell are you talking about?"

"I'm saying we have to do everything we can. I
kept telling myself that it probably had no connection, but I can't run the risk." She glanced at her
watch. "It's eight o'clock in Scotland. I won't wake
Jane if I call her now." She got up from the step.
"I'm going in and making a pot of coffee. Come on
in and we'll talk."


That was Eve." Jane slowly hung up the
phone. "She wants me to meet her in Naples this
evening."

"What?" Trevor leaned back in his chair. "No
way."

She shook her head. "I have to go. Eve never asks
anything of me. She asked this."

"Why?"

"I don't know. She just said it was important to
her. She'll meet me at the airport. Her flight gets in
just after six." She frowned. "God, I'm worried. Eve
doesn't— She sounded—"

"I'm going with you."

She shook her head. "No, she said to come alone."

"The hell you will. She wouldn't want you to come if she knew there was a risk. Is Quinn going to be there?"

"No." She held up her hand to stop the protest she knew was coming. "She said that if you want to send someone to guard me, it's okay with her. She just didn't want any interference."

"I wouldn't interfere."

She gazed at him skeptically.

"Okay, I'd try not to interfere." He shook his head. "I let you go to Lucerne without me. I'm not going to let you go this time. I'll stay in the background. I'll be chauffeur and bodyguard. You can ignore me."

"That's difficult to do. What about Brenner?"

"He didn't turn up anything about Mario's father. I sent him back to Colorado." His lips tightened. "I'm going, Jane."

She gazed at him in frustration. "But Eve doesn't want you."

"Then she'll have to grin and bear it." He flipped open his cell phone. "I'll call and arrange for a helicopter." He added, "And then phone Venable and tell him to back off and not have his men crawling all over Naples airport."

She had forgotten Venable and the bug he had placed on the phone. Better Trevor than the CIA. And she had to admit to herself that she felt more comfortable with Trevor going along. "Okay, but you'd better make yourself invisible, dammit. I'll go tell Mario we're going and then get my bag and passport."

MacDuff was standing in the courtyard when the helicopter landed an hour later. "You're leaving?"

She nodded. "Naples. But we'll be back tonight or tomorrow. How's Jock?"

"Quiet. Very quiet. Almost completely withdrawn." He frowned. "And he had a nightmare last night. I'd hoped they were over."

"My fault?"

"Perhaps. Or mine. Who knows?" He watched Trevor come out of the castle. "But always Reilly's. Why Naples?"

"Eve wants to meet me there."

"Eve Duncan." He frowned. "Why not come here?"

"I'll let you know when I do." She headed for the helicopter. "Tell Jock I'll talk to him when I get back. Tell him I'm—" She wasn't sure what she wanted to tell him. She wasn't sorry she had probed and prodded and possibly opened old wounds, because it had been necessary. She was only sorry for the pain she had caused. "Good-bye, MacDuff. Take care of him."

"You don't need to tell me that."

She smiled. "I know." She repeated the phrase she'd heard him say. "He's one of yours."

"Aye." He turned away. "Mine."

Eve gave Jane a hug when she got out of Customs and then gave Trevor a cool glance. "What are you doing here?"

"What do you think? I watched a man being

beheaded a few days ago. I wasn't going to risk Jane." He took her overnight bag. "But I promised her that I wouldn't get in your way, that I'd fade into the background unless you need me."

"That must have hurt," Eve said dryly.

"Hell, yes. Let's get this over with." He handed Eve a key chain, turned, and walked toward the exit. "Your rental car is parked outside. I'll follow you in another rental car. Unless you can have your conversation here at the airport?"

Eve shook her head.

"I didn't think so. Otherwise you wouldn't have wanted her to come back to Italy. Since Naples is the closest major airport to Herculaneum, I assume that's where you're going?"

"Assumptions are seldom correct," Eve said as she followed him. "That's one of the reasons I didn't want you here. Your mind never stops ticking, and I had no desire to have you leapfrogging and getting in my way. You see, you're already trying to do it." She turned to Jane. "How are you?"

"How do you think I am? Scared. Confused. I don't like to be in the dark. Why the devil are we here, Eve?"

"Because I couldn't be quiet any longer." She nudged Jane toward the rental car Trevor was indicating. "And I've always been better at show-and-tell."

# 15

*Museo di Storia Naturale di Napoli.*

"A museum of natural history?" Jane gazed at the modest stone building set back from an equally modest street. "Eve, what the hell are we—"

"Think about it." Eve turned off the engine. "You were never here, but four years ago Trevor visited this building and persuaded the curator, Signor Toriza, to do him a favor."

Jane stared at her in shock. "The skull."

"The skull. We had to have a skull to draw that homicidal maniac into the trap, and Trevor borrowed one from this museum. I was to do a reconstruction and make sure the finished product resembled the statue of Cira. It went completely against the grain for me to fake it but I did it anyway. We had to catch Aldo before he murdered you."

"And you did it."

She looked away from Jane. "I did it. We called the reconstruction Giulia, and I made it a dead ringer. After we no longer needed it, I did as I promised the museum and did a true reconstruction." She got out of the car. "Come on, let's go see it."

"But I've already seen it," Jane said as she followed Eve up the four steps leading to the front entrance. "There were photos in the newspapers of the phony reconstruction as well as the true one. You did a fantastic job with a skull that dissimilar to the Cira statue."

"Oh, I did a great job. But you've never seen the reconstruction in person." She opened the door. "That's why we're here." She nodded at the small, balding, well-dressed man hurrying toward them. "Good evening, Signor Toriza. It was kind of you to keep the museum open for me."

"It was my pleasure. You know that you have only to call and I will do whatever I can to help you. We are very grateful."

"No, I'm the one who is grateful. You have it ready?"

He nodded. "Shall I go with you?"

"No. If you'll wait here, we'll try not to be long." She strode down the corridor and turned right into a large exhibit room. Glass cases everywhere. Ancient artifacts, swords, bits of rock, and one case devoted entirely to reconstructions.

Jane shook her head. "Good heavens, I had no idea that a museum this small could boast a collection of reconstructions like this. There must be eight or—"

"Eleven," Eve said. "It's what keeps the money from the tourists pouring in, and they need it desperately to buy these specially constructed cases to preserve the skeletons. Those airtight cases are terribly important. That's why Egypt is losing so many of their artifacts and skeletons. This museum had several skeletons recovered from the marina at Herculaneum, but reconstructions of the skulls give everyone a better picture." She moved down the case to the end. "This is Giulia."

"Just like the photos." Jane stared in puzzlement at the reconstruction. The girl must have been in her mid-teens, with fairly regular features except for the slightly splayed nose. Not a homely girl but certainly not a beauty. "What am I supposed to be seeing?"

"Guilt." Eve turned and headed for a door at the end of the exhibit room. "Come on. I want to get this over."

Jane slowly followed her down the length of the room. Guilt?

Eve threw open the door and stepped aside for Jane to precede her. "Good. Toriza has the lights on. This is the museum workroom. I've become very familiar with it in the last few years." She gestured to the reconstruction in the clear rectangular box in the center of the worktable. "Giulia."

"But the reconstruction in the exhibit hall is Giulia. How can—Dear God." She whirled on Eve. "Cira?"

"I don't know." Eve shut the door and leaned against it, her gaze on the reconstruction. "It certainly looks like her. But if this is Cira, then she wasn't the beauty everyone thought she was. The features are coarser, not as cleanly defined as those of the statue. And Toriza says her skeleton showed years of hard labor. Possibly indicating a life of bearing heavy burdens."

"Cira was born a slave." Jane couldn't take her gaze from the reconstruction. "I suppose it could be that—" She shook her head in rejection. "That's not Cira."

"And it's only a coincidence that the features are so similar at first glance?"

Jane shook her head in confusion. "I don't know. I wouldn't think that would be—" She sank down in the chair at the worktable. "But this isn't the Cira I've been living with for the past four years. You've . . . pulled the rug from beneath my feet."

"And what's your first reaction?"

"Why, that I have to find the answers. . . ."

"That's what I thought you'd say," Eve said wearily. "At first I thought it might put an end to that obsession you have with Cira if I left the reconstruction as I did it the night before we left Herculaneum. If you thought the search was over and that she died at that marina, it was possible you might abandon trying to find more about her and the gold Julius gave her." Her gaze shifted to the face. "The resemblance was there, but it wasn't absolute. And I knew that if you had questions, this reconstruction would only spur you on. It would whet your appetite and give you another carrot to lead you down Cira's damn tunnel."

"You . . . lied?" Jane couldn't believe it. "You're the most honest woman I've ever known. You never lie."

"I lied that night. I smoothed out any resemblance to Cira in the reconstruction and did it over. I sent that lie back to the museum."

"Why?" Jane whispered. "My God, that was a violation of your professional ethics."

"It was a two-thousand-year-old skull, dammit." Eve tried to steady her voice. "You were seventeen and going to college the next year. You'd just gone through a horror of an experience with a maniac who wanted to slice your face off. You were having nightmares about Cira. You were tired and confused and the only thing you needed was to get away from Herculaneum and heal."

"You shouldn't have lied to me."

"Maybe not. Probably not. But I made the choice. I wanted to give you the chance to walk away and forget about Cira and everything that had happened to us in Herculaneum."

"Without giving me the choice. I was seventeen but I was no child, Eve."

Eve flinched. "I always intended to tell you later. After you'd had your chance to forget Cira. But you didn't forget. You still went on those archaeological field trips even after you went off to school."

"So why didn't you tell me then?"

She shook her head. "A lie keeps on growing, festering. We'd always been perfectly honest with each other. You trusted me. I desperately wanted to keep that trust." Her lips twisted. "And then Grozak came on the scene and you told me that Cira's gold might be a way to stop Grozak from getting what he needed."

"What's that got to do with this?"

"You didn't look at the artifact case outside in the exhibit room."

"I saw the reconstructions."

"And they rivet the attention so much that most people don't look at the other shelves. There was a small bag of gold coins found at the marina. They were near Giulia's skeleton, but after they examined her and found she was probably a laborer, they decided it must have belonged to one of the other victims in that crowd running toward the sea."

"My God." Her gaze swung back to the reconstruction. "Then it could have been Cira." But it was all wrong. This was not Cira. She felt it.

"Or Toriza could have been correct and the gold didn't belong to her." She added, "But I had to tell you about it, because I didn't want you looking in Julius's tunnel or at Cira's theater when it might be buried somewhere near the marina."

"How did you find out about the pouch?"

"Oh, Signor Toriza and I have become the best of friends during the past four years. You might say we've had a mutual exchange of favors." Her lips lifted in a mirthless smile. "I could stomach a lie only so far. I had to make it right with the museum." She nodded at the reconstruction. "And I had to make it right with her. I made her someone she wasn't, and that wasn't fair to her. I had to try to bring her home. So the summer after we left Herculaneum, I flew back here and talked to Toriza. We made a deal. I got him to agree to let me redo the reconstruction of Giulia and to promise that he would never put her on exhibition until I gave the word."

"And the reconstruction in the case outside?"

"No skull. A bust I sculpted to match the reconstruction we were replacing. After all the publicity we couldn't just let her disappear. She had to be on display."

"I'm surprised Signor Toriza was willing to compromise his principles by suppressing the reconstruction."

"Money. I paid him well." She shrugged. "Not in cash. The sweat of my brow. I told you, we made a deal."

"What kind of deal?"

"Every few months he'd send me one of his skulls to reconstruct. Over the last few years he's acquired one of the best collections of ancient reconstructions in the world."

"How did you do it? You're always overworked."

"I lied. I paid the piper." She met Jane's gaze. "And I'd do it again. Because there was always the chance as long as I didn't feed the flames that you'd forget about Cira and get on with your life. That was worth a few all-nighters to finish Toriza's reconstructions."

"More than a few. Eleven. Did Joe know?"

Eve shook her head. "My lie. My price." She paused. "What are you feeling? Are you angry with me?"

Jane didn't know what she was feeling. She was too stunned to sort out the emotions. "Not . . . angry. You shouldn't have done it, Eve."

"Perhaps if I hadn't been so tired and worried, I wouldn't have made the same decision. No, I won't give myself excuses. I gave you four years to rid yourself of an obsession and have a normal life. Do you know how precious that is? I do. I never had a normal life. I wanted to give you that gift." She paused. "I realize you've always thought you came second with me after Bonnie."

"I told you it didn't matter to me."

"It matters. You were never second, just different. I lied, I violated my professional ethics, and I worked myself to exhaustion for you. Maybe this will show you how much I care for you." She shrugged wearily. "And maybe it won't." She turned and opened the door. "Come on. Toriza is waiting to close up."

"Eve."

Eve looked back at Jane.

"You shouldn't have done it." She moistened her lips. "But it doesn't change how I feel about you. Nothing could do that." She stood up, walked across the room, and stopped before her. "How do I know what I would have done in the same circumstances?" She tried to smile. "We're so much alike."

"Not really." Eve reached out and gently caressed her cheek. "But enough to make me proud and fill me with content. Ever since you came to us, you spread a sort of . . . light over Joe and me. I just couldn't stand the thought of that light dimming."

Jane felt the tears stinging her eyes as she wrapped her arms around Eve. "What the hell can I say to that?" She hugged her quickly and stepped back. "Okay, let's get out of here. May I tell Trevor?"

"Why not? He's probably playing all kinds of scenarios in his mind right now." She started to close the door. "He might as well get the right one."

"Wait." Jane took one last look at the reconstruction on the worktable. "She's close, isn't she? But it's not close enough. There were so many statues sculpted of Cira and they didn't have this . . . crudeness. She could—" She turned to Eve. "The measurements have to be so precise in your work. Could you possibly have made a mistake?"

"Do you think I didn't want this to be Cira? An absolute match to the statues would have solved everything. You would have been convinced you'd found her at last and it would have been over. I was very careful. I did the reconstruction over three times and it came out this way every time." She paused. "Have you considered the possibility that the sculptors who did those statues glorified her, that the real Cira was less than their artistry?"

"I suppose that could—" She shook her head. "It's not—" She turned back to the main exhibition room and let Eve shut the workroom door. "It doesn't feel right."

"But you've lived with the mental image of Cira

for so long that any change would seem wrong. Isn't that true?"

Jane nodded slowly. "But I'm too confused now to decide what's truth or fantasy." She started through the exhibit hall. "Maybe it's all fantasy. Except the gold. The gold is real. That's what I have to concentrate on."

"That's why I asked you to come here," Eve said quietly.

"You say no more gold was found in the recovery at the marina?"

"Not with these victims' skeletons."

"No, I mean no chests hidden in any nearby houses?"

Eve shook her head. "But there's so much of Herculaneum still under that layer of rock. I only hoped to give you a starting place or an alternate place to look."

"Thank you. I know you did." Jane sighed. "I only hope the gold isn't buried under that lava flow."

"You have to face the possibility that it could very well be there."

"I won't face it, dammit. If that was Cira, maybe she was trying to get the gold out of town. Maybe she managed to do it." Her hands clenched into fists. "But it isn't her. I *know* it."

"You don't know it. And the gold is too important to stopping those bastards for us to gamble on instinct." Eve started toward the door. "This could stop us cold. The gold was never a sure thing. I wish to hell it was. But we'd better start looking for another solution to pull out of the hat."

\* \* \*

The marina," Trevor murmured as they watched Eve's plane take off. "Even if it's there, it will be difficult as hell to find and get to it. We'd be a lot luckier if it's in Julius's tunnel."

"But we know she was trying to get the gold out of the tunnel. Perhaps she managed to do it."

"And took it to the marina? Maybe that was just an escape attempt. Maybe she grabbed a pouch from wherever she hid it and ran toward the sea."

"What was she doing at the marina? Julius would have kept watch on her. It wouldn't have been safe for her to—"

"You're talking as if that was Cira." He was silent a moment. "You have to admit the chances are pretty strong it might be. Eve was right. Those statues could have been meant to flatter either her or Julius's taste in women."

"I admit it." Her lips tightened. "I can't do anything else." She turned and headed toward the access for private aircraft. "Until Mario gets that scroll deciphered and we learn what Cira has to say. And what if there's no concrete clue to where she hid the gold or meant to hide it? Eve's right, we can't count on the gold. The chances look slimmer than ever of finding it. And that scares the hell out of me." Her lips tightened. "Let's get back to the Run."

"I've been in contact with Bartlett. He said that everything is status quo. No great urgency."

"Every minute is urgent right now and every possibility is important." She glanced back at the sky where Eve's plane had disappeared into the clouds. "Eve realized that or she wouldn't have flown here to see me. It wasn't easy for her."

"I'm surprised you're not more upset with her. She lied to you."

"She did it because she cared about me. How could I be angry with her when she was whipping herself?" She paused. "And I love her. That's the bottom line. Whatever she did, I'd forgive her."

"That's an impressive blanket statement." He opened the door. "It makes me wonder what it would take to be enfolded in that blanket."

"Years of trust, of give and take, of knowing that no matter what happened she'd be there for me." She glanced at him. "Have you ever had someone in your life like that?"

He was silent a moment. "My father. We were . . . friends. When I was a kid, I didn't want anything more than to live on our farm and tend the fields and be just like him."

"A farmer? I can't picture that."

"I liked growing things. I guess all children do."

"And not now?"

He shook his head. "You put your heart and soul into the earth and it can be destroyed in a moment."

She looked at him. The sentence had been spoken almost casually, but his expression was shuttered. "Is that what happened?" She added quickly, "Don't answer. It's none of my business."

"I don't mind talking about it. It was a long time ago." His pace quickened as they crossed the tarmac. "There was a local racist gang who hated my father because he treated his workers well. One night they raided the farm and burned our home and fields. They killed sixteen workers who tried to fight them off. Then they raped and killed my mother and pinned my father to a tree with a pitchfork. He died very slowly."

"My God. But you survived."

"Oh, yes. I annoyed the gang's leader by trying to stab him, and he had me tied up to watch the slaughter. I'm sure he was planning on killing me later but he was interrupted by the soldiers. Our neighbors had seen the fire and smoke and called them out." He stepped aside for her to climb the stairs of the plane. "They said I was lucky. I'll always remember that as a poor choice of words. I didn't feel lucky."

"Jesus." Jane could almost feel the agony, see the horror of that scene and that boy tied up and forced to watch his parents' murder. "Did they catch them?"

He shook his head. "They disappeared into the bush and the government let them go. They didn't want the bad press a trial would have caused. Understandable."

"I don't think it's understandable."

"Neither did I at the time. It was one of the reasons that I was considered incorrigible during the first year I was in the orphanage. But then I adjusted and learned patience. My father always said that patience won the day."

"Not if that murderer went unpunished."

"I didn't say he went unpunished. Right before I went to Colombia the gang leader came to a nasty end. Someone tied him down, castrated him, and let him bleed to death." He smiled. "Isn't it wonderful how fate has a way of taking a hand?"

"Wonderful," she echoed as she gazed at him. She had never been more aware of how lethal Trevor could be. On the surface he was urbane and sophisticated, and it made her tend to forget the violent experiences in his background. "And they never found out who did it?"

"Some old enemy, they presumed. They didn't look too hard. Considering the delicate balance of the politics at the time, they didn't want to stir up trouble." He shut the cabin door. "Better sit down and buckle up. We'll get this show on the road."

She watched him head toward the cockpit. In the last few moments she had found out more about Trevor than ever before. She wasn't sure if that was good or bad. Now that she could picture the boy he had been, she wasn't sure she would be able to look at him without remembering. It made her heart ache for him.

"No." Trevor was looking over his shoulder, reading her expression. "That's not what I want from you. Sex, maybe even friendship. But not pity. I'm no Mike, who you had to nurture and protect. You asked a question and I answered because it's not fair that I know more about you than you do about me. Now we're even." He disappeared into the cockpit.

Not exactly even, she thought. He knew a lot about her, but she had never confided anything as intimate and hurtful as the story he had just told her.

Stop it. He didn't want pity, and she would have hated it herself. As Trevor had said, that was a long time ago and that boy had grown up and grown armor and fangs.

MacDuff met them at the helicopter when it landed at the Run. "A successful trip?"

"Yes and no," Jane said. "We may have found Cira."

He stiffened. "What?"

"There's a reconstruction in a museum in Naples that resembles her. Her skeleton was found at the marina. Along with a pouch of gold coins."

"Interesting."

Interested wasn't the description she'd give for his expression, Jane thought. He appeared wary, intent, and she could almost hear the thought processes clicking behind that face.

"How close a resemblance?" he asked.

"Close enough to mistake for Cira at first glance," Trevor said. "Or so Jane said. I wasn't privy to the viewing. The reconstruction on exhibition was the counterfeit done by Eve four years ago."

"But according to the news stories and the photo taken of that reconstruction, it looked nothing like—" He stopped. "She faked it?"

"She thought it was for my own good," Jane said defensively. "She would never have— Why am I explaining anything to you?"

"I have no idea," MacDuff said. "I'm sure she had good reasons for what she did." He paused. "How close a resemblance?"

"As Trevor said, at first glance . . ." She shrugged. "But the features are cruder; there are subtle differences. I'm not going to believe it's Cira. Not yet."

"It's always best to take every new fact with a grain of salt," MacDuff said. "Don't just jump in with both feet until you've explored all possibilities."

"And if the chest of gold was hidden in the marina, it's going to make retrieval tough," Trevor said.

MacDuff nodded. "Almost impossible, considering the time factor." His gaze shifted back to Jane. "And you believe the gold might be there?"

"I don't know. The gold coins . . . I don't want to believe it, but I'm afraid not to. As you said, the time factor.

"How is Jock?" Jane asked.

"The same. Not good. But not worse." He hesitated. "Or maybe not the same. I have a feeling something weird's going on in his head." He turned and headed for the stable. "At any rate, I'm keeping an eye on him."

"He seems distinctly skeptical," Jane said to Trevor as she started for the front door. "Since it's the first solid clue we have to Cira, I'm a little surprised."

"It's probably not solid enough for him. He doesn't want us to waste time on long shots. He wants Reilly."

"No more than we do." She opened the door. "I'm going to go up and check on Mario. I'll see you later."

"Where?"

She looked at him.

"Your bed or mine?"

"Pushy."

"I've learned you never take a step back if you've made a successful advance. And last night was damn successful."

Successful wasn't the word. And just looking at him brought back the eroticism of those hours. "Maybe we should slow down."

He shook his head.

Why was she being so hesitant? It wasn't like her. She was usually bold and decisive.

Because it had been too good. There had been times when she had lost control, and that had frightened her. Get over it. She had slept with him because she had realized how fragile life could be and she didn't want to miss one instant of it. She had reached out and grabbed the brass ring and it had not disappointed her. She wanted him just as much now as she had last night. More. Because she knew what waited for her now. And, God knew, tonight she needed a distraction as strong as the one Trevor was offering.

"Your bed." She started up the staircase. "But I don't know how long I'll be with Mario."

"I'll wait." He headed down the hall. "And I have a few things to check out myself."

"What?"

"Brenner, to see if he's managed to find out anything more." He smiled back at her. "Then Demonidas. We didn't get a chance to do any research this morning before Eve called."

"He probably doesn't exist," she said wearily. "It was only a dream. And this Giulia from the marina is more than likely Cira."

He shook his head. "You're tired or you wouldn't be this negative. We're going to give old Demonidas his shot." The door of the library closed behind him.

She *was* tired. And discouraged. She didn't want that poor girl in the museum to be Cira. Yet the coincidence was overwhelming, and she couldn't deny the truth that it might be.

But that girl wasn't *her* Cira, dammit. Not the woman who had lived in her mind and imagination for the last four years.

Then find out the truth. Forget about dreams and give Mario a little more time to give her the reality she needed.

Any progress?" Mario asked when she came in to the study after knocking.

"A skeleton found in the marina that looked like Cira." She walked over to stare at the statue by the window. The determination, the humor, the strength in that face was the Cira she knew. "I suppose it could be her. But what was she doing in the marina if she was in that tunnel on Julius's estate when she wrote those scrolls?" She turned back to him. "How much longer is it going to take you to finish?"

"Not long." He leaned back and rubbed his eyes. "I've been able to piece in most of the missing words. Some of it was guesswork, but I've got the hang of it now."

"When?"

"Don't push me, Jane. I've already stopped training with Trevor and MacDuff to work full-time on it. It will get done as quickly as I can do it."

"Sorry." She glanced back at the statue. "Have you gotten far enough along to tell if it's going to help us?"

"I can tell you it was written in haste and she was planning to leave the tunnel that day."

"The day of the eruption—"

"We don't know that. There's no date on this scroll. It could have been written days before the eruption. She could have left the tunnel and been at the marina that day."

"I guess you're right." Because she'd dreamed Cira was in that tunnel during the catastrophe didn't mean it was true. "And the mention of the gold?"

"Nothing definite."

"Or a ship?"

He gazed at her curiously. "No. Why?"

She wasn't about to confide in Mario about those dreams that were taking on less and less substance. "If she was at the marina, there must have been a reason."

"Survival. She was at the theater and ran for her life."

The logical answer. She should accept it instead of fighting and searching for an alternate solution. Admit that woman in the marina was the dead end Eve had claimed. "Will you have it done by tomorrow?"

"There's a good chance. If I don't sleep." He smiled faintly. "No kindly protest at my sacrifice?"

"It's your decision. I'm selfish enough to want to know right away. It's not going to hurt you to sleep after you finish it." She added soberly, "In my heart I believe I always thought we'd find the gold, and now I'm out to sea and looking for a life raft. I don't know which way to go and I feel helpless. We have to stop this, Mario."

"I'm working as fast as I can."

"I know you are." She headed for the door. "I'll check in with you tomorrow."

"I'm sure you will." He looked back at the scroll. "Good night, Jane. Sleep well."

She didn't miss the faint sarcasm in his tone. She couldn't blame him, but it wasn't characteristic of the Mario she had met when she'd first come here. But then, Mario had changed, forged in the fire of tragedy and loss. He had lost all boyishness and softness, and she wasn't sure she'd recognize the Mario who'd emerge after this was over.

Had she changed too? Probably. Mike's death and this horror hanging over them had shaken her to her marrow. And she'd never had a sexual experience as intense as the one she'd shared with Trevor.

Trevor.

*Intense* wasn't the word for what was between them. Even thinking about him was causing her body to ready. To hell with worrying about how much she or anyone else was changing. Who knew what was going to happen tomorrow. They had to live every moment while they had the chance.

His bedroom. He'd be waiting, he said.

But she'd been with Mario less than ten minutes, and Trevor was probably not finished with the things he had to do. She'd go to her own room and shower and then go to him.

Go to him. Go to his bed. Her pace quickened as she walked down the hall. Electric torches gleamed on the stone walls, casting triangular shadows upward on the arched wooden ceiling and on still another of the many faded tapestries that graced the hall. The MacDuffs certainly liked their tapestries. . . .

It would be strange going to an assignation in this ancient castle. Jesus, she almost felt like the mistress of old Angus MacDuff. If he'd had a mistress. Most of the nobility did, but maybe Angus was the exception. She'd have to ask MacDuff tomorrow.

Her bedroom was dark and she tossed her purse on the chair by the door before reaching for the light switch.

"Don't turn it on."

She froze.

"Don't be afraid. I'm not going to hurt you."

*Jock.*

Her heart was pounding, but she drew a deep breath and turned to the corner of the room from where he'd spoken. The moonlight pouring in the window was faint and it was a moment before she could make him out. He was sitting on the floor, his arms linked about his knees. "What are you doing here, Jock?"

"I wanted to talk to you." She could see his hands clench into fists. "I had to talk to you."

"And it couldn't have waited until tomorrow?"

"No." He was silent a moment. "I was angry with you. I didn't like what you said. For a little while I wanted to hurt you. I didn't tell the laird that. He'd get upset with me if I hurt you."

"Not nearly as much as I would."

"But you couldn't get upset; you'd be dead."

Was there a touch of black humor in those words? It was impossible to tell since she couldn't see his expression. "Does hurt automatically mean killing, Jock?"

"It turns out that way. It happens so fast. . . ."

"What did you want to talk to me about?"

"Rei—Reilly." He stopped and then said again, "Reilly. It's hard for me to talk about him. He—doesn't—want me—to do it."

"But you're doing it anyway. That makes you stronger than he is."

"Not yet. Someday."

"When?"

"When he's dead. When I kill him." The words were spoken with utmost simplicity.

"You don't have to kill him, Jock. Just tell us where he is and we'll let the authorities take care of it."

He shook his head. "I have to do it. It has to be me."

"Why?"

"Because if I don't, the laird will try to do it for me. He won't wait for anyone else. He's . . . angry with him."

"Because he's an evil man."

"Satan. If there's a Satan, it's—Reilly."

"Just tell us where he is."

"I—don't know."

"You have to know."

"Whenever I try to think of it—my head—it hurts so bad I think it's going to explode."

"Try."

"I tried last night." He was silent. "I got—pictures. Flashes. Nothing else." He paused. "But maybe—if I went back I might remember."

"Back to Colorado?"

"Not Colorado."

"That's where they found you."

"Not Colorado. North. Maybe . . . Idaho?"

She felt a leap of hope. "You remember that much? Where?"

He shook his head. "I have to go back."

It was a step closer than they'd been before. "Then we'll go back. I'll talk to Trevor."

"Right away."

"Tonight."

He rose to his feet. "And we have to find Reilly soon or the laird will start looking for him. He's not going to wait much longer."

"We'll start out as soon as we can make arrangements." She frowned, thinking about it. "But no one can know you're with us or Reilly might decide that his position is compromised and flee."

"He won't think that."

"Why not?"

"He probably already knows I'm here and that I haven't been able to tell the laird anything. He'll believe he's safe."

"Why would he believe that?"

"Because he told me I'd die if I told anyone where he was."

"You mean he'd kill you."

"No, I'd just die. My heart would stop beating and I'd die."

"That's crazy."

"No, I saw it happen. Reilly showed—me." He touched his chest. "And I felt my heart pound and pound and I knew that it would stop if he told me it would."

God, it sounded like voodoo. "Only if you believe it. Only if you let him win. If you're strong, it can't happen."

"I hope I'll be strong enough. I have to kill Reilly before he kills the laird." He headed for the door. "I wanted to die once, but the laird wouldn't let me. Now there are times when I don't mind being alive.

Sometimes I even forget about—" He opened the door. "I'll come to you tomorrow morning."

"Wait. Why didn't you go to MacDuff instead of me?"

"Because I have to do what the laird says. He'd want to go after Reilly alone, and if I found Reilly, he'd keep me from him because he wants to protect me. If you and Trevor are with us, you won't do that. I'll get my chance."

"I'd try to protect you, Jock."

He was silhouetted against the light of the hall as he opened the door. "Not like he will." The next moment he was gone.

She stood there a moment, her mind whirling with a mixture of excitement and hope. There was no guarantee that Jock would remember Reilly's location, but it was possible. He seemed to be coming back, and he'd already remembered it wasn't in Colorado and might be Idaho.

And his answer when she'd asked him why he hadn't gone to MacDuff had shown a maturity and perception that surprised her. He had clearly thought about the consequences and worked out his own solution. If he'd come that far, then there was hope indeed.

And they had to act on the gift he'd given them right away. Only tonight she'd told Mario how helpless she felt about finding another avenue to explore since discovering the gold was now in question. Well, now they had an opportunity, and they had to grab it and run with it.

But there were many pitfalls to just taking Jock

back to the U.S. where MacDuff had found him with no preparations for fallout. They'd need all the help they could get.

She opened the door and went to the library to find Trevor.

# 16

"We can't just wander around the U.S. on the chance Jock will find Reilly," Trevor said. "The Run is being watched by Grozak. We take off and we'll be followed. If we're followed, then Grozak will tell Reilly, and Reilly will close the deal and give Grozak what he wants."

"Jock said that Reilly won't be worried about him," Jane said.

"I won't bet on it. Jock broke through his training to escape Reilly. Reilly would have to be a true egomaniac to be positive that he wouldn't ignore that self-destruct command."

"Christ, that couldn't happen, could it?" She shook her head. "It violates every law of self-preservation."

"I've heard of suicide experiments by the Nazis in World War Two that were supposed to be successful.

The mind can be a powerful weapon. At any rate, Jock believes it."

"And he's willing to risk his life to save MacDuff." She was silent a moment. "And we're going to let him do it."

"To possibly save several thousand more people than Jock's laird."

"I know that. Why do you think I'm here? But I don't have to like it." Her hands clenched on the arms of the chair. "So how do we make it work? How do we get away from here without letting Grozak know we're gone?"

"With great difficulty."

"How?"

"I have to think about it. And there's Venable, who's practically parking on our doorstep. We can't bring him into it or there would be no hope of keeping our departure secret. We can't afford any leaks."

"It's the CIA, for heaven's sake. They should be able to handle a clandestine operation."

He looked at her without replying.

No, Jock had trusted her, and she didn't want to shift that responsibility to strangers either. "Okay, no ideas?"

"I have a few glimmers." He leaned back in his chair. "Let me think about it."

"Can we use MacDuff?"

He smiled. "He'd deny that anyone could use him. But we'll almost certainly have to bring him into the mix. We'd have to kidnap Jock to get him away from his laird."

"I'm not sure about that. He didn't want Mac-Duff near Reilly."

"And you believe MacDuff wouldn't raise hell and track us down if we tried to interfere with Jock without his supervision?"

"No, I guess not."

"And I made a deal with MacDuff about Reilly."

"Reilly's head on a platter?"

"Let's say I promised him that if I found Reilly, he'd get his chance at him." He tilted his head. "It was a bargain I had no qualms about making considering Reilly's character." He reached for the phone. "Sorry to wake you, Bartlett. We have a situation. Will you come to the library?" He hung up. "Don't talk to Eve or Quinn for the time being, Jane."

"Why not?"

"When I called Venable tonight, he said that his tech crew intercepted an unknown electronic signal in the area yesterday. Grozak may have been able to get a fix to tap the phone line."

"That's great," she said in disgust. "That's all we need right now."

"We'll get around it. We may even be able to use it." He spoke to Bartlett as he came in to the room. "We're going to the U.S."

"You want me to arrange transport?"

"Not yet. I'll let you know. We can't be seen leaving here, so we may have to meet the pilot somewhere away from the Run. We'll have to use a different pilot this time. Probably Kimbrough. He operates out of Paris."

"When do we leave?"

"You don't leave. You stay here."

Bartlett frowned. "Why should I? I'm doing nothing here. I've been very bored lately."

"I've an idea that that won't continue." He turned to Jane. "You'd better get to bed."

Was he trying to get rid of her?

He shook his head as he saw her expression. "Tomorrow may be rough sledding. You can stay if you like, but I'm just going to go over the routine running of the security of the castle and my business affairs with Bartlett." He smiled faintly. "I promise I'm not going to go anywhere without you."

She stood up. "You bet you aren't." She headed for the door. "When are you going to talk to MacDuff? I want to be there."

"Eight?"

She nodded. "Eight."

But it was only a little after six the next morning when Bartlett knocked on her door. "I'm sorry to wake you," he said apologetically. "But MacDuff just blew into the library like a hurricane and Trevor sent me to get you."

"I'll be right there." She jumped out of bed and grabbed her robe. "Give me a minute to wash my face."

"I'll wait." He watched her run to the bathroom and called after her. "But MacDuff seems very impatient. He's not waiting for anyone to vent. I believe Jock must have decided to break his news to him."

"I'm not surprised." She was dabbing at her damp face with a towel as she came out of the bathroom and headed for the door. "I don't know how unpredictable Jock was before, but he's volatile as hell now."

"No more than MacDuff," Bartlett murmured as he hurried after her.

She saw what he meant when she entered the library. MacDuff was standing, hovering over Trevor like the wrath of God. His lips were tight and his eyes glittering as he turned to her. "Why did I have to hear it from Jock? Were you trying to shut me out?"

"I considered it. Jock didn't really want you along," she said curtly. "But Trevor said he'd made a deal."

"How honorable," MacDuff said with sarcasm. "Am I supposed to be grateful? Our deal was for you to find Reilly. It turns out Jock is going to find Reilly for me. I don't need you."

"But Jock won't find Reilly for you," Jane said. "He's afraid for you. He wants us along."

"So he told me." He scowled. "I could push him."

"And do you want to do that?" Trevor asked. "He appears to be pretty finely balanced. He could break or slip over the edge."

MacDuff didn't speak for a moment. "Dammit, I don't want you interfering."

"Tough," Jane said. "You're not the only one affected by that scumbag. Jock wants us and we're going." She met his gaze. "And I don't care about your deal with Trevor. You're apparently willing to disregard it to get rid of us."

"True," Trevor murmured.

MacDuff continued to glare at her for another moment before he said through his teeth, "Very well. We go together. But I don't promise it's going to stay that way. If Jock tells me where I can find Reilly, I'll leave you in my dust."

"Then I think it would be fair for us to have the same choice," Trevor said. "But I believe we should put our minds to getting away from here unnoticed rather than what will happen after we zero in on Reilly."

"No CIA," MacDuff said flatly. "Nothing that will tip Reilly off and scare him into making a move to stop us."

"No argument," Trevor said. "And Grozak is watching the castle—there's a good chance he has our phone tapped now. We can't just call for a helicopter to pick us up."

"No, we can't." MacDuff turned on his heel. "Pack what you have to carry and meet me at the stable in an hour."

"What?"

"You heard me." MacDuff glanced over his shoulder. "If we have to leave, we'll leave."

"I told you that we—"

"We'll leave. This is *my* castle, *my* land. I won't be kept a prisoner by anyone. Not your fine CIA or Grozak or anyone else."

Jane flinched as the door slammed behind him. "He's a little irate, isn't he? But he doesn't seem to have a problem with the logistics of the situation. Do you think he can come up with a way to get out?"

"Evidently he thinks he can. It won't hurt to meet him at the stable and see what he has to say once he's cooled down." He got up from his chair. "Get moving. Pack and meet me in the hall. Stop by and give a heads-up to Mario and tell him we'll be in touch."

"What are you going to be doing?"

"Bartlett and I have set up a little diversion." He smiled at Bartlett. "We should have enough time to do the final."

She moved toward the door. "I don't know how Mario's going to take this. He's not pleased about being stuck in that study since his father was killed."

"Too bad. You seem to be the negotiator these days." He crooked his finger for Bartlett to come in. "Persuade him."

Persuade him, she thought in exasperation as she climbed the staircase. Mario was bound and determined to avenge his father, and she was supposed to tell him he should forget it and stay at his desk. The only thing that had kept him at work so far had been the promise of making him competent enough to exact that revenge successfully. Now his work was almost completed and they were leaving him to—

She stopped outside Mario's study and drew a deep breath before she knocked on the door.

No," Mario said curtly. "Hell, no. I'm going with you."

"Mario, we don't even know where we're going or whether we'll find Grozak or Reilly."

"You have a lead." He got to his feet. "And that's more than you had before."

"You can't help."

"How do you know?" He took the top paper from the pile on his desk and shoved it into his pocket. "I'm going." He shoveled the rest of the papers into the top drawer. "No arguments."

"I am going to argue. And so will Trevor."

"As you please." He patted his pocket. "But you're not going to make any headway. And you might ruin your chance of reading the translation I just finished."

She stiffened. "You finished it?"

He nodded. "And very interesting it is. There were a few surprises."

"Did she mention the gold?"

"Absolutely." He headed for the bedroom. "I have to brush my teeth and take a shower. I've been working all night. I'll meet you at the stable."

"Mario, dammit, what did she say?"

He shook his head. "If I've learned one thing from this horror, it's that weapons are important, even against the people you believe are your friends. We'll talk about Cira after we find a way to get Grozak and Reilly."

"We may be able to negotiate with Reilly if you can tell us where the gold may be."

"I don't want to negotiate. I want to chop off those bastards' heads like they did my father's." His lips tightened grimly. "Ugly, isn't it? The priests would be praying for my soul now." He opened his bedroom door. "But then, no one was there to pray for my father's soul, were they?"

"We're not going to put up with this, Mario. We can't. Trevor will take that translation away from you in the blink of an eye."

"If he can find it. By the time you go get him I'll have it tucked away so well that Sherlock Holmes wouldn't be able to come up with it. Maybe I'll even destroy it and re-create it later."

She stared after him for a moment with a mixture of pity and frustration before heading for the door. He'd made up his mind and was willing to withhold Cira's scroll to get his way. In her heart she couldn't blame him. She wasn't sure she wouldn't have done the same thing.


Jock was standing in the doorway of the stable when Jane and Trevor arrived an hour later. "The laird said to tell you he'd be back soon."

"Where is he?"

"He had to talk to the guards. He said it was important." He turned to Jane. "He's not angry with me. I thought he would be, but he's angry with you instead. I'm sorry."

"It's not your fault. He'll just have to get over it." She watched MacDuff stride toward them. "He's feeling as frustrated as the rest of us, and he cares about you."

"My, how generous," Trevor murmured.

"It doesn't take generosity. Understanding, maybe.

MacDuff may be hard, but he's doing all this for Jock. In a way, that's admirable."

"I'll admire him too, if he can get us out of here," Trevor said. "What about it, Jock? Can he do it?"

"Of course." Jock said to Jane, "I watered my plants, but do you think you could get that Bartlett to do it again in a few days if we don't come back?"

"I'm sure he'll be glad to." She turned and started back to the castle. "I'll run back and tell him to—"

"Where are you going?" MacDuff was only a few feet away.

"Bartlett needs to be told to water Jock's plants."

"I've already told Patrick," MacDuff said. "No one else need be involved in Jock's business."

"What were you telling the guards?" Trevor asked.

"That they're to behave absolutely normally, as if we were still here."

"Can you trust them?"

MacDuff gave him a scornful glance. "Naturally. They're my people. If anyone approaches the castle, they're to deny entrance." He paused. "Even if they claim to be CIA."

"I've no objection. I phoned Venable this morning and told him that he might not hear from me for a day or two since Mario was close to finishing the scrolls and everything was on hold until we found out if we had anything to work with to find the gold."

"And what if he phones you?"

"Bartlett and I worked out a voice-over substitute last night, and he'll take the calls."

"What do you mean?" Jane asked.

"It's a very clever little gadget you attach to the phone and it makes anyone talking on it sound exactly like you." He smiled. "I assure you it works. It's not the first time Bartlett has had to cover for me."

"That doesn't surprise me," Jane said. She braced herself and said to MacDuff,  "Mario is coming with us."

"The devil he is." He whirled on Trevor. "What the hell are you doing?"

"Don't blame me." Trevor held up his hands. "I had the same reaction, but Jane says that Mario finished the scroll and may have a lead on the gold. He won't come through with the info if we leave him behind."

"A lead on the gold," MacDuff repeated. "Do you believe he's telling the truth?"

Jane nodded. "But I'm not sure. He's changed. He might even be manipulating us to suit himself."

"To get his father's killer." MacDuff was silent a moment, thinking. "The gold is important. If Mario comes, you'll have to be responsible for him not getting in the way, Trevor. I'm going to be too busy with Jock to hold his hand."

"Mario's not a child," Jane said. "You can reason with him."

"Like you did?" MacDuff asked.

"That's different. We were closing him out. Any of us would have felt the same. And he had an ace in the hole with the gold. It stopped me in my tracks.

As you say, it's important." She met his gaze. "How important is it to you? I thought you were all about righting wrongs."

"I'm no Galahad. Yes, I'm going after Reilly." He glanced across the courtyard at the castle. "But Trevor promised me a share of that gold, and I'm going to need it. I'm going to *have* it."

"Not if we can work a deal with Reilly," Jane said. "If we can't find a way to get that bastard, we'll bargain. And I don't care about your fine, great castle, MacDuff."

"You don't have to," MacDuff said. "I care enough for all of us." He nodded at Mario coming down the steps. "And here's your scholar who wants to be a superhero. I'm tempted to just squeeze the information out of him and leave him here. And you can't tell me you don't feel the same way, Trevor."

"It occurred to me," Trevor said. "But he has a mission, and it would take time to shake him up enough to—"

"No," Jane said.

MacDuff shrugged. "It appears that's the end of it for now. But there will be more opportunities later if he's a problem." He turned away and entered the stable. "Tell him to get his ass moving if he's coming with us, Trevor. Come along, Jock."

Jane nodded quickly at Mario before hurrying after MacDuff and Jock as they strode down the stall-lined corridor. "Where are we going?"

"Angus's place," Jock said. "Isn't that right?"

"Aye," MacDuff said. "And a fine cozy place it is."

He went in the third stall from the end. "If you don't mind mud and the stink of mold." He moved a tackle box and three saddles to open a dirt-encrusted trapdoor. "Though in the old days the stink would have been considerably more disgusting. Angus made sure no one wanted to mess around in here. There was always a layer of manure covering the floor."

"And where does this door lead?" Trevor had caught up with them and was peering down into the darkness. "Stairs . . ."

"Yes, they wind down at an angle and reach the bottom of the cliff where it meets the sea." MacDuff opened a box beside the trapdoor and grabbed a flashlight from the several the box contained. "Everyone take a flashlight. There are no lights, and the stairs curve too much to rely on a leader with one flashlight. You'd round a curve and find yourself in the dark, and those steps are wet and slippery as glass." But MacDuff was negotiating the winding stairs surely, quickly. "Be careful or you'll end up with a broken head. My great-grandfather got a little tipsy one night and took a fall that laid him up for two years. He almost died before he crawled back up the stairs to the stable."

"No one was with him?"

"Of course not. Angus's passage is the family secret, passed on from father to son. Angus built it at the same time he built the castle. It was to be an escape hatch that led to the sea, and there's another passage that doubles back to the hill outside the gates that would let him get behind an attacking army. He lived in perilous times and always wanted to be prepared."

"That was centuries ago." Lord, the steps were slippery, Jane thought as she balanced herself by holding on to the curving wall. They seemed to lead down and down. . . . "And you're telling me that no one else knew about it?"

"There's such a thing as honor. We were all bound not to tell anyone outside the immediate family. In later years it wasn't so crucial, but we're a family who believes in tradition."

"It appears Jock knew about it."

"He didn't until I brought him back from Colorado. And Jock would rather die than tell anything I don't want him to. Two yards and veer left. That's where it branches off and becomes a tunnel leading to the hills."

She dimly saw the branch off to the right as she veered left as he'd told her. "How much farther?"

"Not far. The steps get steeper here as they approach the surf. Be careful."

"And what are we going to do when we reach the sea?" Trevor asked. "Swim?"

"Actually, Angus was strong enough to swim the four miles around the headland, but his descendants weren't quite that Spartan. There's a motorboat in a camouflaged boat deck at the foot of the steps. We'll use oars, not the motor, and if we keep close to the cliffs, we should be able to reach a safe distance in twenty minutes."

"And what then?" Trevor asked.

"I shouldn't have to do everything for you,"

MacDuff said. "I have Colin, one of the villagers, meeting us with a car to take us to Aberdeen. I trust you can arrange for transport to the U.S. from there?"

"I'll call Kimbrough in Paris as soon as we get on the road. I haven't used him in a few years and Grozak won't have a fix on him."

"How long will it take him to get here?"

"If he's not on another job, a few hours. If he is, I'll phone someone else."

Jane heard Mario cry out and then begin cursing behind her. "Dammit, how much farther, MacDuff? I almost broke my ankle."

"Too bad," MacDuff said. "The uninvited have no right to complain."

Neither Trevor nor she had been invited either. She wondered what MacDuff would—

She heard a watery slushing ahead of her. "What's that?"

"The bottom steps are covered with water when the tide comes in," MacDuff called back from around a curve in the stair. "I'm having to wade through it to get to the boat. Nothing to worry about." He added slyly, "Except the occasional eel or crab that manages to come in with the tide. You'll be okay. You're not barefoot."

"How comforting." She turned the corner of the spiral and saw MacDuff and Jock ahead of her. They were thigh-high in water as they waded down the final steps toward a sleek black-and-cream motorboat tied to a steel post. A short distance away she could see a narrow opening leading to the sea.

"Okay?" Trevor was a few steps behind her. She hadn't realized she had stopped.

She nodded and again started down the steps, holding her small duffel over her shoulder.

Three steps down she was waist-high in cold salt water that sent a shock through her. She suppressed a gasp and kept on going. A moment later she had reached MacDuff and Jock, who were climbing onto the boat.

Jock turned and held out his hand. "Give me your duffel and I'll pull you up."

"Thanks." She threw him the duffel and then let him pull her on board. MacDuff was opening a box by the steering wheel and getting out oars. "You know your way pretty well down here, Jock."

"The laird wanted me with him when we first came back here. He had work to do and he didn't want me to be alone."

Because Jock had been suicidal and MacDuff had been afraid to leave him. "I'm sure you were a great help."

"I tried," Jock said gravely. "I did what he told me, but I didn't know all the things that Angus and the laird knew. It was Angus's place, Angus's room."

"Room?"

"All those steps and the dark . . . I got lost. My head was all fuzzy and the laird had to pull me out of the water once."

Lost? Was he speaking mentally or—

"Jock, I need you," MacDuff called, and Jock immediately went to him.

"You're soaking wet." Trevor was climbing onto the boat. "Any towels, MacDuff?"

"In the box under the wheel." MacDuff handed Jock an oar. "She can dry off later. Let's get out of here."

"I can row," Mario said as he got on the boat. "I crewed at my university."

"By all means. Earn your way." MacDuff gave him an oar. "But you'll find this rowing a bit more unwieldy."

Trevor found the towel and handed it to her. "Dry off. We don't need you sick."

"I'm okay." She tried to absorb a little of the water from her clothes with the towel. She made a face. "Nary an eel, MacDuff."

"Really? How fortunate."

"Let's hope it continues that way." Trevor untied the boat. "Get us out of here, MacDuff."


Kimbrough met them at the airport outside Aberdeen where Trevor had landed when they'd come from Harvard. He was a small, fortyish man and all business. "Ready to take off," he told Trevor. "I've filed a phony flight plan to New Orleans. We'll have to take on fuel in Chicago, but we should arrive in Denver in about nine hours."

"Good." He turned to MacDuff. "You said you had a house outside Denver that you used when you came after Jock. Do you think it would help jog his memory to be in semifamiliar surroundings?"

"I have no idea. But it couldn't hurt. We have to

have a place to start. I'll phone the leasing company once I'm on the plane."

"You can't do that. They'll recognize your name from when you were there before. We can't have any way to trace—"

"They'll recognize the name of Daniel Pilton. Do you think I'd have taken a chance on Reilly knowing where I took Jock?" He gestured to Jock and Mario. "Get on the plane. I'll be right with you." After Jock and Mario had disappeared into the plane he said grimly, "For all I know, Jock will freeze up once he's back in Reilly's backyard."

"Isn't this a waste of time? According to Jock, Colorado isn't Reilly's backyard," Jane said. "He mentioned Idaho."

"But we don't know where to start there. He's too damn vague about it." MacDuff's lips tightened. "Believe me, he's not vague about Colorado. If you could have seen him during that month after I found him, you'd realize that."

"But you said he didn't have any idea what he was doing there."

"I didn't push it. Whatever happened there was enough to shove him over the edge." He started up the steps. "He had enough trauma to get over without my digging into that wound."

"You might have to do it," Jane said as she followed him up the steps. "If he doesn't remember that, how can he remember what went before?"

"My God, you're hard," MacDuff said as he disappeared into the plane. "And I thought I was being callous."

Was she hard? The words she had spoken had come without thinking. She wanted the best for Jock. She'd help him if she could, but the importance of finding Reilly outweighed every other consideration. So maybe she was as hard as MacDuff thought.

"The bastard hurt you," Trevor said roughly from behind her on the steps. "Screw him."

"No." She tried to smile. "He's probably right. I've never been the gentlest person in the world. I'm not sweet or tolerant. I was even rough on Mike when he wasn't behaving the way I thought he should."

"Good God, now you're having a backlash and feeling guilty?" He stopped her with a hand on her shoulder before she could enter the plane. "No, you're not sweet. You're intolerant as hell. You may be gentle on occasion but it's usually reserved for dogs and Eve and Quinn." He stared her directly in the eye. "But you're honest and smart and you make me feel as if I'm looking at a sunrise every time I see you smile."

She couldn't speak for a moment. "Oh." She didn't know what to say. "How . . . poetic. And completely unlike you."

"I agree." He smiled. "So I'll temper it by saying you're probably also the best lay I ever had and I'm shallow enough to have wished Jock didn't have his breakthrough on a night when I was planning on screwing the hell out of you. How's that for frankness?" He pushed her through the doorway of the plane. "More later. I have to go up front and talk to Kimbrough."

"I have to call Eve."

"I expected that. It's actually best you phone them. There's no telling what they'd do if they didn't hear from you or couldn't reach you. But you can't tell them where we are or what we're doing. Just let them know you're safe and you'll contact them later. Agreed?"

Jane thought about it. "For now. They'll be upset with me, but there's not much to tell anyway. But I won't keep them in the dark for long."

"I hope to hell you won't have to. Either we find out what we need from Jock or we don't. But wait until we land in Chicago to make the call."

She watched him walk down the aisle as she sat down beside Mario. Trevor had been kind and comforting, and it had surprised her in this tense moment. So much of their relationship was based on the sexual attraction that had dominated them both for years. Even now she could feel that response that quickened her pulse as she gazed at him. But now there was more than that mindless heat; there was warmth. She forced herself to shift her eyes away from Trevor. "You've been very quiet since we left."

"I decided it would be foolish to try to join in the conversation when no one wants to hear me." Mario made a face. "I managed to push my way into this trip, but I'm not welcome. So I'll watch and listen and find a way to make my contribution."

"Contribution?" Jane repeated. "You didn't sound like you were opting for a joint operation."

"I'm not foolish. I know my limitations." He gazed at Jock. "But he has more limitations than I do. We're risking a lot on the chance that he won't shatter."

"We don't have a choice." She paused. "Unless you decide to give us something to negotiate with."

He shook his head. "You don't understand. I'm not callous. I don't want to cause a catastrophe like 9/11. But I have to have my chance at those sons of bitches." He leaned back in the seat and closed his eyes. "Now I'm going to take a nap. So don't keep jabbing at me. It's not going to work."

"I'll keep jabbing and jabbing and jabbing," she said. "Maybe sometime in a moment of mental clarity you'll realize that chance isn't worth the price."

He didn't answer and kept his eyes closed. He was obviously going to ignore her.

Well, let him, she thought. She'd get her opportunity to nag at him when they reached Colorado. She smiled ruefully at the thought. MacDuff had accused her of pushing Jock, and now she was doing the same to Mario. Evidently her period of self-doubt had vanished with those words Trevor had spoken.

No, those words had warmed her, but she had bounced back quickly because that was her nature. All her life indecision had been the enemy. You had to go forward, not take a step back or stay in place. She didn't know any other way.

So to the devil with MacDuff and Mario. She'd do

what she'd always done. She'd try to shape her
world to suit herself. It was the only way to—

"Come with me." Trevor was standing beside her.
"I need to talk to you."

"Why should—" She broke off as she saw his expression, and got to her feet and followed him
toward the cockpit. "Problem?"

"Maybe." His lips were tight. "I just got a call from
Venable. He said one sentence and hung up: 'Sorry,
I warned her.'"

"What's that supposed to—"

"Call Eve," he said. "Now. See if she knows anything."

She dialed the number. "Eve, Jane. Something
odd is—"

"Hang up," Eve said curtly. "And get out of there.
Joe just found out that Homeland Security is taking
over and pushing the CIA out of the picture.
They're planning on scooping up everyone at
MacDuff's Run, questioning you all, and conducting
their own investigation."

"Shit, they can't do that. It would tip off Grozak
and tie our hands."

"It's going to happen. John Logan tried to talk
them out of it, but he did his job of stirring them up
too well. They're panicky about looking bad if they
don't take some action. Get off the phone. Our line
is bugged and they'll trace you."

"Good. Then they'll realize that we're not at
MacDuff's Run any longer. It would be senseless for
them to pour into the castle and try to arrest us."

"No arrest, just quest—"

"It's the same difference. They'll tie our hands. And we can't afford that right now. We have a chance, Eve." She glanced at Trevor. "I'm going to hang up and have Trevor call you. They can trace him and tell he's not at the Run either. Try to get through to someone at Homeland Security and tell them that they're going to blow everything for nothing."

"They've heard you tell them," Eve said. "And I'll have John put it to them in the way they understand best. A monumental blunder will stick them right smack in the political hot seat. It may keep them away from the Run, but don't count on it stopping them from trying to find you. Keep safe." She hung up.

"Call her," Jane said to Trevor. "Homeland Security's taken over and bugged her line. We've got to try to keep them away from MacDuff's Run."

Trevor nodded and dialed his phone. Jane leaned against the wall and listened to him talk to Eve for a few minutes and then hang up. "That should do it. I'll be right back."

"Where are you going?"

"To have MacDuff call his government friends in London and have them put all kinds of roadblocks in place to keep Homeland Security from touching the Run. They'd have to have special permission to operate on foreign soil, and they have no concrete proof of any crime. The government isn't going to want to believe anything bad about MacDuff."

"That's right, you said MacDuff was some kind of folk hero."

"And it may prove to be an ace in the hole."

She watched him walk over to where MacDuff was sitting and talk to him. MacDuff nodded and pulled out his phone and started dialing.

A moment later Trevor was back with Jane, opening the cockpit door. "Now we have to get the hell out of here. Give me your phone." She handed it to him. "We'll have Kimbrough fly low and eject them over the Atlantic as soon as we get airborne. I'll have Brenner arrange to get us other satellite phones when we reach Colorado."

"They can trace our phones that closely?"

"It's an electronic world, and there are spy satellites used by all the agencies. They can zoom in on practically anything. They probably have a fix on us now." He said to Kimbrough, "We've got to get moving. See if you can hurry up the tower." He closed the cockpit door and turned back to her. "Sit down and buckle up."

She nodded but didn't move. She felt dazed and was trying to take in the implications of what had happened. "Can we get Venable to explain everything to them, get them off our back?"

"He's probably talked until he's blue in the face. Homeland Security is all-powerful these days, and sometimes they don't play well with others." He grimaced. "And like he said, he did warn you."

"Then we can't count on the CIA's help," she said slowly. "And we don't know anyone at Homeland Security; we can't count on them believing anything we say or letting us do anything but what they tell us to do. We're on our own."

"That about covers it." He raised his brows. "But then, we were pretty much on our own before."

"But we had Venable for a strong backup. I felt safer."

"It's not as if we won't try to bring them back in as soon as we zero in on Reilly." He added, "Of course, we could call Homeland Security and tell them to meet our plane if you'd rather forget about Jock and put yourself in their capable hands."

"No!"

"I didn't think so." He opened the cockpit door. "Try to get some sleep. I have to get Kimbrough to change our flight plan. We'll get fuel in Detroit, and I'll call Bartlett and see if Eve was able to keep Homeland Security from making a raid on MacDuff's Run."

# 17

Trevor placed the call from Detroit to Mac-Duff's Run only minutes before they were due to take off.

He turned away from the phone booth. "No sign of anyone at the Run. And since it's been several hours, we're probably in the clear."

"Thank heavens."

"Thank Eve and her friend John Logan." He was striding toward the plane. "But that doesn't mean they won't try to pick us up if they can trace us. We're on their turf and violating it to boot. They're not going to be as cooperative as Venable was." He made a face. "I never thought I'd be wistful about losing Venable."

"Because you could control him," Jane said.

"No, because, believe it or not, I respected him." He smiled faintly as he followed her up the steps.

"And, *yes*, I could control him. I hope to hell the bastard didn't get in trouble with Sabot."

The chalet was a small three-bedroom bungalow nestled between two mountains. It was one of several cottages scattered around an ice-covered lake.

Jock got out of the rental car, his gaze on the front door. "I remember this place."

"You should," MacDuff said. "It's not been that long." He strode up the stairs and unlocked the door.

"Do you remember where you were when he found you?" Jane asked Jock as she got out of the car.

"Doctors." Jock slowly climbed the stairs. "They didn't understand. They wouldn't let me— Blood . . . They strapped me to the bed and wouldn't let me do what I had to do."

"Because it was wrong," Jane said. "To take your life is wrong."

He shook his head.

"Leave him alone," Trevor said as he and Mario got out of the car. "Let him get his bearings."

Jane nodded. "I wasn't pushing." She made a face. "Well, I didn't mean to push. It just sort of happened."

"Jock and I will share the first bedroom off the living room," MacDuff said over his shoulder. "There's an office with a Murphy bed down the hall.

And another bedroom with twin beds adjoining it. You decide among you who sleeps where."

"I don't think we should be here at all," Mario said. "Dammit, we can't settle into this cozy little place. When do we start *doing* something?"

"Tonight." MacDuff gave him a cool glance. "Jock needs to rest and have dinner. We'll go out after that."

"Sorry," Mario muttered. "I'm a little on edge." He passed MacDuff and Jock and went into the cottage. "I'll take the Murphy bed. I'll see you all later."

"Go build a fire, Jock." MacDuff whirled on Jane and Trevor when Jock had gone inside. "This isn't going to work. Mario's on edge? What about Jock? He's already shaky, and he has to deal with a committee every step of the way? All of you go back to the Run and leave him to me."

"That's not what Jock wants," Jane said. But she could see why MacDuff would object. That moment on the porch had shaken her a little too. It was clear Jock was remembering the suicide attempt in the asylum and it was filling him with confusion. "What were you planning for tonight?"

"Jock was picked up by the police on a road outside Boulder. I'm taking him back there and setting him loose."

"You're not staying with him?"

"I'll be close enough. But I want him to feel alone."

"And you accuse me of callousness?"

"That's different. He's one of—"

"Yours," Trevor finished for him. "Then all is supposed to be forgiven?"

"Ask him," MacDuff said. "It should be the two of us. You're all outsiders."

"Jock wants this particular outsider along." Trevor gestured to Jane. "And since this is simply a preliminary foray with Jock, I'll volunteer to stay here with Mario and keep him from interfering if you'll take her with you."

MacDuff was silent a moment. "I'm surprised. I thought you'd give me more of an argument."

"Why? It's not a bad plan. You want to shake Jock up, and too many bystanders would interfere with his concentration. Mario is a problem. The only danger in this situation should be from Jock and, with you standing by, Jane should be okay." He met his gaze. "Just don't try to shut me out when we get close to Reilly."

MacDuff shrugged and strode into the house.

"I'm surprised too," Jane said quietly. "You're not one to stay and play babysitter."

"It's to prove to you how reasonable and self-sacrificing I can be."

She gazed at him skeptically.

"The truth?" His smile faded. "I've had a bad feeling since we boarded that plane at Aberdeen. This entire scenario could go completely wrong."

"But we're moving, something's happening."

"I know. That's why I'm giving MacDuff a little now, to cement more cooperation later. While you're out there tonight I'm going to see what I can do about convincing Mario to talk to us about Cira's scroll. Maybe I'll try splinters under his fingernails. Just joking." He gave her a quick, hard kiss. "Be careful with Jock. He may believe he's ready to help but he could blow at any moment."

D o you recognize any of this, Jock?" Jane could feel the ramrod tension of his muscles on the seat beside her. They'd been driving around for over two hours, and only during the last few miles had she seen any change in Jock. She glanced out the car window. It was a fairly populated area on the outskirts of Boulder, and the houses they were passing seemed to be in golf communities and upscale subdivisions. "Have you been here before?"

He jerkily shook his head, staring straight ahead.

"How close is this to where the police found him?" she asked MacDuff.

"Six, eight miles. Close enough to walk." He studied Jock. "He's definitely having a reaction. He's drawing up inside like a clam." He suddenly pulled over to the side of the road. "Let's see if we can open him up. Get out, Jock."

Jock shook his head.

"He's terrified," Jane whispered.

"Get out, Jock," MacDuff repeated. His voice cracked with whiplike sharpness. *"Now!"*

Jock moved sluggishly to open the door. "Please . . ."

"Go. You know why you're here."

Jock got out of the car. "Don't make me do it."

MacDuff put his foot on the accelerator and drove off.

Jane twisted around to look back at him and felt her heart ache. "He's just standing there. He doesn't understand."

"He understands," MacDuff said roughly. "If he doesn't, he'd better learn. It's got to end. You want Jock to save the world. I only want him to save himself. And he won't do it by burying his head in the sand. This is his chance and, by God, he's going to take it."

"I'm not arguing." Jane forced herself to look away from Jock. "How long are we going to leave him out there?"

"Thirty minutes. We'll go to the next exit and double back."

"Thirty minutes can be a long time."

"A lifetime. His lifetime." He stepped on the accelerator. "Or his sanity."


I don't see him." Jane's gaze frantically searched either side of the road. Three times Mac-Duff had driven slowly down the stretch where they had left Jock, and there had been no sign of him. "Where is he?"

"He could have wandered into one of the subdivisions. We passed by Timberlake golf community and Mountain Streams subdivision on this stretch. We'll do one more pass and then we'll start searching—"

"There he is!" Jane had caught sight of a figure

sitting in the ditch by the side of the road. "Oh, God, do you suppose a car hit him or—" She jumped out of the car as MacDuff screeched to a stop. "Jock, are you—"

"Four eight two." Jock didn't look at her. He was staring straight ahead. "Four eight two."

"Is he hurt?" MacDuff was beside her, dropping to his knees and shining his flashlight on the boy. "Jock, what happened?"

Jock stared blindly at him. "Four eight two."

MacDuff was running his hands over Jock's arms and legs. "I don't think he was struck by a car. No obvious injury."

"I think his injury is pretty damn obvious." She tried to steady her voice. "My God, what have we done?"

"What we had to do." His hands grasped Jock's shoulders and made him look at him. "We're here now. Nothing is going to happen. You don't have to be afraid."

"Four eight two." He suddenly bent double in agony and closed his eyes. "No. Can't do it. Little. Too little. Four eight two."

"Jesus," she whispered.

MacDuff handed her the flashlight. "We have to get him back to the chalet." He scooped Jock up in his arms. "You drive. I'll get in the backseat with him. I don't know what he's going to do next."

"I'm not afraid. For God's sake, he's hurting."

"You drive," he repeated, and straightened. "If there's a risk, I'll take it."

Because Jock was one of MacDuff's people. She

could tell by the possessive way he was holding Jock that there would be no arguing with him. And she had no desire to do anything but get the boy back to the chalet as soon as—

482.

The beam of the flashlight MacDuff had given her had fallen on the earth where Jock had been sitting.

482. The numbers were etched deep in the earth. The numbers were repeated over and over. 482. 482. 482.

"Jane."

Her head rose at MacDuff's call and she hurried toward the car.

How is he?" Mario asked as she came out of Jock's room.

"I don't know." She glanced back at the door. "He seems almost catatonic. Poor kid."

"It may be my religious upbringing, but I'm having trouble pitying a murderer." His lips tightened. "And when you think about it, if he worked with Reilly then he's one of them." He held up his hand. "I know. I'm in a minority here. But I can't give him either understanding or forgiveness."

"Then you'd better stay away from MacDuff," Trevor said. "He's a little touchy right now."

Mario nodded. "I've no desire to antagonize him. He may still be able to get something out of Jock." He headed for the kitchen. "I'll make a pot of coffee."

"Four eight two," Trevor repeated, his gaze on the bedroom door. "Is he still saying it?"

She nodded. "Like a mantra."

"But that mantra didn't start until he hit that particular stretch of road. Has MacDuff tried to ask him any questions?"

"Not yet. Would you?"

"Probably not. We don't need the boy going into meltdown."

"It's pretty sad that we have to worry about what we need, not what Jock needs." She stopped him as he opened his lips to speak. "I know," she said wearily. "It's necessary. And I'm the one who was all for pushing him to get the answers. It just breaks my heart to see him hurting like this."

"Then the remedy is to either keep on until he comes through it, or back off and let him go back into his shell. He might get better in a few years. Then again, he might not. And can you justify the consequences of waiting?"

"No."

"I didn't think so." He turned away. "But you'll be better prepared if you know what he's up against. I'll work on it."

"Four eight two?"

He nodded. "I'm no good at nurturing and soothing, but give me an abstract problem and I'm in my element. I've written down exactly what you told me Jock said tonight, and I'll try to find a match for his obsession with that number. It may not be easy. Four eight two could be a lock combination, a partial number on a license plate, a speed-dial on a telephone, an address, a lottery number, a code for a security system, a password to get into a comput—"

"I get your point," Jane said. "And if you continue to go through the options, I'll get more depressed than I am now. Just do it."

He nodded. "I'll take the easiest first and work down." He paused and put his hand gently on her arm. "Go and get a cup of that coffee from Mario. You look like you need it."

"Maybe I will." His touch felt warm and comforting and she didn't want to move away from it. She gave herself a moment before she straightened away from him. "And I'll take one to MacDuff too. He's not going to leave Jock. He's hovering over him like a mother with a baby. It's weird to see a man as strong as MacDuff act that maternal."

"He may have thought he was acting for the best by throwing Jock on his own tonight, but there's always an element of guilt in situations like this. I'll get back to you as soon as I come up with a list of possibles."

Wake up."

Jane opened drowsy eyes to see Trevor kneeling beside her easy chair, his hand touching her cheek. "What . . ."

"Wake up." He smiled. "I may have found something. No guarantees, but it's worth a try."

She straightened in the chair and shook her head to clear it of sleep. "What's worth a try?"

"Four eight two. I fooled around with telephone speed-dials for a while and then went to the addresses. You said Jock didn't start freaking out until you began driving down the stretch of road that bordered the two subdivisions. I accessed the street maps on the Internet. No four eighty-two in the golf community, but Mountain Streams subdivision has a four eighty-two." He gave her the printout. "Four eighty-two Lilac Drive."

Excitement surged through her, but she tried to be coolly reasonable. "It could be a coincidence."

"Yes."

To hell with being reasonable. She wasn't going to rob herself of hope. "Could it be Reilly's address?"

He shook his head. "According to the Net the present residents are Matthew Falgow, his wife, Nora, and daughter, Jenny. Falgow is a local union leader, with a reputation as clean as a whistle." He handed her another sheet. "Here are their photos at the last union election they attended. Cute kid."

She nodded absently as she gazed at the photos. An attractive couple in their forties with an adorable fair-haired little girl who looked to be four or five. The dossier on Falgow was as squeaky clean as Trevor had indicated and certainly contained no hint of a subversive taint. "No connection with Reilly . . ."

"Maybe. Maybe not." He sat back on his heels. "Remember everything Jock said tonight. Then approach it from a different direction."

She met his gaze and a chill ran through her as she realized where he was going.

Stop being a coward. Face it. She'd known it wouldn't be pretty. Everything about Reilly was corrupt and hideous.

She drew a deep breath and looked back down at the photo of Falgow.

Is he awake?" Jane asked MacDuff, her gaze on Jock. The boy's eyes were closed but there was a tension about his muscles that showed he was anything but relaxed.

"He's awake," MacDuff said. "He won't answer me when I speak to him, but he's not catatonic and he knows I'm talking to him."

"May I try?"

"Be my guest."

"Will you leave us alone?"

MacDuff's gaze narrowed on her face. "Trevor wouldn't like that."

"For God's sake, he's helpless."

"That could change in a heartbeat." He glanced at the paper in her hand. "Why do you want to be alone with him?"

"Trevor came up with a possible answer to four eight two. Jock loves you and he has a lot of inward conflict because of that love. But he doesn't love me. I may be able to break through to him."

His gaze was still on the paper. "I want to see it."

"Afterward."

MacDuff was silent a moment. "Trevor knows you're doing this?"

"He doesn't know I'm asking you to leave. He's out on the porch with Mario."

"And you don't want me to join them." He slowly rose to his feet. "I'll be outside the door. If you see any sign of aggression don't wait to call out. Thirty seconds and it could be over."

"The only person I've noticed him willing to commit violence for is you. I'll be careful not to let him think I'm a threat to you."

"We pulled the rug out from under him. He may have reverted to the time before I found him in that hospital."

"Comforting."

"I don't want you comfortable. Comfort can be fatal." He opened the door. "Call if you need me."

She wasn't at all comfortable. As she stood and stared down at that beautiful boy, she was sad and angry and filled with horror. "Jock, do you hear me?"

No answer.

"You might as well answer me. I know you probably heard and understood what I was saying to MacDuff."

No answer.

She sat down on the side of the bed. "Four eight two."

His muscles stiffened even more.

"Lilac Drive. You once told me you didn't like lilacs. Such a beautiful flower. I didn't understand why."

His hands closed into fists on the coverlet.

"Four eighty-two Lilac Drive."

The tempo of his breathing was altering, quickening.

"Four eight two, Jock."

He was panting, the pulse in his throat jumping crazily. But he wouldn't open his eyes, blast it. She had to find a way to shock him out of this withdrawal.

"You kept saying 'little,' 'too little.' There was a little girl in that house on Lilac Drive. Pretty, rosy-cheeked, with fair hair. Her name was Jenny. Four years old."

His head was thrashing back and forth. "No, three . . ."

"You should know better than I do." She paused. He was still too withdrawn. Okay, hit him hard. Any way she could. "You killed her."

"No!" His eyes flew open. "Little. Too little."

"You went there to kill her."

"Four eight two. Four eight two. Four eight two."

"Reilly told you the address and what to do. You managed to get into the house and you went to her room. It wasn't difficult; you'd been trained well. Then you did what Reilly told you to do."

"I didn't." His eyes were blazing in his taut face. "Stop saying that. I should have done it but I couldn't. Too little. I tried but I couldn't—touch her."

"But you always do what Reilly tells you to do. You have to be lying to me."

"Shut up." His hands closed on her throat. "I

didn't do it. I didn't do it. Wrong. Wrong. Reilly said I should but I couldn't."

She could feel his hands tightening with every word. "Let me go, Jock."

"Shut up. Shut up."

"What was wrong, Jock? Was it not killing that little girl? Or was it Reilly telling you to do it?" What was she doing? She should be calling for MacDuff. Her throat was so tight she was almost croaking. No, she was too close. "You know the answer. Tell me."

"Reilly's—always—right."

"Bullshit. If he'd been right that night, you'd have killed that child. You realized that night how terrible he was and how many terrible things he'd already made you do. But when you walked away from that house, it was over. His conditioning might have lingered and confused you, but he doesn't own you any longer."

Tears were running down his cheeks. "Not over. Never over."

"Okay, maybe it's not over." Jesus, she wished he'd take his hands away from her throat. There was no telling when she might say something that would trigger him. "But you were on your way back when you left four eighty-two Lilac Drive that night. Reilly can't control you any longer. It's only a matter of time now."

"No."

"Jock, it's the truth. MacDuff and I have both noticed that you're changing, getting stronger."

"The laird?" He stared into her eyes. "He said

that? Are you lying to me? You lied about me killing the little girl."

"It was the only way I could think to jerk you back. You had to confront what you'd done. Or rather what you'd not done. When you broke Reilly's conditioning, you were feeling almost as guilty about disobeying him as you would have been if you'd killed that child."

"No, couldn't do it."

"I know you couldn't. But I had to shock you into talking to me. And I did it, didn't I?"

"Yes."

"And you realize I did it for your own good. Right?"

"I . . . suppose so."

"Then will you please take your hands from around my throat? MacDuff and Trevor would not be pleased with either one of us if they came in here and saw you throttling me."

He looked at his hands grasping her throat as if they didn't belong to him. He slowly released her and dropped them to the bed. "I think . . . they'd be more displeased with me."

Was there the faintest hint of humor in his tone? His expression was bleak, tears were still shimmering in his eyes, but at least the raw violence had vanished. She took a deep breath and rubbed her throat. "As well they should be. There's such a thing as accountability." She sat down in the chair beside the bed. "Not only for you. Reilly has a big account coming due."

"Not . . . the laird. My fault. All my fault."

"The important thing is bringing him down."

"Not the laird."

"Then it's up to you to force yourself to remember where Reilly is so that we can go after him."

"Try . . ."

"No, you have to do it, Jock. That's why we brought you here. That's why we put you through this hell. Do you believe we'd do it if we saw any other way of jarring you into remembering?"

He shook his head. "I'm tired now. I want to go to sleep."

"Are you trying to avoid talking to me, Jock?"

"Maybe." He closed his eyes. "I don't know. I don't think so. I need to be alone with him."

She felt a chill go through her. "Him?"

"Reilly." He whispered, "He's always with me, you know. I try to get away but he's still there. I'm afraid to look at him or listen to him, but I have to do it."

"No, you don't."

"You don't understand. . . ."

"I understand he controlled you in the most evil ways possible. But he's gone now."

"If he was gone, you wouldn't be here making me try to remember. While he's alive, he won't ever leave me alone." He turned his head. "Go away, Jane. I know what you want from me and I'll try to give it to you. But you can't help me. I'll either be able to do it or I won't."

She stood up. "Do you want me to send MacDuff in?"

He shook his head. "I don't like him to see me like this. Reilly makes me weak. I'm . . . ashamed."

"You shouldn't be ashamed."

"Yes, I should. Forever. Black soul. Never be clean again. But MacDuff won't let me die. I tried but he brought me back. So if I can't die, I have . . . to be strong." His voice harshened. "But sweet Jesus, it's hard."

She hesitated. "Are you sure you don't want me to stay and—" He was shaking his head. "Okay, I'll let you rest." She headed for the door. "If you need me, I'll be here. Just call me."

"You weren't in there very long." MacDuff rose from his chair as the door closed behind her.

"Wasn't I?" It had seemed like an eternity. "Long enough."

"Does he need me?"

"Probably. But he doesn't want you. He doesn't want anyone right now. And I don't believe he's in any immediate danger."

His glance was on the paper still in her hand. "Any response?"

"Oh, yes. Is it enough to jump-start his memory of Reilly? I don't know. From now on, it has to come from him. He seems . . . different."

"How?"

She frowned, trying to puzzle it out. "Before, he reminded me of that scroll Mario was working on. There were certain sentences and phrases missing that Mario had to replace with educated guesswork so that he could make sense of the whole document. I think that's the point that Jock is at now."

"Then you must have jarred the hell out of him." His lips tightened grimly. "I want to see that paper."

"I want you to see it." She headed for the kitchen. "I'll tell you about it while I get a cup of coffee. I need it."

"No doubt. Button up your shirt."

"What?"

"Try to cover up those bruises on your neck. I don't want Trevor going after Jock."

She touched her throat. "He didn't hurt me. Not really. And he didn't mean—"

"Tell that to Trevor. You're alive, and if you were too stupid to do what I told you to do, then you deserve a few bruises." He sat down at the kitchen table. "Now tell me about four eight two."


Four eight two. Too little. Too little.

*She's evil. Devil's spawn. Kill her.*

Child. Child. Child. Jock could feel the word tear him, scream from him.

*It doesn't matter. Do your duty. You're nothing without duty. Fail and you'll displease me. You know what that means.*

Pain. Loneliness. Darkness.

And Reilly waiting in that darkness. Jock could never see him but he knew he was there. Bringing the fear. Bringing the pain.

*Four eight two. Kill the child. Go to the house. It's not too late. It will bring you my forgiveness.*

"No!" Jock's eyes flew open. His heart was pounding, hurting. He was going to die. Reilly had told him that he'd die if he ever betrayed and disobeyed him, and now it was going to happen. "I didn't die when I didn't kill that little girl. You can't hurt me."

*Die.*

His heart was growing bigger, swelling, he couldn't breathe.

*Die.*

He could feel himself slipping, growing colder, dying. . . .

Weakness. Shame. Not worthy of living.

*Die.*

If he died, if he gave in to shame, the laird would also die. He would go after Reilly, and Jock wouldn't be there to help.

*Die*

I will *not.*

*Die.*

He could see Reilly more clearly now. Hovering in the shadows. Not a ghost. Not a ghost. A man.

*Die. Stop fighting. Your heart is bursting. It will stop soon. You want it to stop.*

Reilly wanted it to stop. And Jock didn't want to do anything that Reilly wanted him to do. That path led to the shame.

Don't panic. Think about stopping the pain. Slow the heartbeat.

*Die.*

Screw you.

"Jock." MacDuff was shaking his shoulder. "Answer me. Dammit, Jane told me you were okay. I should never have—"

Jock slowly opened his eyes. "It's not— I'm not going to die."

MacDuff sighed with relief. "Everybody dies." He tousled the boy's fair hair. "But you've got a long way to go."

"I didn't think so. Reilly didn't want—" His expression was full of wonder. "But it doesn't matter what he wants, does it? I can do anything."

"You can't jump off buildings with a single bound." MacDuff cleared his throat. "But anything within reason."

"He's still there, waiting for me. But he can't hurt me if I don't let him."

"That's what I've been trying to tell you."

"Yes . . ." He turned his head on the pillow. "I want to go back to sleep. I'm tired. . . . He wouldn't stop. But I didn't give in to him."

"That's good." He paused. "Can you tell me where to find him?"

"Not yet. I can see pictures but there's no connection. And he may not still be there. He moves around a lot."

"Idaho?"

He nodded his head. "I keep thinking that it's Idaho."

"Where?"

He was silent a moment. "Near Boise."

"You're sure?"

"No. Sometimes Reilly could give me memories of things that had never happened. But I was working at an equipment shop at a ski resort near there when I first met him. He offered me a job and we went out for a drink at a bar in the town. After the third drink I passed out. At least, I suppose I did. After that it was all Reilly."

"What ski resort?"

He was silent a moment. "Powder Mountain."

"And the name of the bar?"

"Harrigan's." He frowned. "But I told you, sometimes I couldn't be sure what was real and what was—"

"I'll check it out." He rose to his feet. "I'll let you know. You just keep on trying to remember."

"I can't do anything else." Jock smiled without mirth. "I can't shut down. It just keeps going round and round with Reilly in the center."

"We need to know everything we can about him."

"I'll try. But there's too much that gets in the way. Roadblocks . . ."

"Jump over them." MacDuff turned away. "You can do it."

"I know," Jack said quietly. "But maybe not in time."

A week ago MacDuff wouldn't have bet on it happening at all. But he was encouraged and exhilarated that at least Jock was able to weigh consequences, and he was more normal than MacDuff had seen him since he'd known him as a boy. "Nonsense. I have faith in you."

"Do you?"

"Would I have gone through all we have together if I didn't?" He smiled at him over his shoulder. "Do your job. Make me proud of you, lad."

"It's too late for that. But I'll do my job." He closed his eyes. "It may take a while."

"We'll give you time."

"Good. He keeps getting in the way. I can't see. . . ."

"You will. Just let it come."

# 18

"Well?" Trevor asked when MacDuff came out of the bedroom. "Do we have a fix on Reilly?"

"Maybe. He's still leaning toward Idaho. Where's Jane?"

"In the kitchen with Mario. Where in Idaho?"

"He's not sure." He moved toward the kitchen. "Near Boise. I'm not going through this twice. I want to make sure everyone knows that I don't want Jock harassed."

"May I point out that it was you who sent him around the bend?"

"With help from Jane."

"She's giving you a little too much help. I saw those marks on her throat."

"And did she complain?"

"She said it was worth it. I don't agree."

"You would if you'd seen Jock just now. He's coming out of the fog."

"Good for him. It's still not worth it." Trevor preceded him into the kitchen, where Jane and Mario sat at the table. "MacDuff says that Jock is zeroing in on Boise as a possible location."

"Really?" Mario's body tensed with eagerness. "Where exactly?"

"He's not sure. You can't expect everything to come back to him right away."

"Can't you talk to him, push him?"

"No. He's doing the best he can. I don't want him to have a setback."

"How was he?" Jane asked.

"Tentative. Like a baby taking its first steps." He smiled. "And so goddamn close to normal it was bloody incredible."

"Then he should be able to tell us something soon," Mario said.

"Back off," Trevor said. "It's what we all want."

"How long?" Jane asked.

MacDuff shrugged. "As long as it takes."

"That's not acceptable." Mario frowned. "What if Grozak and Reilly find out what we're doing? And even if they don't, there's only a week left. Grozak could close the—"

"I'm not pressuring him," MacDuff said. "And neither are you."

"I don't want to hurt him, but you need to—" Mario threw up his hands in frustration as he met MacDuff's gaze. "Never mind." He strode out of the room.

"He's right," Trevor said. "We can't twiddle our thumbs and wait for time to cure Jock."

"We'll see. There has to be a compromise." MacDuff went to the counter and poured himself a cup of coffee. "I'm not going to destroy Jock because Mario wants his revenge yesterday. We can afford a couple days. It will come."

"And we don't want Mario striking out on his own and blowing what little cover we have," Trevor said.

"He won't do that." Jane stood up. "I'll talk to him."

"By all means," MacDuff said. "You hold his hand. I'm not about to do it." He glanced at Trevor. "And I don't believe Trevor's in a mood to do it."

"At least I'm not going to have to worry about Mario choking the life out of her," Trevor said. "It's a step forward from the way you put her head into the lion's den with Jock." He glanced at Jane. "I could do it if you don't want to deal with him."

"Neither of you is remembering that Mario is hurting too." Jane moved toward the door. "All he wants to know is that there's an end in sight."

Trevor's brows rose. "That's all we all want to know."


Have you been sent on a mission of diplomacy or as a teacher to slap my hands?" Mario asked. "I'm not sorry. I spoke the truth."

"No one sent me," Jane said. "And you should be allowed to speak your mind." She paused. "But not before you think it through. My first impulse was the same as yours. Jock could be the only way to stop this. Just a few words and he might be able to lead us to them."

"Then tell Trevor and MacDuff."

"I will. But not until we give Jock his chance. We're not savages. We don't want to destroy a mind if we can save it by letting Jock find his own way back." She met his eyes. "Do we, Mario?"

He stared at her, a multitude of expressions crossing his face. He finally said curtly, "No, dammit. But there has to be a way of getting him to—"

"No pressure."

"Okay, okay. I hear you. But what if I spent some time with him, got to know him? Just a couple days. Maybe I could get him to talk, nudge him a little."

"No pressure."

"I wouldn't even mention Reilly. Unless he mentioned him first. I'm not dumb. I can be subtle."

"When you're not traumatized yourself."

"I promise, Jane. I'm not cruel. I don't want to hurt Jock. I feel sorry for the kid. Just let me help. Let me *do* something."

She gazed at him thoughtfully. She could see the desperation in his expression. "It might not be a bad idea. You'd be a new voice in the mix. Trevor, MacDuff, and I have been pushing Jock. Every time he sees us, it's a reminder. You're close to his age. Someone else to distract him. A change of pace . . ."

"That's right," Mario said eagerly. "It makes sense, doesn't it?"

"Perhaps." She paused. "If I can trust you."

"I promise. I don't break my word." He grimaced. "The priests made sure I believed in eternal damnation if I broke any of the commandments."

"You're planning on breaking a big one if you kill Grozak and Reilly."

"Some things are worth chancing damnation. And I believe the Church would weigh my sin against the greater one they're going to commit. I won't break my promise, Jane."

She made up her mind. "You'd better not. If you upset Jock, MacDuff will send you to that eternal damnation without a second thought."

"You'll let me do it?"

"On one condition. We need to make a deal. You can have your two days with Jock if you give me Cira's letter at the end of that time."

"I didn't bring it with me." He added quickly, "But I can tell you what it said."

"Then tell me."

"After I spend my time with him. That's only fair. When can I see Jock?"

"When he wakes up." She turned to leave. "But don't be surprised if he doesn't want to talk to you. He's not exactly sociable. This is purely an experiment."

"I understand that. I'll just be a sounding board. If he wants to talk, I'll be there."

"I'm trusting you, Mario."

"Within limits." He smiled. "And with a backup in case I don't come through. I don't care. As long as I can see a way to help."

For the first time since they'd started on this journey, Mario seemed almost cheerful, the brooding and bitterness lessened. Purpose could work miracles. Perhaps throwing the two young men together would work out. "MacDuff may not be needed if you foul up," she murmured. "Jock is extremely well trained to take care of anyone who upsets him."

Hello, Jock. Do you know who I am?"

Jock shook his head to clear it of sleep before studying the man in the chair beside his bed. "You're the man who lives in the room with Cira. Mario . . ."

"Donato." The man smiled. "And I don't exactly live with Cira. Although I sometimes feel as if I do. I'm trying to decipher her scrolls."

"You live with her statue, the one that belongs to Trevor. MacDuff let me go up and see it before you came to the Run."

"Without Trevor's permission?"

"It's the laird's castle, and he knew I wanted to see it after he showed me the photo on the Internet."

"And you just walked right in?"

"No, I know how to get into places." His expression clouded. "It was easy."

"I'm sure you wouldn't have had to use your cat-burglar skills to see the statue. Trevor's never objected to me having her in my study."

He shrugged. "The laird didn't want me to bother him."

"But not enough to tell you not to trespass and go to see her?"

"It wasn't trespassing. It was his right to give me permission to see her."

"Trevor wouldn't agree, I'm afraid." He smiled. "The castle is under lease and the statue of Cira is his."

He shook his head. "It was the laird's right."

"Well, we won't argue about it," Mario said. "I'm glad we share a passion for Cira. She's beautiful, isn't she?"

Jock nodded. "I feel . . . close to her."

"So do I. Would you like to read her letters?"

"Yes." Jock studied Mario's expression. Although the fog that clouded his mind was lessening, sometimes clearing entirely, it was still difficult to focus. He forced himself to concentrate. "Why are you here?"

"I thought we should get to know each other."

He shook his head. "You're being nice to me. Why?"

"Does there have to be a reason?"

"Yes." Jock thought about it. "You want what the rest of them want. You want to know about Reilly."

"Why should I—" Mario nodded. "I won't lie to you."

He said wearily, "I can't tell you what I don't know."

"It will come back to you. I want to be there when it does."

He shook his head.

"Look at it this way. I promised I'd ask you no questions. You'll be able to relax with me. If you want to talk about Reilly, I'll be willing to listen. No, I'll be eager as hell to listen."

Jock searched his face. "Why?"

"Grozak and Reilly killed my father. He was beheaded."

That's right, Jock remembered Jane saying something about Mario's father's death. "I'm sorry. It wasn't me. I've never been told to behead anyone."

Shock crossed Mario's face. "We know who did it. I didn't think it was you."

"That's good. It would complicate things."

Mario nodded. "I'd say that's an understatement." He was recovered enough to force a smile. "You're not what I expected. But that doesn't mean we can't come to terms and help each other."

Jock didn't speak for a moment, his gaze on Mario's face. This man wanted to use him and thought he was simpleminded enough to let him do it. He couldn't blame him. When the fog closed down, he was barely capable of functioning even on the simplest level. But now there were periods when the fog lifted and he felt keen and sharp as a dagger.

"Don't you want to know what's in those scrolls?" Mario asked persuasively. "I've just translated one that I haven't let anyone else read yet. I could tell you about it. You'd be the first."

He was trying to bribe him. Jock could sense the desperation that was driving Mario. Revenge and hate and the urgency that went along with that desperation. It was strange being able to know how others were feeling when he'd been turned inward for so long.

Accept it. He was still weak and everyone around him was strong. He had to build his strength. Take whatever Mario was willing to give him. Let him use him.

Until the fog vanished entirely.

I didn't think it would work." Trevor's gaze was fixed on Mario and Jock walking down to the pier. "I thought you had let Mario influence you. But it's been two days and they seem to be best buddies."

"He did influence me. I felt sorry for him. But not enough to let it go on if I saw any sign of him disturbing Jock. I had to fight too hard to get MacDuff to let Mario even talk to him. But it was a way to make him a deal to give us Cira's scroll, and I knew I could yank him away if he upset Jock." Jane shook her head in wonder. "And Mario seems gentle with him. He reminds me of the way he was when I first came to the castle. Jock tells me he jokes with him and tells him stories of his life in Italy. I don't believe he's asked Jock any questions at all."

"Yet."

"Yet." Her hands clenched into fists at her sides. "But we'll have to start asking questions ourselves soon. It's been driving me crazy sitting here and waiting for Jock to get around to remembering something that could stop this horror. We can't wait much longer for him to heal. Have you heard anything from Brenner?"

"Only that he checked out the resort where Jock worked. He sold equipment in the ski shop for three months and then just didn't show up one day. The owner was pretty upset. He didn't think Jock was that unreliable. He even thought about filing a missing-persons report."

"But he didn't do it?"

He shook his head. "Drifters come through those resorts all the time. They stay to earn a few bucks and enjoy the skiing and then move on."

"Nothing on Reilly?"

"Not yet. He's tapping a few sources, but he has to be careful not to tip off anyone that we're looking for Reilly. Leaks are too dangerous right now."

Everything was dangerous now. Including this waiting on Jock. Lord, she wished there was something else they could do. "Have you talked to Bartlett lately?"

"Last night." He smiled. "Homeland Security hasn't invaded MacDuff's stronghold. So they're basically watching and waiting."

"And so are we." She paused. "I don't suppose you could rig my new phone with some kind of block so that I could talk freely to Eve and Joe?"

"Too risky. You know that."

She had known that would be his answer. And it was the right answer, dammit. As much as she wanted to confide in Eve and Joe, it would be foolish to run that risk. "Okay."

"Look, this is tearing you apart. It was your decision, but we all went along with it. You were right, if we'd pushed Jock he might have closed down. But if you're having second thoughts, then say the word and I'll have a talk with him."

"You mean you'll use force."

"If I think it's the only way. He's our only hope and our primary stumbling block. I don't want you having regrets for the rest of your life because you were too soft to do what you had to do."

"I won't be too soft." It was true. She knew herself well enough to know that in spite of the agony, she'd make the decision she had to make if there was no other way. But, God, how desperately she was hoping there was another way. She gazed back at Mario and Jock. "But Mario had better get something from Jock pretty soon. If he doesn't, we'll do whatever we have to do. Including bringing in Homeland Security, the CIA, anyone who has a chance of helping. And they won't be either understanding or gentle with him. They'll take whatever they can get, even if they break his mind."

"I'm not arguing. Let's hope it won't be necessary." Trevor changed the subject. "But I do have another interesting bit of information you might want to know about. Demonidas."

Her gaze flew to his face. "What?"

"I've been trying to keep myself busy and I found a reference to a Demonidas on the Internet. He did live during the same period as Cira."

"That's all?"

"Not much more." He paused. "But he came to public attention when his ship's log was found in Naples two years ago. It was supposedly in a good state of preservation and was going to be offered at auction by the government to benefit the local museums. There was quite a buzz about it. Collectors were lining up to bid."

"Can we see it?"

He shook his head. "It disappeared a week before the auction."

"Stolen?"

"Unless it walked out of that safe in Naples."

"Damn."

"But at least it did exist, and so did Demonidas. Does that make you feel better?"

"Yes. Anything in this mess that has a basis in concrete fact is to the good."

"I'll keep on looking, but I thought you'd like to know something definite. It's been a pretty frustrating time for all of us."

"That's an understatement." She smiled. "Thanks, Trevor."

"You're welcome. It's worth it. That's the first time you've smiled at me in days." He reached out and took her hand. "I missed it."

She looked down at their joined hands. It felt warm, nice. . . . "I've been a little on edge."

"We've been balanced on that edge since the day we met. I don't know how it would feel to be able to have dinner, go to a show, maybe sit around and watch TV together. Normal stuff."

He was right. Normal was a state they knew nothing about. They hadn't had the time or opportunity to discuss, explore, and truly get to know each other. It had all been sexual tension, a fine balance between trust and suspicion, and literally walking on the wild side of violence. "And do you want that?"

"Hell, yes. I want the whole nine yards. I want to *know* you."

She glanced away from him. "And what if you're disappointed when you do?"

"You're backing away from me."

He was right. His hand felt too good and she needed the comfort and companionableness he was giving. It made her want to cling, and she couldn't allow herself to do that. If she didn't have her strength and independence she had nothing. "What do you expect? This is too new. I didn't expect to— When I was a kid on the streets, what I saw of the man-woman relationship wasn't pretty. I suppose . . . it scarred me. I'm afraid of what you make me feel. You're not like anyone I've ever known, and I'm not sure if you'll even be here when this is all over."

"I'll be here."

She pulled her hand away and stood up. "Then we'll worry about going to dinner and watching TV together then." She headed for the door. "I think I'll go down and sketch Jock and Mario together. They're an interesting contrast, aren't—"

"Jane."

"Okay. I'm avoiding talking about it." She stared

him in the eye. "You want sex? Fine. I love it with you. I just can't— It's going to take me time to become close to anyone. And if you can't accept that, you'll have to deal with it."

His lips tightened. "I can accept it." He suddenly grimaced. "And I'll damn well take the sex." He turned back to the house. "I'll hit the computer and see if I can come up with anything else on Demonidas."

They must be just sitting around twiddling their thumbs," Wickman said when Grozak picked up his call. "No sign of any action at all. Why don't I take a few men and go in and stir things up?"

"Because it would be stupid," Grozak said. "I'm surprised you'd even suggest it. I told you I wanted the woman, and the minute you try to use force, they'll start circling the wagons to protect her. And if you don't succeed, it will show Reilly how inept we are. The bastard respects strength."

"I'm *not* inept."

"I know you're not," Grozak said quickly. "It would only be an appearance."

"Five days, Grozak."

"You don't have to remind me. I'm in Chicago now arranging the shipment of the explosives to Los Angeles. Then I go to Los Angeles and make sure the bribes are in place."

"All your fine plans won't do any good if we don't give Reilly what he wants." Wickman hung up the phone.

Grozak's lips tightened as he hung up the phone. Wickman was becoming more arrogant every time he talked to him. He was beginning to regret the day he'd hired the son of a bitch. Wickman might be smart and efficient, but there were moments Grozak felt as if he was losing control.

Have him killed?

Not yet.

He glanced at the calendar on the desk and felt the muscles of his stomach clench.

Five days.

## Four Days

Hello, Jock." Jane sat down on the porch steps beside him and gazed out at the splendor of the sunset before flipping open her sketchbook. "It's peaceful here, isn't it? It reminds me of Joe's cottage on our lake at home."

"Do you have mountains there?"

"No, just hills. But the peace is the same."

He nodded. "I like it here. It makes me feel clean inside. And free."

"You are free."

"Right now. But I always wonder if I'll stay that way."

"I know how you feel." She held up her hand as he started to shake his head. "Okay, no one could know unless they'd gone through what you did, but I can imagine. I don't think there's anything worse than being controlled like a slave. It's my worst nightmare."

"Is it?"

She nodded. "And Trevor told me that Reilly would just love to try his hand at controlling me. It made me sick."

He frowned. "But there weren't any women there at the compound except Kim, and she works for Reilly."

"I was evidently going to be the exception."

He nodded. "Maybe it's because you look like Cira. He liked her. He kept asking me about her and if the laird had found out anything about her gold or—"

"He did?" Her gaze flew to his face. "You remember that?"

"Yes, little things have been coming back to me in the last few days."

"What else?"

"Four eight two."

She felt a surge of disappointment. "Oh."

"That's not what you wanted me to say."

"I just thought that you'd already come to terms with that."

"Now I have. Now that I've remembered that I did all I could."

"Would you like to tell me what happened that night?"

"There's not much to tell. Reilly gave me the address and the victim and I went to do what he told me."

"Why a child?"

"To hurt Falgow. Something to do with the Mafia. I think Reilly had been paid by them to punish Falgow for not cooperating."

"But a little girl . . ."

"It would hurt him. It hurt me. I couldn't do it. But if I didn't do it, Reilly would send someone else. I knew it. I had to do something. . . ."

"What?"

"Anything. They thought she was safe. She wasn't safe. She'd never be safe if they didn't protect her. I turned over a table. I broke a window and went out that way. They had to know someone was there, that she wasn't safe."

"It must have worked," Jane said gently. "She's still alive, Jock."

He nodded. "But no one's really safe from him. He might have given up, but then, he might just be waiting. He's very patient."

"Have you been remembering anything else?"

"Yes."

She drew a deep breath. "We have to talk, Jock. We've left you alone as long as we could. It's time."

Jock smiled. "Not quite alone. You sent Mario to remind me what my duty is."

"I told him not to bug you."

"He didn't. He's been very nice. I like him."

"So do I."

"But sometimes you don't have to say anything. I know what he wants. What you all want."

"And are you going to give it to us?"

He was silent a moment. "I . . . may give it to you."

Her gaze flew to his face. "You remember where Reilly is?"

He nodded. "It's coming back to me in bits and pieces."

"Idaho?"

He nodded.

"Where?"

He didn't answer.

"Jock."

He shook his head. "You'll tell the laird. Or Trevor. Or Mario."

"They all want to help."

"I told you the night I came to you that the laird can't know, that I have to do it myself."

"Yes, but you didn't say that you were going to close us all out."

"I had to get here," he said simply. "You wouldn't have brought me if you hadn't thought I'd tell you if I could."

She gazed at him in amazement. "So you manipulated us?"

"I had to get here," he repeated. "I'm very grateful to you for making it happen."

"Thanks a lot." She paused. "Then help us. You know what terrible things could happen if we don't find Reilly and Grozak."

"Yes."

Her hands clenched. "Then *talk* to me."

"I will." He stared at her, troubled. "But only to you, Jane. And not now."

She gazed at him with narrowed eyes. "What are you saying?"

"I won't tell you. I'll take you there. And when we're almost there, I'll let you call the police or anyone you like. Except the laird."

"Jock—"

"Only you."

"And will you wait for the police to get there before you go after Reilly?"

He didn't answer.

She looked at him in frustration. "Jock, you can't go after him yourself."

"Why not? I know how to do it. He taught me."

"We don't know how many of his men will be there. For all we know Grozak may be there too."

"I know how to do it."

The words were simple but absolutely confident, and they sent a chill down her back. His expression was serene and his eyes were clear and honest as a child's.

"Look, if you don't do it right, Reilly will be able to give warning, and we won't get Grozak."

"I don't care about Grozak."

"I do."

"So does Mario. But without Reilly, Grozak can't do anything. You can catch him later."

"And what if we can't?"

Jock shook his head.

Lord, he was stubborn. And she couldn't reason with him, because he saw only one path, one goal. "What would you do if I said no and went back to the chalet and told Trevor and MacDuff what you've remembered?"

"If you say no, then I won't be here when they

come to find me." Jock gazed out at the snowy peaks. "I know about hiding in the mountains. MacDuff might find me, but it would be too late for you."

"Jock, don't do this."

"Only you."

He meant it. His lips were tight with determination.

She gave in. "Okay." She asked curtly, "When?"

"Tonight. Dress warmly. We may have to be outside. Can you get the keys to the car?"

"I'll manage." She got to her feet. "One in the morning."

He nodded. "That would be good. And bring a credit card. We'll need gas and other things." He stared at her with a troubled frown. "Are you mad at me?"

"Yes. I don't want to do this. I'm afraid for you." She added, "And, dammit, I'm afraid for me."

"Nothing will happen to you. I promise."

"You can't make that kind of promise. We don't know what's going to happen."

"I thought you wanted to go. I could go alone."

"No, you can't. I have to take the chance of getting him." Jane gazed at Jock over her shoulder as she started up the path. "But I'm going to leave a note." When he started to speak, she interrupted. "Don't tell me no. I'm not going to just abandon them without a word and let them worry about us. It's not going to hurt you. You haven't told me anything of value."

"I suppose you're right," he said slowly as he

started down toward the pier. "I don't want to worry anyone."

"Then don't do this."

He didn't reply as he moved down the path.

No, he didn't want to worry anyone, but he was willing to throw a stick of dynamite into the mix, Jane thought as she moved toward the chalet.

Okay, don't let her concern and nervousness show. Stay out here for a little while longer and by then it would be time to go to bed. She cast a quick glance at the car parked beside the chalet. Someone was bound to hear them when they left in the early-morning hours.

Well, by that time it would be too late to stop them.

She had to ignore the surge of panic the thought brought. At least they were doing something toward finding Reilly. Jock had promised her that she could bring in help as soon as they reached their destination.

Yeah, and he'd also promised her she'd be safe. Not likely. Jock would be focused on getting Reilly and not on protecting her.

Then she'd have to protect herself. What was different about that? She'd taken care of herself all her life. Jock probably wouldn't have been much help anyway. He was like a bell that sometimes rang crystal clear and sometimes exploded in a cacophony of thunderous sound.

She just had to concentrate on keeping that explosion from killing her.

Lakewood, Illinois

The four smokestacks of the nuclear plant pierced the horizon.

Grozak pulled to the side of the road. "We can only stay here a minute. There are security patrols cruising the entire area every thirty minutes."

"I didn't have to see this," Carl Johnson said. "All you have to do is tell me what to do and I'll do it."

"I thought it wouldn't hurt." And Grozak wanted to see Johnson's reaction to the place where he was going to meet his death. When he'd picked Johnson up at the airport, he'd been shocked. The man was young, clean-cut, and good-looking, and spoke with a Midwestern twang. Of course, that all-American look was good, but it made Grozak uneasy. He couldn't see Johnson driving the truck through that gate. "The truck is a catering van and it visits the plant at noon every day. It's security-cleared but it's searched as soon as it gets to the checkpoint."

"Is the checkpoint close enough?"

"There's enough firepower to take down the first two towers. After that, the entire plant will blow."

"You're sure?"

"I'm sure."

Johnson stared thoughtfully at the smokestacks. "Reilly told me that the radiation would take out Illinois and Missouri. Is that right?"

"That's right. Probably more than that."

"It has to be worthwhile, you know."

"I assure you that it will be—"

"If it's not, Reilly will tell me. He said he'd call me."

"Then I'm sure he will."

"May I go to the motel now? Reilly told me to go to the motel and stay there."

Grozak started the car. "I just thought you should see—"

"You wanted to see if I'm afraid." Johnson gazed at him without expression. "I'm not afraid. Reilly taught me to control fear. You can't be afraid and win. And I will win, and all those bloodsucking bastards will lose." He leaned back and closed his eyes. "Just make sure that blast will do the job."

## Three Days

"Don't start the engine," Jock said in a low voice as Jane got into the car. "Take off the brake and I'll push you down to the road. We may get enough distance so that they won't hear us."

"Not much chance." The night was very still and icy cold so that her breath plumed with every word. "We can try." She disengaged the brake. "Let's go."

She didn't have to tell him twice. She felt the car move sluggishly on the ice beneath the tires as he pushed the car carefully and laboriously toward the road.

No sign of stirring from the chalet.

She was half hoping that someone would hear them. Maybe if they did, Jock would give up the idea of—

They reached the gravel road.

Jock was breathing harshly as he jumped into the passenger seat beside her. "Don't gun it. Slow. Very slow."

The gravel crackled beneath her tires like BBs spat from a child's gun.

No sign of life from the chalet.

Or was there?

Yes, a light illuminated one window.

"Go!" Jock said. "Get on the highway but get off at the first exit. They'll expect us to stay on it. We'll access another highway later."

Her cell phone rang.

She glanced at Jock and then punched the button.

"What the hell are you doing?" Trevor asked. "And where's Jock?"

"Sitting beside me." The highway was just ahead. "I left you a note."

"Get back here."

"Read the note." She entered the highway. "I'm sorry, Trevor." She hung up the phone.

"I'm sorry too," Jock said gently as he held out his hand for the phone. "I want to trust you, Jane. I promise I'll give the phone back to you when we get to Reilly."

She slowly put the phone in his palm. The surrender made her feel very vulnerable.

"Thank you." Jock turned off the ringer and stuffed the phone in his jacket pocket. "Now get off at the exit coming up."

Goddamn her." Mario's expression was as violent as his tone. "She's cheating me."

"Watch your mouth," Trevor said. "You read the note. Jock didn't give her much choice. She said she'd let us know something as soon as she's verified Reilly's location."

"There's always a choice," MacDuff said. He reached for the phone. "She should have come to me. I'd have managed to make Jock cough up everything he knew."

"What are you doing?" Trevor said.

"Arranging for a rental car to pick me up and take me to the airport. She said Idaho. I'm going to Idaho."

"*We're* going to Idaho," Trevor said.

"Why not just take off after them?" Mario said impatiently. "We might be able to intercept them before they find Reilly. And maybe Jock lied to her and intends to change the destination once they're on the road."

"Jock made a deal with her," MacDuff said. "And right now I doubt if he's capable of any complicated deceptions."

"Or is he?" Trevor asked Mario. "You've been spending a lot of time with him."

Mario thought about it and then slowly shook his head. "He kept going in and out. Sometimes almost normal, other times he was sort of blurred."

"Then it's Idaho." Trevor picked up his duffel and started stuffing clothes into it. "Let's get the hell out of here."

# 19

## Two Days

"We'd better stop for gas," Jane said. "There's a truck stop up ahead. They usually have good food in their restaurants."

"Yes." Jock looked at the brightly lit gas station. "And very good coffee." He smiled. "It's strange how well I remember little things and have trouble with the big things. They must slip under the wire somehow."

"How long were you with Reilly?"

"It's hard to remember. The days blurred together." He frowned thoughtfully. "Maybe . . . a year, eighteen months . . ."

"That's a long time." Jane pulled into the gas station. "And you were pretty young."

"I didn't think so at the time. I thought I was old enough to do anything, be anything. Cocky. Very cocky. That's why I had no problem taking the job

Reilly offered me. I couldn't imagine that my judg-ment could fail." He grimaced. "But Reilly showed me, didn't he?"

"Evidently Reilly is very good at what he does." Jane got out of the car. "I'll pump the gas. You go in and get us coffee. It's going to be a long drive."

"Don't get too much gas." Jock got out of the car. "Just enough to get us to the next big town."

"What?"

"We'll have to abandon this car and rent another one. The laird will be checking to get the license number of this one."

"That's very astute of you."

He shook his head. "Training. You never stay in the same rental car for any length of time." He smiled sardonically. "Reilly wouldn't be pleased, and that meant punishment."

"What kind of punishment?"

He shrugged. "I don't remember."

"I think you do. I believe you remember more than you tell me. Whenever you don't want to an-swer, you conveniently 'forget.'"

Jock gave her a troubled glance. "I'm sorry. I don't remember," he repeated. "I'll get the coffee."

Jane didn't speak again until they were back on the road. "I didn't mean to make you feel uncom-fortable. I guess I'm a little nervous. We're getting so close. You're sure you know where Reilly is lo-cated?"

"As sure as I can be." Jock lifted his coffee to his lips. "We'll go to the place where I had my training. He's so sure that I won't break my basic training that I'd bet he's never left it. It would be an admission of failure, and Reilly's ego wouldn't permit it."

"What if you're wrong?"

"I have a few more places to search that he doesn't know I know about."

"And how did you manage that?"

"I didn't manage anything. That wasn't an option during that time. His housekeeper, Kim Chan, dropped information about them between her training bouts with me."

"What kind of training?"

"Sexual. Sex is a driving force. Reilly used sex along with everything else to maintain control. And Kim was very well versed in sexual pain of every sort. She enjoyed it."

"I'm surprised Reilly would tolerate anyone around him who would talk out of turn."

"Kim wouldn't dare let him know that she'd let anything slip. She might not even remember she did. She had perfect confidence that Reilly's conditioning would hold and that she didn't have to be careful with me. She's been with him for over ten years."

"A personal relationship?"

"Only in that they feed on each other. He lets her have a certain amount of power and she does whatever he tells her to do."

"You seem to remember her very well," Jane said dryly. "No blanks there."

"Kim liked me wide awake and drug free when she had her turn at me."

"But you'll have your payoff now."

"Yes."

"No enthusiasm? You told me you hated Reilly."

"I hate him. But I can't think about it now."

"Why?"

"It would get in the way. When I think about Reilly, it's hard for me to think of anything else. I have to find him and make sure he doesn't hurt the laird." He changed the subject. "According to the map, the next city is Salt Lake. If we dump the car at the airport, it may not be found for days. We'll pick up another car and do the same thing at—"

"You have it all planned." A hint of sarcasm inflected Jane's words. "I feel like a chauffeur."

He gave Jane an uncertain glance. "You don't believe we should do it that way?"

She made a face. "Of course I do. I'm a little on edge. It's a good idea. We'll stop in Salt Lake. I'm actually feeling a little more optimistic about this, though I still don't condone your blackmail. Even if you're on automatic, you have a heck of a lot more experience at this than I do. It's a little like turning Reilly's weapons against him."

Jock gave her a pleased smile. "It is, isn't it? It makes me feel better when I remember that." He glanced down at the map again. "We should probably get a four-wheel-drive SUV next time. The radio weather said there was going to be a blizzard in the Northwest in the next few days. The roads get pretty rough in bad weather in the area we're going to."

\*  \*  \*

## One Day

"How much farther?" Jane's eyes strained to see through the windshield. "I can't even see the white line on the highway." The snow was spinning across the tarmac in front of their SUV like a whirling dervish.

"Not far." Jock looked down at the map on his lap. "Another few miles."

"This area is pretty desolate. I haven't even seen a gas station for the last twenty miles."

"That's the way Reilly likes it. No neighbors. No questions."

"Trevor told me the same thing about MacDuff's Run." She glanced at him. "But the other side of the coin is that it's difficult to get help to isolated places like this. You said that you'd let me call out the police or anyone I wanted to contact the minute we got to Reilly. You didn't tell me that they'd have to brave a snowstorm and the wilderness primeval to get here."

"You're not being fair. I didn't know there'd be a snowstorm. Though this isn't a blizzard yet. The squalls have been coming and going. Give it another couple hours." He smiled. "And, clever as he is, I don't believe Reilly has the technology to create it. It's just bad luck."

"You don't seem upset about it." She studied his face in the lights of the dashboard. His expression was tense, alert, and, good God, eager. His eyes were gleaming with excitement and he looked like a boy going off on a great adventure, she realized in shock.

"Why should I be upset? I don't mind the snow. Reilly had me taught to perform my function in all kinds of weather. He always said that no one expected attack by an enemy when they were already being attacked by nature."

"But then, Reilly will be expecting it."

"Perhaps. But he thinks we're still back at the Run. There's a road branching off to the right just ahead." He squinted, trying to see out the windshield. "Take it. About a mile down the road you'll see a shack."

She stiffened. "Reilly?"

"No, it's an old hunting shack. It's a run-down ruin of a place, but there's a propane heater and you'll be able to keep warm until you get someone to come. There's a fireplace too, but don't light it. I don't think anyone could see the smoke in this storm but you wouldn't want to take the chance."

She could see the shack now, and it was as dilapidated as he'd said it would be. Boarded-up windows and a front porch that had missing planks. "And this is where you're dumping me?"

"It's the safest place I know. And it's only safe if you're very careful."

She pulled over in front of the shack. "How close are we to Reilly's place?"

He didn't answer.

"Jock, you promised me. I have to be able to tell Trevor where he is. You've got your head start. Now, dammit, give me the information I need."

He nodded. "You're right." He got out of the SUV and moved toward the front door. "Come in. I have something to collect and I don't have much time." He gave her a faint smile. "Can't waste that head start."

The furniture in the lodge consisted of a rickety wood table, two chairs, the propane heater Jock had mentioned, and, tossed in a corner, a moth-eaten sleeping bag. Jock lit the heater and then unrolled a state map on the table. He pointed to a spot in the north central corner of the state. "That's where we are now." He took off his gloves and skimmed his finger along the map to a spot near the Montana border. "That's where Reilly's headquarters is located. It used to be an old trading post, but Reilly bought it, remodeled, and added another two thousand square feet. The new addition is half underground, and that's where Reilly's personal quarters are located. He has a bedroom and office with a special records-filing room. Adjoining it is his favorite place, the antiquity room."

"Antiquity?"

"He has an office with shelves containing all sorts of artifacts from Herculaneum and Pompeii. Records, ancient documents, books. Coins. Lots and lots of books of ancient coins." He tapped another spot. "There's a back door leading from this office to the helicopter landing pad."

"How many of his men are there?"

"Usually only one or two guards at the most. The main training camp is across the Montana border. The only people who occupy the house are Reilly,

Kim Chan, and the training prospect Reilly is most interested in at the moment." His lips curved in a bitter smile. "His favorite."

"Like you."

"Like me." He pointed at the camp across the border. "But if he gets a chance to call the camp, a swarm could come across that state line like killer bees. Tell Trevor not to let him make that call."

"Surprise?"

"It's hard to surprise him. He has video cameras in trees all over the woods surrounding the post and land mines planted at regular intervals. There's a security room at the house where the cameras can be monitored and the land mines activated. Any stranger approaching would be an easy target."

"But could he see them coming in this snowstorm?"

"Not well. But maybe well enough."

"And only a couple sentries?"

"Sometimes not even that when I was here. With the video cameras it's not necessary." He moved toward a paneled wall across the room, placed his hands at two points, pressed, and a six-foot section slid back to reveal a cavity containing a large rectangular wooden box. "That's the layout. Good luck to them."

"They'd have better luck if you'd wait and lead them to Reilly."

He shook his head. "I've given you all I can." He lifted the lid of the box. "Come here."

She followed him across the room and looked down into the box. "Jesus, you have enough weapons here to start a war." The box was filled with automatic rifles, hand grenades, knives, pistols . . .

"Reilly always liked me to be prepared. He has weapon stashes all over the state. This one was closest to his headquarters. For every mission he'd send me here to choose the weapon of choice. I wasn't sure the cache would still be here." He smiled mirthlessly. "But why get rid of it when he was sure I'd never be able to function as a thinking human being again? He probably used it to train his current subject." He took a pistol, rifle, wire, dynamite, and plastic explosives from the box. "You know how to use a gun?" When she nodded, he gave her the pistol and reached into the box for another for himself. "Keep it with you. Don't lay it down for a minute."

"Don't worry."

He handed back her cell phone. "You're on your own."

"And so are you. It doesn't have to be that way."

"Yes, it does. Because I choose it. And, God, it's good to be able to have the will to choose my own path." He moved toward the door. "Stay here and be quiet and you'll be safe." The door opened and let in a blast of cold, snow-wet wind. The next moment he was gone.

Gone after Reilly. Taking his head start and running with it. God help him.

She flipped open her phone and dialed Trevor's number.

\* \* \*

Stay where you are," Trevor said. "We're in Boise. We'll get to you as soon as possible."

"I'm not going anywhere on my own. I'd be wandering around in the snow and probably set off one of Reilly's booby traps or video cameras. Jock's in enough danger without me putting that bastard on the alert." She looked out at the falling snow. It seemed to be getting heavier. "Can't you call Venable and get him to have the CIA or Homeland Security set up a ring around this entire area?"

"Not until I know you're safe."

"I'm safe now."

"The hell you are. You're sitting on Reilly's doorstep. Besides, they wouldn't be able set up an operation that big in the blink of an eye. Particularly with all the conflict going on between the agencies. They might slip and tip off Reilly and cause him to call that Montana training camp Jock told you about. And if Reilly has as many bolt-holes as Jock claims, he could slip away from them." She heard him say something away from the receiver. "Mac-Duff is looking at the map. It looks like you may be an hour by road. Fifteen minutes by air. We're on our way. MacDuff says he'll set up a helicopter if this damn weather permits." She heard more conversation in the background. "Mario is renting an SUV with snow tires and heading out right away. One way or another, we'll get to you." He hung up.

She felt a little warmer, comforted, as she pressed the disconnect. She wasn't really alone. She could dial Trevor and hear his voice.

Who was she kidding? She'd never been more alone in her life than she was in this rickety shack only miles from Reilly's lair.

Okay, but she had a weapon. Her hand grasped the hilt of the .357 Magnum more tightly.

She propped a chair beneath the knob of the front door, curled up in the corner near the heater, and wrapped her arms around herself to keep warm. That propane heater might save her from freezing, but it was pitifully inadequate for warmth.

Come on, Trevor. Let's get this bastard.


There was someone near.

Jock stopped, still, listening.

He'd only gone a few hundred yards from the shack when he'd sensed . . . something.

Now he could hear it too. The crunch of snow beneath a foot.

Where?

From the road, from where he'd come.

Who? The sentries were always stationed around the house, not this far away. But Reilly might feel more cautious now that he was involved with Grozak.

But if this was a sentry, he shouldn't be able to hear him. Silence was paramount in Reilly's training. Noise was clumsy, and Reilly didn't permit clumsiness.

Another step crunching the snow.

Moving toward the shack where he'd left Jane.

Dammit, he had no time for this.

Make time.

He whirled and moved silently over the snow.

The driving snow kept him from seeing anything until he was only a few yards away.

Up ahead, a dark blur. Tall, very tall, long legs . . .

Gauge your distance.

Silence.

Remember, silence.

Where were they? Surely an hour had passed since she'd called Trevor. Jane checked her watch. An hour and fifteen minutes. It wasn't time to panic. The roads were terrible and the snow had increased in the last thirty minutes. It was pelting down now. Maybe Trevor's estimate had been optimistic.

A pounding on the door. "Jane!"

She jerked upright. She knew that voice. Thank God, they were here. She jumped to her feet, ran across the room, and pushed the chair from beneath the doorknob. "What kept you? I was afraid—"

The edge of a hand came down on her wrist, and the gun in her numbed hand fell to the floor.

"Sorry, Jane." Mario's voice was regretful. "I wouldn't have chosen to do this. Life can be a bitch." He turned to the man standing next to him. "Delivered as promised, Grozak."

Grozak. Jane stared at the man uncomprehendingly for a moment. But these were the features of the man in the photo Trevor had shown her that day in the study. "Mario?"

He shrugged. "It was necessary, Jane. You and Cira's gold appear to be sharing the spotlight for the most popular prize with Grozak, and I had to—"

"Stop yammering," Grozak said. "I didn't come here to have you waste my time." He lifted the hand at his side and pointed a gun at Jane. "Out. We need to pay a visit to Reilly. I can't tell you how eagerly he's waiting for you."

"Screw you."

"I want you alive, but I really don't care if you're damaged. You can either come with me or I'll shoot off your kneecap. I'm sure Reilly wouldn't mind you helpless for what he has in mind."

Jane was still staring in disbelief at Mario. Mario a traitor?

"Mario, you did this?"

He shrugged. "Do what he says, Jane. We don't have much time. I was afraid that Trevor would get here ahead of me, but they grounded his helicopter at a podunk airport near here and he's scrambling for a rental car."

"I was disappointed," Grozak said. "I was looking forward to turning you both over to Reilly. It would have been insurance."

"If Trevor shows up and I'm not here, he'll call the authorities."

"If Trevor shows up, he'll run into Wickman, and Wickman will be delighted to dispose of him before he has a chance to call anyone."

"Wickman is here?"

"He'll be here. He was supposed to meet me ten minutes ago. The snow must have delayed him." He smiled. "Now stop trying to delay me. I have a lot to do today. Tomorrow is showtime."

"You can't get away with this. You're going down, Grozak."

Grozak chuckled. "Did you hear her, Mario? I'm pointing a gun at her, but I'm the one going down."

"I hear her." He pointed the gun he'd taken from Jane at Grozak. "Actually, you are going down, Grozak."

He shot Grozak between the eyes.

"My God." Jane watched Grozak slump to the floor. "You killed him. . . ."

"Yes." Mario gazed down at Grozak with no expression. "Isn't it strange? I thought I'd feel some satisfaction, but I don't. He shouldn't have killed my father that way. I told Grozak that I had no affection for him and that he could dispose of him if he needed to do it. But he shouldn't have done it that way. It disturbed me. It made it very . . . personal."

She stared at him in disbelief. "Patricide is very personal."

"I never considered him my father. Maybe as a small child. But he went away and left my mother and me in that stinking village where we both had to work from morning to night just to stay alive."

"Desertion shouldn't mean a death sentence."

He shrugged. "I didn't plan it that way. Grozak wasn't even certain he'd have to do it. Only if he thought my position might need reinforcing. But he couldn't touch anyone at the castle, and I wasn't making the progress with the scrolls he needed in finding the gold. I was the only one who might be able to do what he needed at the castle. So I had to be completely suspicion-free."

She shook her head. "But I know you were shocked when it happened. No one could be that good an actor."

"I was shocked. I had orders to have no communication with Grozak unless it was to tell him that I knew where to find the gold. He didn't want me to blow my cover. Laudable plan, and I suppose it did make my reaction to my father's death more realistic. Bastard."

"You were working for Grozak all along?"

"From the day Trevor hired me. I was due to leave for the Run the next morning, but Grozak paid me a visit that night and made me an offer I couldn't refuse."

"The gold?"

He nodded. "But I soon found out that was a lie. Why should he give me the gold when he could use it as a bargaining chip?"

"Why indeed?"

"Actually, I was very popular that night. Reilly called me too and told me he'd give me a bonus if I could let him know when Jock left the castle. He evidently didn't trust Grozak. I didn't trust the cheap bastard either. So I had to start making plans of my own."

"A little double-dealing?"

"It was obviously the way the game was played. After we left the Run I called Grozak and told him that you were heading for the U.S. I also called Reilly to make a deal of my own. Reilly wanted to make sure

Jock didn't talk and he wanted either you or the gold. Or both."

"And that's why you wanted that time with Jock. Were you planning on killing him?"

He frowned. "Not if I was sure he wasn't going to remember. I'm not like Grozak or Reilly. I don't kill indiscriminately. And if Jock did remember, Wickman was watching the chalet from the foothills and I could have called him to take care of it."

"But Jock fooled you. He didn't tell you that he'd remembered. Was Grozak upset with you?"

"Yes, but Wickman was following you. I told Grozak that he should let Jock take you into the lion's den and I'd let him know when and where to pick you up."

"And that's what you did."

He shook his head sadly. "You don't understand. I don't want to do this. But I'm not like you. I need nice things. A fine house, beautiful old books, paintings. It's a hunger."

"It's corruption."

"Perhaps." He motioned with the gun. "But I'll probably appear pristine-clean to you after you meet Reilly. I understand he's a very unpleasant man."

"You're really taking me to Reilly?"

"Of course, and very quickly." He checked his watch. "Trevor and MacDuff won't waste time. They should be on my heels."

"Why are you doing this? You can't get away with it."

"But I can. I turn you over to Reilly. I tell him the

info about the gold that was in that last Cira scroll and where to find the transcript at the Run. He gives me the money he promised me and I take off. If I run into Trevor and MacDuff, I tell them Reilly has you and that I was on my way to the police."

"And I'll tell them exactly what you did."

"I doubt if you'll get the opportunity. Reilly will get out of this and probably take you with him. He's spent half his life preparing hideouts and bolt-holes, and the CIA hasn't been able to find him for the last decade. There's no reason to think they'll succeed this time." He motioned again. "No time for talk. We have to move."

"If I don't, I suppose you're threatening to shoot off my kneecaps too?"

"I'd hate to do it. I'm very fond of you, Jane."

But he would do it. A man who'd stand by and let his father be butchered would have no real compunction. She'd probably have a better chance with Reilly. At any rate, standing here with his gun pointed at her was a lose-lose situation. She started toward the door. "Let's go. We wouldn't want to keep Reilly waiting."

The snow was stinging cold as he opened the door. Mario led her past the three cars parked before the shack.

"Aren't we going to drive?"

Mario shook his head. "Reilly said that unless you had the deactivation codes for the driveway, the car would set off the explosives. And there was no way he was going to give those codes out. He said to walk through the woods. I was to call him as soon as I reached them and he'd turn off the booby traps as the video cameras showed us coming through the trees."

She could barely see three feet ahead of her through the snow. How the devil could Reilly see anything on camera?

"Change your mind, Mario," she said over her shoulder. "So far the only criminal thing you've done is kill a murderer."

"And become an accessory to a terrorist. They either shoot you or put you in jail and throw away the key for that. I made a choice that night when Grozak hired me. I was going to be rich. I can still make it work." He halted. "Stop. We've almost reached the tree line." He dialed his phone. "Mario Donato, Reilly. I've got her. We're coming in." He listened for a moment. "Okay." He hung up the phone. "We're going to have a welcoming committee when we reach the house. Kim Chan and Reilly's latest protégé, Chad Norton." He grimaced. "Another Jock. Another weakling."

"Jock isn't a weakling. He's a victim."

"He has to have a basic flaw in his character to be manipulated like that."

"You don't think it could happen to you?"

"No way." He gestured with the gun. "And I doubt if it can happen to you."

"But you're willing to let Reilly try."

"If you turn out to be of the same weakling stock, then you'll deserve it." He smiled. "Maybe you'll get lucky and that half-wit Jock will save you." He nodded at the woods ahead. "Move."

She hesitated. Once she reached that tree line the video cameras would pick her up and she'd be in Reilly's court.

"Jane."

"I'm going." She started toward the woods. "I respect that gun. I'm not about to let you shoot—" She spun, her leg lifted in a roundhouse kick. Her boot hit the gun, sending it flying, and she followed through with another kick to Mario's gut. "Weakling? You son of a bitch."

He grunted and fell to his knees.

She hit him in the back of the neck and he fell to the ground. "You egocentric excuse for a—"

Christ, he'd fallen too close to the gun. He was reaching for it!

She dove into the snow. Her hand closed on the handle. It was cold, wet, slippery. . . .

He was on top of her, reaching down to grab the gun from her. "Bitch. You are a weakling. Reilly will be—"

She pulled the trigger.

He jerked upright like a marionette, gazing down at her in disbelief. "You—shot—me." A tiny rivulet of blood trickled out of the corner of his mouth. "Hurts . . ." He collapsed on top of her. "Cold . . . cold. Why am I—" He shuddered and went still.

She pushed him off her and looked down at him. His eyes were wide open in disbelief—and death. She shuddered as she sat up in the snow. She couldn't seem to move. She should get out of here. They were only a few miles from Reilly's headquarters. Maybe they'd heard the shot.

In a minute. She'd killed a man, and the realization was just hitting her. She kept remembering the Mario she'd first met, the man she'd thought him to be. In death his features were softer, boyish, as they'd been that night.

All pretense. All deception.

Get a grip. Get out of here.

She got to her feet.

"What the hell happened to—" A voice behind her.

She instinctively whirled with the gun raised.

"Hold it!"

MacDuff. She dropped her arm to her side.

"Thank you." He moved forward to stare down at Mario. "Grozak or Reilly?"

"Me."

He swung around to look at her. "Why?"

"He was in Grozak's pay and made a deal with Reilly on the side. He was going to turn me over to Reilly."

He smiled faintly. "And you didn't choose to go." His smile faded. "What word of Jock?"

"I haven't seen him since he left me at the shack. Where's Trevor?"

"Here." Trevor came toward them. "I was farther back than MacDuff. I ran into an encumbrance." He looked down at Mario and his lips tightened grimly. "I wish the bastard was alive so that I could kill him myself. Did he hurt you at all?"

She shook her head. "What encumbrance?"

"Wickman. His body was under a pile of snow

near the shack." He looked at Jane. "We found Grozak at the cabin. Mario?"

She nodded.

"And Wickman?"

"I don't know. I don't think so. Grozak was supposed to meet him. I guess Mario could have killed him." She shook her head. "I don't know. But we have to get out of here. Someone might have heard the shot."

MacDuff shook his head. "I barely heard it and I was close to you. Maybe it's this snow muffling the sound." He glanced at Trevor. "What do you think?"

"I heard it. But very dimly." He looked at her. "So tell us what happened while we're on our way back to the car."

"Back to—" She went still, her gaze on the tree line. "I'm not going back." She turned quickly to Trevor. "Mario arranged with Reilly to take me through the trees toward the house. Reilly was going to deactivate the booby traps as the video cameras sensed our passage. We could still do it." She held up her hand as Trevor started to protest. "The video cameras won't be able to tell the difference between you and Mario in this snowstorm. You're about the same height and weight. If you keep your head covered and down and the gun visible, I'll be going first so I'll be the first one they see."

"And what do you do once you reach the house?" MacDuff asked.

"Play it by ear. We were supposed to be met at the door by Kim Chan and another of Reilly's protégés, Norton. If we can get past them, I doubt if there are any booby traps inside the house. Maybe we'll get to see the great man himself right away." She started toward the tree line. "Let's go."

"No way," Trevor said roughly. "Get the hell back to the car and out of here."

She shook her head. "It's a good plan considering the circumstances. We can nail Reilly and get the information we need to stop Grozak's attack."

"It's a lousy plan," Trevor said.

She turned to MacDuff. "Will you go with me? You're not as good a physical match, but it could work. Jock is probably positioning himself somewhere near there. You'll be able to contact him. That's all you care about, isn't it?"

He smiled. "That's all I care about. Lead on."

"No!" Trevor drew a deep breath. "Okay, I'll go with you." He pulled the hood of his anorak up. "Go. We should know by the first hundred yards whether they can tell the difference between me and Mario."

MacDuff shrugged. "It seems I'm out of a job. I guess I'll just have to go after Jock on my own."

"How?"

"I'm pretty good with booby traps. I had a lot of experience with land mines in Afghanistan. It will take me a long time to block the cameras and deactivate the land mines, but I'll get there eventually."

"If you don't get blown up," Jane said.

He nodded. "But then just think of the distraction I'd give you." He moved toward the tree line, angling to the left. "I'll wait five minutes after you start through the woods. With any luck they'll be concentrating all their attention on you as soon as the video camera picks up on you."

"I could go with him," Trevor said as he watched MacDuff walk away from them. "You should go back to the car and let us do it, dammit."

She shook her head. "They're expecting Mario and me. If they don't see us, they'll come looking." She started toward the tree line. "I'd rather go looking for them instead of trying to hide in those woods in a snowstorm."

# 20

Another camera.

MacDuff studied the angle at which the camera was pointed and moved to the left to avoid the shot.

Careful.

Slow.

Stay close to the trunk of the trees. Most of the time booby traps were set up on the most likely traveled paths.

Most of the time.

Christ, he was sweating blood in these frigid temperatures. Booby traps had always been one of his pet hates. He'd lost too many men to land mines. You couldn't see them. You couldn't fight them. You just had to try to avoid them and hope. Or pray.

He couldn't have gone more than twenty yards

since he'd left Jane and Trevor, and this excruciatingly slow pace was not making him a happy man.

Better a patient man than a dead one.

Another video camera up ahead. Christ, they were hard to see through the driving snow and camouflage Reilly had set up.

He studied the angle; it was aimed at the path to his left.

But that didn't mean there wasn't another camera behind that pine close to—

"Don't move."

MacDuff's head whipped around to see Jock standing a few feet away.

"It's a triple." Jock carefully stepped across the snow. "Every now and then Reilly planted three land mines in a row across the paths. It would catch anyone trying to avoid the main booby traps." He was right next to MacDuff. "You shouldn't be here. You could have gotten hurt."

"Tell me about it," MacDuff said grimly. "I could say the same about you."

"I know these woods. I know where every one of those land mines is planted. I can't tell you how many times I've come through here in the pitch dark." He turned. "Come on. I'll take you out of here."

"No, but you can take me to Reilly."

Jock shook his head.

"Don't say no," MacDuff said roughly. "I'm taking him out, Jock. Take me to him or I'll go by myself."

"There's no reason to go. I've taken care of it."

MacDuff stiffened. "You've killed him?"

He shook his head. "Soon."

"I can't wait. It has to happen now."

"Soon."

"Look, you like Jane. She and Trevor are on their way to Reilly's headquarters now. They don't know what's going to happen when they reach there, but it won't be easy."

Jock went rigid. "How long ago?"

"They should be there any time." His gaze narrowed on Jock's face. "Why?"

"They shouldn't have gone. I told her to stay at the shack." Jock wheeled and started in the direction of Reilly's headquarters. "Follow me. Hurry. Step in my footprints."

"Believe me, I will." He carefully placed his boot in Jock's print in the snow. "Go ahead. I'll keep up."

"You'll have to. I took out both the sentries, but that won't keep her from—" Jock was flying over the snow. "She'll die. I told her. She shouldn't have gone. . . ."

They had to be close to the house, Jane thought. It seemed as if they'd been trekking through these woods forever. Her gaze rose to the branches of the tree in front of her. The cameras were so well camouflaged that she'd only been able to spot two on the way here. How was MacDuff going to take them out if she couldn't even see them?

Let him worry about that. She and Trevor had their own problems.

"There it is." Trevor's low voice in back of her. "Straight ahead."

She could see the lights too. About a hundred yards from where they were standing. "The snow's lessening again. Keep your head down."

"It's so low it's practically up my ass now," Trevor said. "I can't do any— Get down!"

A shot.

"Jesus." Jane hit the ground. "The video cam— They know. They saw—"

Another shot.

Trevor grunted with pain.

She looked back at him. Blood. High on his chest. Panic knifed through her. "Trevor?"

"I'm hit," he said harshly. "Dammit, get the hell out of here. They'll be streaming out of that house any minute."

Christ.

"Get out of here!"

"Can you walk?"

"Hell, yes. It's a shoulder wound." He was wriggling on his belly toward the trees. "But not as fast as you. Run."

"You run. They're not going to shoot me. They were aiming at you. Reilly wants me alive." She got to her knees. "I'll run toward them with my hands up and give you time to get away. And don't you dare argue with me. Find MacDuff. Call the CIA. Do something. I want someone to be out here to come after me when I'm in there with Reilly."

Another shot.

She heard the thunk of the bullet in the snow close to Trevor's head.

Her heart jumped to her throat.

No more time.

She sprang to her feet, raised her hands above her head, and started running toward the house.

"No!"

"Stop yelling and move your ass, Trevor. I'm not doing this for nothing." She glanced over her shoulder and relief surged through her as she saw him rising to a low crouch and running behind the trees.

Relief? He might be dodging those bullets, but what about those damn land mines?

Oh God, be careful.

Someone was standing in the driveway. A man?

No, a woman. Small, delicate features and a slim, compact body that still managed to appear strong.

And a pistol in her hand pointed straight at Jane.

"I'm not resisting," Jane said. "I've no weapon and I can't hurt—"

An explosion shook the earth!

She looked over her shoulder at the place where Trevor had disappeared. . . .

Smoke was curling up to the sky.

The tall cedar trees were on fire.

"No," she whispered in horror. "Trevor . . ."

The land mines.

Dead. He had to be dead. No one could live through that inferno.

But she couldn't accept that and give up. He might have survived. There might be some way she could help him. She took a step back toward the woods. He could have been thrown by the blast and—

Pain.

Darkness.

Stone walls. Creamy beige, cracked, and appearing very, very ancient.

"You really shouldn't have tried to run away. I was disappointed."

Jane's gaze swung to the man who'd spoken. Fiftyish, fine features, dark hair with white sideburns. And he'd spoken with an Irish accent, she realized suddenly. "Reilly?" she whispered.

He nodded. "And that's the last time you'll be allowed to address me with such disrespect. We'll start with 'sir' and progress from there."

She shook her head to clear it and then flinched as pain shot through her. "You . . . hit me."

"No, Kim hit you. You're lucky she didn't have Norton shoot you. She doesn't approve of my interest in your reprogramming and would be delighted to be rid of you." He turned to a far corner. "Isn't that right, Kim?"

"It's an indulgence."

Jane's gaze flew to the small woman sitting in the chair by the window. It was the Eurasian woman who'd met her in the driveway. From this close she looked even more fine-boned and delicate and her voice was soft, gentle. "And she was too expensive.

You may never see that gold and you sent two of our best-trained men to Grozak to pay for her."

"I can afford to be self-indulgent." There was an edge to Reilly's voice. "And it's my decision what I wish to pay. You might remember that, Kim. You've been getting entirely too arrogant of late. I tolerate it because you're—"

"Trevor!" Jane sat upright as memory flooded back to her.

An explosion that shook the earth.

Trees burning.

Trevor. She had to get to Trevor.

Her feet swung to the ground and she struggled to get to her feet.

"No." Reilly pushed her back down on the couch. "You probably have a concussion and I don't want you damaged any more than you are."

"Trevor. He's hurt. I have to see if I can help him."

"He's dead. And if he's not, he will be soon. It's freezing cold out there. Hypothermia is dangerous to a healthy man; a wounded man has no chance at all."

"Let me go and see for myself."

He shook his head. "We have to leave here. After you appeared with Trevor, I sent my man Norton out to see where Mario Donato had gone. Lo and behold he found a body. Who killed him? Trevor?"

"No, I did."

"Really? Interesting. I approve. It shows a quality that's rare in a female. There was also another body. Your work too?"

She shook her head. "Wickman. Mario probably did it."

"His neck was broken. I wouldn't think Donato would be capable of killing like that. Now, my Jock was very accomplished in that type of murder. He came with you?"

"What did Donato say?"

"Nothing about Jock. Donato was trying very hard to cover all the bases. He knew I wouldn't be pleased if I knew that he'd let Jock come this close and not handed him over to me."

"I'm sure he would have betrayed anyone if he'd been able to do it."

"I'm sure too. Is Jock out there now?"

She didn't answer.

"I'll take that as a yes. It casts a new light on the situation."

She changed the subject. "Let me go and see if Trevor's alive. He can't hurt you if he's wounded."

"But he can't help me either. Sorry, I can't appease your curiosity now. It may be getting a little uncomfortable for me soon. Even though Trevor may be dead, Mario Donato told me when he called me that MacDuff may be heading in this direction."

"And you're afraid of MacDuff?"

"Don't be absurd. Not afraid. Just cautious. Even though it's not in his best interests, MacDuff might decide to call in the authorities if he thought Jock was in danger. He seems to be very protective of him."

"Somebody has to be. You nearly destroyed his mind."

"He did that to himself. He could have gone on for years performing the function I ingrained in him. It was the rebellion that broke him." He shrugged. "Actually, I'm more wary of Jock than of MacDuff. Jock's my creation, and I know the damage he can cause. Of course, if I could confront him face-to-face I could sway him, but that might not be possible. And I'm a man who doesn't take chances."

"You took a big one when you made a deal with Grozak. The U.S. government would never have stopped hunting for you if you'd gone through with it."

His brows rose. "But I did go through with it. The men are all in place and will carry out their designated duties as soon as I call and tell them it's a go."

She gazed at him in shocked horror. "But it would make no sense to do that. Grozak is dead. You don't have a deal any longer."

"But I do. When Grozak started to quibble about payment and Mario offered his services, I contacted a few of my extremist Islamic friends. There was no use letting a lucrative project go down the tubes if I decided to shut Grozak out of it. The Middle Eastern contingent will be taking over the operation and supplying me with all the protection I need."

"We should get out of here," Kim said as she rose to her feet. "You have her, now let's go."

"Kim's a little impatient," Reilly said. "She's been nervous since Jock wandered away from us. I told her that I could control him, but she didn't believe me."

"I was right," Kim said. "In the end he broke free. I always knew he was stronger than the others."

"It's not a question of strength." He looked pained. "How many times do I have to tell you that? I can control any subject with the right amount of exploration and effort. I didn't have quite enough time to search out that little foible he had or he wouldn't have broken."

"Little foible?" Jane stared at him incredulously. "Objection to killing children is a 'little foible'?"

"It's all in the way you look at it." He smiled. "The whole world rises and falls on the way we see the events that take place around us. If I'd had more time, I'd have been able to convince Jock that killing that child would make him a hero."

"Good God, that's sick."

"Cira would probably have admired me for being able to control those around me. She was a manipulator herself."

"Cira would have recognized you as the slimeball you are and ground you into the dirt."

His smile faded. "It's true there would probably have been a few battles. But I'm the one who would have won. I always win." He turned to Kim. "Call for my helicopter and start packing up the personnel records. Then call the compound and tell everyone there to disperse immediately until I call them. Don't panic them. Tell them it's just a precaution."

Kim headed for the door. "Where are we going?"

"Canada first and then North Korea. I have contacts there. After that, I'll play it by ear. Those religious terrorists are volatile. I'd prefer to deal with them at a distance."

"You'll never be able to get away with it," Jane
said.

"But I will. You don't understand. It's a different
world, and wars are different too. The man who can
control the mind and will can do anything. Those
soldiers in Iraq aren't afraid of regular combat, but
they're terrified of a man who will wander in to a
mess tent and blow himself up. A suicide with the
right papers and cover is everyone's worst nightmare." He tapped his chest. "I'm their worst nightmare."

"The CIA will pick you up before you get out of
the country."

Reilly shook his head. "I don't think so."

"The helicopter should be here in five minutes."
Kim came back in the room carrying a large brief-
case. "I have all the psychological subject files.
Should I pack up those historical documents?"

"No, I'll do it myself. I want to show my collection
to the lady."

"We don't have time to pack up all those artifacts.
You'll have to leave them."

"No, I'll take the coins and tell Norton to pack
the rest up and take them across the border for a
pickup." He held out his hand to Jane. "Come
along. I want you to see my collection."

"I'm not interested."

"You will be. You'll be very interested before I'm
done with you."

"No, I won't. You couldn't make me do anything." She stared him in the eye. "And you can't

make me remember something I never knew. You're crazy if you believe that."

"We'll see. The more I'm with you the more eager I am to get started." He opened the door and gestured for her to go inside the room. "You're going to prove very interesting. How many women could have managed to kill Mario Donato? As for the gold, look at your behavior pattern in the last years. You're completely fascinated by Cira. Those archaeological expeditions to digs in Herculaneum, your obsession with the scrolls. Every day you look in the mirror and see her. Perhaps deep down you want to protect her and her gold. Maybe you know where it is and are being selfish. Or you may have stumbled on the clue that can lead us to it and won't admit it to yourself." He smiled. "But I can correct that given enough time. I can do almost anything." His eyes glittered with pleasure. "And then the fun begins."

She felt a cold chill. He'd almost convinced her he could do it. And the frightening thing was that he didn't know how close she was to Cira. He didn't know about the dreams. . . . "Very flimsy reasoning, Reilly. I can't believe you'd actually make a deal with Mario to bring me here when there's no evidence I know anything at all."

"Believe it. And there is evidence. Come look at Cira's world." He gestured at the softly lit shelves that gave off an ambient glow across the room. "I've been collecting artifacts from Herculaneum and Pompeii for the last twenty years."

And it was an impressive collection, she thought,

as she saw a multitude of various artifacts that in-
cluded bowls, crude knives, scrolls, and stone reliefs
depicting exaggerated sexual acts. "You'd have gotten a lot of pleasure from Julius Precebio's scrolls,"
she said dryly. "He was into porn too."

"It was his right. The master always sets the rules.
And I do identify with Precebio. We have a lot in
common." He led her forward. "But you've missed
the most interesting exhibit." He nodded at the
stand in front of her. "Your personal contribution."

"What the devil are you—" She inhaled sharply.
"My God."

Her sketchbook. The one Trevor had stolen from
her two years ago. She'd only been concerned
about the sketches of Trevor, afraid that it would reveal her feelings for him. She hadn't remembered
this sketch that Reilly had chosen to place on exhibition.

"Extraordinary, isn't it?" Reilly murmured. "The
detail is so minute that it would be incredible for at
least part of it not to have been sketched from real
life."

It was a sketch of Cira, one of the many she'd
done since she'd come back from Herculaneum
four years ago. Cira was standing in profile in the
doorway of a room with rocky walls and ledges on
which various vases, bowls, and jewels were placed.
On a ledge farther away, displayed by itself, was an
open chest overflowing with gold coins.

She moistened her lips. "Real life? Sorry, I wasn't
around to sketch Cira two thousand years ago."

"But you might have found where she hid that chest and sketched the place."

"That's crazy. The sketch was purely imaginary."

"Perhaps. But I've been studying that sketch closely for weeks. I did a lot of research, and those striations in the rocks are found in formations in Italy near Herculaneum. As I said, the detail is truly amazing."

"Where did you get my sketchbook?"

"Grozak stole it from Trevor's hotel room and sent it to me. He thought it might intrigue me." He smiled. "It did. It raised all kinds of interesting possibilities."

"Listen, I don't know anything about that gold."

"We'll see. In a few weeks I'll know everything you know."

He gestured at the glass case in the center of the shelf. "Some of those coins are worth a fortune, but I've never found the one that the whole world would envy me having. It's been my dream for years. You just may be able to provide me with that final triumph."

"What?"

"A coin from the purse given to Judas for betraying Christ could be among the gold in that chest."

"That's crap."

He nodded at the book on display on his shelf. "Not according to rumors that have drifted down through the centuries. What a coup that would be." He smiled. "I'll have it all. The gold, the fame, Cira's statue that Trevor stole from me."

"You'll have a hard time stealing that from North Korea."

"Not really. I have people all over the world who only want to do whatever I wish."

"By that time MacDuff will have taken the statue for himself. He's as obsessed with Cira as everyone else."

"I know. He almost got in my way a couple years ago when we went after the same document."

"What document?"

He nodded at the file case in a corner of the bottom shelf. "I have the original in a specially sealed case, but the translation is there. It opened a brand-new school of thought to me regarding Cira and the gold." He smiled. "If you're good, I may let you see the translation during one of the latter stages in your training."

She stiffened. "I won't be good, you son of a bitch. I won't do anything you tell me."

He clucked softly. "Such disrespect. Now, if I was Grozak, I'd slap you. But I'm not Grozak." He turned to Kim, who'd just come into the room. "Tell Norton to go out to the place where the mine exploded. If he finds Trevor alive, kill him."

"No!" Panic soared through her. "You can't do that."

"But I can. I can do anything. That's what you've got to learn. Go ahead, Kim, tell him."

Kim turned to leave the room.

"No!"

"Since you're new at this, if you ask me politely I

might tell Kim to forget Trevor." He smiled. "But you'd have to say please."

He was staring at her with malicious satisfaction, waiting for her to give in. Submission. She wanted to break his neck.

But pride wasn't worth the chance of Trevor being killed to teach her a lesson. "Please," she said through her teeth.

"Not gracious, but I'll consider it a lesson learned." He gestured and Kim left the room. "Though Cira would have probably let me kill Trevor rather than give me the satisfaction."

"No, she wouldn't. She'd have given in and then waited to get her own back later."

"You seem very certain." He tilted his head. "Promising. Very promising."

Another ripple of fear went through her. God, he was clever. In the space of minutes he'd managed to make her surrender to his will when she'd never thought that possible.

"You're afraid," he said softly. "That's always the first step. I have to find the key and then turn it. You're not afraid for yourself, but you're afraid for Trevor. It's really too bad he's probably dead. He might be a valuable tool." He turned and picked up a briefcase on the desk. "But there's always Joe Quinn and Eve Duncan." He carefully put the cases with his coins in the briefcase before opening the file cabinet and putting the translations into the same briefcase. "One tool may be as efficient as the other."

"Is that how you trained Jock? Did you threaten people he loved?"

"Partly. But I had information to gather from him, so it had to be a combination of drugs and psychological training. I'll be following on those lines with you too, but every case is different."

"Every case is a horror story. You're a horror story."

"But aren't the most fascinating stories in literature all with their element of horror? Frankenstein, Lestat, Dorian Gray." He fastened the briefcase. "Come along. I wonder if I should take the original manuscripts instead of letting—"

His telephone rang and he pressed the button to answer it.

I can't do it," Jock said. "It's too late."

"You set the damn charge," Trevor said. "Now fix it."

"He can't fix it," MacDuff said as he finished wrapping a make-shift bandage around Trevor's shoulder. "He's already activated it. He wasn't planning on being here. If he gets near the landing pad, it will blow him to kingdom come."

"Why the landing pad?" Trevor's gaze shifted to the concrete landing pad half buried in snow. "Why not set a charge near the house?"

"I couldn't get close enough to the house," Jock said. "There's a ring of land mines around the entire perimeter. I had to wait for an increase in the snowfall, set the charge, and get out quick before I was seen." He looked at Trevor. "You were supposed to be going after Jane, not Reilly. Not right away. Neither Jane nor you was supposed to be here. I should have had at least another thirty minutes and then it would have been over."

"Too bad. Everything doesn't always work out like you think it will. And what's to keep the helicopter from blowing up the minute it sets down?"

"I set the wire a foot from the pad and covered it with snow. The vibration won't set it off, but direct foot pressure will."

"You're sure?"

Jock stared at him in bewilderment. "Of course I'm sure. I don't make mistakes."

"And what if Reilly doesn't use the landing pad?"

"He will. In less than ten minutes," Jock said. "Reilly is a very cautious man. He might not be alarmed about dealing with us, so I put on some pressure."

"What kind of pressure?"

"I called the police and told them about the training compound across the Montana border." He checked his watch and then his gaze focused on the back door. "About forty minutes ago. If Reilly hasn't gotten a call from the compound already, he'll get one soon. He'll be off and running. He'll have that helicopter here ASAP."

"Christ." Trevor turned to MacDuff. "You said you were good with mines. Jane's bound to be with Reilly. He may even make her go first. Can't you do anything about that charge?"

"Not in five minutes. I'd get out there just in time to meet Reilly and his crew."

"Shit. Then we try to go in after them."

"No." Jock was shaking his head. "I told you. We can't risk—"

"We can't risk Jane being blown up," Trevor interrupted. "So find us a way to get in there before that helicopter comes."

"I'm thinking about it." Jock's forehead was furrowed as he reached down and picked up his rifle. "The distance is a little too far for a safe shot. It was going to be fine. You shouldn't have been here. Now I'll have to— Shit!"

"What's wrong?"

"The wind has picked up and is blowing the snow away from the wire. I can see a little bit of it from here."

Trevor could see it too. "Good."

"No. If he sees it, then everything is ruined. I can't let him get on that helicopter. This may be our last chance." He started forward. "Maybe if I'm careful I can go out and try to cover the wire again." His head lifted and he looked up at the sky. "Too late. Time's run out."

Trevor could hear it too. The beat of the rotors of a helicopter.

"Hell's bells." His gaze flew to the house.

The back door was opening.


Hurry. Get out there." Reilly pushed Jane through the doorway and said over his shoulder to

Kim, "You stay here and make sure Norton packs up everything into the truck and go with him."

"You're not taking me? That wasn't the plan." Kim looked at him, outraged. "You're leaving me behind?"

"If the police are at the compound, they'll be all over this place soon. They'll seize my collection. I have to be sure—" He stopped as he saw her expression. "Very well. Just tell Norton to pack everything and get out of here within the next half hour."

"I'll tell him." She handed him the personnel records. "You wait for me."

"Arrogant bitch," Reilly muttered as he pushed Jane ahead of him. "If I wasn't afraid she'd torch my collection, I'd leave her here to rot. She's not going to be that useful from now on anyway."

"That's loyalty." Jane watched the blue-and-white helicopter land. "Can't you see that everything's going down the tubes for you? The police are closing in. Forget about the agreement you made with the Muslims. Cut a deal."

"If you could see what's in these personnel records, you wouldn't even suggest that. They wouldn't deal." His pace quickened. "And as soon as I get in the air, I'm going to make those calls to my men in Chicago and Los Angeles, and within two hours I'll have a very happy partner who will meet us in Canada and whisk us to North Korea."

Jesus. She couldn't let him get on that helicopter. He mustn't make those calls.

What the hell could she do to stop him?

Stall. She halted. "I'm not going."

He pointed the gun at her. "I've no time for this nonsense. I've gone to a lot of trouble and I've no intention of losing you now. It's not an—"

A shot.

*Pain.*

She fell to the ground.

# 21

What the hell did you do?" Trevor said. "You shot her, you idiot."

"Only a flesh wound in the upper arm." Jock was aiming down the barrel of the rifle again. "She was in my way. I couldn't get a clear shot at Reilly."

"You still can't. He's weaving like a football player toward that helicopter." MacDuff started to laugh. "And leaving Jane behind. Jock, you son of a bitch, that's what you meant to do."

"It seemed very reasonable. If I can't get the shot, then it will distract him enough so that the explosion will get him. Reilly always taught me to have a backup." He zeroed in on the back of Reilly's head. "It's a gamble," he murmured. "Will he move left or right next? I'll . . . guess . . . left." He pulled the trigger.

* * *

Jane stared in horror as Reilly's head exploded.

"Son of a bitch." Kim Chan was standing a few feet away, staring at the monstrosity that a moment before had been Reilly. "I told him—" She was shaking with rage as she turned toward Jane. "You. He should never have— The fool." She lifted the gun in her hand. "Your fault. You and that idiotic Cira. You were—"

Jane rolled over in the snow and struck Kim in the knees, bringing her down.

Get the gun.

She had it.

But Kim was on her feet and running toward the helicopter. Christ, did she know those phone numbers to call? Would the suicide bombers pay attention to her if she did? She worked closely with Reilly. There was a chance she might want to step into his shoes. Jane struggled to her knees. "Stop. You can't do—"

The earth shook as Kim stepped on the snow-covered wire bordering the helicopter pad.

*Whoosh.*

An explosion.

Flames.

The woman was suddenly no longer there.

Then the helicopter exploded.

Shards of metal and rotors were hurling in every direction.

Jane buried her face in the snow and tried to flatten herself into the ground.

When she looked up seconds later it was to see the burning hulk of the helicopter.

"Are you okay?" It was Trevor kneeling beside her, unzipping her anorak to look at her arm.

He was alive!

Thank God. "I thought you were dead," she said shakily. "The land mine . . ."

"Jock set it off to make everyone think I'd bought it. MacDuff and he were staking out the house and he saw me crawling away. I was grateful." His lips tightened. "Until the looney kid shot you because you were in the way of him getting Reilly."

"I don't think I'm hurt much." She looked at the burning remains of the helicopter. "And it was worth it to stop Reilly from getting on that helicopter."

"I don't agree." He was looking at the wound. "Just a little bleeding. Jock said it was a flesh wound."

"Where is he?" Then she saw Jock and MacDuff heading for the house. She called, "Be careful. Norton's in there and he'll—"

"Don't worry," MacDuff said. "We'll be careful. But Jock doesn't want the police to hurt this Norton. He wants to get to him first. He's feeling a bit of empathy."

"Will he feel the same empathy for those suicide bombers at the compound?" Jane murmured as MacDuff and Jock disappeared into the house. "Jesus, what do you do with people like that?"

"Leave it up to the government. They'll probably put them in a hospital and try to deprogram them."

"If they can find them. Reilly called and told them he wanted all of them to 'disperse.'" She got to her feet. "But he took the personnel records with him." She moved slowly toward Reilly's body. "The records must have some information about those people." She carefully kept her gaze from the bloody corpse as she took the briefcase from Reilly's hand. "He had another one with his translations of documents from Herculaneum. I don't see— There it is." The other briefcase had been flung several yards away by the blast.

"I'll get it." Trevor moved across the field and picked up the briefcase. "Now let's get you to an emergency room to look at that wound." He smiled. "And I wouldn't mind a little first aid myself. MacDuff did a pretty makeshift job of bandaging."

"Complaints, complaints." MacDuff was coming toward them. "You're lucky we were there to save your ass. You can't expect everything." He glanced at the briefcase in Jane's hand. "What's that?"

"Personnel records from the compound."

He went still. "And what are you going to do with them?"

"Turn them over to Venable."

He shook his head. "Not Jock's." He held out his hand. "You can do what you like with the rest. But not Jock's records."

She hesitated.

"I'll take care of him," MacDuff said quietly. "You know I will. He's very close to crossing over to being normal. Whatever normal is supposed to be. I won't have that blasted to hell. You don't want that either."

No, she didn't want that to happen. She snapped open the briefcase and looked through the contents. She slowly held out the briefcase. "Only Jock's file, MacDuff."

MacDuff riffled through the file and drew out a folder. "That's all I care about." He glanced at the briefcase Trevor was holding. "What's that?"

"Copies of the translations of Reilly's Herculaneum documents," Trevor said.

MacDuff's eyes narrowed. "Indeed. I'd really like to see those."

"So would I," Jane said. "And I've earned the right for first look."

"Why not let me—"

"Back off, MacDuff."

She thought he was going to continue arguing but he smiled instead. "Consider me backed off." He handed the personnel briefcase back to her. "But keep me in mind for the second look. And you'd better get out of here with it or it will be impounded as evidence and buried for a decade or so in red tape. Neither one of us wants that. Can you drive?"

She nodded.

"There's a truck in the garage that Norton was packing up. Get to a hospital and get those wounds tended."

"I can drive," Trevor said.

"You lost more blood than I did," Jane said. "Jock

was trying to inflict as little damage as possible with me." She shook her head ruefully. "Jesus, I can't believe we're arguing about who has the worse wound."

"Whatever. You win. Who's going to wait here for the police?"

"I'll do it," MacDuff said. "Call Venable and have him call the local authorities and pave the way. I don't want to end up in jail." He looked at Jane. "Did Mario give you any idea what was in that last Cira scroll?"

"Only that it gave a clue about the gold. He was going to sell the translation to Reilly." She frowned as she recalled that conversation with Mario. "No, that's not right. He was going to tell him where to find the translation." She glanced at Trevor. "We have to go back to the Run."

"It's still there?"

"That's what he said." She glanced at MacDuff. "So it seems we'll still be your guests for a while."

"If I let you come back."

Trevor stiffened. "I have a lease, MacDuff. Don't pull that crap."

"It's very tempting to just close the gates and go after that translation myself. It's my home, and possession is nine-tenths of the law." MacDuff added softly, "Why, you even left the Cira statue there, Trevor. How can I resist?"

"Try," Jane said dryly. "You're not old Angus and we're not about to put up with you playing robber baron."

MacDuff laughed. "Just a thought. I'm actually

glad to have a little on-hand support from both of you. I'm taking Jock back with me, and we may need help if Venable finds out it was him who caused all this carnage."

"Venable should be grateful," Jane said.

"But government agencies ask questions, dig deep, and sometimes gratitude is lost by the wayside," MacDuff said. "Suppose I meet you at the airport and we'll go together? I'll phone you as soon as I'm free here. Believe me, it will be much easier getting through my guards at the gate if I'm with you."

Trevor shrugged. "Suit yourself. But don't make any calls to your people about searching Mario's study before we get there."

"How suspicious you are. I never gave it a thought." MacDuff turned away. "I'll wait here and keep a lookout for the police. Before you leave send Jock out to me. I've got to brief him on what he should say to the police."

"I'm not sure he'll listen to you," Jane said. "He seems to be operating under his own agenda these days."

MacDuff's lips tightened grimly. "I'll make him listen."

Jock was standing over Norton's body when they reached the garage. He looked up guiltily. "I didn't kill him. He'll wake up soon."

Trevor knelt and checked Norton's pulse. "What happened?"

"He's trained to protect Reilly. I knew I wouldn't

be able to persuade him to give up." He shrugged. "So I shut off the blood flow to the carotid artery and put him down." He turned to Jane and said earnestly, "I'm sorry I had to shoot you. I was very careful."

"I'm sure you were. You did what you thought best. Anyway, it stopped Reilly." Jesus, how bizarre to be comforting someone who'd just shot you. "But we have to leave and get to a hospital. MacDuff said to take this truck and he told me to tell you he wants to see you. The authorities are going to be asking questions and he wants you to have the right answers."

"There aren't any right answers," Jock said. "MacDuff wants to protect me, but he'll only get in trouble himself."

"That's up to him," Trevor said. "MacDuff can take care of himself. That's what he's been trying to tell you." He turned and got in the cab of the truck. "Personally, up to the point where you shot Jane, I was damn grateful you were around. Get in the truck, Jane."

"In a minute." She hesitated, gazing at Jock. "It doesn't matter about my wound. You did the right thing. You couldn't take a chance of not getting Reilly. He was too dangerous to too many people."

"I know. At first it was only about MacDuff, and then it was about me too. And then I got to thinking about you and all the other people Reilly was hurting. It was like tossing a pebble in a lake and seeing the ripples go out farther and farther. It was strange. . . ." Then Jock smiled at her, that radiant smile that had first drawn her to him. "Thank you for not being angry with me. I'll never hurt you if I can help it."

"That's comforting." She gently touched his cheek before taking a step back. "And what would be even more comforting is if you could turn off those land mines in the driveway and the road out here."

He laughed. "I've already done it. I went to the security room after MacDuff left me." He pressed the wall button and the garage door opened. His smile faded as he gazed outside. "The only thing you'll have to worry about is the storm. The blizzard they predicted seems to be here at last."

He was right. The wind was whipping the snow into a blinding veil.

"If you're going, it had better be now." Jock was still looking out at the storm.

Jane was already in the cab and starting the truck. She stopped and said impulsively, "Come with us, Jock."

"Why?"

"I don't know. I just don't want to leave you here. It seems as if we've all been telling you what to do since I met you. We could talk about what you want to do."

He shook his head.

"You're sure?"

He smiled as he started out of the garage. "MacDuff wants me to come to him. Don't I always do what MacDuff says?" He disappeared into the swirling snow.

"Dammit." Jane finished backing out of the

garage. "What if he gets scared and those police think he's going to hurt—"

"Stop borrowing trouble," Trevor said. "MacDuff will take care of him. And Jock is far more threat to anyone else than they are to him."

She'd reached the road and couldn't speak for a moment while she concentrated on staying on the road until she reached the relative shelter of the trees. "But he's changed. He doesn't want to kill. He never really wanted that. But he has to have help and guidance."

"And MacDuff will give it to him. You heard him. He always does what the laird says."

She suddenly remembered something. "He didn't call him the laird. He called him MacDuff. He never calls him that."

"You're looking for trouble. It doesn't matter what he calls MacDuff as long as he does what he tells him to do. And he's always obedient to him."

*I promised the laird I wouldn't go near you. . . . But if I go ahead and you follow me I won't really be near you.*

"Not all the time," she whispered. "Not always, Trevor."

What a bloody mess you've made of everything, Trevor." Brenner walked into the treatment room where Trevor and Jane were sitting after being dismissed by the physician. "With an emphasis on bloody."

"Thanks for your sympathy," Trevor said dryly as he shrugged back into his shirt. "But since you were out of the action entirely you have no right to criti-cize."

"I'm sympathetic." He turned to Jane. "I feel very sorry that Jane had to put up with your incompe-tence. Are you okay?"

"Fine. Hardly a scratch."

"Good." He turned back to Trevor. "And I was hardly out of the action. Who do you think shep-herded those police units to the compound?"

"Jock."

"Be for real. What do you think the odds are that any small-town police department would send their men out in a snowstorm on an anonymous tip? I heard them debating over my police-band radio when I was driving toward Reilly's place and took it upon myself to persuade them that glory and pro-motions waited for them at the compound."

"And how did you do that?"

"Well, I did borrow Venable's name and told them that the raid was planned by the CIA and it was to be a joint effort."

"And they bought it?" Jane asked.

"I'm an amazingly persuasive fellow." He smiled. "Though my Australian accent gave me a little trou-ble. They don't trust foreigners in these parts. But it only goes to show you how good I am. So what's next?"

"Next I call Eve and Joe and let them know what's going on," Jane said. "Then after we leave the hospi-tal we head for the airport and get the first flight out. We have to go back to MacDuff's Run."

Brenner glanced at the window. "It's snowing like

hell. I wouldn't be in too much of a hurry to go to the airport." He held up his hand as she opened her lips to protest. "I know. You want out of here. Okay, I'll see about a charter. But no sane pilot is going to take off until it's safe." He took out his phone and started dialing.

"Safe," Jane murmured. "Did we stop them? Are we all safe, Trevor? I'm afraid to believe it."

"I don't know. There are still too many loose cannons to worry about." Trevor took her hand in comfort and support. "We'll have to wait until we hear from MacDuff."

MacDuff didn't call for twenty-four hours and his tone was curt when he did. "I'm through here. Venable smoothed the way, but they didn't let me leave until he arrived six hours ago. He wants to see you but I stalled him. I said you'd call and give him a statement within forty-eight hours. He didn't like it. But he agreed."

"The suicide bombers?"

"No action taken by them. Without Reilly the job was evidently like a snake without a head. There were a few notes in the personnel folder that might lead the CIA to identify those particular suicide bombers. We did find reference to the targets, and they were put on alert."

"Thank God."

"I'll be at the airport within two hours if I can get there through this damn blizzard. It's got to stop sometime."

"No hurry. The flights are grounded anyway."

"The hell there's no hurry. I'm going to be there when the airport opens."

"I'm? Not we?" Her hand tightened on the phone. "Jock's not coming?"

"Not now."

"Venable? He has Jock in custody?"

"No, though he wants him damn bad. Jock took off before the police showed up last night."

"Took off? Where?"

"Into the woods. I tracked him for six hours but then I lost him."

"He could die out there."

"He won't die. That bastard Reilly taught him to operate in fair or foul weather. We just have to find him. And right now Venable has half the local police force looking for him. I'll come back here when I'm not stumbling over everyone." He hung up.

Jane hung up the phone. "Jock's on the run."

"So I heard," Trevor said. "Is MacDuff worried?"

"He won't admit it if he is." She frowned. "I'm worried. I don't care how good he is at living off the land. Maybe he doesn't want to live. He tried to commit suicide before. MacDuff's safe from Reilly now, and that gives Jock one less reason to live."

"Perhaps he's far enough along that self-preservation has kicked in."

"Maybe." She looked out the huge glass windows at the planes parked at the gates. "We'll have to wait and see."

"You can't do anything for Jock now. Focus on what you can do."

"Finding Mario's translation." He was right. If MacDuff had abandoned the search because he didn't want to find Jock and reveal his presence to the other searchers, then she was even less likely to be able to help Jock right now. She glanced down on the chair beside her at Reilly's briefcase containing the copies of his Herculaneum documents. "And afterward I'll go through these and see if I can find out anything that Reilly knew about Herculaneum. He mentioned that one of these documents made him look at Cira in an entirely new way. . . ."

MacDuff was right. The guards at the gate of MacDuff's Run challenged them at once, and only when MacDuff got out of the car and they recognized him did they let the car go in to the courtyard.

MacDuff waved at Trevor to go on without him and turned back to talk to Campbell, the guard.

"We're in," Trevor said. "I was wondering if we were going to have a problem with MacDuff honoring that commitment."

"He was just playing with us. He's not stupid. This place and his family name mean too much to him to risk being accused of not keeping to a contract."

"You seem very sure." He parked the car in front of the castle. "But then, you've gotten to know him pretty well through Jock."

She did feel as if she knew MacDuff. He was tough and hard and he'd never been either easy or tolerant with her. Hell, who wanted tolerance? Tolerance was degrading and made her want to punch someone in the nose. She'd always wanted to be accepted on level ground with all her merits and faults. "He's hardly an enigma." She got out of the car. "Like the rest of us, he does what he has to do to get what he wants." She wrinkled her nose. "He just happens to want a bloody castle."

Trevor changed the subject as he followed her into the castle. "Do you know where you're going to look for the translation? Did Mario give you any hint?"

"Not much." She started up the stairs. "I don't know. Maybe. I'll have to think about it."

"I'll be up to help you as soon as I finish checking with Venable on their progress in finding Jock. He brought in some trackers from Special Forces. They'll probably be able to locate him."

"You think so? Who is it that compared him to Rambo? I'm not so sure."

"And you don't want them to find him."

She stopped on the stairs to look down at him. "Do you?"

He shook his head. "But even though MacDuff destroyed Reilly's records about him, there could still be a backlash. Jock showed how dangerous he could be. It might be a good idea for him to get hospital care."

"The hell it would. Do you want him to try to commit suicide again?"

"Maybe he's healed enough to not—" He shrugged. "Okay, it would be a chance." He headed down the hall. "But I don't want him dying in a snowstorm either."

It was what she had been worrying about too. "I believe he'll be all right." Jesus, she hoped he would be. "He's tough. And maybe Reilly's training will save his life. God knows, he deserves some payback from that bastard." She started up the stairs again. "If Venable's men don't corner him and make him react instead of think."

Trevor had already gone into the library and didn't answer.

She opened the door of Mario's study and stood there looking at the familiar room. The desk piled high with papers. The statue of Cira by the window. The chair in the corner where she'd spent so many hours. Everything was the same and yet everything was different. Nothing was as she'd perceived it to be.

Snap out of it.

She straightened her shoulders, threw the briefcase containing Reilly's Herculaneum papers on a chair by the door, and strode toward the desk. Finding Cira's letter was first on the agenda. She started to go carefully through the papers on Mario's desk. Ten minutes later she gave up and went to his bedroom.

Nothing there either.

Dammit, he hadn't had that much time to hide that translation. Maybe he'd destroyed it. . . .

No, it had meant too much to him. Even if he hadn't considered the translation a bargaining coin, there had been a part of Mario that had been proud of his work, and he'd been thoroughly engrossed in the Cira legend. He'd even insisted that Trevor give up—

She stiffened. "Christ." She left Mario's bedroom and went back into the studio and over to the Cira statue by the window.

"Did he give it to you?" she murmured.

Cira stared back at her, bold and unflinching.

"Maybe . . ." She carefully lifted the bust and set it on the floor.

A few sheets of folded paper lay on the pedestal.

"Yes!" She took the sheets of paper, replaced the statue, and dropped down in the easy chair. Her hands were shaking as she unfolded Mario's translation.

*My dear Pia,*

*I may die tonight.*
*Julius is behaving strangely and he may have found that the gold is missing. Though the guards I persuaded to do my will are still serving Julius, he may be trying to disarm me until he can find where I sent the gold. I will not send this to you unless I think it safe. Take no chances. You must not die. You must live long and enjoy every minute of it. All the velvet nights and silver mornings. All the songs and laughter. If I don't survive remember me with love and not bitterness. I know I should have found you sooner, but time flies by and you can never get it back. But enough of this gloominess. It is staying with Julius that is making me think of death. I need to talk to you of life, our life. I will not lie. I cannot promise you that it will be either—*

# 22

$\overline{\phantom{22}}$

W here are you going?" Bartlett asked Jane as she tore down the stairs. "Is everything okay?"

"Fine. Tell Trevor I'll be back soon. I have to see MacDuff. . . ." She trailed off as she ran out the door and down the front steps. No, not MacDuff. Not yet. She flew across the courtyard and into the stable. A moment later she was lifting the trapdoor, grabbing a flashlight, and starting down the steps that led to the sea.

Cold. Wet. Slippery.

Angus's place, Jock had called it. And later also Angus's room. She had thought it odd when there was no room. . . .

Not where she was.

She had reached the narrow passage that doubled back to lead to the hills instead of the cliffs. She started down the passage.

Darkness. Suffocating narrowness. Slick stones underfoot.

And an oak door about a hundred yards down the corridor.

Locked?

No, it swung open on oiled hinges.

She stood in the doorway, the beam of her flashlight shining into the darkness.

"Why are you hesitating?" MacDuff asked dryly from behind her. "Why not one more trespass? One more invasion of privacy?"

She stiffened and turned to face him. "You're not going to make me feel guilty. Hell, I may be entitled to know why Jock said you spent so much time here."

He didn't change expressions. "Trevor isn't leasing this part of the estate. You have no right to be here."

"Trevor's invested a lot in trying to find Cira's gold."

"You think it's here?"

"I think there's a chance."

His brows lifted. "I'm supposed to have found Cira's gold on one of my trips to Herculaneum and hidden it here?"

"Possibly." She shook her head. "But that's not my guess."

He smiled faintly. "I'll be fascinated to hear your speculations." He gestured. "Let's go into Angus's room and you can tell me all about it." His smile widened as he saw her expression. "Do you think I'm going to indulge in foul play? I might. Cira's gold is a great instigator."

"You're not a fool. Trevor would tear this place apart if I disappeared." She turned and went into the room. "And I came here to see what was in this room, and now I have an invitation."

MacDuff laughed. "A reluctant invitation. Let me light the lanterns so that you can have a good look." He moved across the room to a table against the wall and lit two lanterns, illuminating the room. It was a small room that contained a desk with an open laptop computer, a chair, a cot, and a number of cloth-draped objects leaning against the far wall. "No chest overflowing with Cira's gold." He leaned lazily against the wall and crossed his arms over his chest. "But you don't really care about the gold, do you?"

"I care about everything connected with Cira. I want to *know*."

"And you think I can help you?"

"You were very eager to grab Reilly's Herculaneum files. You didn't like it at all when I wouldn't let you have them."

"True. Naturally, I was concerned that they might give a clue to where the gold was."

She shook her head. "You were concerned that there was a ship's log written by a merchant captain Demonidas among those documents."

His gaze narrowed on her face. "Was I? Now, why?"

She didn't answer. "I didn't realize myself how

important that log might be until I read Mario's translation of Cira's last letter."

"You found it?"

She nodded and reached into her pocket. "Would you like to read it?"

"Very much." He straightened away from the wall and held out his hand. "You know I would."

She watched him unfold the pages, and she tried to decipher his expression as he read the words that were engraved in her memory.

> *I need to talk to you of life. Our life. I cannot promise that it will be either easy or safe, but we will be free and answer to no one. That I can promise you. No man crushing us beneath his heel. Achavid is a wild land, but the gold will make it tamer. Gold always soothes and comforts.*
>
> *Demonidas still has not agreed to take us past Gaul, but I will persuade him. I don't wish to waste time finding another ship to take us farther. Julius will be on our heels and he will never stop.*
>
> *Let him look. Let him venture into those rough hills and confront those wild men that the emperor calls savages. He's not a man who can survive without his fine wines and soft life. He's not like us. We'll live and thrive and thumb our noses at Julius.*
>
> *And if I'm not there to help you, then you must do it yourself. Be bold with Demonidas. He's greedy and you must never let him know that we've hidden the gold among the boxes that we're taking with us.*

*By the Gods, I'm telling you how to handle him,
yet I hope with all my heart that I'm there to do it for
you.*

*But if I'm not, you will do it. We are one blood.
Anything I can do, you will be able to do. I trust in
you, my sister.*

*All my love,
Cira*

MacDuff folded the letter and handed it back to
her. "So Cira did manage to get the gold out of the
tunnel."

"And put it on a ship captained by Demonidas
sailing to Gaul."

"Perhaps. Often plans go awry, and she wasn't
sure she'd even live through the night."

"I believe she did. I think she wrote that letter the
night the volcano erupted."

"And your proof?"

"I don't have proof." She reached into her pocket.
"But I have Reilly's translation of Demonidas's
log. He refers to a Lady Pia who paid him well to
transport her, her child, Leo, and her servants to
Gaul and then to southeastern Britannia. They
left on the night of the eruption, and he brags about
his bravery in the face of calamity. They wanted him
to take them on to what he called Caledonia, the
place we call Scotland, but he refused. The Roman
army was warring with the Caledonian tribes, and
Agricola, the Roman governor, was launching ships
to attack the northeast coast. Demonidas wanted no

part of it. He left Pia and company in Kent and returned to Herculaneum. Or what was left of Herculaneum."

"Interesting. But it refers to this Lady Pia, not Cira."

"As you read, Pia must have been Cira's sister. They were probably separated as children and Cira was too busy surviving to search for her. And when she did find her, she didn't want to involve her in her battle with Julius and put her in danger."

"And then Cira died and Pia sailed away with the gold."

"Or Pia died in the city and Cira took her name and identity to escape Julius. It was the kind of thing she would do."

"Any mention of the names of the servants who accompanied her?"

"Dominic . . . and Antonio. Cira had a servant, Dominic, a lover, Antonio, and she'd adopted a child, Leo."

"But wouldn't her sister have taken care of Cira's family if Pia was the one who survived?"

"Yes. But, dammit, Cira *didn't* die."

He smiled. "Because you don't want it to have happened that way."

"Antonio was Cira's lover. He wouldn't have left her and gone sailing off."

"My, how certain you are. Men leave women. Women leave men. It's the way life is." He paused. "And why did you run over here after reading those documents and break into Angus's room?"

"I didn't break—well, not technically. But I was prepared to do it."

He chuckled. "I do love that honesty. From the moment I met you, I knew that I—"

"Then be honest with me. Stop playing word games." She drew a deep breath and then went for it. "You knew what Demonidas had written in that log."

"How could I know that?"

"I don't know. But Reilly said that you'd almost stolen a document from him. It had to be this document. Because Reilly tracked and took Jock for a reason. You told me that Reilly probably thought you'd discovered something about the gold on one of your trips to Herculaneum. That Jock was in and out of your castle and that he might know something more."

"Isn't that reasonable?"

"Absolutely. That's why I didn't question it. Until I read Cira's letter and Demonidas's log. Until Reilly told me that after reading the document he'd come to new and different conclusions regarding Cira."

MacDuff looked at her inquiringly.

"Don't play with me. You knew that Reilly had that log."

"How could I?"

"You went after Demonidas's log at the same time Reilly did. But Reilly got his hands on it first. And after Reilly had it translated, he remembered that you had wanted it too. Very badly. He became curious. But Jock wasn't able to tell him anything, so he put you temporarily on the back burner. He was busy trying to get hold of Cira's scrolls and manipulating Grozak."

"Not quite on the back burner," MacDuff said. "He had me followed and once sent one of his trolls to try to knock me on the head and kidnap me."

She stiffened. "You admit it?"

"To you. Not to Trevor or Venable or anyone else."

"Why not?"

"Because this is between the two of us. I'm still going to get that gold and I don't want interference."

"You don't have it yet?"

He shook his head. "But it's there and I'll find it."

"How do you know it's there?"

He smiled. "You tell me. I can see you're working your way through it."

She was silent a moment. "Cira and Antonio left Kent and came here to Scotland. It was a warring, savage country and she was still on the run from Julius. They decided to go inland, deep into the Highlands. They could lose themselves there and bide their time until they could become more visible and set themselves up in the style Cira had always wanted."

"And did she?"

"I'm sure she did. But she had to be careful, and a little gold would have gone a long way in such a primitive place. It wouldn't have taken much of her store of gold to set herself and Antonio up quite comfortably, even luxuriously by the standards of those wild Scots. Isn't that right, MacDuff?"

His brows lifted. "It sounds reasonable. I'd think you were right."

"Don't you know?"

He didn't speak for a moment and then he slowly nodded and smiled. "It would have taken only a mere pittance, and Cira was very, very canny."

"Yes, she was." She smiled back at him. "And she stayed there and prospered and she and Antonio changed their names and raised their family. Their descendants must have liked it there, because they never moved to the coast even when it was safe. Until Angus decided to build this castle in 1350. Why did he do that, MacDuff?"

"He was always a wild man. He wanted to strike out on his own and carve his own niche. I can understand that, can't you?"

"Yes. When did you find out about Cira's background? Was that another old family secret?"

"No. Cira must have turned her back on Herculaneum when she settled in the Highlands. There are no tales of Roman revelry. No stories of Italy passed down from father to son. It was as if they sprang from the ground there and made it their own. Angus and Torra were wild and free and, on occasion, as savage as the people surrounding them."

"Torra?"

"It means *from the castle.* A good name for Cira to choose, and it exactly mirrored her intentions."

"And Angus?"

"He was the first Angus. It's not too far from Antonio."

"If there weren't any family stories, then how did you know about Cira?"

"You told me."

"What?"

"You and Eve Duncan and Trevor. I read the story in the newspaper."

She gazed at him incredulously.

He chuckled. "You don't believe me? It's true. Shall I prove it?" He grabbed one of the lanterns and moved across the room toward the draped objects leaning against the far wall. "Life is strange. But this was a little too strange." He pulled the drapery off to reveal a painting—no, a portrait, she saw, as he turned the painting to face her. "Fiona."

"My God."

He nodded. "It's a mirror image."

He stepped back and held the lantern high.

The woman in the portrait was young, in her early twenties, and dressed in a low-necked green gown. She wasn't smiling but gazing out of the portrait with impatience. But there was a vitality and beauty that was unmistakable. "Cira."

"And you." He began stripping the draperies off the other paintings. "There's no other similarity as close as Fiona's but there are hints, traces of resemblance." He pointed at a young man dressed in Tudor clothing. "His mouth is shaped like Cira's." He gestured to an older woman with a lorgnette, and hair in a bun. "And those cheekbones were passed down in almost every generation. Cira definitely left her stamp on her descendants." He grimaced. "I had to take down every portrait and hide them here when I knew I was leasing the place to Trevor."

"That's why there were so many tapestries on the walls," she murmured. "But you don't bear any resemblance to her at all."

"Perhaps I take after her Antonio."

"Maybe." Her gaze was moving from portrait to portrait. "Amazing . . ."

"That's what I thought. I was only curious at first. I began to probe a little and did start to do a little intensive research into family history."

"And what did you find out?"

"Nothing concrete. Cira and Antonio covered their tracks very well. Except for one old, tattered letter I found buried with some papers Angus had brought from the Highlands. Actually, it was a scroll in a brass container."

"From Cira?"

"No, from Demonidas."

"No way."

"It was a very interesting letter. You'll be glad to know it was addressed to Cira, not Pia. It was couched in flowery terms but it was basically a blackmail letter. Evidently when Demonidas returned to Herculaneum he heard about Julius's search for Cira and decided that he'd see if he could get more money from her than he could from Julius for telling him where she was. He was agreeing to meet with Cira and Antonio to receive his pound of flesh." He smiled. "Big mistake. Nothing was heard from Demonidas again."

"Except the ship's log."

"That was written three years before he tried to feather his nest. He must have left it at his home in Naples. But when I heard it existed, I knew I had to try to get hold of it. I didn't know what was in it, but I didn't want to risk it connecting Cira with my family."

"Why?"

"The gold. It's mine and it's going to stay mine. I couldn't let anyone know that it might not be in Herculaneum. If they knew there was even a chance that it was here, they'd find a way to tear this place apart."

"And would they find it?"

"Maybe. I haven't yet."

"How do you know that it wasn't found by one of Cira's descendants and spent?"

"I can't know for sure. But there have always been tales of a lost treasure in the family. It was vague, more fairy tale than anything else, and I never paid any attention to it. I was too busy coping with the real world."

"Like Grozak and Reilly." She gazed at the portrait of Fiona. MacDuff's kinswoman might have had her share of trials and tribulations, but Jane doubted she'd had to deal with monsters who cared nothing for human life or dignity.

"You're shivering," MacDuff said roughly. "It's cold in here. If you intended to breach Angus's stronghold, why the devil didn't you grab a jacket?"

"I didn't think. I just went for it."

"What you always do." He went over to the desk and opened a drawer. "But I can take care of it this time." He took out a bottle of brandy and poured a small amount in two shot glasses. "I've been known to need a wee drop myself when I've been working through the night."

"I'm surprised you admit it."

"I always admit my faults." He grinned as he handed her the shot glass. "That way I don't intimidate anyone by the sheer volume of my talents and accomplishments."

"And your incredible modesty." She drank the brandy and made a face as the liquid burned through her. But in a moment she did feel warmer, steadier. "Thank you."

"More?"

She shook her head. She didn't know why she'd accepted the liquor to begin with. She wasn't sure she trusted him, and he'd already told her that he wanted no one to know that his family had any connection with Cira. He was a tough, ruthless bastard, and that might mean she was in danger of violence. Yet here she was sharing brandy with him and feeling very comfortable about it. "It wasn't really about the cold."

"I know." He tossed off his brandy in one swallow. "It's been a hard time for you. But brandy is a cure-all for more than the chill." He took her glass and carried it back to the chest. "And it will make you more mellow toward me."

"The hell it will."

"A tiny jest." His eyes were twinkling. "Mellow is not how I'd ever describe you." He put away the glasses and brandy. "So are you going to tell Trevor that I may be sitting on his pile of gold?"

"You consider it your pile of gold."

"But Trevor believes in the luck of the draw and finders keepers. So do most of the people who'll come after it if you let the cat out of the bag."

"You can keep outsiders away from the castle."

"But what if it's not in the castle? I don't believe it is. I've searched for a long time for some trace or clue to where it's hidden and I know every nook and cranny. Of course, it could be somewhere on the grounds or even buried back in the Highlands where Angus lived before he came here."

"Or not exist at all."

He nodded. "But I won't accept that. Cira wouldn't want me to give up."

"Cira died two thousand years ago."

He shook his head. "She's here. Can't you feel it? As long as her family exists, as long as the Run still stands, she'll live too." He met her gaze. "I believe you know that."

She pulled her gaze away from his. "I've got to get back to the castle. Trevor will be wondering where I am. I didn't tell him where I was going."

"And he probably didn't question you because he didn't want to offend your independence. He's still not sure of you. Though he'd like to be."

"I've no intention of talking to you about Trevor."

"Because you're not sure of him either. Sex isn't everything." He laughed. "Though it's a hell of a lot. Is the bond there, Jane? Does he make you feel what Cira wished Pia? What were her words? *Velvet nights and silver mornings?* Do you feel as if you're the most important person in his life? You need that."

"You don't know what I need."

"Then why do I feel as if I do?"

"Sheer arrogance?" She turned and headed for the door. "Stay out of my business, MacDuff."

"I can't do that." He paused. "Ask me why, Jane."

"I'm not interested."

"No, you're afraid of what I'll say. I'll say it anyway. I can't stay out of your business because it goes against both my nature and my training."

"Why?"

"Haven't you guessed?" He added simply, "You're one of mine."

She stopped short, rigid with shock. "What?"

"Mine. Turn around and look at Fiona again."

She slowly turned around but stared at him instead of the portrait. "Fiona?"

"Fiona wed Ewan MacGuire in her twenty-fifth year and moved to the lowlands. She bore him five children and their family lived a prosperous life until the late 1800s, when Fiona's descendants fell on hard times. Two of the younger sons left their home to seek their fortune, and one of them, Colin MacGuire, boarded a ship for America in 1876. He was never heard from again."

She was staring at him, stunned. "Coincidence."

"Look at her portrait, Jane."

"I don't have to look at her portrait. You're crazy. There are thousands of MacGuires in the U.S. I don't even know who my father was. And I'm sure as hell not one of 'yours.' "

"You are until proven otherwise." His lips twitched. "I believe you're casting aspersions on the House of MacDuff. You'd rather be a bastard than a member of my family."

"Did you expect me to be honored?"

"No, just tolerant. We're not such a bad lot, and we do stand by our own."

"I don't need anyone to stand by me." She whirled and headed for the door. "Shove it, MacDuff."

She heard him burst into laughter as she ran down the hall toward the steps leading back to the stable. She was confused and shocked and . . . angry. The anger took her by surprise, and she couldn't see any reason for—

Yes, she could. She had been alone all her life and been proud of the independence that isolation had bred. MacDuff's sudden revelation did not make her feel warm and cozy. It seemed to take something away from her.

Damn him. He'd probably concocted a kinship just to keep the blasted gold in the family, to keep her from talking to Trevor.

And what was she going to do? How much was she going to tell Trevor?

And why was she even considering limiting what she told Trevor?

Of course she'd tell him everything. Except that nonsense about her being related to MacDuff. What Trevor chose to do about pursuing Cira's gold was his affair, and she wouldn't make him feel any reluctance because he might be dipping into her family's treasure trove.

She had no family but Eve and Joe. She certainly didn't need to invite an arrogant, paternalistic MacDuff into her life right now.

But *paternalistic* wasn't the right word. MacDuff's attitude had been—

She wouldn't think about MacDuff's attitude. It disturbed her, and she had enough emotional trauma to deal with right now.

She had reached the courtyard and she saw Trevor standing on the front steps.

*Velvet nights and silver mornings.*

Screw you, MacDuff. The sex was grand and Trevor was a unique man who stimulated her mind as well as her body. That was all she needed or wanted.

Her pace quickened. "I have something to tell you. I found Cira's letter, and it's no wonder Mario didn't want to tell us about what she . . ."

W hat do you want me to do about it?" Trevor asked quietly when she'd finished.

"The gold? Whatever you want to do about it," Jane said. "You've searched for it for a long time. Your friend Pietro died in that tunnel trying to find it."

"Some would say that MacDuff deserves the gold since technically it's his family's fortune."

"Yes. And how do you feel?"

"He deserves it if he can find and hold it."

"He said you'd say something like that."

"He's a perceptive man." He paused. "I won't go after it if you don't want me to. It's only money."

"Don't give me that. It's a damn fortune." She started up the steps. "And you'll have to make up your own mind. I'm not going to be responsible for influencing you one way or another. I'm tired to death of being responsible."

"And I believe I'm getting tired of being irresponsible. Don't you think we'd make a great match?"

She felt a surge of happiness, followed immediately by wariness. "What are you saying?"

"You know what I'm saying. You're scared to admit it. Well, I'm way past that point. You'll have to catch up. How did you feel when you thought I was blown to bits?"

She said slowly, "Terrible. Frightened. Empty."

"Good. That's progress." He took her hand and kissed the palm. "I know I'm rushing. I can't help it. I've got years of experience on you and I know what I want. You're having to work your way through this. You don't know whether you can trust what we have." He smiled. "And it's my job to show you that this feeling isn't ever going to go away. Not for me and, I hope to God, not for you. I'm going to dog your footsteps and seduce you at every opportunity until you decide you can't live without me." He kissed her palm again. "What are you going to do after you leave here?"

"I'm going home and be with Eve and Joe. I'm

going to sketch and rest and forget everything connected to MacDuff's Run."

"And am I invited to come along?"

She stood looking at him and felt that wave of wild happiness soar through her again. She gave him a quick, hard kiss and then smiled. "Give me a week. And then, hell yes, you're invited."

$M$acDuff met them in the courtyard when the helicopter landed two hours later.

"Leaving? I take it you're terminating your lease, Trevor?"

"I haven't decided. Don't hold your breath. I may need a base if I choose to go after the gold. MacDuff's Run might suit me very well."

"And it might not." He smiled faintly. "My place, my people, and I won't roll out the welcome mat this time. You could find it uncomfortable." He turned to Jane. "Good-bye. Keep well. I hope to see you soon."

"You won't. I'm going home to Eve and Joe."

"Good. You need it. I'm leaving too. I have to go back to Idaho and find Jock."

"Venable may beat you to it," Trevor said as he started to climb the helicopter steps.

MacDuff shook his head. "I only have to get within calling distance and Jock will come to me. The reason I came back here was to pick up Robert Cameron. He served under me in the service, and he's the best tracker I've ever met."

"Another one of your people?" Jane asked dryly.

"Aye. It comes in handy on occasion." He started to turn away. "You'll see."

"I doubt it. But good luck with Jock." She started to follow Trevor, who'd disappeared into the helicopter.

MacDuff called after her, "I'll let you know when I find him."

"How do you know I won't call Venable? You're making me an accessory after the fact."

He smiled. "You won't call him. Blood is thicker than water. Jock's one of yours—cousin."

"The hell he is. And I'm not your cousin."

"Aye, you are. I'd be willing to bet my DNA on it. But a very distant cousin." He winked and tipped his hand to his brow. "Thank God."

She watched with exasperation and frustration as he strode across the courtyard toward the stable. He looked perfectly assured, arrogant, and at home in this ancient relic of a castle. Old Angus would have had just that cocksure attitude.

"Jane?" Trevor had come back to stand at the door of the helicopter.

She tore her gaze away from that damn Scot and started up the steps. "Coming."


Y*ou bastard," Cira said through gritted teeth. "You did this to me."*

"*Yes." Antonio kissed her hand. "Forgive me?"*

"*No. Yes. Maybe." She screamed as another pain tore through her. "No!"*

"*The woman from the village swears that the child will*

*come in minutes. It's not unusual for a first babe to take this long. Be brave."*

*"I am brave. I've been trying to give birth to this child for thirty-six hours and you dare to tell me that? When you sit there so smug and comfortable. You don't know what pain is. Get out of here before I kill you."*

*"No, I'll stay with you until the child is born." Antonio's hand tightened around hers. "I promised I'd never leave you again."*

*"I could have wished you'd broken that promise before this child was conceived."*

*"You mean that?"*

*"No, I don't mean that." Cira bit her lower lip as another pain washed over her. "Are you stupid? I want this child. I just don't want the pain. There has to be a better way for women to do this."*

*"I'm sure you'll think of something later." His voice was unsteady. "But I'd be grateful if you'd just give birth to this child and have it over."*

*He was frightened, she realized dimly. Antonio, who wouldn't admit to fearing anything, was frightened now. "You think I'm going to die."*

*"No, never."*

*"That's right, never. I complain because I have a right to complain and it's not fair that women have to bear all the children. You should help."*

*"I would if I could."*

*His voice was a little steadier but still shaky.*

*"On second thought, I don't think I could ever lie with you again if I saw you with a swollen belly. You'd look ridiculous. I know I couldn't bear to look at myself."*

*"You were beautiful. You're always beautiful."*

*"You lie." She rode the next spasm of pain. "This land is hard and cold and not easy on women. But it won't beat me. I'll make it mine. Just like this child. I'll bear it and raise it and give it everything that I missed." She lifted her hand to gently touch his cheek. "I'm happy I didn't miss you, Antonio. Velvet nights and silver mornings. That's what I told Pia to search for, but there's so much more." She closed her eyes. "The other half of the circle . . ."*

*"Cira!"*

*"By the gods, Antonio." Her lids flipped open. "I told you I wasn't going to die. I'm just tired. I've no time to comfort you any more now. Shut up or go away while I go about having this child."*

*"I'll shut up."*

*"Good. I like you with me. . . ."*

MacDuff answered his phone on the fifth ring. He sounded sleepy.

"How many children did Cira have?" Jane asked when she picked up.

"What?"

"Did she have just one? Did she die in child-birth?"

"Why do you want to know?"

"Tell me."

"According to family legend Cira had four children. I don't know how she died but she was a very old lady."

Jane breathed a sigh of relief. "Thanks." She had a sudden thought. "Where are you?"

"Canada."

"Have you found Jock?"

"Not yet. But I will."

"Sorry to wake you. Good night."

MacDuff chuckled. "My pleasure. I'm glad you're thinking about us." He hung up.

"Everything okay?" Eve was standing in the doorway of Jane's bedroom.

"Fine." Jane pressed the disconnect. "I just had to check on something."

"At this hour?"

"It seemed urgent at the time." She got out of bed and put on her robe. "Come on. We might as well go get a hot chocolate since we're both awake. You've been working so hard that I've scarcely had a chance to talk to you since I got home." She made a face as she headed for the door. "Of course, some of that is my fault. I've been going to bed early and getting up late. I don't know what's been wrong with me. I feel as if I've been on narcotics."

"Exhaustion. Backlash from Mike's death, not to mention what you went through in Idaho." She followed Jane to the kitchen. "I was glad to see you resting for a change. When are you going back to school?"

"Soon. I missed too much time this quarter. I'll have to do some catching up."

"And then?"

"I don't know." She smiled. "Maybe I'll hang out here until you kick me out."

"That's no threat. Joe and I would like that." She spooned instant cocoa into two cups. "But I don't believe we have a chance in hell." She poured the hot water. "Another dream, Jane?"

She nodded. "But not a scary one." She wrinkled her nose. "Unless you call having a baby scary."

Eve nodded. "And full of wonder."

"I thought the dreams would stop when Cira got out of the tunnel. It seems I'm stuck with her."

Eve gave Jane her cup. "And that upsets you?"

"No, I guess not. She's become a good friend over the years." She headed for the porch. "But sometimes she leaves me hanging."

"You're not upset about her any longer." Eve half sat on the porch rail. "Before, you were pretty defensive."

"Because I didn't know why I was having those damn dreams. I couldn't find any logical sequence that would have explained them."

"And now you have?"

"Demonidas was on record. He might have had other records than the ones we found. I might have picked up something about Cira from him."

"Or you might not."

"You're a great help."

"If MacDuff told you the truth about you being a descendant of Cira's, then there might be an answer there." Eve looked out at the lake. "I've heard there's such a thing as racial memory."

"Translated into dreams that I can almost step into? That's reaching, Eve."

"It's the best I can do." She paused. "You told me once that you wondered if Cira was trying to make contact, trying to stop the use to which her gold was being put."

"In one of my nuttier moments." She sat down on the porch step and patted Toby, who was lying stretched out on the step below her. "Not that I've had many coolly rational moments since Cira started paying me nocturnal visits. It's okay, I've gotten used to her. I even missed her when she stopped coming for a while."

"I can understand that," Eve said.

"I know you can." Jane looked up at her. "You understand everything I've ever gone through. That's why I can talk to you when I can't to anyone else."

Eve was silent a moment. "Not even Trevor?"

Jane shook her head. "It's too new, just scratching the surface. He makes me pretty dizzy, and that doesn't help for analyzing a relationship." She hesitated, thinking about it. "Cira wrote about velvet nights and silver mornings. She was talking about sex, of course, but the silver mornings meant something else to her. I've been trying to puzzle it out. A relationship that changed the way she saw everything?" She shook her head. "I don't know. I'm too hardheaded. It would probably take a long time before I let myself feel like that."

"A long, long time."

Jane wasn't sure if Eve was talking about Jane or her own experiences. "Maybe it won't ever happen to me. But Cira was pretty hardheaded herself, and she was the one who told Pia what to look for."

"Silver mornings . . ." Eve put her cup down on the railing and sat down on the step beside Jane.

"Sounds nice, doesn't it?" She put her arm around Jane. "Fresh and clean and bright in a dark world. May you find them someday, Jane."

"I already have them." She smiled at Eve. "You give one to me every day. When I'm down, you bring me up. When I'm confused, you make everything clear. When I think there's no love in the world, I remember the years you gave me."

Eve chuckled. "Somehow I don't believe that was what Cira was talking about."

"Maybe not. She never had an Eve Duncan, so she might not have realized that silver mornings aren't restricted to lovers. They can come from mothers, fathers, sisters, and brothers, good friends . . ." She contentedly put her head on Eve's shoulder. The breeze was chilly but brought with it the scent of pines and the memory of years past when she had sat like this with Eve. "Yes, definitely good friends. They can change how you see your world too."

"Yes, they can."

They sat in silence for a long time, gazing out at the lake in contentment. Finally Eve sighed and said, "It's very late. I suppose we should go in."

Jane shook her head. "That makes too much sense. I'm tired of being reasonable. It seems all my life I've forced myself to be practical and sensible, and I'm not sure I haven't missed a heck of a lot by not letting in a little whimsy. My roommate, Pat, always told me that if your feet are planted firmly on the ground then you'll never be able to dance." She smiled at Eve. "Hell, let's not go to bed. Let's wait for the dawn and see if it comes up silver."

Turn the page for a preview of
Iris Johansen's next tale of intrigue
and deception, introducing a
remarkable new heroine.

# KILLER DREAMS

Coming in hardcover from
Bantam Books in June 2006

#1 NEW YORK TIMES BESTSELLING AUTHOR

# IRIS JOHANSEN

TAKES YOU TO THE EDGE OF SUSPENSE

# Killer Dreams

# KILLER DREAMS

## On sale June 2006

Fentway University Hospital
Baltimore, Maryland

W hat's going on? You're not supposed to
be here."

Sophie Dunston looked up from the chart to see
Kathy VanBoskirk, the head night nurse, standing
in the doorway. "An overnight apnea study."

"You worked all day and now you're monitoring
an overnighter?" Kathy came into the room and
glanced at the bed on the other side of the double
glass panel. "Ah, an infant. The light dawns."

"Not so much an infant any longer. Elspeth's
fourteen months," Sophie said. "She'd stopped having incidents three months ago and now they're
back. She just stops breathing in the middle of the
night and her doctor can't find any reason for it.
Her mother is worried sick."

"Then where is she?"

"She works nights."

"So do you. Days *and* nights." Kathy gazed at the sleeping baby. "Lord, she's beautiful. Makes my biological clock start ticking. My kid is fifteen now and there's nothing lovable about him. I'm hoping he'll turn back into a human being in another six years. Think I have a chance?"

"Don is just your typical teenager. He'll get there." Sophie rubbed her eyes. They felt as if they had sand in them. It was almost five and the sleep study would be over soon. Then she'd run the errand that was on the top of her list before getting to bed and grabbing a few hours of shut-eye before she had to get back for her one o'clock session with the Cartwright child. "And he offered to clean my car last week when you had him at the office."

"He probably wanted a chance to swipe it." Kathy grimaced. "Or maybe he wanted the chance to score with an older woman. He thinks you're cool-looking."

"Yeah, sure." Right now, Sophie felt older than her years, frumpy, and ugly as sin. She turned back the chart and checked Elspeth's case history. She'd had an apnea episode about one a.m. and nothing since. There might be something there that would help her pin down—

"There's a message for you at the nurses' station," Kathy said.

Sophie stiffened. "Home?"

Kathy quickly shook her head. "No. God, I'm sorry. I didn't mean to panic you. I didn't think. The message came in during the shift change at seven and they forgot to give it to you." She paused. "How is Michael?"

"Sometimes terrible. Sometimes okay." She tried to smile. "But all the time wonderful."

Kathy nodded. "Yes, he is."

"But in five years I'll probably be pulling my hair out like you're doing." She changed the subject. "So who left the message?"

"It's from Gerald Kennett again. Aren't you going to call him back?"

"No." She checked Elspeth's meds. Allergies?

"Sophie, it wouldn't hurt you to talk to him. He offered you a job that will pay you more in a month than you make in a year here at the university. And he might even up the salary since he keeps after you. I'd jump at it."

"Then you call him back. I like my work here and the people I work with. I don't want to have to answer to any pharmaceutical company."

"You worked for one before."

"When I first got out of medical school. It was a big mistake. I thought they'd free me up to do research full time. It didn't happen. I'm better off doing the research in my spare time." She circled one of the medications on Elspeth's chart. "And I've learned more dealing with people here than I'd ever learn in a lab."

"Like Elspeth." Kathy's gaze was on the baby. "She's stirring."

"Yes, she's been in nREM for the last five minutes. She's almost there." She put down the chart and headed for the adjoining door to the test room. "I've got to get in there and remove those wires before she's fully awake. She'll be scared if she wakes up alone."

"When's her mother supposed to get here?"

"Six."

"Against the rules. Parents are to pick up their children promptly at the end of the session and this one ends at five-thirty."

"Screw the rules. At least she cares enough about the kid to have the tests. I don't mind staying."

"I know," Kathy said. "You're the one who's going to have the night terrors if you don't stop exhausting yourself."

Sophie made the sign to ward off demons. "Don't even talk about it. Send Elspeth's mom in as soon as she gets here, will you?"

Kathy chuckled. "Scared you."

"Yes, you did. There's nothing scarier than night terrors. Believe me, I know." She went into Elspeth's room and went over to the bed. It took only a few minutes to remove the wires and then she sat down on the bed beside her. The little girl had dark hair like her mother and her skin was a silky olive now flushed with sleep. Sophie felt a familiar melting as she gazed at her. "Elspeth," she called softly. "Come back to us, sweetheart. You won't be sorry. We'll talk and I'll read you a story and we'll wait for your mama . . ."

She should get back to work, Kathy thought as she looked through the glass at Elspeth and Sophie. Sophie had picked the baby up and wrapped her in a blanket, and was sitting down in the rocking chair with the baby on her lap. She was talking and rocking the child and her expression was soft and glowing and loving.

Kathy had heard other doctors describe Sophie as brilliant and intuitive. She had a double doctorate in medicine and chemistry and was one of the best sleep therapists in the country. But Kathy liked this Sophie best. The one who effortlessly seemed to be able to reach out and touch her patients. Even Kathy's son had responded to that warmth the one time he'd met her. And Don was definitely a hard sell. Of course, the fact that Sophie was blonde, tall, and slim and bore a vague resemblance to Kate Hudson probably had a lot to do with her son's admiration. He wasn't into the maternal types. Unless Madonna was the one on the album covers.

But Sophie didn't look like Madonna anymore than she did the statue of the Holy Virgin. In this moment she was very human and full of love.

And strength. Sophie would have had to be strong to be able to endure the hell she had gone through in the last few years. She deserved a break. Kathy wished she'd take the Kennett job, scoop up the big bucks, and forget about responsibility.

Then she shook her head as she glanced at Sophie's expression again. Sophie couldn't shunt responsibility, not with this baby and not with Michael. It wasn't in her nature.

Hell, maybe Sophie was right. Maybe the money wasn't as important as the payback she was getting in there with that kid.

* * *

Bye, Kathy." Sophie waved as she headed for the elevator. "See you."

"Not if you have any sense. I'm on night duty all this month. Did you find any cause for the increase in apnea?"

"I'm changing one of the meds. It's mostly trial and error at Elspeth's age." She stepped inside the elevator as the doors opened. "We just have to monitor her until she grows out of it."

She leaned back against the wall of the elevator as the doors shut and closed her eyes. She was too tired. She should go home and forget about Sanborne.

Stop being a coward. She wasn't going home yet.

A few minutes later she was unlocking the door of the van. She avoided looking at the gun case with the Springfield rifle in the back of the Toyota. She'd checked it earlier to make sure it was in order. Not that she really had to do it. Jock always took care of the weapons and he wouldn't let her go with a faulty rifle. He was too much the professional.

She wished she could say the same for herself. She'd blocked the thought of Sanborne all night but she was trembling now. She leaned her head on the steering wheel for a few minutes. Get over it. It was natural that she'd feel like this. Taking a life was a terrible thing. Even a vermin like Sanborne.

She drew a deep breath, raised her head, and started the van.

Sanborne would be arriving at the facility at 7 a.m.

She had to be there waiting for him.

* * *

Run.

She heard a shout behind her.

She skidded down the slope of the hill, fell, picked herself up, and flew down the bank of the creek.

A bullet whistled by her head.

"Stop!"

Run. Keep on running.

She could hear a crashing in the brush at the top of the hill.

How many were there?

Duck into the bushes. The van was parked on the road a quarter of a mile from here. She had to lose them before she reached the van.

The branches were whipping her face as she tore through the shrubbery.

She couldn't hear them anymore.

Yes, she could. But they sounded farther away. Maybe they'd gone in another direction.

She'd reached the van.

She jumped in the driver's seat and threw the rifle into the back before she peeled out onto the road.

Her foot stomped on the accelerator.

Get away. It could still be okay. If they hadn't gotten a good look at her.

If they weren't close enough to put a bullet through her head . . .


Michael was screaming when Sophie came into the house an hour later.

Shit. Shit. Shit.

She threw her bag down and raced down the hall.

"It's okay." Jock Gaven looked up when she ran into the room. "I woke him as soon as the sensor went off. He didn't get much of it."

"Enough."

Michael was sitting up, panting, his thin chest heaving. She flew over to the bed and gathered him into her arms. "It's okay, baby. It's over," she whispered. She rocked him back and forth. "It's all gone."

Michael's arms tightened desperately around her for an instant before he pushed her away. "I know it's okay," he said gruffly. He drew a deep breath. "I wish you wouldn't treat me like a kid, Mom. It makes me feel weird."

"Sorry." Every time she swore to herself that she wouldn't act this emotional, but she'd been caught off guard. She cleared her throat. "I'll watch it." She smiled shakily. "But some people would think you were a kid. Imagine that."

"I'll go make you some breakfast, Michael," Jock said as he headed for the door. "Get a move on. It's eight."

"Yeah." Michael got out of bed. "Cripes, I've got to get ready for school. I'll be late for the bus."

"No hurry. I can drive you if you miss it."

"Nah, you're tired. I'll make it." He looked back over his shoulder. "How's that little baby?"

"One episode. I think it's one of the meds she's on. I'm going to try to substitute."

"Great." He disappeared into the bathroom.

And when he closed that door, he was probably leaning against the sink and giving himself a minute to fight the nausea the terror brought. She had taught him how to do that but lately he was closing her out of the process. Perfectly natural reaction and there was no reason for her to feel hurt. Michael was ten and growing up. She was lucky they were still as close as they were.

"Mom." Michael had stuck his head out of the bathroom, a grin lighting his thin face. "I lied. It doesn't really make me feel weird. I just thought maybe it should."

He was gone again.

Warmth and overpowering love poured through her as she headed for the kitchen.

"Nice kid." Jock was standing at the counter. "Guts, too."

She nodded.

His smile faded as he looked at her. "You have a scratch on your cheek."

She kept her hand from flying to her face. She'd cleaned up at a gas station but there was no way to hide the scratch. She should have known Jock would notice. He noticed everything. "It's nothing."

His eyes were narrowed on her face. "I expected you an hour ago. Where were you?"

She didn't answer directly. "You could have reached me if there was a problem with Michael."

"Where were you?" he repeated. "The facility?"

She wouldn't lie to him. She nodded jerkily. "He didn't come. He's shown up by seven on Tuesdays for the last three weeks. I don't know why he didn't come today." Her hands clenched into fists at her sides. "Dammit, I was *ready*, Jock. I was going to do it."

"You'll never be ready."

"You taught me. I'm ready."

"You may kill him, but it will still tear you apart."

"Killing didn't tear you apart."

He made a face. "You should have seen me a few years ago. I was a basket case."

"All the more reason to kill Sanborne," Sophie said. "He shouldn't be allowed to live."

"I agree. But you shouldn't be the one to do it." He paused. "You have Michael. He needs you."

"I know that. And I've made arrangements with Michael's father to take care of him if necessary. He loves him but he couldn't take it during that first year. But Michael's much better now."

"He needs *you*."

"Shut up, Jock. How can I . . ." She rubbed her aching temple and whispered, "It's my fault. They're still doing it. How can I let them go on?"

"MacDuff knows a lot of important people. I could ask him to call someone with your government."

"You know I tried that. I called everyone I knew. They patted me on the head and told me that I was understandably hysterical. That Sanborne was a respected businessman and there was no proof he was the monster I said he was." Her lips twisted. "By the time I got to the fifth bureaucratic bastard of a senator I was hysterical. I couldn't believe they wouldn't believe me. Yes, I could. Payoffs. All the way up the line." She wearily shook her head. "Your MacDuff would run into the same wall. No, it has to be this way." Her lips tightened. "And you're wrong, it wouldn't tear me apart. I wouldn't let Sanborne hurt me anymore than he's done already."

"Then let me kill him for you. That's a much better solution."

Jock's tone was casual, almost without expression, she thought. "Because it wouldn't bother you? That's a lie. It would bother you. You're not that calloused."

"Aren't I? Do you know how many kills I've done?"

"No, and you don't know either. That's why you're helping me." She pressed the start button on the coffeemaker and leaned against the counter. "One of the guards saw me. Maybe more than one guard. I'm not sure."

He stiffened. "That's bad. Were you caught on video camera?"

She shook her head. "And I was wearing a coat and my hair was tucked under a cap. I'm sure no one saw me until I started to leave and then only for a minute. It could still be okay."

He shook his head.

"Yes, it *will*." Her lips tightened. "I'll make it work. No one's going to call the police. Sanborne doesn't want to call attention to anything out of the ordinary at the facility."

"But they'll be on the alert now."

She couldn't deny that. "I'll be careful."

Jock shook his head. "I can't allow it," he said gently. "Maybe MacDuff has infected me with his sense of responsibility. I killed my personal demon years ago, but I pointed you in the right direction to get Sanborne. You might never have found him if I hadn't led you to him."

"I'd have found him. It would have just taken me longer. Sanborne Pharmaceuticals has facilities all over the world. I would have checked every one of them."

"And it had taken you eighteen months to get that far."

"I couldn't believe it. Or maybe I couldn't accept it. It was too ugly."

"Life can be ugly. People can be ugly."

But Jock wasn't ugly, she thought as she gazed at him. He was perhaps the most beautiful human being she had ever seen. He was slender, in his early twenties with fair hair and features that were completely remarkable. There was nothing effeminate about him, he was totally masculine and yet that face was . . . beautiful. There was no other way to describe it.

"Why are you looking at me?" Jock asked.

"You wouldn't want to know. It would offend that manly Scottish pride of yours." She poured herself a cup of coffee. "I had a patient last night whose name was Elspeth. That's Scottish too, isn't it?"

He nodded. "And did she do well?"

"I think so. I hope so. She's a sweet little girl."

"And you're a good woman." He paused. "Who's trying to avoid an argument by changing the subject."

"I'm not arguing. This is my battle. I pulled you into it to help me, but I'm not going to let you run any risk or accept any guilt."

"Guilt? Lord, if you'd thought it through, you'd

realize how silly that is. My soul must be as black as hell's own cauldron by now."

She shook her head. "No, Jock." She bit her lower lip. Lord, she didn't want to say this. "I appreciate all you've done but maybe it's time you left me."

"That's not going to happen. We'll talk later. Good day, Sophie." Jock was heading for the door. "I promised to pick up Michael from his soccer game this afternoon, so you don't have to bother if you're tied up. Get to bed and try to sleep. You told me you had a one o'clock appointment."

"Jock."

He glanced over his shoulder and smiled. "It's too late to try to rid yourself of me. I can't have you killed. I'm being entirely selfish. I have too few friends in this world. I seem to have lost the knack. It would hurt me to lose you."

The door slammed behind him.

Dammit, she didn't need this reaction from Jock. She should have kept her mouth shut about being seen. She knew how protective he could be. And she should have sent him away after he'd taught her what she needed to know. He'd said he was being selfish, but she was the one who'd been selfish. Having him here to keep an eye on Michael when she had to work late had been a blessing in itself. She'd felt terribly alone and Jock had been a comfort. But she had to force him to go now.

She'd find a way to protect Michael. Go to bed. Go to sleep. Then go back to the hospital, where she could keep herself busy doing what she'd been trained to do.

Help people, instead of planning to kill them.

# IRIS JOHANSEN

*The #1* New York Times *Bestselling Author*